Wednesday's Woes

Wednesday's Woes

a novel by
Gayle Jackson Sloan

Q-Boro Books
WWW.QBOROBOOKS.COM

An Urban Entertainment Company

Published by Q-Boro Books
Copyright © 2006 by Gayle Jackson Sloan

ISBN-13: 978-1-933967-50-9
ISBN-10: 1-933967-50-1
First Printing November 2006
Mass Market Edition July 2008

10 9 8 7 6 5 4 3 2 1

LCCN: 2007933677

This is a work of fiction. It is not meant to depict, portray or represent any particular real persons. All the characters, incidents and dialogues are the products of the author's imagination and are not to be construed as real. Any references or similarities to actual events, entities, real people, living or dead, or to real locales are intended to give the novel a sense of reality. Any similarity in other names, characters, entities, places and incidents is entirely coincidental.

Cover Copyright © 2006 by Q-BORO BOOKS all rights reserved
Cover Layout & Design—Candace K. Cottrell
Photo by Ted Mebane; Cover model—Aura Harewood
Editors—Melissa Forbes, Candace K. Cottrell, Stacey Seay

Q-BORO BOOKS
Jamaica, Queens NY 11434
WWW.QBOROBOOKS.COM

Dedication

This novel is dedicated to my mother, the late Nannett A. Jackson, who continues to be my inspiration. And my husband, Ronald Sloan, who still believes I can fly.

This novel is also dedicated in loving memory of my granddaughter, Bianca: December 9, 2004 - July 17, 2005. I know you are with your great-grandmom, Nan, so I know I don't have a thing to worry about!

Acknowledgments

I hate this part because I am always afraid I will forget someone and I dislike hurting anyone's feelings, but here goes:

First and foremost, thank you Melissa Forbes for an outstanding job of editing. Your suggestions and direction were invaluable. I look forward to working with you for a very long time.

Ronnie, I love you and thank you for always being there for me and understanding the times I couldn't talk because I was too busy having conversations with my characters. Every woman should be so lucky to have a husband like you. My wife, I think I'll keep him. LOL.

Dad, I love you and I am grateful to still have you.

Charlotte, ditto. Now do whatever is necessary to keep it right.

To our kids, Rhonda, Ronnie and Rachel, what wonderful adults, parents and people you have become. Ronnie and I are both so proud of you all and love you more than we can say. Remember God didn't bring you this far to leave you now. Believe that!

To my grandchildren, Keturah, Robert, Travis, Nicholas and Kiersten, I love you and I am so proud of you all! To my youngest granddaughter, Bianca Worrell. You were a gift and an angel sent from heaven and your daily struggle to live inspired me, awed me and humbled me.

Betty: you are alright with me!

Reda and Lanie, my ace-boon sisterfriends. Thanks for being my friends and for being my read-through ladies again! I deeply love you and deeply appreciate your feedback.

Thanks Rich for you legal input and allowing me to be me. Never forget that when one door closes, a window opens. Thanks for having my back, cause you know I got yours.

Terisa, you are a saint for listening to me for two years bounce ideas off you and putting up with me whining about trying to finish this book, even though I had to wait to talk to you after ten! (Wink-wink. Don't pluck me!) LOL Thanks, homie!!

Lorraine, you have got to be the strongest woman I have ever met and I am so glad we are sister friends.

Thanks, Nakea for always believing in me and for being a wonderful friend who also happens to be my publicist. Never let 'em see you sweat. Your dreams are just a wish away.

Marlo and Angie, thanks for the early feedback, it was invaluable and just the confidence booster I needed to get this book done.

Thanks to everyone at my old law firm who supported me with my first book, even though I am sure I shocked a few of you. I hope you will continue to support me in my literary efforts. I truly appreciate it.

To Tee C. Royal and RAWSISTAZ: again I have to say thank you because without you and your support, I don't know what I would have done. Tee, you are one of the most amazing young ladies I have every had the pleasure of meeting. You are a literary angel. Never give up, but I'm glad you have learned to take that superwoman cape off e'ry now and then!

To my online groups, hanging out with you guys have been a blast and a constant source of inspiration during my many trials and tribulations over the last few years. I don't know how I would have made it without your outpouring support, friendship, encouragement and prayers. I love you guys!!

Thank you, Candace, for my beautiful website. You took some disjointed ideas and turned them into something wonderful.

Last but not least, I'd like to thank my publisher, Mark Anthony, for believing in me and really wanting to do this project and for letting me vent! You professionalism, vision, and drive is a beautiful thing to see. Let's take this baby to the top!

CHAPTER ONE
The Ex Hex

*F*unny how trouble brings more trouble. Just when you think it can't get any worse, something or someone is sure to come along and kick the shit out of you. It was bad enough that Zoe was still recovering from that nasty injury she suffered at work. Now all she did was eat pain medication and fight with worker's comp for benefits that were rightfully hers. If she was smart, she would have left that fat-ass woman right there on the floor when she missed her wheelchair by a country mile. Zoe tried to tell her to wait until after the orderly returned to put the prosthesis back on her leg so that he could help her into her chair. But *nooo*. The woman had to be so damn quick, insisting that she could move herself. Then *BAM!* The next thing Zoe knew, the woman was sprawled out on the cold hospital floor, looking very much like a beached whale.

The moment Zoe reached down to assist the woman, she realized she had made a horrible mistake. First she heard a sick popping noise, and then she felt a pain like someone had suddenly driven a branding iron *through* her lower back. Not only that, but then the woman wrapped her arms around Zoe's neck and Zoe knew the wrenching feeling in her back couldn't be good. It wasn't. So here she was, months later, just barely getting by on the reduced check from the good folks at We-Don't-Believe-Shit-You-Have-to-Say-But-Here-Is-a-Stipend-Until-We-Prove-You-Are-Lying-And-Then-We'll-Make-You-Pay-It-All-Back, and what Vaughn laughingly called child support for their daughter Shanice.

Thinking of Vaughn now made Zoe mumble a curse under her breath as she tried to hurry up her daughter.

"Shanice, your father will be here any minute. Hurry up and finish getting ready now. You know how he hates to wait," Zoe said, glancing at her stainless steel tank watch and rushing her daughter to move a little faster as Zoe stuffed Shanice's pajamas into her overnight bag.

Actually, it wasn't Vaughn having to wait that was the problem. The problem was, Zoe hated to have him in her house any longer than necessary. Just the sight of him worked on her last, frayed nerve. Even though they had been divorced for almost four years, she still didn't like being around him if she didn't have to be. The wounds and bitterness went too deep. Had it not been for their daughter, she would have told him the day they divorced to go fuck himself and never darken her doorstep again. As much as she wanted to change her name back to Livingston, Zoe decided to keep using Knight for her daughter's sake. Besides making Shanice feel better, it created less confusion for her daughter at school.

From Zoe's perspective, whenever Vaughn came to pick up their daughter, he always seemed as if he was inspecting her house, like he half expected to see evidence of wild parties and uninhibited sex in her damn living room. He just couldn't get over the fact that she was in love with a man almost fifteen years younger than her. And no matter how hard he tried—which wasn't *that* hard—he always had something snide to say about Antonio. So Zoe usually tried to make sure Shanice was ready to run out the door when Vaughn pulled into the driveway.

No such luck today. Vaughn managed to get there before Shanice was ready.

"Hey, Babe. How you doin'? Looking like Betty Crocker as usual I see," Vaughn told his ex-wife, eyeing her up and down and taking in her still firm, slim figure.

Today Zoe was sporting black velvet leggings, black suede ankle boots, a yellow turtleneck, and a yellow and black checked oversized moleskin shirt. She also had on black onyx and gold checked earrings and a gold Rollo chain around her neck with a pendent that spelled out *Super Bitch* in rhinestones. Her makeup, as usual, was flawless, even though her thin, high cheek-boned face was presently frowning at Vaughn.

"Betty Crocker?" Zoe asked, frowning at the object of her lack of desire.

"Ummhmm, moist and delicious!" Vaughn quipped, pleased to see Zoe's face scrunch up like a cat's behind. Swallowing a laugh, he told her, "Stop frowning so much, Zoe. Damn, is it that hard looking at me? Didn't your mother ever tell

you frowning could cause you to get early wrinkles?"

"It's eleven forty-five, Vaughn. You weren't supposed to be here until twelve," Zoe snapped, not
bothering to hide her displeasure.

"What can I say? Traffic was unusually light. I
got here faster than I thought I would."

"Humph." Zoe grunted, and then yelled up the
steps, "Shanice! Hurry up. Your father is here," before turning and walking back toward the kitchen,
leaving Vaughn to decide if he wanted to sit down
or stand where she had left him by the front door.
Instead, he chose to follow her. The house, he
noted, was spotless as usual. He missed living in
this house. He and Zoe had worked hard to make
it what it was today.

From the soft, floral, apple green wallpaper in
the living room, with the same colors done in
stripes in the dining room, to the new kitchen with
washed oak cabinets he made himself, the house
was custom designed. Then there were the black
granite counter tops, which they really couldn't afford at the time, but Zoe *had* to have because her
sister Sara had granite counter tops in her brand
new house. From the black appliances in the kitchen, to the gleaming inlaid hardwood floors with
the thick, wool area rugs, the house looked good.
Even the fireplace in the living room, with its cheery
fire going to take the chill off the dreary February
day, reminded him of how hard he had worked to
take the many layers of paint off to reveal the
golden brown oak underneath that he stained and
varnished to a high glossy shine. He remembered
how they had scrimped and saved, replacing every
window and door, redoing the driveway, the plumb-

ing, and the electrical wiring and even replacing the roof. Now she was living comfortably in a house that he had practically rebuilt, and he was stuck in a tiny-ass, one-bedroom apartment in Germantown. At least in the summer, when she knew she wasn't going to be home, she would occasionally let him come over to take a dip in the pool with Shanice and Jonathan. Whoopee.

"So, Tony's not here?" he asked, looking around the kitchen like he expected his ex-wife's boyfriend to suddenly pop out of the kitchen cabinets.

"His name is Antonio. Not Tony, not Tone. How many damn times do I have to tell you that? And why do you care if he's here or not?" Zoe snapped.

"Whatever. I just asked a simple question. Where are the boys?"

Zoe's sons, Christopher and Jonathan Tillman, were from a previous marriage. Their natural father was just a vague memory. Jonathan had no real memories of him at all. Chris, however, still longed to have his father in his life. He understood that his parents loathed each other, but still, he wished he had some kind of contact with his father. He had always resented Vaughn in his mother's life. Although Chris tolerated Vaughn, as he was becoming older he realized that they didn't like each other on many levels. Chris could never like anyone who hurt his mother. The rational part of him realized that his father had also hurt her, but he had been much too young to actually *see* that. Therefore, he felt he couldn't judge it. Consequently, Chris and Vaughn avoided each other as much as possible.

Jonathan, however, adored Vaughn. Since he was just a baby when Zoe and Vaughn had gotten together, Vaughn was really the only father he ever knew. Jon was not handling the breakup too well, so Zoe was considering letting him live with Vaughn for a while. He had been nothing but difficult since the breakup. Now, at age fourteen, he was starting to have serious problems in school. He resented his mother for leaving Vaughn and he had not been shy in letting her, or anybody else in the family, know exactly that.

Chris had been ambivalent about the whole thing. As long as his mother was happy, he could care less. At least he didn't have Vaughn raggin' on him anymore. Besides, he was into his own thing. At seventeen, he was only concerned with one thing: getting laid. And with his huge, hazel green eyes and sculpted body, that was not a problem. Girls practically threw themselves at him, and Chris was always happy to oblige. With his looks, extremely deep voice, and well toned body, women in their twenties, and sometimes even in their thirties, were starting to sit up and take notice.

"I'm ready, Daddy," Zoe's nine-year-old daughter announced as she came into the kitchen.

"There's my baby! Don't you look pretty today?" he gushed.

Shanice rolled her eyes and just said, "I'm not a baby anymore, Daddy. I wish you would stop calling me one."

"You'll always be my baby, Shay-boo," he told her with false heartiness.

"*Daddy*! I've asked you *not* to call me that!" Shanice told her father impatiently, rolling her eyes again and sucking her teeth.

Vaughn just laughed. Shanice was a smaller version of her mother. It didn't help that their birthdays were within days of each other. Vaughn loved his daughter to death, but as she was getting older, he could see that she was getting to be just as prickly and opinionated as her mother. However, he lived for the times they could spend together. He missed having his daughter around every day.

As quiet as it was kept, Vaughn probably had a harder time adjusting to the divorce than his daughter and stepson had. But he wasn't willing to acknowledge his part in pushing Zoe to the point of divorce. He kept telling himself that he had no idea why their marriage had fallen apart.

Vaughn was never one to admit when he was wrong. Just because he had a fling or two or three was no reason to throw a perfectly good marriage out the window, as far as he was concerned. It wasn't like he hit her or anything. Well, there was that one time when he'd finally found out about Antonio.

Even he had to admit that he had lost his mind. He still cringed to himself when he remembered how he tapped his own phone and talked a couple of his friends into following his wife. When it was proven that she was actually cheating on him, he was like a man possessed. He conveniently forgot the many times Zoe caught him doing the same thing. He still couldn't understand that maybe his actions had forced her hand. To this day, he couldn't believe he had actually picked Zoe up and slammed her to the floor like he was reenacting a scene from a popular wrestling show.

That incident was the result of his confronting her about her affair, and her telling him she had done it on purpose, as a result of *his* affair. She taunted him by saying in no uncertain terms that she didn't give a fuck if he liked it or not. She berated him and told him exactly how she felt about him and their farce of a marriage. She called him everything but a child of God. Before he realized what he was doing, he had slapped her. Zoe, never one to back off from anybody, went at him, clawing at his face in a rage. Then he grabbed her and threw her on the floor. It was the first and last time he had ever seen Zoe afraid of him. He was still ashamed to admit to himself that he felt an unreasonable sense of power and control when he briefly saw fear in her widened eyes. As a cop, he knew better than to have let it get that far. He reacted as a husband, not as an officer of the law. However, after she picked herself up, silently raced up the stairs, and came back down brandishing his gun, he was the one who was afraid. The look in her eyes was no longer one of fear, but one of unmitigated hatred. For a minute, he forgot he had taught her to be a crack shot. But when he was looking down the barrel of that gun, it all came crashing back. He barely got out of the house alive.

After the dust settled, Zoe ended up with the house, the car, and alimony every month while he just barely held onto his badge. It didn't help that what he thought was only a passing fancy between her and Antonio had endured longer than he would have ever believed. It stuck like bile in his throat that she was still with that young gigolo. No man liked to think about his woman being with a man who was still young enough to be able to get it up two or three times a night.

Zoe would have been horrified to know the thoughts that were roaming around her ex-husband's mind. All she wanted was for him to

leave, and quickly. Antonio was due back soon, and she didn't want another confrontation between her man of yesterday and her man of the here and now. To help him leave faster, Zoe told Shanice with forced cheerfulness, "Give Mommy a kiss, and you behave yourself, Miss."

After planting a kiss on her mother's smooth cheek and giving her a quick, tight hug, Shanice promised, "I will, Mom. I'll try not to drive Daddy *too* crazy this weekend!"

Zoe laughed at her daughter. She knew no matter what she said, Shanice was going to do whatever she wanted to do anyway. Her daughter figured out a long time ago how to work her father's guilt over her parents no longer being together. Shanice would come back on Sunday tired, but Vaughn's pockets would be considerably lighter with all the things he hadn't been able to deny her.

Ushering them toward the front door, down the steps, and to Vaughn's car, Zoe finally breathed a sigh of relief when they left. No sooner had they turned the corner than Antonio was pulling into her driveway. Zoe stood in the doorway admiring him as he unfolded his tall, lean, muscular body out of his cherry-red Jeep Cherokee. From his spotless black Timberlands to his baggy black FUBU jeans, turtleneck Polo sweater, and bright yellow First Down jacket, the brother was fly. No matter how many times she saw him, she was always fascinated with his exceptional physique and looks, not to mention his flawless milk chocolate skin and his smooth bald head. Damn. He always looked like a piece of delicious Godiva chocolate to her. Always smooth, rich, and good enough to eat. And Lord, she had done that more times than she cared to count. There was something to be said about having experience. She had definitely blown his young mind. At twenty-six, Antonio had been in awe of Zoe since day one.

When they first met in a mall, Zoe was with her younger sister Sara. In all honesty, Zoe believed that Antonio initially approached them because he was interested in Sara. Sara, however, blew him off quick, fast, and in a hurry. She was so in love with her then-boyfriend, Theo (who was now her husband) she couldn't give any other man the time of day. Feeling sorry for Antonio, Zoe took up the conversation in the awkward silence that followed. Sara rudely wandered off to a clothing store, leaving Zoe to deal with Antonio. Before she knew it, Zoe had his phone number and had called him to meet for drinks. They had been to-gether almost ever since. Sara and Antonio joked about it now. Even though Sara wasn't interested and initially disapproved of Zoe and Antonio's re-lationship, Sara and Antonio got along fine now. Well, most of the time.

In any event, Zoe still found it hard to believe, but she was totally, completely, recklessly in love. She just hoped to God that Antonio was every-thing he seemed to be and not a figment of her imagination.

Her first husband—her sons' father—was noth-ing more than a teenage crush, really. And Vaughn? Vaughn was a means to an end. He never knew it, but she never really loved him. In the beginning, because he was so nice and sweet to her and her boys, she convinced herself that with time she would grow to love him. Sadly, she never did. She was very *fond* of Vaughn at one time, but after all of his affairs, he proved to be an overwhelming disappointment. Now she was in her forties, drooling at just the sight of Antonio, with her heart at the mercy of a man in his twenties.

When she first got together with Antonio, he was a means to get back at Vaughn for his infidelities. She admitted to herself that she originally used Antonio to tweak Vaughn's nose. In the process, she got her groove back so tough, she could have given Stella lessons. Somewhere along the way, she fell first in lust, and then in love, with Antonio. However, as much as she loved him, she constantly worried about him leaving her for a woman closer to his own age. But she pushed all those thoughts from her mind as she admired Antonio's stroll to the front door. She never tired of watching him walk. He reminded her of a sleek jungle cat, like a panther or jaguar.

Smiling at him, she pushed open the black, wrought iron, security door, shivering slightly as a blast of cold, damp air whipped around the open door.

"Hey, Baby. Lucky you, you just missed Vaughn," Zoe said as she stood on her toes to brush his lips with her own as he entered the warm house.

"It wasn't by accident. I tried to time how long I thought he might be here before coming home." He grimaced, shrugging out of his jacket, then hanging it in the closet. He had been with Zoe long enough to know the rules. You *never* walked into Zoe's house without hanging up your coat. That, along with some of her other idiosyncrasies, were hard to get used to at first, but after all this time he found he did it automatically. So much so, he even surprised his mother and grandmother when he would do it at their houses.

"I know, Baby. He can be such an asshole sometimes. But the good news is that by some stroke of luck, we've got the whole weekend to ourselves," Zoe said.

"Cool! How did you pull that one off?"

"Chris is visiting a friend up at a private school in the Poconos and Jonathan is hanging with T.J. this weekend. Whatever the reasons, I'm not going to question our luck." She laughed, kissing him again, happy to have a rare weekend with no kids. "Hungry? I was just getting ready to fix some fish sticks and fries. Want some?"

"I have a better idea. Let's go to Applebee's in Jenkintown. I've been tasting one of their burgers all week," he told her, rubbing his six pack.

"You? Eating red meat?" Zoe asked him in surprise. Antonio, for the most part, avoided red meat like the plague.

"Every now and then I have to succumb, Babe. This is one of those times." He laughed, pulling her into his strong embrace before planting a kiss on her lips. The kiss, which was supposed to be brief, soon turned into something more as Zoe molded her slim frame into his muscular one. Before long, Zoe felt the evidence of Antonio's desire as it pressed insistently against her belly. Zoe rubbed herself sensuously against his hardness, feeling herself becoming moist and hot like she always did around Antonio.

"Baby, if you keep that up, we won't be going anywhere. I'll be wanting to eat something else."

Laughing in triumph, Zoe told him through

eyes that were heavy with desire, "Bring it on, Baby. Bring it on!" before pulling him up the stairs to her bedroom.

After almost ripping his clothes off, Zoe laid Antonio down on her bed, before leaning over him to softly kiss his lips. She kissed him deeply, letting her tongue sensuously play with his before gently sucking on his throat, having taught him a long time ago to take it slow and easy. As she kissed her way down his eager, hard body, she let her hands lead the way. Soon her mouth met and replaced the hand that was curled around his more than adequate maleness. Then she softly, surely, stroked him to an iron hardness. She let her tongue swirl around the head of his penis and dip down his shaft, feeling him gyrate in and out of her hot, eager mouth.

"Oh *Baby*! Keep that up and I won't be responsible for what might happen," he panted.

Zoe just smiled as she looked up at him with gray eyes that had become dark and smoky and looked decidedly more feline than human. She reluctantly let him slip from her lips with a final kiss on the tip of his penis before she quickly climbed up his body. After positioning herself, she sighed as she let herself slide down onto his hardness until her soft bottom rested on his muscular thighs. She moaned in pleasure as she rocked back and forth and up and down on his body, teasing him with her small round breasts. Antonio played with her deep brownish-red nipples until they became hard and sensitive, marveling again at their color against her fair skin. He called them his cherries on his french vanilla ice cream scoops. Wetting his fingertips, he strummed them across her sensitive peaks, causing Zoe to gasp with the pleasure he was giving her body inside and out.

Antonio continued to let her ride him for a few more minutes, his own hips rising and falling beneath her body as he felt her walls stroking and tightening on him, making it hard for him to maintain his control. For being such a small woman, she rode him well. After another few minutes of struggling to keep from climaxing too soon, he grabbed her by her hips and quickly reversed their positions. Before Zoe knew it, she could feel herself slipping away as she rode the crest of a powerful climax. Zoe was so lost in the throes of her own climax that she barely heard Antonio as he shouted his own release.

Moments later, after they regained the ability to breathe normally, they snuggled together in Zoe's queen-sized bed, idly stroking each other wherever their hands landed with light willowy touches on overly sensitive, sexually stimulated skin.

"I guess we should get up and find something to eat," Zoe murmured.

"I thought we were going to Applebee's."

"I forgot all about that. I can cook us something if you don't feel like going out," Zoe offered.

"As much as I love your cooking, Baby, I think I would rather go out. Maybe we can hit a movie after we eat. What's the point in not having any kids around if we don't get out and enjoy ourselves?"

"Getting buck wild wherever and whenever we feel like it?"

"So who says you can't get buck wild in the movies?" he teased.

"I *know* you talkin' out the side of your neck

now! You know I don't go for public displays of affection, especially *that* kind of display."

"You should try it, Boo. It's a kick, knowing somebody could bust you at any moment."

Zoe remained silent as she quickly got out of bed and padded toward the bathroom inside her bedroom.

"If we want to beat the dinner crowd, then we better hurry up," was all Zoe said as she disappeared into the bathroom, firmly shutting the door behind her.

Antonio knew that meant she wanted to shower alone. Sighing, he reached over to Zoe's bedside table to retrieve the remote control for the television. Flicking it on, he channel-surfed until he came to an action-adventure movie, quickly forgetting about his conversation with Zoe.

Zoe, however, was disturbed by it. That wasn't the first, second or third time Antonio brought up the subject of them getting freaky in public. She wondered if it was a *young* thing or just Antonio's thing.

Zoe was from the old school. She might have been in her early forties, staring middle age in the face for real, but she had come up in a different time and place. She always believed that what went on behind closed doors should remain just that: behind closed doors. Once again she worried that maybe she was just too old for Antonio and she was living in a fool's paradise.

As Zoe waited for the water to get hot enough in the shower, she brushed her teeth, rinsed, and spat before examining her face closely in the mirror above the sink. She turned her face this way and that, always on the lookout for any signs of aging. The small face with its high, sharp cheek-bones that stared so solemnly back at her was as smooth as it had ever been. Zoe grimaced slightly at her pale complexion, thinking that it wouldn't be summer soon enough for her. Then, thank God, she would get that golden color she wished she had been blessed with, like her sister Sara, instead of her own pale, parchment color. At least she inherited her paternal grandmother's gray eyes. Growing up, she hated them. The kids at school used to make fun of her and call her a cat or a witch. But after kicking enough ass, that finally stopped. Now she liked her eyes.

By now, the mirror was fogging over as the steam from the shower rolled across the small bathroom. Zoe added cold water until the temperature was right and stepped in, shutting the calla lily etched glass door behind her. Looking over the shelves in the corner of the stall, she finally selected the *Bijon* shower gel she loved so much. Of course, she also had gels of *Beautiful, Burberry's for Women, Glamour, Red and White Diamonds* and various other scents from Victoria's Secret. Zoe liked to layer her scents; first with shower gel, then lotion, and finally, perfume of the same scent. This, she learned long ago, made the fragrance last all day, with maybe a tiny spritz to touch it up, depending on which fragrance she chose to wear.

As she lathered up, she didn't even notice the rich fragrance that mixed with the steam around the small bathroom as she continued to think about Antonio's comment. He had been trying for a while to get her to *indulge* in some type of public sexual act. She flatly refused. Now, whenever he brought it up, she simply ignored him. But that didn't stop her from worrying about it. Hell, she had even been reluctant to have sex in her own living room, in front of the fireplace. The only reason she finally agreed was because of a conversation she had at her sister Sara's house. Thinking back to that night, all Zoe could do was shake her head, especially as she remembered Tamika's contribution to the conversation.

It was ladies' night at Sara's house, something they did every couple of months. The ladies present that night were Zoe, Sara, Sara's grown stepdaughter Chelsea, Sara's friend Danita, Gina and Stephanie, Zoe and Sara's sisters, and Zoe's friend and main roadie, Tamika.

They were on their second pitcher of Mudslides and the ladies were talking a lot of shit. As usual, the conversation finally got around to men and sex. Stephanie declared a need for a cigarette, grabbed her drink and took a seat onto the deck outside of Sara's breakfast room. Knowing what a prude Steph could be, no one paid her any attention other than to throw a little friendly ribbing her way. Zoe's friend Tamika was the most rambunctious of the group. Although Tamika was tiny, her small size was deceptive. A lot of people thought because of her stature, Tamika could be pushed around. Wrong. She may have been short and petite, but she would quickly put you in your place. She was also unbelievably beautiful. She had smooth, coffee colored skin, a perfect build for her size, and incredible, doe shaped, long-lashed eyes that she used to her advantage on any man she met. Her hair was styled to fit whatever her mood was that day.

One day it would be a weave down to her trim waist; the next day it might be a short, twisty style. Tamika changed her hair like other people changed their underwear.

As for her sexual exploits, she always had tales that either had them cracking up or dropping their jaws. Girlfriend had plenty of encounters and experiences and was never ashamed to talk about them. Tamika's attitude was that she did it so she had no shame in her game. Zoe, however, sometimes secretly wondered how much was fact and how much was fiction. As much as Zoe liked Tamika, sometimes even she was taken aback by some of the things Tamika would say. She and Tamika had been friends for years, and yet Tamika still had the ability to shock her. She supposed that some people would think Tamika was a hoochie, and even though sometimes the things she said made her sound like one, she really was a good person. Tamika just believed that men served one purpose and one purpose only: to provide her with the style of living she felt she deserved, which happened to be a very expensive one. Tamika was the original material girl. If a man didn't have the money, she didn't have the time.

Zoe listened in growing amusement, along with the other ladies, as Tamika regaled them with tales about some of the losers she had met via the Internet. She also told them about some of her more intimate encounters with those she met in person. One of her stories had them gasping for air from laughing so hard.

"Girl, this one guy I met was hung like a horse, which should have been no surprise since he kind of looked like one. You know I would never have given him the time of day if he didn't have some *serious* ducats. And believe me, I had his *entire* portfolio checked out before he *ever* crossed my door! He's an investment banker or some such thing. Anyway, we were in my family room, and after all the shit he had been talking online, about his sexual skills and all, I wanted to see if he was lying or not. He was a real Mr. Straight-Up guy during the day, and a freak at night online. I mean he wasn't the best looking brother I'd ever seen, but he wasn't the worst either. But I figured since he wasn't all that fine, he had to have something to back him up besides his fat wallet. So at first we're sitting on the sofa watching this porno flick he brought over and the next thing you know we were fooling around. He's rubbing all over my titties and begging me to let him taste them and shit. So I let him taste these 36Cs and then the next thing you know, brother man is making that trip downtown.

"Guuurl, let me tell you! He had some serious skills. I thought he was trying to lick me hairless! Not that there was that much to lick off, cause you know I keep my shit shaved anyway. He got a liplock on my stuff and turned it every which-a-way but loose. I must have cum about five, six times. By this time, I'm all hot, wet, and *ready*. I'm thinking I'm gonna fuck this Wall Street wanna-be stupid silly. I reach down and I'm feeling around and my hand kept going further and further down his leg trying to feel the tip of his dick. Finally I said, 'Well damn Baby, how big is that bitch?' He gets up and unzips his pants and that's when I saw he didn't have any drawers on, and he reaches down *into* his pants leg and pulls out the biggest dick I have ever seen in my life! Chile, let me tell you. It looked like it should have been somebody's damn arm and the tip was as big as my balled up fist," she demonstrated, waving her fist in the air. By this time all the ladies were laughing hysterically.

"That's," Tamika continued, "when I remembered he told me that he came from down south, raised on a farm. And you *know* them farm grown nuccas be big as shit, but his stuff was *whacked*! I was like, 'Shee-eet! You ain't putting that mother up in me, fuckin' up my shit! Niggah, you must be crazy!' And he was like, 'What you mean? Aw, come on Baby. You know you can handle this.' I was like, 'Think again, motherfucker. Ain't no way in hell you are coming anywhere near *this* pussy with *that* dick!' And do you know what he had the nerve to say then?" At our collective negative shakes, she said, "He had the nerve to say, 'Well, you could give me some head then.' I was like, 'I know I got a big mouth, but do I look like Paul Bunyan's mama to you? Niggah, please.'"

The other ladies were rolling on the floor, tears running down their faces from laughing so hard while Tamika just shook her head with an exaggerated disgusted look on her face at the memory and calmly went back to sipping her drink and searching for some more nachos. By the third pitcher of Mudslides, the conversation was really getting deep. Zoe was shocked when Sara confessed to a night of great sex with her husband Theo in front of the fireplace. What was really shocking were the details Sara gave up.

But this night with the ladies was enough to plant a seed of curiosity in Zoe. That particular get-together happened during the summer. At the first sign of a chill in the night air and no kids at home, Zoe decided to try something a little different with Antonio.

After a romantic dinner in the candlelit dining room, Zoe and Antonio carried their glasses of wine into the living room to sit on the sectional in front of the blazing fire. While some soft jazz played in the background, they both got comfortable with Zoe's head resting on Antonio's shoulder. They talked quietly about this and that and just relaxed and enjoyed each other's company and the unusual quiet of the house. Soon, however, after a few more glasses of wine, and a change of the CD player to a more sensuous disc, things began to heat up.

Almost before Zoe knew what was happening, Antonio had her cream cable knit sweater on the floor and was unsnapping the front of her bra, exposing her small breasts with her unusually large, chocolate colored nipples, to the heat of the fire. He loved how large her nipples were, as well as how sensitive. Before she could protest, the warmth of his mouth soon replaced the warmth of the fireplace, causing other fires to ignite and burn within her. He licked and sucked her nipples like a starving baby, seemingly trying to draw her into him.

Zoe started to tell him to stop. But suddenly remembering her resolve, she forced herself to keep from imploring Antonio to move things upstairs.

Feeling emboldened, she sat up and quickly divested Antonio of his clothes. Before long, they moved from the sofa to the floor. Somehow, she ended up on top of Antonio with her legs wrapped around his head and her mouth firmly wrapped around his hardness. When neither could wait any longer, they changed positions. But before Antonio slipped into her eager body, he jumped up and walked over to stand as close as possible to the fire.

Zoe was confused until Antonio suddenly turned around and quickly moved between her legs. She understood when he entered her quickly, and she gasped as his heated hardness penetrated her. From standing in front of the fire, he felt much like a hot poker. Over and over he suddenly stopped and heated himself up like that until finally it got to the point where neither one of them could stop. Zoe felt herself climax with an intensity she had never known.

Remembering that night, Zoe smiled, thinking that maybe tonight would be a good night to repeat such a performance.

By now she was out of the shower, dried off, and standing in front of her closet trying to decide what to wear. Applebee's was pretty casual, and even though she had a lot of casual clothes, she wanted to wear something that was fashionable as well as comfortable. Antonio took her place in the shower and she finally decided on a pair of black jeans, a fushia turtleneck sweater, and black, faux alligator short boots when the phone's insistent ringing had her scurrying to answer it.

Thinking it was Shanice calling to check on her, she answered with a breezy "Hello?"

"Zoe? Oh, thank God you're home!"

"Sara?" Zoe asked, recognizing her sister's distraught voice, causing her own throat to tighten. Some premonition told her that Sara was going to tell her something she didn't want to hear.

"What's wrong?" Zoe asked, instinctively knowing that something *was* wrong.

Zoe had to wait before Sara could answer her, she listened helplessly to Sara sobbing on the other end of the line. Finally, not able to take it anymore, Zoe screamed, "*What is it, Sara? What's wrong?*"

"Oh, God, Zoe, it's Mom. She's gone, Zoe. Mom's gone."

CHAPTER TWO

Life's Passage

Zoe stared out of the passenger-side window, not really seeing anything that flashed by her window as Antonio zoomed up Route 309 to Sara's house in Horsham. She wasn't aware that the tissue she was holding had been torn to shreds until Antonio placed his warm hand over hers to still their restless motions. When she looked down, she was shocked to see bits and pieces of tissue all over her lap. Wordlessly, she looked up and into Antonio's sympathetic eyes before he returned his attention to the road. Silent, fat tears rolled down her face again, prompting her to reach between the two front seats and snatch another tissue from the box on the floor. She swiped at her already swollen, red-rimmed eyes, trying to pull herself together.

In a flurry of tearful phone calls, she spoke to her sisters, Gina and Stephanie, and everyone agreed to meet at Sara's house to discuss what to do next. The hardest phone call was to their father, Phillip, who was alone in Athens, Pennsylvania, where her parents lived. Zoe saw her father cry on more than a few occasions, usually when he was begging Amanda's forgiveness, but never like this. He sounded like a wounded animal. When he finally pulled himself together, Zoe learned that Amanda had suffered a massive heart attack. Her father found her on the floor of the bedroom. He said he was downstairs watching television when he heard Amanda call him. By the time he got upstairs, she was on the floor. He called 911, but by the time they got there it was too late. And for the second time in his life, his wife died in his arms. His first wife died from leukemia, and now Amanda from a massive heart attack.

But the person Zoe really worried about was Sara. Sara and their mother were always close, probably closer than Zoe or any of the other girls ever were. Maybe they were so close because Sara was the youngest and the last one at home. She had years of having their mother all to herself. From the time Sara was eleven, until she finally left home at almost twenty, she was the only child at home. Zoe, Gina, and Stephanie were long since gone. Zoe moved to California, Gina was living in Philadelphia, and Stephanie moved to Pittsburgh. The only time they all made their way to Akron, Ohio, where their parents were living at the time, was for Mother's Day, unless it was one of the times Amanda was sick enough to be in the hospital.

It had been a few years since Zoe last saw their mother. She realized now that she had no one to blame but herself. Ever since Sara had met and married Theo, Amanda and Phillip visited quite often. Sara always made it a point to let all the sisters know when their parents were coming to visit. Occasionally, Zoe would make the effort to go see them. A few years ago, however, Amanda had chastised one of Zoe's children and it had really pissed Zoe off. Zoe felt the only person who had the right to tell her children anything was her. Words had been exchanged and for some reason, she stopped making the effort to visit her parents. She was even too stubborn to call. She convinced herself that if they really wanted to talk to her, they would call.

Looking back, Zoe realized that her stubbornness was another test to make Amanda prove that she loved Zoe as much as she loved Sara. Everyone in the family felt that Sara was Amanda's favorite. While it may or may not have been true, it was probably one of the reasons she, Steph, and Gina were always so hard on Sara. Being a mother of three, Zoe now realized that more than likely, by the time Amanda had Sara, she was too tired to be as strict with her as she was with her three older children.

Still, that was no reason for Zoe to stop speaking to her mother. She felt ashamed. Her regret caused fresh tears to sting her eyes. Foolishly she thought that there would enough time to get it together, but there always seemed to be something else to do. Where had the time gone? And now it was too late. There were no more tomorrows.

Thinking about that caused a sob to choke in Zoe's throat. Suddenly all the hurt, misunderstandings, or whatever else there may have been between her and her mother seemed silly and trivial.

It didn't even seem important to remember right now that technically, Amanda wasn't Zoe's mother. Zoe's natural mother died when she was little more than a baby. And even though her father married Amanda, Zoe knew that he always continued to mourn her mother. What was worse, Amanda knew it too. Sometimes, Amanda would be angry with Phillip because of his cheating or because he kicked her ass again. But as much as Zoe used to feel sorry for Amanda, there were times when she hated Amanda because it seemed to Zoe that Amanda always took her anger out on Zoe. Once she tried to talk to Sara about it, but they got into an argument because Sara didn't remember it like that and didn't want to hear it. Sara and Amanda were as close as a mother and daughter could be, and Sara didn't want to hear one disparaging word against her mother.

However, as much as Zoe sometimes resented Amanda, in a lot of ways she was more like Amanda than Sara or Stephanie, her natural daughters. Gina used to tell her that all the time.

Gina rarely got caught up in the family dynamics. She used to say that because she was adopted, she had a different take on the family. As far as she was concerned, she was happy to even have a family. Gina was forever grateful that Amanda had saved her from the crazy woman who was her natural mother. When Gina's natural mother had tired of being a mother, she thought it might be a good idea to shove Gina in front of an oncoming train. Amanda, who happened to be there at the time, had seen everything and literally snatched Gina from death's door. It had all been a bigger shock when Amanda realized that Gina was a schoolmate and friend of Stephanie's.

Gina used to say that Zoe had naturally taken

after Amanda because Zoe was the one who was usually in the kitchen or at home with Amanda. Steph was into sports, Gina used to hang out with Phillip, and Sara would be somewhere playing with her baby dolls or listening to her records. Consequently, Amanda came to depend on Zoe to help with the cooking and cleaning. Working side-by-side with Amanda, Zoe learned how to be a little Amanda. Especially when it came to housework and pushing herself until a job was done. Sara and Steph would quit when they got tired and start again the next day. Not Zoe. Like Amanda, once she started something, she was compulsive—obsessive really—about finishing it before she could allow herself to stop.

As these thoughts finished running through Zoe's head, she and Antonio pulled into Sara's driveway. Zoe noticed that Gina and Stephanie's cars were already there. Antonio barely rolled to a stop when the front door was snatched open and Zoe could see Sara silhouetted in the doorway, looking to all the world like a lost child, and very much like Amanda. Sara stood there holding her hands across her middle just like Amanda would do when she was upset.

Jumping out of the Cherokee, Zoe quickly crossed the distance between them. As soon as she stepped across the threshold and embraced her sister, the tears began to flow. However, Sara quickly pulled away and Zoe watched in amazement as she saw Sara fight to pull herself together. Looking past Zoe, Sara moved into Antonio's hug and quiet words of condolences.

When Gina and Stephanie joined them in the foyer, Antonio moved to the side as the four sisters once again gave in to their grieving, totally ignoring the others in the house as their tears overcame them. Everyone left them alone, understanding that they needed that moment to grieve together.

After a bit, the sisters wiped their faces, blew their noses and moved into Sara's family room and kitchen where Antonio, Sara's husband, Theo, Gina's new husband, Frank, and Sara and Theo's kids, T.J. and Bethany, were already stationed.

"So, what's the plan?" Zoe asked no one in particular.

"I guess everyone can get things settled with their jobs and on Monday, we'll go up to Athens. Dad shouldn't be up there by himself. He was a wreck when I spoke to him," Gina said.

"But that means it'll be two days before we can get to him," Sara fretted.

"I know, but what choice do we have?" Steph asked.

"I guess." Sara frowned.

"Besides, it'll be better to make all the necessary calls down here rather than running up their—I mean Dad's—phone bill," Gina reasoned.

"Yeah, that's true. So did Dad say where the funeral is going to be?" Zoe asked.

"At the funeral home. He grew up with the funeral director and wants to do everything there," Gina told them.

"Well, I don't know why. I think it should be at a church," Stephanie huffed.

The other three sisters surreptitiously looked at each other. This was just the kind of thing Amanda had said she wanted to avoid.

On her last visit down, it was almost like Amanda knew she was going to die. At one time or another she told Zoe, Sara, and Gina: "Don't let Stephanie take over my funeral. Right or wrong, Phil is still my husband and he has a right to have a say in how things go. You know Stephanie will try to bulldoze over everybody else and just have her way. I don't want that. Respect your father's wishes."

Trying to avoid an argument, Sara said, "Why don't we wait until we get there and talk to Dad?"

Gina and Zoe agreed and shot Stephanie a look telling her to drop it. She did, but they could see it coming. They would have a difficult week ahead of them. They continued to discuss what needed to be done and who still had to be contacted. They all took turns fielding phone calls. At one point, Theo was on the phone taking messages and everyone else was on his or her cell phone calling people. Sara looked around, and for some reason the scene struck her as funny. When everyone saw her laughing, they were convinced that she had finally snapped. After phones were either hung up, turned off or flipped closed, they all kind of moved in around her, cautiously, like she might flip out at any moment.

"What's so funny, Sara?"

"What the hell did people do before cell phones? I mean really. I just happened to look up and there's Theo with the cordless, Zoe with her cell over in one corner, me with mine in this corner and even *Stephanie* has a cell over there. I can just see Mom somewhere laughing at all the fuss being made." Suddenly, Sara's smile of amusement changed to a small smile of regret and loss.

"Whenever I've had to go through something hard, Mom has always been there for me. How can I get through the most difficult thing I've ever dealt with in my life, which is losing her, without her?" Sara cried. Theo, ever sensitive to his wife, caught her just as she crumbled to the floor, crying hysterically.

Zoe felt her own eyes well up with tears and she pushed her balled-up fist against her lips in an effort to keep it in and hold herself together. Watching her sister fall apart was harder than dealing with her own loss. Looking around, she saw that Bethany had rushed to her mother who was being gently rocked in Theo's strong arms on the kitchen floor where he had eased down with Sara in his lap. Zoe watched as Theo repeatedly rubbed Sara's back in small circles as he tried to get her to calm down. The front of his shirt was soaked through. And now he was trying to comfort not only Sara, but Bethany as well, as he ignored his own silent tears running down the lean planes of his face. For the first time since meeting him, Zoe noticed how much older Theo was. Amanda's death seemed to have aged him overnight. She noted the tired puffiness under his eyes. For a moment, he looked up and she was startled again by the intensity of his green eyes. She could see that he was trying to deal his own pain while also worrying about his wife.

Pulling her eyes away, Zoe noticed Stephanie by the patio doors. Only the slight shaking movement of Stephanie's shoulders indicated that she was also crying. Zoe felt sorry for Stephanie at that moment because she had no one other than her sisters to console her. Out of all of them, Stephanie was the only one without a man or any significant other that they knew of. And having not had one for so long, it was just generally accepted that Stephanie was never getting married. Everyone privately thought perhaps she was gay, although no one ever said so out loud, except through innuendo. Her best friend, Paula, was a single, nondescript white woman—a nun actually—who no one really liked, but all tolerated for Stephanie's sake. Amanda once told Zoe that she couldn't stand Paula. Something about her just worked Amanda's nerves. Zoe was surprised to see that when Steph walked in earlier, Paula wasn't there. Usually, if you saw Stephanie, Paula wasn't far behind.

Looking around, Zoe noted that Gina had made her way to the family room bar and was knocking back glass after glass of wine.

Zoe shrugged away Antonio's hand when he tried to pull her into his comforting arms. Instead, she stumbled down the short hallway to Sara's powder room and firmly shut the door behind her. Leaning against the door, she gulped in air, feeling the beginning of a panic attack. Before she knew it, she was gasping for air as if she were an asthmatic. She could feel her throat tightening, choking off her air supply. Her mind told her to calm down, but her body wasn't listening. A panic attack. She hadn't had one of those since all that drama she went through with Vaughn and her divorce. As she gulped in air, she fought to slow her heartbeat and make herself calm down. Finally, after a few minutes, she noticed the weight seemed to ease up on her chest. When she felt relatively normal again, she checked her face in the mirror and opened the door to rejoin the others.

Everyone seemed to have pulled themselves together again, and offered each other watery smiles. At the same time, they all decided to leave and return to their own homes, leaving Sara and her family to themselves.

When Zoe got back home, she walked into her house and stopped, not sure what to do with herself. Antonio took the decision out of her hands. He gently pulled her coat off, led her into the living room and made her sit down on the sofa. Wordlessly, he started the fire again, put on her favorite Dave Koz CD, pulled her alligator skin boots off, and told her to chill while he went into the kitchen to fix them something to eat.

Zoe doubted she could eat anything and keep it down. Her appetite was always the first thing that went when she was upset. Not that she could afford to lose a pound. She was small as it was, and it didn't take much for her clothes to hang on her.

However, watching the dancing flames and letting the soothing music wash over her had the desired effect. She didn't even realize she had drifted off to sleep until she felt Antonio gently shaking her awake.

For a moment, she felt disoriented and was about to tell Antonio that she wasn't hungry until she caught a whiff of something delicious wafting out of the kitchen. When her stomach grumbled, she realized she actually was hungry.

"Damn, that smells good, Baby. What did you fix?"

"Come in the kitchen and find out," he told her before smiling broadly.

Zoe got up, stretched, and padded into the kitchen. She started smiling when she saw the table set with plates, silverware, and linen instead of the usual foam plates, plastic ware, and paper napkins. He had even gone out back and snipped some foliage and dried flowers from her long-since hibernating garden to make a lovely winter arrangement for the center of the table.

"Antonio, this is so sweet. You didn't have to go through all of this trouble!"

"No trouble, Miss," he said, calling her by his sometimes pet name for her. "I thought you might need a little something different, that's all," he told her, not wanting to remind her of why she was so sad.

Before either could dwell on that, he told her to sit down as he grabbed her plate and went to the stove to fix it for her. He returned with a plate covered with smothered pork chops, rice with pan gravy, and steamed broccoli.

"I thought you couldn't cook. Looks like you've been holding out on me," Zoe mocked-fussed. "All these years we've been together and you let me think you didn't know your way around a kitchen. Makes me wonder what other secrets you've kept from me!" Zoe joked.

Opening up the side-by-side refrigerator door, Zoe missed the discomfited look that passed over Antonio's face. By the time Zoe closed the door, the look was gone.

Instead, Antonio joked, "I still can't cook. I called my grandmother and she talked me through it. I think I did pretty good, if I do say so myself." He was smiling with satisfaction as he fixed his own plate.

Zoe took a few bites, and then had to refrain from eating like she didn't have any home training.

"Baby, this is delicious! I think you'll be calling your grandmother more often," she warned as she continued to devour the food. She realized with a start that it was the first time she ate all day, and here it was already dark outside.

Not long after they finished cleaning up the kitchen, and moved into the living room, Zoe announced that she was going to bed. It had been an emotionally exhausting day and she just wanted to take a shower and crawl between the sheets. She wasn't looking forward to what the rest of the week had in store. She thought about calling her father again, but decided that she just couldn't deal with him at the moment. That would all come soon enough.

CHAPTER THREE
The Week From Hell: The Beginning

"*W*hy don't they drive faster?" Sara complained as she turned around again to see how far behind them Stephanie, Zoe, and Gina were.

"Because if they drive any faster Gina's piece of shit is going to fall apart from all the shaking and rattling it's doing. Talk about shake, rattle and roll!" Theo laughed.

Sara sucked her teeth. "I told them we should all ride together, but does anyone ever listen to me? No!" Sara fumed.

If Antonio and Frank were going with them, it wouldn't have been an issue. At least they would have had Antonio's Cherokee and Frank's Lexus. Stephanie could have just ridden with one of them. Unfortunately, due to their work schedules, the men wouldn't be coming up until the day before the funeral. Why Frank hadn't let Gina take the Lexus was beyond Sara's understanding. He couldn't go a couple of days without stylin' and profilin'?

"Jesus H. Christ. It's going to take us forever to get to Dad's at this rate. They act like they've never been up here before. I say we just leave their asses and they get there when they get there."

"Now you know we can't do that, Sara. What if the car breaks down? Then they would be stuck and we would only have to come all the way back to get them."

"I guess," Sara grumbled, crossing her arms over her chest in disgust. She had been in a foul mood since having words with Stephanie before they left.

Everyone had agreed to meet at Sara's house since she wasn't that far from Route 309 where they would have to go anyway to get on the Pennsylvania Turnpike. Sara assumed that they would all ride up together. But Stephanie shot that idea to all hell. She insisted that they needed to take Gina's car. If there were a number of things that had to be done, Steph thought they could be done faster with two cars. That would have been fine except Gina's car was a piece of shit that developed a serious case of the palsies if pushed to go faster than 45 miles an hour! Sara kept waiting for the doors, body and everything else to fall off leaving the three of them sitting in a car that was just wheels and a floor.

This was why Sara kept turning around to see how far back the other three were lagging. She had forgotten what a lousy driver Stephanie was. She drove like a scared old lady, cautious and jerky, with her body all hunched over the wheel.

Finally, after almost five hours, instead of the usual four, they pulled into their parents' driveway. Theo tooted the horn to let his father-in-law know they had arrived. Everyone got out of their respective cars and indulged in much needed stretches.

"I should have ridden with y'all. My back is killing me," Zoe complained to Sara.

Phillip came out on the porch and hugs and kisses were exchanged all around.

"Y'all come on in. I have some details to go over with you. I thought you would be here earlier. We have to go to the funeral home in about an hour, so Ma's clothes have to be picked out."

"We thought we would have been here sooner too, Dad," Sara grumbled.

"What happened?"

"It's a long story," was all Sara would say as she shot her sisters a look. Gina just shrugged her shoulders.

"Whatever. Just go on upstairs and pick out Ma's outfit."

"In a minute, Dad," Sara told him, dreading walking into the kitchen. Looking around at each other, they seemed to be trying to find the courage to go inside. Finally, Sara mumbled, "I can do this," as she purposefully marched up the steps and snatched open the kitchen door. Sara crossed the threshold, her sisters on her heels, with Theo bringing up the rear. He was as reluctant as his wife and sisters-in-law about going into the house. Sara walked into the kitchen and stopped dead in her tracks.

Like a chain reaction, they all collided into one another, then quickly stepped apart from each other. Silently, they surveyed the kitchen and almost as one, their eyes were drawn to the empty rocking chair in the corner of the kitchen by the basement door. Freshly ironed and stiffly starched aprons hung on hangers from the light sconce behind the chair, waiting to either be worn or put away upstairs. Plants nestled in Amanda's macrame or hand-crocheted holders hung in the kitchen windows, which were adorned with starched window swags. The stove was spotless as usual, waiting for the old, but dully gleaming pots that hung on the opposite wall to take their places on the burners. Worn, but familiar rugs rested in front of the stove, the sink, and under the glass-topped table with the white, wrought iron chairs that sported robin's egg blue vinyl seats.

Sara was far enough into the kitchen to look down the hallway to the front door and the stairs. Usually, whenever they came to visit, if Amanda wasn't in the kitchen, she would come bustling down the stairs, her face split into a wide smile, arms outstretched for hugs. Only this time, she wasn't coming down that hallway. She wasn't waiting in the kitchen, rocking in her low rocker, a piece of knitting or embroidery in her lap. There weren't any tantalizing aromas coming from the top of the stove or inside the oven.

As expected, everyone experienced a moment of profound grief. However, to their credit, they quickly tried to pull themselves together. Unheard, Phillip had wandered back into the kitchen and stood in the doorway watching his daughters grapple with something he had been trying to deal with by himself for two days.

Once again, Zoe heard Sara say to herself, "I can do this. I can do this." Zoe looked at her sister oddly, but didn't say anything.

"I guess we should go upstairs and pick out Ma's things," Gina suggested.

"What time do we have to be there again, Dad?" Sara asked.

"Five o'clock. So we better hurry up. Pick out her things and any jewelry you think is appropriate."

After everyone took turns going to the bathroom, they all assembled in Phillip and Amanda's bedroom.

"Didn't Dad say that he found Mom on the floor?" Zoe asked.

"Yeah," Stephanie said. "I wonder where."

"I don't want to know," Sara told them.

"Let's just get this over with. Sara, what do you think we should pick?" Zoe asked. She knew if anyone was the most familiar with Amanda's clothes, it would be Sara. She and Theo, along with Bethany, were frequent visitors to their parents' home.

"This," Sara said holding up a beautiful cream suit with gold threads woven throughout the jacket and skirt. "We gave her this suit last Christmas for a dinner dance she was supposed to go to with her friend Mary. She was too sick to go. I don't think she ever got a chance to wear it," Sara said, shaking her head sadly.

"She didn't," Phillip told them. "By the way, you girls can have any of Ma's jewelry that you want, except I want Ma's wedding ring."

"Are you sure, Dad?" Zoe asked, surprised.

"Yes, take whatever you want, but I want that

ring," he told them as he headed back down the stairs to wait for them in the living room.

"I guess we should pick out jewelry for Mom too," Zoe told them.

Looking through Amanda's things on her dresser, Sara picked up a strand of pearls that Amanda wore almost constantly and two rings, one for each hand. Both of the rings had large stones, one with five stones across the top, the other with three princess cut stones.

"Are those real?" Stephanie asked, looking at the rings Sara had chosen.

"Knowing Mom, I wouldn't be surprised, but I don't think so. They are probably her fabulous fakes. The pearls are real though. At least I think they are."

"Let me see," Gina said as she rubbed them against her teeth. "Yeah, I think they are. I remember hearing something about rubbing them against your teeth. If it feels rough, then they're real, and these feel real. Fake pearls are too smooth."

Theo was still quietly standing in the doorway, the ever protective presence in his wife's life. He knew how things could get sometimes with Sara and her sisters, especially between Sara and Stephanie.

"Okay, what else do we need?" asked the ever practical Zoe. Without waiting for an answer, she started pulling open drawers, looking for undergarments. "Look at her drawers. Everything is so neat," Zoe commented in awe.

As they opened drawer after drawer, the sisters stared in amazement at Amanda's organization and neatness. In her nightgown drawer, every single gown was pressed and folded. The same thing was true for her slip, stocking, bra and underwear drawers. It made it easy to find everything they needed. They weren't sure if they needed those things but as Sara said, "I am *not* burying my mother without her underwear!"

Once they gathered everything together, they joined their father downstairs and headed around the corner to the undertakers.

"Damn, we could have walked around here," Zoe said when she saw how close it was to the house, causing everyone to laugh nervously, not because it was particularly funny, but because everyone could feel the tension building as they filed into the funeral home.

The director, an old classmate of Phillip's, led them into a conservatively modern looking conference room.

After listening to what choices they had, they struggled through the various decisions that had to be made. Every time something had to be decided, Stephanie immediately let her wishes be known. Zoe, Gina, and Sara, however, would defer to Phillip, asking what he wanted. Surprisingly, their father often conceded to their wishes, but they wanted to make sure that everything was how he wanted it to be. By silent accord, three of the sisters remembered what their mother had requested: not to let Stephanie take over and push Phillip's feelings aside. And even though he seemed to want to let them decide everything, they made him actively participate in the myriad of decisions.

Once they were finished, Sara asked to see the coffin they selected. Because their mother only had a tiny funeral policy, the choices were slim.

When the director showed them what the policy would cover, all of the sisters were dismayed. After looking at the other coffins, they decided to upgrade to a better one.

Sara and Theo offered to buy the best one there, but everyone said that wasn't fair. They all wanted to help pay for any upgrade, but it had to be within everyone's budget. What Sara and Theo could afford to pay was not what everyone else could. After a few words, they finally picked a coffin with which everyone felt comfortable. At least, cost-wise. Sara was pissed, but Theo quietly told her to let yet another thing go.

When they returned to the house, everyone realized how hungry they were. Looking in the refrigerator, they discovered slim pickings. The freezer wasn't much better. There would have been enough to feed Amanda and Phillip, but not all of them. They informed their father they were going to the store, and he declined to go with them. Maybe it was the stress of what they had just been through, but this shopping experience soon turned out to be the strangest one they had ever had.

It started out normal enough. Stephanie and Sara were discussing whether to buy fruit. Gina wandered over to the fresh vegetable section, while Theo went to the bread section. Suddenly Zoe came over to Stephanie and Sara, munching on a stolen cherry.

"These cherries are sweet!" she exclaimed and then she suddenly spit the pit out near Stephanie's foot, causing Stephanie to jump out of the way to avoid the pit missile.

"Zoe! What the hell is wrong with you?" Sara asked, looking at her like she had lost her mind.

Zoe, with her eyes wide and jaw dropped, said, "I don't know what possessed me to do that! I've never done anything like that in my entire life!"

This only made Steph and Sara look at each other, then at Zoe, as they all started laughing hysterically and rushed over to tell Gina. Wiping their eyes from laughing so hard, they caught up with Theo near a display of wind chimes.

"Oooh, I've always liked wind chimes!" Zoe said, brushing some and cocking her head to the side, listening to their tinkling sound.

Imitating a whining child, Theo chimed in with, "Mommy, can I have a wind chime? Can I? Huh? Can I?" causing Stephanie, Gina, and Zoe to explode with peals of laughter. Sara looked at Theo like he had lost his mind before she finally cracked up herself.

"I don't believe you did that! Theo, will you stop?" She laughed as he continued to act up.

Suddenly, Zoe spotted the candy display and said, "Ooh! Look! Candy!" They all rushed to the candy like they had never seen it before. They grabbed plastic bags from the roller above the display and started shoveling in their favorite candies, totally ignoring the weight. It didn't matter anyway since they all started eating it as they continued going up and down the aisles shopping.

Sara picked up some aspirin and went to put it in the cart. Zoe quickly scanned the piece of paper where she had written down what they needed and exclaimed, "It's not on the list! It's not on the list! If it's not on the list, you can't get it!" as she jabbed at the piece of paper with the pen she was using to check off each item, like a deranged, anal retentive, drill sergeant. That only sent them all into more peals of laughter.

Suddenly, Theo started skipping and then riding on the cart, saying, "Wheeee!" By now they were almost ready to pee on themselves from laughing so hard. Thankfully, the store was practically deserted, but they didn't really pay any attention to the other patrons anyway.

When they finally got in line, there was a small argument over payment of the grocery bill, as every one of them wanted to pay. They finally split the bill up before exiting the store, still happily munching on their now much lighter bags of candy.

After they got back into Theo's Navigator, Sara turned around and asked, "What the hell was that? What possessed us to act like that in a grocery store?"

"It was your mother," Theo said sagely, causing the sisters to nod solemnly, like that explained everything.

Zoe thought maybe he was on to something. Or maybe it was because of what they just went through at the funeral home. It was strange that they all got so silly at the same time. Maybe they were more alike than they realized.

After unpacking all of the bags, they quickly had chicken frying to a golden brown, sweet bread baking, butter corn boiling in the pot, and one of Gina's awesome salads cooling in the refrigerator.

"Is somebody going to fix Dad's plate and take it in to him?" Sara asked, putting a clean towel on the TV tray their father used to eat in front of the television in the living room.

"I'm not fixing shit. He can get off his ass and come fix his own damn plate," Zoe said.

"Zoe," Sara admonished, trying to keep the peace.

"Zoe, what? I mean it. Mom used to do that. I always hated it. I'm not doing it. Either he can come get it his damn self, or one of y'all can do it." With that, she got herself a plate and filled it before plopping down in one of the chairs around the table to eat.

Gina, Sara, and Stephanie looked at each other.

"Oh hell, I'll do it!" Sara grumbled, as she fixed the plate, set it on the tray, arranged the silverware just so, filled a glass with iced tea, and put a slice of bread on a smaller plate with a pat of butter. Picking up the tray, she carried it into the living room to her father who grunted his thanks.

"Better you than me," Zoe commented when Sara came back.

"Zoe, don't you think he's been through enough these last couple of days? I mean, come on."

"He might as well get used to it. Mom is not coming back. He's got nobody to wait on him hand and foot anymore. And while I'm here, it damn sure won't be me!"

Before anyone could comment, there was a knock at the door. One of their parents' neighbors was dropping off a dish of something none of them recognized. Stephanie thanked her sweetly for her generosity before closing the door and turning around with the dish to hand it to Zoe who was busy eating.

"Here, Zoe, take this. Write down the lady's

name and what she brought for the thank-you cards.

"I'm eating, Stephanie. When I get done."

"No, I want you to do it now, before you forget."

"Well damn! Who made you the Commander? Shit! I *said* I would do it after I'm finished eating. I'm hungry just like everybody else. I'll do it when I'm done, and not you or any-damn-body else is going to make me do it before then!"

Stephanie rolled her eyes, but decided she would leave Zoe alone; for now. They all knew that you didn't fuck with Zoe when she was trying to eat. And for God's sake, *do not* attempt to take her plate before she's finished. One move toward it could find you with a fork stuck in the back of your hand.

Needless to say, the rest of the meal was eaten with little conversation. Finally, Gina asked, "So, where is everybody sleeping tonight?"

"Well, Theo and I always stay in the room across the hall from Mom and Dad. Dad will probably sleep on the couch. So that leaves their bedroom and the back bedroom that Dad uses as a dressing room," Sara told them.

"I'll take the back bedroom, if no one objects," Gina said.

"That means that Stephanie and I have to share the same bed. I don't like sleeping with women. I don't even sleep with my own daughter. Damn!" Zoe complained. After sighing heavily, she continued, "but I guess there's no other choice. *Shit!*"

For once, Stephanie had no comment.

After the dishes were done and the kitchen cleaned up, they made their way into the living room to spend some time with their father. Trying to have a conversation with Phillip was never easy for any of them. Out of the four sisters, Gina seemed to have the easiest rapport with their father. Those two had always been drinking and hanging out buddies. However, after a while each sister got up on some pretense or another and ended up back in the kitchen.

"I need to go for a walk. Anybody want to join me?" Zoe asked.

"I'll go," Sara said, grabbing her cigarette pouch. Gina and Stephanie declined, stating they were going to take their showers and probably turn in. Theo, thankfully, stayed in the living room with Phillip to watch a game and just generally keep him company.

After they both had taken drags on their cigarettes and exhaled mightily, Zoe told Sara, "I had to get out of there. Stephanie has been working on my freakin' nerves all day. What was with all that bossing around? Damn! I love her to death, but sometimes she can be a bit much. And as hungry as I was, I was in no mood for her shit!"

"I know what you mean. She's been pretty cool and I was wondering when the real Stephanie was going to show up. Bet before the week ends, it'll get a lot worse."

"Tell me about it," Zoe sighed.

CHAPTER FOUR
The Week From Hell: The Middle

*E*arly the next morning, after everyone ate their breakfast of choice, the sisters opted to walk around the corner to the florist. Their father declined to join them, saying that he had already made his selection before they arrived.

After almost two hours, they finally agreed on two arrangements: one from the daughters and one from the grandchildren. The one from the daughters included four carnations, each in a different color, to represent each daughter.

"Now what?" Zoe asked.

"We can go back to the house for now, I guess. We have to meet with the caterer later to discuss the menu for the repast," Gina reminded them.

"What time were we supposed to be meeting them?" asked Stephanie.

"Oh, in about fifteen minutes." Sara told them.

"Well, we can forget about walking then," Gina said.

"Theo, we've got to get to the caterer's. Would

you mind driving us?" Zoe asked as they rushed into the house.

"No problem," Theo replied, getting his keys off the kitchen table. So much for needing separate cars. They had only been using Theo's car since they got there. Zoe was grateful. The thought of getting back into Gina's rattle-trap made her shudder.

"Dad, do you want to go?" Zoe inquired, knowing that he was probably going to say no.

"Y'all go ahead. I've got to go over to the Legion. I'll meet you back here later," Phillip told them, waving them out the door.

"Coming, Gina?" Zoe asked her sister.

"I have a raging headache. You all go on. I think I'm going to lay down for a little bit."

"Okay, Sis. I saw some Tylenol on the table. Take a couple of those and we'll see you when we get back. Want anything while we're out?"

"No, I'll just take some fruit juice upstairs with me. Catch y'all later," Gina told them as she headed toward the stairs.

"Where is this place anyway?" Zoe wanted to know.

"Where else? On Main Street." Sara laughed, while Stephanie just grunted a disinterested, "Figures."

When they got to the caterer's, which was really just a deli shop, the three sisters found the place empty with the exception of a young, pimply-faced youth behind the meat counter who looked like a cross between John-Boy Walton and Richie from *Happy Days,* right down to a smattering of freckles across his nose.

"Can I help you?" he squeaked.

"Yes, we're here to check on the order for the Livingston funeral," Sara told him.

"Uhmm, let me check. That name doesn't sound familiar at all," he told them.

"What do you mean it doesn't sound familiar? Jesus Christ! Can't anybody get anything right in this damn town!" Stephanie shouted.

"Chill, Steph. Dag. Give him a chance to check," Sara told her.

"He shouldn't have to check! We had an appointment; we got here on time. What the fuck is there to check?"

"Ma'am, I'm sorry, but I don't see an appointment with that name," he stammered, taken aback by Stephanie's outburst.

"*Shit!* Goddamnit, where is the manager?" Stephanie demanded, sending the clerk scurrying out of the storefront to somewhere in the back.

"Okay, Steph, that's enough. You don't have to get ugly," Zoe told her.

"Don't tell me what to say. I'm tired of these small town crackers. They're gettin' on my fuckin' nerves!"

"For God's sake, Stephanie, keep it down," Sara hissed between clenched teeth.

Before Stephanie could say anything else, the red-faced youth came back to tell them to follow him to his father's office.

Once they got in the office, a rather nice looking Caucasian man with chestnut brown hair and warm brown eyes identified himself as the owner of the store.

"I apologize for the mixup. My son didn't know

the name of the deceased. The person who called in to make the appointment, a Leslie McMann, gave her name, not yours."

"Oh, Leslie. Right. She was a friend of my Mom's. She just told us what time to be here." Sara smiled as she shook his hand.

"Well she must have told you where the damn food had to go, which means she would have told you our name," Stephanie huffed.

"That's enough, Stephanie," Zoe said, cutting her off.

"Okay, that's it. I'll meet y'all in the car," Sara snapped, leaving Zoe to deal with Stephanie.

When she got to the car, Theo asked, "What's the matter? You look mad enough to fry an egg on your head."

"Not a what, but a who!"

"Stephanie, I assume. What did she do now?"

"She went in there and lost her fuckin' mind," Sara said as she proceeded to fill Theo in.

"You don't get ugly with folks who fix your food," Theo said, shaking his head.

Zoe, meanwhile, was stuck in the store with Stephanie, trying to cover for her obnoxious behavior. She wanted to smack Sara for leaving her alone with Steph. She shot Stephanie one of those 'don't say another word' looks, concluded their business, smiled prettily at the owner, and hustled Stephanie's ass out of there as fast as she could. The minute they got out the door, they went at it.

"What the hell is the matter with you, Stephanie? There was no cause for you to act like that," Zoe spat.

"Well, they should have . . ."

"I don't want to hear it," Zoe snapped, climbing

into the Navigator on one side, Stephanie on the other.

"Why did you do that, Stephanie?" Sara asked. You don't get up in people's faces who handle your food. You just don't."

"Well I *did*," she answered in a nasty tone.

"All I know is, I'm not eating shit from here now. And I will tell my kids not to eat it either," Zoe snapped. "No telling what they may do to that food."

"For real," Sara concurred.

Stephanie just sucked her teeth and sulked.

When they got back, they discovered that Phillip hadn't returned yet. Gina, who felt much better, was up and had started dinner.

"How did it go?" she asked, pulling a roast out of the oven.

"Don't ask," snapped Sara, heading straight up the stairs to her and Theo's room.

Gina turned back to look at Stephanie and Zoe. When she saw Stephanie stomp upstairs, her eyes got wide and she looked at Theo and Zoe for an explanation.

"Don't ask me, I wasn't there," Theo told her, throwing his hands up before going into the living room to watch television.

Once again, Gina's eyes swung to Zoe, who was now sitting at the kitchen table, furiously puffing on a cigarette.

"Well?"

"You wouldn't believe the way she acted up in there, Gina. She embarrassed the hell out of Sara and me. She just went the fuck off for no reason."

"Oh, so in other words, Stephanie was being Stephanie," Gina said with a sigh.

"Exactly!" Zoe then proceeded to tell Gina what happened. As she filled her in, she got up and helped Gina finish getting the meal together.

"Girl, I thought Sara was going to deck her right there in the store," Zoe said, laughing. "And speaking of Sara, can you believe how she's handling all of this? I just *knew* she was going to be a wreck and we'd be holding her hand all week. I'm amazed at how well she's holding up."

"Sara's grown up a lot, Zoe. I think the only one of us who won't admit it is Stephanie. As far as Steph's concerned, Sara is still her baby sister who used to adore her, and she refuses to let Sara out of that position. When any of us butt heads with Steph, she feels that because she's the oldest, everybody, especially Sara, has to do what she says. She knows that shit doesn't work with us! We've both cussed her out too many times for her to try that with us. I don't think Sara ever has."

"No, I don't think so either. You would think that with Steph and Sara having the same mother, they would be trying to get each other through this. Instead, it seems like Steph is almost baiting Sara. At least she's been civil to Dad, even though he's not her father. But I'll tell you what, if Stephanie keeps acting like she is, she just might meet a whole new side of Sara. And that ain't no joke. And if she keeps fuckin' with me like she has, she's going to end up getting her feelings hurt. Shit, she ought to know me by now," Zoe said.

Gina laughed, "Yes, we all know you and your temper, Zoe. I guess we should call them and tell them dinner's ready."

"I'm not telling them shit. They saw you fixing dinner when they came in. I will tell Theo to tell

Sara, though. If Stephanie is hungry enough, she'll bring her mad ass down here."

"Zoe. Now you need to stop. Forget it, I'll go tell them myself," Gina said, striding out of the kitchen. She popped her head in the living room to tell Theo on her way up the stairs. Knocking gently on Sara's door, she told her that dinner was ready. She heard Sara say she would be right down. Repeating the action, she listened at Stephanie's door but got no response. Shrugging her shoulders, she was on her way back down when she heard someone behind her. Turning her head, she saw that Sara was following her down the stairs.

"Smells good, Gina. I'm starved," she laughed.

Phillip returned, and as usual he ate his dinner in the living room. Theo found another tray and volunteered to eat in there with Phillip so he wouldn't have to eat alone. Everyone was already eating before Stephanie finally showed up.

Silently, Stephanie fixed her plate and sat down to eat. Gina, Zoe, and Sara exchanged a look, but no one said a word. Finally, Stephanie started a conversation about something inconsequential, and after a while the sisters were laughing and talking again.

When Theo came back into the kitchen with both dinner trays, he was relieved to see the sisters laughing, and not at each other's throats.

While the others cleaned up the kitchen, Zoe, who was more in the way than helpful, went upstairs for some alone time and to call Antonio. Zoe felt much calmer after talking with him and catching him up on all that had happened since they arrived.

Next she called Vaughn's house so she could

check on the kids and confirm when Antonio would be picking them up to bring them to the funeral.

"I'm coming to the funeral, Zoe," Vaughn informed her.

"What? Why?"

"I always liked your mom and while we were married, she was always nice to me. Besides, the kids want to come, so I'm bringing them."

Even though she didn't like it, Zoe just said, "Fine, Vaughn. I'll see you in a couple of days." She didn't bother to tell him Antonio would be there. At this point, she didn't care and she didn't feel like dealing with it.

After a long, hot shower, Zoe fell into bed, trying hard to ignore Stephanie's snoring presence on her other side.

The next morning, Zoe got up early, dressed, and went downstairs to fix herself a cup of Amaretto and Cream coffee. She was surprised to find her father already up.

"Hey, Dad. What are you doing up so early?" Zoe asked as she got a mug from the cup cabinet. After setting the teapot on the stove to boil, she looked in the refrigerator for something to go with her coffee. Spotting some danish, she pulled one out and popped it in the microwave to warm up.

"You know me. I'm used to getting up early. Retirement hasn't changed fifty-some years of habits."

"I hear you." Zoe poured the now boiling water into her mug with the gourmet flavored coffee she liked already inside. Inhaling its sweet aroma, she carefully brought it over to the table. They sat in an uncomfortable, all too familiar silence as Zoe munched on her pastry and gingerly took an occasional sip of the steaming coffee.

"So . . ." they both said at the same time, and then nervously laughed.

"Go ahead . . ." they both said again, this time chuckling for real. Phillip held out his hand, indicating ladies first.

"I was just going to make sure you knew what the agenda was for today. We're supposed to go view the body at eleven o'clock. Antonio should be arriving sometime this evening and Vaughn is coming up later with the kids. Frank should be here sometime today with Gina's kids and Theo's daughter, Chelsea, should be here with Bethany and T.J."

"Where are all of those people going to fit? This house isn't big enough for that!"

"We know that, Dad. We're going to make reservations at the nearest hotel in Sayre. I think Stephanie is staying here with the kids. Everybody else will probably come up just for the funeral and then leave immediately afterward."

"When are you guys all leaving?"

"Probably the day after."

"Oh. Well. Hhmm."

Silence settled between them again. Zoe didn't want to feel sorry for her father, but she did. She could see he was dreading being in the house by himself. But what were they supposed to do? They all had lives back in Philadelphia. Lives, jobs, and homes. Surely he understood that. Thankfully, before the silence became too painful again, Gina and Sara came bustling downstairs. Both sisters greeted them with a tired sounding "Mornin'."

Sara declared she was in desperate need of a cup of coffee, while Gina quietly went about fixing herself a cup of the specially mixed herbal tea that she carted around with her everywhere she went, along with her crystals and worry stones. Gina believed a good cup of herbal tea cured everything from cramps to a grumpy disposition, bad back, or gallstones. And what the tea didn't cure, the crystals would. Not to mention the ton of vitamins she took every day. Gina was into holistic healing and had volumes and volumes of books on how to cure just about everything naturally. Of course, this was also a woman who believed in keeping a stash of the best damn marijuana money could buy.

"Where's Steph?" Zoe asked.

"She was just coming from her shower when we were on our way down," Sara said, lighting up her cigarette and then letting out a satisfying sigh as she gratefully sipped her coffee.

"Next best thing to a drink: a cup of coffee!" she declared.

Both Zoe and Gina frowned and Zoe admonished, "You're not drinking again, are you?"

"Chile, please! Hell no. I was just saying, that's all. Nope, been clean and sober for years now."

"Just checking, Girl."

"I know, Sis. This," Sara waved her hand in the air, encompassing everything that had happened in the last few days with her gesture, "has made me pretty damn tempted, but I've been holding steady. It's what Mom would want. She wouldn't want me to compromise my sobriety because I can't cope with her dying. Hell, if I could live through that other mess, I guess I can make it through this," she said quietly, looking into her coffee mug for answers.

Gina and Zoe glanced at each other. Nobody really liked to talk about what had happened to Sara. Sometimes they could almost pretend it never happened. They knew how hard it was for her to deal with her attack and rape. They could only imagine what she must have gone through. They even tried to pretend they didn't know that she was still going through therapy in order to deal with it. It just simply wasn't talked about. At least not among them.

"You know, I used to talk to Mom about it all the time. Sometimes for hours on end. Who am I going to talk to now?" Sara wondered sadly.

"You can talk to us, Sara."

"No, I can't. You know it and I know it. Y'all didn't want to deal with it then, and I know you don't want to deal with it now. It happened. I'm okay. Well, as okay as I'm ever going to be, that is. I almost never have to make Theo stop when we're having sex anymore, and my therapist says that's progress."

Zoe glanced around to see what their father was thinking about this conversation and noticed that he had eased out of the room. It was just as well. It was as hard on him as it had been on everyone else. Zoe had never seen such murderous rage in her father's eyes as she saw that day when she picked her parents up and brought them back down to Philly after Sara's attack.

When they got to the hospital they found Sara still in a coma. Her face was ravaged with ugly purple, black, and brown bruises and a swollen jaw and she had bruising on her arms and wrists. Zoe was sure that if Frankie or Terrell, Sara's attackers, were standing there, Phillip would have killed them both with his bare hands.

Phillip then pulled down the sheet that was covering Sara and they both gasped in horror when they saw the bruises that snaked up her legs from her ankles to under the gown they were sure hid more hideous bruising. Phillip gently re-covered Sara with the sheet and muttered an expletive before turning on his heel and exiting the room. Zoe was left to comfort Amanda as best she could. That was when Zoe realized that Phillip really did love his daughters. He may not have always said it or shown it, but in that moment, she had not one doubt.

Once again, Zoe and Gina's eyes met over Sara's head.

"I know that y'all are looking over my head. I don't know why y'all never want to talk about it, but, hey, shit happens."

"Sara, you know we don't mean any harm. We just don't always know what to say to you."

"Yeah, I know, Sis."

Before Sara could say anything else, Stephanie came bobbin' into the kitchen. Surprisingly, she seemed to be in good mood for a change.

When they arrived at the funeral home, the funeral director discreetly greeted them and ushered them inside. Once again, they milled around the lobby, reluctant to walk into the room where their mother was laid out. When they could no longer put it off, they collectively took a deep breath as they slowly entered the room and hesitated a moment before walking to the front of the room to view their mother's body.

Sara immediately began fiddling with the pearls

around Amanda's neck, giving the rest of her mother's body a cursory look.

Gina heard her mumble, "If I keep playing with these pearls, I don't have to deal with the fact that this is Mom," as she noticed her sister's hand tremble over the pearls.

For a moment, no one said anything as they viewed Amanda's body. Zoe thought that she looked really good and said so. The other sisters quickly agreed. Phillip said nothing as he stood at the side of the casket. Zoe noticed him reach out and squeeze Amanda's lifeless, stiff hand. Wordlessly, he turned around and left the room, leaving the sisters to their own thoughts.

Still, Sara fiddled with the pearls, trying to get them to lay just right. Despite her best efforts, they kept rolling up under Amanda's neck, and wouldn't lay the way she wanted them to. She was surprised to see that they weren't even clasped behind her mother's head.

"Sara, the suit is beautiful," Gina told her.

"Thank you," Sara replied, her voice barely above a hoarse whisper.

"Where is the plaque?" Stephanie asked.

The funeral director and his assistant, who had joined the sisters, looked confused.

"Plaque?"

"Yes, the plaque," Stephanie snapped.

"I'm not sure I understand what you mean," the director stammered.

"The goddamn plaque that's supposed to be on the casket with her name," Stephanie barked at the poor man.

"Steph, they may not do that up here," Gina tried to reason.

"Oh for Chrissake! Can't they do anything right in this goddamn backwater town?" Stephanie railed.

"I'm sorry, but we don't do that here," the director tried to explain in the soothing voice funeral directors use for distraught relatives.

"Shit! I knew we should have found a way to bring Mom down to Philly! They can't do shit right up here!"

"We are not having this, Stephanie! Not here, and not now," Sara told her firmly but quietly through clenched teeth, gesturing over her mother's body, as her eyes bore into her oldest sister's eyes.

"Sara's right. Cut it out, Steph," Zoe admonished.

Nervously clearing his throat, the funeral director asked if they wanted the jewelry removed after the service.

Hesitantly, Sara said, "Well, if no one minds, I'd like to have Mom's pearls for Bethany. It's her birth stone, and Mom always told Bethany she could have her pearls."

"I'm sure *no one* would have a problem with that. Isn't that right, Steph?" Gina asked, looking Stephanie in the eyes, seeming to convey more than what she was saying.

"Sure, I don't care." Stephanie shrugged, but Zoe noted how she fingered their mother's pearls. Zoe also noted the look of relief on Sara's face, correctly guessing that she was relieved not to have to fight about it.

"And the rings," the director prompted.

"I think we should bury Mom with them," Sara commented.

"I can just hear her saying, 'I know them niggahs ain't gonna bury me without some jewelry!'" Zoe laughed, then clapped her hand over her mouth when she realized what she had said in front of the director and his assistant, who were both a bright red.

The comment, however, helped to diffuse the tense atmosphere in the room. But Stephanie only let her tight smile fade, still pissed off about the plaque.

After making final arrangements, Sara and Zoe took a moment to thank the funeral director and his assistant for how well they had made their mother look. Being one of the very few black people in Athens, they were surprised with how well Amanda had been turned out. Even her hair looked good. Sara expressly thanked the assistant for that. They hadn't been sure what they would find, but with the exception of Stephanie, they had all been pleased with Amanda's appearance.

Just before leaving, Sara turned around to look at their mother one more time and cried out in dismay, "Where are her breasts?" While everyone looked at Sara like she must have lost her mind, Sara felt her mother's chest, frantically trying to find her breasts, saying, "I know Mom never had that much; but now they're completely gone!"

"It's the embalming, Sara," Gina gently told her, like that explained everything.

"I don't see what that's got to do with her losing her breasts," Sara grumbled. Sara noted that once again the director and his assistant were looking at them like they had just landed on Earth from Mars.

Needless to say, the ride back home was tense. The minute they hit the door everyone scattered to their own space. Zoe and Sara took off for their rooms. Gina went to her small sanctuary in the back bedroom. And Steph stayed downstairs in the kitchen to stew in her own juices. Theo opted to hide out in the living room with Phillip.

Later, when Zoe came back downstairs, she immediately picked up on the strained atmosphere. Sara and Theo were in the living room with their father, while Gina seemed to be in a deep discussion with a disgruntled looking Stephanie. Their conversation, however, seemed to come to an abrupt halt when Zoe entered the room. Looking around, Zoe thought she saw a 'behave yourself' look pass from Gina to Stephanie.

Zoe didn't care. As long as she wouldn't have to deal with any more of Stephanie's shit.

"You got the directions to the hotel, Gina?" she asked instead.

"Yup, right here. Let me go get Sara and Theo and we'll be ready to roll."

"I'll go get them," Zoe volunteered, not wanting to be in the kitchen with Stephanie.

"What's wrong with her?" Stephanie asked Gina with a raised eyebrow.

"Do you really need to ask, Sis?" Gina responded with a slight smile.

Stephanie, not bothering to answer, grabbed her down jacket and went out on the back steps to wait for the others.

Gina looked after her, started to follow, then changed her mind and just shook her head.

The ride to the hotel was short, and in a matter of minutes they were all checked in. Zoe even thought to ask the desk clerk to hold a room for Vaughn, since he was insisting on coming.

They'd just returned to the house and settled around the kitchen table to discuss what else needed to be done when a very pleasant woman knocked at the kitchen door.

"Can I help you?" Zoe asked politely.

"I knocked at the front door. I guess no one heard me. I'm here to speak with Amanda Livingston about some life insurance," she replied with a smile.

Looking at the faces of her sisters, Zoe was speechless for a moment.

"Is something wrong?" the lady asked, nervous as she looked around at the stunned faces.

Finding her voice, Sara told her, "Our . . . our mother just passed away a few days ago."

"Ohmygod! Ohmygod!" the woman cried, falling back against the nearest wall. She looked like she was getting ready to burst into tears. Sara immediately tried to comfort *her*, instead of the other way around.

"It's okay. You had no way of knowing."

"I just spoke to her last week, when I arranged for this meeting. She said she didn't have enough insurance in case . . . in case she died," she finished on a whisper. "I am so sorry. Are all of you her daughters?"

"Yes, we are." Zoe gently smiled.

"You have my most sincere condolences. She seemed like such a nice lady on the phone," the woman stammered.

"She was," Sara said firmly.

"Well. Well. I guess I should be going then," the flustered woman said.

"Yes, well, under the circumstances, I guess so," Sara told her, as she watched the woman beat a hasty retreat.

"I guess she's never had that happen before," Sara said, chuckling at the absurdity of it all.

"Damn, that was strange. Like Mom knew she was going to die," Zoe said.

"I know. It was kind of creepy, wasn't it?" Gina remarked, watching the woman repeatedly try to get her key in the ignition. When she finally succeeded, she sped up the street like the Hounds of Baskerville were chasing her.

"Bet she's going to the nearest bar." Stephanie smirked. The others silently nodded their agreement.

CHAPTER FIVE

The Week From Hell: Laid To Rest

"**W**ell, that went well," Sara volunteered as they sat around Gina's room, discussing the day's events.

Ex-spouses, children, significant others, and one spouse had all descended on the house at once, in one long caravan. The small street was ill-equipped to handle all the various vehicles, so sympathetic neighbors came to their rescue and permitted some of them to park cars in their driveways. It was a courtesy that stunned everyone. In the city—especially Philadelphia—people would get cursed out for taking up too many parking spaces, and parking in someone else's driveway was unheard of.

Zoe was delighted to see her children and Antonio, but she was on the verge of saying something smart to Vaughn until she saw the sheen of tears in his eyes after he broke his embrace with Phillip. She bit her tongue instead and withstood Vaughn's awkward display of condolences when he first arrived.

The viewing, to say the least, was strange. As one particular group came in, Zoe thought she was going to choke when she overheard Sara say, "talk about coming from central casting!" One man looked like a bad imitation of Jed Clampett, covered from head to foot in dirt, teeth missing and a face that looked like a piece of crumbled parchment. His friend wasn't much better. The women with them all looked like tired, worn out mountain women with really bad home perms, the kind the television commercials used to warn people about. However, to their credit, the women told the sisters that they all just heard about Amanda's death and viewing and came straight from the fields.

But the scene of all scenes was the one staged by Stephanie herself. At one point, each of the sisters had gotten up to get some air or smoke a cigarette. Sara was just coming out to join the other three when she saw Stephanie throw down her cigarette, curse and rush back into the funeral home.

"What was that all about?" Sara asked, looking as confused as Zoe, as they stared at the empty space Stephanie had just occupied.

"Wait, you'll see," Gina said mysteriously, a smirk playing about her lips. A few minutes later, Stephanie's best friends, two white nuns, strolled around the corner of the parking lot next to the funeral home.

"Oh. I get it," Zoe whispered to Gina, before being engulfed in a massive hug from Paula and then another one from the nun they called Phil behind Stephanie's back, because she looked like Phil Donahue.

"Well I don't," grumbled Sara, as they followed the newcomers into the funeral home.

"I'll tell you later," Zoe whispered back before stopping dead in her tracks. Sara ran into Zoe's back, wondering what was wrong. She looked around Zoe to see Stephanie at the front of the parlor, kneeling on the small prayer bench that was placed cattycorner to their mother's open coffin. There knelt Stephanie, with one hand up to her forehead, head bent, eyes closed: the picture of overwhelming, silent grief.

"What the hell?" Sara muttered, looking at her sister in disbelief. Of course, Stephanie's friends, who were a couple of steps in front of Zoe and Sara, rushed to the front where Stephanie seemed not to notice them until one gently placed her hand on her shoulder in silent support. Stephanie turned and looked up with grief-stricken eyes. She then stumbled up, like the act of moving was just too much for her weary body, before collapsing into her friends' waiting arms.

"Give me a break!" Zoe said, while Gina silently laughed, saying, "*That's* what I was talking about, Sara."

"Jesus. She should get an Academy Award for that performance," Sara whispered to Zoe, causing Zoe to snort out a short laugh.

Thankfully, the wake was soon over and everyone trooped back to the house, tired and with nerves more than a little frayed.

Zoe, Gina, and Sara, after stepping out of their heels in the dining room, hurried into the kitchen to fix plates for their kids who all wanted to be fed *yesterday*. They then hustled them all upstairs to get ready for bed.

Ever efficient Zoe remembered to bring her steam iron back to the house and was busy steaming out all of the kids' clothes while Gina and Sara handled bath detail.

Finally, everyone was settled and they returned downstairs to sink tiredly into kitchen chairs. On her way through the dining room, Zoe found Steph still talking with her two friends. Zoe spotted a bottle of wine on the dining room table in one of those snazzy wine baskets.

"Oh, this is nice," she commented, picking up the bottle.

"That's mine!" Stephanie snapped, snatching the bottle from Zoe's hands, ignoring her startled look.

"Well, damn! I can see that, Steph. I was only commenting on how nice the basket is. Damn! Nobody asked you for any!"

"Yeah, well, I thought you might have thought it was for the house. It's a gift from Paula," Stephanie said defensively, trying to clean it up.

"Whatever," Zoe said, walking out of the dining room before she said something nasty.

"Y'all ready to go to the hotel?" she asked no one in particular. Gina and Sara had heard the whole exchange and silently sent Zoe sympathetic glances.

"Yeah, we are," Gina answered.

"Cool. See you guys at the hotel," Zoe said, not bothering to wait for a response before striding out the kitchen door and into Antonio's car.

"Okay, then," Gina said to the empty space that had been Zoe. "Steph, the kids are down, their clothes are hanging on the doors, and we'll be here as early as we can to give you a hand," Gina told her sister.

"Yeah, sure. Thanks," Stephanie mumbled.

"I'm sure Mother Rebecca will be up early, and

will certainly help you," Gina said as she laughed, referring to her daughter. Becca loved having an opportunity to lord over her cousins. She was the oldest and had recently adopted a 'motherly' attitude which drove her younger cousins crazy.

Even Stephanie had to smile, knowing how Becca acted since she was now a teenager—especially with Shanice and Bethany. Actually, Stephanie was glad Becca was there. As much as she loved doing hair, she knew that would be one chore she wouldn't have to deal with in the morning. She had already decided to hand the task over to Becca.

"Okay, Sis. I'll call you in the morning to make sure y'all are up in time," Stephanie told her as she followed Gina out the back door.

"You gonna be okay here tonight?" Gina asked, concerned.

"Yeah. I'll be fine. Paula and Gerri will be leaving in a few minutes and Dad said he was going to turn in soon himself."

"Okay, Sis, see you in the morning," Gina said before climbing into Theo's Navigator. Frank had gone back to the hotel right after the viewing, saying he was tired from the long drive and the long day. Gina wanted him to come back to the house for moral support, but she let him go.

The ride to the hotel was quiet, as Gina, Sara, and Theo seemed to be lost in their own thoughts.

On the elevator ride upstairs, Gina said, "I've got a bottle of wine in my room. You guys want to stop in for a drink?" At first, she was puzzled when no one said anything. Then she remembered that Sara couldn't drink.

"Oops, sorry, Hon. For a minute, I forgot. What about you, Theo? You're not on the wagon."

At Theo's hesitation, Sara told him, "Go ahead, Boo. Don't let me stop you. Why don't you call Zoe? I'm sure she's ready for a drink and more!" Sara laughed. "But I'll have a diet soda if you have any. Just let me go get out of these shoes before I hurt somebody!" Sara groaned, ready to do a Patti LaBelle and kick her shoes down the hall that led to their rooms.

Sara and Theo changed clothes and met Zoe and Antonio, who were also headed for Gina's room, in the hallway. After Frank let them in, Sara noticed Gina sitting at the table in the far corner of the room, busily rolling a joint. She glanced at Theo to see what his reaction was. Theo never liked being around pot. To Sara's surprise, he just shrugged his shoulders and accepted the cold beer that Frank handed him.

"Well, that went well," Sara offered.

Zoe snorted, and Sara was unsure whether it was from the pot she was smoking or just her general disgust.

"You're kidding, right? After that performance Steph put on tonight? And what was up with those strange people? For a minute I thought we were in a bad Stephen King movie," Zoe quipped.

"Which performance? At the funeral home or the one at the house?" Gina asked.

"At the funeral home. Lord, I have never seen anything like that in my entire life!" Sara giggled.

"What are y'all talking about?" Theo asked.

"Oh that's right, you missed it. That must have been when you were in the bathroom," Sara told him. At his continued look of confusion, they proceeded to demonstrate Stephanie on bended knee, bowed head, pitiful look and all. Theo just shook his head.

"And let's not forget how she bit my head off at the house," Zoe snapped.

"Well, thank goodness we just have to get through tomorrow and then we can all go home."

"Is everybody leaving tomorrow?" Sara inquired.

"No, I thought we were all going to leave the day after, just to make sure Dad is okay," Zoe answered.

"That's what I thought," Sara said.

"Except Frank is leaving tomorrow to take Becca and Sean home," Gina said.

"Same here," Antonio spoke up.

"I thought the boys were going to go home with their father and I would be riding back with you," Zoe told him, frowning.

"They are, but I never got a chance to tell you that I have to leave after the funeral. My boss wants me to come in tomorrow evening to do some overtime. They're short-handed."

"Nice damn time to tell me," Zoe snapped. It was things like this that sometimes got on Zoe's nerves.

"I was going to tell you, Baby. I just forgot all about it until now," he soothed.

"Uh-huh. Damn, so how am I supposed to get home? No offense, Gina, but I refuse to get back in that hoopty of yours. Not to mention, I can't promise that I won't haul off and smack the mess out of Stephanie if she says one more out of the way thing to me."

"None taken," Gina smiled, knowing that Zoe and Stephanie were damn close to having a confrontation. She was actually glad to be riding back alone with Stephanie. Trapped in the car for four hours, Stephanie would have no choice but to listen and talk to her. She felt there were things that needed to be said. She probably was the only one out of the four of them who could talk to Stephanie without her acting like a fool.

Laughing, Sara said, "No problem, Zoe. You can ride with us."

"Thanks," Zoe said, glaring at Antonio. She would have some choice words for him when they got back to their own room.

However, by the time Zoe finished showering, Antonio was fast asleep. Or at least he was *pretending* to be. She remembered how Amanda used to always say "every goodbye ain't gone and every closed eye ain't sleep." Zoe debated waking him. Exhaustion finally won the battle and she slipped into bed and was practically asleep before her head hit the pillow.

Zoe awoke the next morning with the sun streaming into the room and the loud jangle of the phone reverberating through her head. Groping for the phone she mumbled an incoherent "Yeah?"

"Zoe? You're still in bed? Chile, you're going to be late!" Sara practically screamed into the phone, prompting Zoe to lift it away from her ear.

"What time is it?"

"Time for us to be getting out of here," Sara huffed.

"Okay, give me twenty minutes. Thirty, tops. I'll meet you in the lobby."

"Just hurry up!"

"I *said* okay!" Zoe snapped, instantly awake.

Nudging Antonio, she jumped up from bed, hollering for Antonio to hurry up as she slammed the bathroom door behind her.

Forty-five minutes later, Zoe was in the lobby, looking flawless as usual.

"You look nice," Zoe told Sara and Theo. She smiled at them, ignoring Sara's scowling face.

"Well it's about damn time. But thanks, you do too. That hat looks cute," Sara commented.

All of the sisters had decided to wear hats. They were going to do this funeral Philadelphia style. They might have been mourning, but they were going to be sharp while doing it! Zoe wore a smoke gray cashmere jacket that flared at her small waistline and brought out her gray eyes. Her long, smoke gray cashmere skirt was paired with black nappa leather boots. Under her jacket she wore a black silk turtleneck sweater. Her accessories were chunky pieces of silver jewelry at her ears, throat, and wrist, along with her ever-present stainless steel tank watch. Her hat of choice today was a small, wool felt topper trimmed in faux silver fox, with a small asymmetrical brim that she wore cocked to one side, the brim dipping slightly over her right eye.

Sara chose to wear a deep cognac wool suit trimmed in faux mink along the collar, with a long column skirt and dyed-to-match suede Michael Kors stiletto-heeled boots. Her gold hoops, bracelet, and watch glowed warmly in the hotel light. Her hat of choice was a wool felt hat with a cutaway lampshade brim that she also wore dipped to one side of her beautiful face. The cognac color of the suit went well with her smooth, honey-colored skin. Sara's outfit was completed by her real golden ranch mink that she casually draped over her shoulders.

Theo's chocolate brown Armani suit, Thomas Pink golden yellow shirt, silk tie, Armani leather trench coat, and brown Ferrogamo slip-ons complimented Sara's outfit beautifully. And looking at Antonio, Zoe had to admit that he looked like the panther she often likened him to be in his black Hugo Boss suit and Bruno Magli loafers. She smiled again at his sleek and sexy look as she noticed the small diamond he wore in his right ear twinkling at her.

Zoe noted that quite a few people passing through the lobby turned to look in their direction. Whether it was because of how well they were turned out, the unusual sight of black folks, or a combination of both, she couldn't say. However, both she and Sara seemed to stand a little taller and preen just a bit.

Turning her attention back to the group, Sara volunteered, "Gina and Frank went on ahead to make sure the kids were ready and weren't being terrorized too badly by Steph."

"Let's roll then," Zoe told her, taking a deep breath as if she were steeling herself.

"Oh yeah, Stephanie said for all of us to meet at the house so we could have a car procession to the funeral home," Sara told them as she smirked.

"Well that's stupid! We have to pass the damn funeral home to get to the house!" Zoe exclaimed.

"I know. I told her we would meet them there if we had the time, but you were just getting up and we might be a little late. You know she sucked her teeth and bitched all over the place. Look at it this way, with all the kids there, at least those limos she insisted we get will be used."

"Humph. What time are they leaving from the house?"

Glancing at her gold watch, Sara said, giggling slightly, "About now!"

"Darn! What a shame! I guess it's off to the funeral home then," Zoe said with false regret.

Antonio and Theo looked at the sisters, who seemed delighted to have thwarted Stephanie's wishes. They just shook their heads as they followed their women out of the hotel.

When they reached the funeral home they were surprised the parking lot seemed full. Somehow they hadn't thought that many people would be there. Over the last few years, with Amanda's health declining, she had kept very few friends. Their father, however, was very active in both the Legion and the VFW, so they supposed most of the people who came were his friends.

"I hate funerals," Zoe heard Sara mumble under her breath as they went into the room where the services were being held. They hurried down the aisle to join Gina and Stephanie. Steph was craning her neck looking for them, so her face showed relief when she spotted them.

Zoe had to admit that even Steph and Gina, who generally seemed to care less about their appearances, had outdone themselves today.

Stephanie was in a deep purple suit with metallic gold embroidery on the cuffs of the jacket. She wore a pair of *clean* pumps that were designed in contrasting black and purple suede with metallic braiding on one side, giving the shoes an asymmetrical look. Her hat was large brimmed wool felt with dyed-to-match feathers sweeping around the brim. Girlfriend's purse even matched her shoes! Zoe was impressed. She didn't know Stephanie had it in her.

Gina opted for head to toe black: black silk turtleneck, black six panel suede skirt, black suede boots, silver jewelry, and a silver fox full length coat. Her hat was black wool with a huge, silver grosgrain bow on the brim. It went well with her salt and pepper curly hair.

The service itself went smoothly. Everyone read except Sara, who besides having a fear of public speaking, wasn't sure she could hold it together long enough to get any words out. Zoe and Sara sat next to each other, and whenever their eyes would fill up, they would gently joke about not ruining their makeup. Somehow, it worked to keep them from completely losing it.

Stephanie, however, gave a wonderful speech about who Amanda Livingston was. But what Zoe remembered the most was her closing sentence. *"May you finally rest in peace, Mom. You've certainly earned it!"* Zoe almost winced. They all knew what Stephanie was alluding to. After all the years with Phillip, all the years of abuse, all the years of waiting on him hand and foot, Amanda was finally free. It was Stephanie's final dig at their father. None of them had known what Stephanie was going to say. She had kept it to herself until now. Zoe glanced over at her father, noticing his stoic look as he continued to look straight ahead, acting as if he hadn't heard Stephanie. But Zoe knew better. There wasn't much that Phillip ever missed. Glancing over his head to Gina, she saw Gina slightly shake her head as if she were saying, "Let it go."

Zoe was glad when the funeral finally ended.

That is, until it was time to put the cloth over Amanda's face. For a moment they hesitated as each took a final look at their mother. Considering she died from a massive heart attack, she looked remarkably at peace. Zoe glanced at Sara, afraid that she was going to lose it. Surprisingly, Sara almost single-handedly put the cloth over Amanda's face before turning away quickly and walking out of the funeral home altogether, not even waiting for Theo's assistance. Zoe was impressed with the strength Sara exhibited, but what she didn't know was when Sara got outside, she had to take great gulps of air into her lungs. Nor did she see Sara clinging to the railing as she stumbled down the stairs, blinded by her tears.

When they reached the cemetery, Theo, Antonio, Frank, Vaughn, Christopher, and a distant cousin of their father's served as pall bearers. Zoe was so proud at how well Christopher handled his first real grownup act. At the funeral when Christopher bent down and kissed Amanda goodbye, Zoe was shocked and touched. And he was so handsome and properly somber when it came time to carry the casket from the hearse to the grave site. At seventeen, she didn't think she could have done something like that. But Christopher and Amanda always had a special bond, and he cried like a baby when he learned of Amanda's passing.

Zoe now stood next to her father, watching him and expecting him to fall apart. But he didn't. He stood silent and dry-eyed, except for one moment when Zoe saw him dash at his eyes. She was relieved not to have an emotional wreck on her hands, but she was perturbed by his seemingly granite facade.

When they returned from the cemetery, Zoe breathed a sigh of relief, glad to have it all over. However, when they went downstairs at the Legion, where the repast was being held, she made sure to tell her people not to eat the food. She was still suspicious that the caterer may have tampered with the trays. After Stephanie's performance, she wasn't taking any chances. She told her children she would feed them when they returned to the house. When they finished that little fiasco, most people opted to go upstairs to the large barroom. Phillip in particular declared that he was ready for a drink. Gina and Stephanie accompanied him there to keep an eye on him.

Zoe and Sara helped all the kids change out of their dress clothes and into sweaters, sneakers and jeans for the trip home. Gina and Frank had already said their farewells to one another. Zoe noticed that Frank was pacing back and forth, waiting for Becca and Sean to load their things into the car. He kept looking at the sky, anxious to get on the road before the weather turned bad.

Vaughn left soon after with Jonathan, Christopher, and Shanice. Zoe was grateful that he had stayed out of the way and out of her face, other than to express his condolences. She was mildly shocked at his open display of grief. She had forgotten how well Amanda and Vaughn got along. He used to tease her mother unmercifully whenever they would all get together. Like Theo, he could have her giggling like a schoolgirl. Zoe supposed that she never realized before how much Vaughn cared for her mother.

She felt a little uncomfortable when she saw

Vaughn and Antonio standing together to serve as pallbearers, along with the others. She was shocked and amazed when it appeared that each man was trying to console the other with awkward pats on the back.

Although she hated to see her children leave, she was quite relieved to see Vaughn go. Now that the grief of the funeral had started to wear off, she noticed the dark looks he was throwing Antonio's way. And she only had one more day before she returned to her own home and kids.

"Okay, Babe. I've got to go, too," Antonio said, smiling at Zoe.

"See you tomorrow, Boo. I can't wait to have this week behind me," Zoe sighed. "Be careful going home. The weather looks like it may turn ugly." After a passionate kiss goodbye, Zoe waved to him as he went down the street, turned the corner, and was gone. She walked up the driveway and sat for a quiet moment on the back steps.

What a week! she thought to herself. Her eyes wandered over the dry, barren patch of land that would have been her mother's carefully tended flowers and herbs growing on the side of the house in the spring and summer. Any minute she expected Amanda to come swinging out of the kitchen door, the smells of something delicious and the strains of one of her favorite operas, usually *Madam Butterfly* or *I, Pagliacci*, wafting on the air behind her as she wiped her hands on her ever-present, crisply starched apron. Sadly, she realized she would never see that image or smell those smells again. For some unexpected reason she thought with regret about how she never got her mother's recipe for homemade rolls. She always loved those rolls. Right now she would kill for just one of the mouth watering, buttery confections.

"Hey, Zoe. Whatcha doin' out here? Missing Antonio already?" Sara asked as she came out and sat on the step next to her sister. For the first time since they arrived, they were alone in the house.

"Actually, I was sitting here wishing I could taste one of Ma's rolls," Zoe responded, turning her head to discreetly brush away a sudden, unexpected tear. When they were all young, they had called Amanda "Ma." However, once they got older and supposedly more sophisticated, they called her "Mom." But all of them still called Amanda "Ma" when they were upset.

Sara became very still for a moment, suddenly at a loss for words as she too remembered her mother's famous rolls.

"Damn! I haven't had one of Ma's rolls in ages. She stopped making them because of her arthritis. Dag. Why did you have to mention them? I'd kill for one right now!" Sara said, unaware that she had voiced Zoe's exact thought.

"Me too. That's what I was thinking. And I'm pissed now that I never bothered to get her recipe."

"Me neither. Dag. We always think we have enough time. You know what I wish I had her recipe for?" At Zoe's negative shake, Sara said, "Her sweet potato souffle. I loved that! And her ice box cake! And what about her macaroni and cheese?"

"Yeah. And what about her homemade soups? She had one vegetable soup that I swore had butter in it, but she said it didn't. Remember all those Christmases where we either had a lot of food and not many presents or lots of presents and small dinners? But we always had those rolls and her sticky buns!"

"Yeah, I remember. And don't forget her sweet potato pies that she added scotch, brandy, rum, or whiskey to."

"Oh yeah," Zoe said, remembering. "It depended on what she was sipping as she was cooking!" Zoe added before chuckling at the memory of Amanda in her kitchen, slightly tipsy with that silly smile on her face she would get when she was drinking. Amanda made some of her best meals when she was tipsy.

"I remember one year I was on a cookie baking kick, pulling recipes out of the Sunday paper every week. It was a food Christmas, not a present one. I think Dad was laid off from yet another job. Anyway, Ma and I got in that kitchen and had a ball making cookies all day one Sunday. I wanted to make these candy cane cookies I found a recipe for. I don't remember the other recipes, but I never forgot those peppermint candy cane cookies. I gave Ma a list with the ingredients and she got everything on that list. It was great," Sara said wistfully, lost in memories of the past.

Before they knew it, each was lost in her own tears, but they smiled too, as they remembered images of Amanda bustling around her kitchen, busy cooking up a storm.

Zoe placed her arm around Sara's shoulders, feeling closer to her than she had in years. With a start, she realized that Sara had grown up. She smiled to herself, thinking that Theo had indeed been very good for Sara. She was much calmer and steadier now. Zoe used to think Sara, while sweet, was a bit flighty. Not the case now.

Out of them all, Zoe realized that Sara was probably going to miss their mother the most. They were always very close. Zoe supposed that because Sara was the baby of the family, Amanda tried not to repeat any of the mistakes she had made with the rest of them. Whatever it was, sometimes Zoe was almost envious about Amanda and Sara's relationship. And maybe it was that envy that caused her to withdraw from Amanda. Looking at it that way now, she deeply regretted that she had let small, petty things stand between her and Amanda's relationship.

"You know Dad wants us to divvy up the jewelry before we leave. We might as well get it over with tonight after dinner," Sara said, breaking into her thoughts. "Or do you think we should take a look now?"

"I guess we could. But shouldn't we wait for Gina and Steph?" Zoe wondered.

"Chile, ain't no telling how long it will be before they get back. At least we can see what we have to deal with."

"Maybe," Zoe said. "Why don't we walk around to the Legion instead and find out what Dad and n'em are doing?"

"Okay. I'm going to let Theo know where we're going," Sara agreed. She found him dozing in their father's favorite chair. After telling him where they were going, she picked up her and Zoe's purses on her way out the kitchen door.

When they got to the Legion, they quickly spotted their father, Stephanie and Gina across the room. None of them were feeling any pain. Stephanie and Gina muttered "Oh shit!" at the same time when they saw Zoe and Sara walk in.

"Here's my other two daughters!" Phillip roared jovially. "Hey Sweeties! Y'all want a drink?"

"Naw, Daddy. We just came over to see what you guys were up to," Sara told him.

"I'm getting drunk! Told myself that the minute the funeral was over, I was going to get pissy-eyed drunk! I earned it, Goddamnit!" Phillip exclaimed, slapping his knee.

"Yeah, Dad, I guess you did," Zoe said indulgently. She had to admit, Phillip had been holding up well. He was busy over the last few days, but she could tell that he was holding everything at bay. Zoe supposed that Phillip getting drunk was his way of releasing some of what he'd been holding in so tightly.

"Alright, Dad, we're going to the Dandy Mart and then we're going back to the house to start dinner," Sara told him.

"Okay, Sweetie! I'll see ya when I see ya!" he said, then laughed uproariously like he had just said the funniest thing.

"Is he okay?" Zoe whispered to Gina, who was weaving slightly on her stool.

"He's fine," Gina said softly. "He needed this. And if we have to get drunk right along with him, we will. Steph and I will look out for him."

Relieved, Zoe and Sara said their hurried good-byes, glad to get out of the alcohol and smoke-filled room, although for two completely different reasons. For Zoe, it was because she didn't like being around all those white folks. Other than her sisters and father, there wasn't another black person to be found anywhere nearby. She never felt that comfortable anywhere where there wasn't an abundance of people with similar melanin content in their skin.

Sara was glad to leave because the overwhelming smell of alcohol was not a good thing for her. Every day was a test of her sobriety. Her emotions were fragile enough as it was, and being in a place with nothing but alcohol was *not* a good place for her to be. She thought she might be strong enough to have a couple of drinks, but why chance it? So it was no surprise to see Theo just arriving when they got outside. Once he realized where they said they were going, he hightailed it over there. He was terrified, although he would never admit it, that he would find Sara happily ensconced at the bar, her sobriety completely forgotten.

At her raised eyebrow and unasked question, he said, "Uh, I just came over in case Pop needed a ride home."

"Oh, then you might as well stay here. He's in no condition to walk home," Sara told him, choosing to believe what he said rather than what she knew was the real reason for him being there.

"You staying?" Theo asked, trying to sound casual.

"No, we're going back to the house to start dinner. But first we're going next door to the Dandy Mart. Want me to put your numbers in?"

"Yeah. Just play my usual numbers. I'll see you when I get back to the house."

"Okay, Babe," Sara answered with a smile before Zoe hurried her along. The wind had picked up and Zoe looked up, hoping those weren't snow clouds gathering in the thickening sky.

"It's not supposed to snow, is it? I'd hate to think of everybody on the road in the middle of a snow storm," she fretted, shivering slightly in her leather bomber jacket. She pulled her chenille scarf a little tighter around her neck in an effort to block the frigid air.

"I don't know. I missed the weather this morning, rushing to get ready."

"Damn, it's getting cold out here! It's been pretty good this week until today. I just hope it doesn't snow so much that we end up stuck here for another couple of days."

"Yeah, I know what you mean. I'm ready to go home too," Sara agreed as she waited for the old lady at the machine to finish punching in her numbers from the sheet Sara handed her.

After Zoe played her own numbers they walked quickly back to the house to get out of the rapidly dropping temperature.

When they returned to an eerily quiet house, Sara pulled out the small boom box she had brought with her, and after popping in Maxwell's latest CD, she and Zoe efficiently set about fixing dinner, having forgotten about looking at the jewelry. The sisters talked little as they worked, but the silences were calm and companionable. That ended, however, with the loud and boisterous return of their father, Theo, and their other two sisters.

"Are you all right, Dad?" Zoe asked, watching her father weave back and forth as he tried to get his balance to walk up the stairs to the second floor.

"I'm fine!" he roared, then laughed, the sound coming out harsh and wicked. With a broad grin he added, "I promised myself I was gonna get drunk, and by God, I did!" With that, he lurched upstairs. Zoe assumed he had to go let out some of that beer and whatever else he had been drinking. She headed into the kitchen.

"Is he okay?" Sara whispered. Why she felt the need to whisper, she didn't know.

"He's three sheets to the wind, as Mom used to say. I guess he needed that," Zoe told her, but to Sara's ears, she sounded a little disgusted.

"Well, I don't like it. It's just not normal, to be that jovial after burying one's wife!" Sara exclaimed, wringing her hands.

"And how would you know? You bury any wives lately?" Zoe cracked.

"Don't be such a smart ass, Zoe! You know what I mean," Sara snapped.

Peeking into the hallway, Zoe saw their father as he turned the staircase and moved into the living room. After a few seconds, the television blasted on.

"Is he sure he can hear that?" Gina asked as she came into the kitchen.

"Well you know he's getting older. Mom used to say those speakers he mounted on the wall by the television used to drive her nuts," Stephanie said as she followed Gina into the kitchen.

"Smells good in here. What did y'all cook?" Gina asked as she began lifting lids off pots and pans, not really waiting for a response.

"Well, if you're going to stick your nose in all of the pots, why bother to ask?" Zoe told her, laughing.

"Ooh, cornbread. Did you make this, Sara? You know I love your cornbread," Gina told her, almost dropping the pan, which she found extremely funny.

Sara, failing to see the humor of almost seeing her cornbread end up as bird breakfast, none too gently took the still warm pan from her sister and said "Thanks. Yeah, I did."

"Good, 'cause I'm starved," Stephanie said, her words slightly slurred.

"I wonder why?" Zoe mumbled under her breath, but Sara caught the sarcastic undertone and smothered her own quick grin.

"I know you are not getting ready to get into that food without washing your hands first?" Zoe fussed, tapping her foot.

"Oh yeah," Gina and Steph said in unison, which struck them as funny and they gave into peals of laughter. Zoe and Sara cut their eyes at each other and just shook their heads. But then the sudden sound of an anguished cry from the living room rendered them all speechless and rooted to their respective spots. Just as suddenly, they all rushed out of the kitchen together, only to skid to a halt at the living room door. There they found their father, tears streaming down his face, as he cried, loudly and almost hysterically with his mouth wide open.

"I can't believe she's gone! Ma! Ma! She can't be gone!" he howled, sounding lost and broken. They stood there, helpless as to how to comfort him, when Theo, who was coming down the steps, waved them back as he sought to calm Phillip down and comfort him. Sara supposed it was some male-bonding-we-take-care-of-our-own kind of thing. Relieved, the sisters quietly withdrew from the room.

"I was wondering how long it was going to take before it hit him," Gina said quietly.

"I guess him getting drunk made it easier to let it all out, huh?" Sara speculated, not really needing an answer.

Silence descended in the small kitchen as they listened intently for any more flare ups from the living room. Their father seemed to have gotten himself together and quieted down. Dinner, forgotten and now unwanted, congealed in the pots unnoticed. Still, they were all reluctant to leave the haven of the kitchen. Silent looks were passed around as they each tried to elect the other to act as scout. Their election was aborted, however, when Theo stepped into the kitchen.

"Well?" was all Sara could manage.

"He's asleep," Theo said, sounding weary as he slumped into the nearest chair. He knew what his father-in-law was going through. He had put it out of his mind for years, especially since he was with Sara, but tonight brought it all back. He felt it slam into him when he saw Phillip's breakdown.

Theo was with his first wife for twenty years when she died from complications of reconstructive surgery to her left breast, which she lost to cancer. He was furious with her for having the surgery. He didn't care about her lack of a breast. But interfering relatives had convinced her that she was less of a woman because she only had one. Foolishly, she scheduled the surgery without his consent or consultation. As a result of receiving the wrong anesthesia, she went into a coma and after two of the most agonizing weeks of his life, she finally succumbed to death. She was only in her thirties.

Theo thought his life was over and had retreated into his own brand of hell, virtually ignoring his son and daughter who were grappling with their own grief. That is, until he met Sara. Sara with the hard edges and even harder heart. Sara with the sizzling sensuality. Sara, his sunshine. She brought him out of his darkness and back into the light. He put his grief behind him and learned to live again. That is, until tonight. Although he wasn't exactly grieving for his lost wife, he completely understood Phillip's grief, anguish, and confusion. At least Theo had two weeks to prepare for the possibility of his wife's death. Phillip had no time to prepare. Theo didn't know a lot about their marriage, but he had heard enough over the years. Tonight, though, he simply saw a man who was grieving for his wife. Whether some of it was guilt or not, wasn't for him to judge.

"Do you want something to eat, Baby?" Sara asked in concern, as she rubbed his tense shoulders.

"Ah, yeah. I guess I could go for a little something," he told his wife, placing his hand over hers as he twisted around to give her a tired smile.

Sara smiled in spite of herself as she watched Gina and Zoe suddenly spring into action before she could even move from behind Theo's chair. Gina piled a plate with short ribs, greens, and corn and popped it in the microwave to warm while Zoe grabbed a glass from the freezer, filled it with ice, and poured Theo a glass of soda. She then cut Theo a huge piece of cornbread and got him some silverware.

"This is too much," Theo protested when Stephanie placed the warmed plate in front of him. "But thanks."

"No problem, bro-in-law," Gina told him, glad to have something to do.

"Can I get some of that?" Phillip said from the doorway.

"Dad! We thought you were asleep. Sure, no problem," Sara told him, fixing him a plate, warming it and placing it on the table, where he sat opposite Theo.

"Dag, I'm hungry now too," Gina told no one in particular.

"Me too."

"I could go for a bite."

"Damn, those ribs smell good."

"You okay, Daddy?"

"Yeah, Babygirl. I'll be fine."

CHAPTER SIX
Picking Up The Pieces

"**A**lright. Okay. I'll talk to you next week, Dad. Okay. You too. Bye-bye," Zoe said, as she hung up the phone. Lord, she spoke more to her father now than she had in years. She and Sara felt like they had to check up on him, especially since he was all alone up there. Thank goodness for his friend Pete. He and Pete were hang-out buddies. Pete would pick Phillip up on check day to take him shopping and they were always going to some function or other at the Legion or VFW.

Sighing, Zoe looked around her bedroom, trying to decide what it was that she wanted to do next. Getting motivated seemed to be getting harder each day. However, life refused to stop long enough to let her catch her breath. Dinners still had to be cooked, clothes still had to be washed, and homework still had to be checked.

She mentally ticked off what she had done so far today and was pleased with her handiwork. The last of the laundry was in the dryer, dinner was warming in the oven, and the kids' clothes were pressed and ready for another school week. Zoe still had to drop off Shanice at her friend Marketta's house for a sleepover and pick up Jonathan from football practice. Christopher was, well, wherever Christopher was. Probably over at the house of that little bimbo Zoe couldn't stand. That girl was trouble. She could feel it in her bones. What was her name again? Oh yeah. Tribby, short for Tribecca. Zoe wasn't going to go there. She guessed Chris couldn't see past her big chest and even bigger behind. She was cute in a hoochie-in-the-making sort of way: clothes tight and small, always sporting the latest hairdo. Zoe just *knew* that wasn't all of that girl's own hair on her head. At least it didn't scream *FAKE* at you like some of those weaves did. Her mother must have been paying a pretty penny for her to get it done right. But it was her sloe-eyed looks that bothered Zoe the most. She looked like she knew too much for her age, or like an oversexed man-eater. Zoe often caught her running her too-pink tongue over her too-full, too-glossed lips when she looked Chris' way. Chris didn't think Zoe noticed, but he was practically a walking, breathing erection whenever *that girl* was around.

"Humph. I guess he doesn't think I was young once!" Zoe grumbled under her breath. Pushing herself up from the side of the bed where she was sitting, she grabbed her purse and car keys before walking across the hall to Shanice's room.

"You ready, Honey?"

"Yeah, Mom. All set!" Shanice smiled at her mother.

"Got your toothbrush?"

"Yes, Mom!" Shanice said in exasperation. "You always ask me that!"

"Well, I don't want you to have funky breath and run those poor people out of their own house. You know what a dragon you are when you first wake up," Zoe teased her daughter.

"Gee, thanks, Mom. I love you too," Shanice flipped as she followed her mother downstairs. After grabbing their jackets, she added, "And yours isn't exactly peppermint fresh either, you know!"

"Alright, Miss Smarty. Let's go." Zoe laughed as she pulled the front door closed.

After dropping Shanice off and picking Jonathan up, Zoe made a quick stop at the supermarket before heading back home to feed Jonathan, who declared he was starving. Eyeing his almost six feet, one hundred eighty pound frame, Zoe supposed he was. Feeding Jonathan was like throwing food down a bottomless pit. With his shoulder pads on, the boy looked more like a professional football player, rather than the 14-year-old he was. That is, until you looked at his baby face. Still so open and honest, Zoe worried that Christopher's influence would change her middle child's innocence.

After stuffing himself, Jonathan disappeared upstairs to his room to play with his Playstation2 while Zoe was left to clean up the kitchen. She was about to run down to the basement laundry room when the ringing phone stopped her.

"Heeey! Whatcha' doin' girl? Getting cute for tonight I hope," Tamika drawled on the other end.

"Heeey. Girl, I told you, I do not feel like going out tonight. Besides, Chris is God knows where, Shanice is at a sleep over and I can't leave Jon here by himself."

"Chris is at the junior hoochie's house?"

"Probably. I just don't know what he sees in that girl!"

"I would imagine it's those big-assed titties of hers. And you know she's puttin' out. You can see it all over her."

"From one hoochie to another?" Zoe joked.

"You damn skippy!" Tamika said, and then laughed.

"Chile, please. I will not voluntarily relinquish my son to that little slut!"

"Now, Zoe, you know as well as I do that the more you try to keep teenagers from the object of their desire, the more you push them to it. Leave it alone. He'll figure it out sooner or later; or at least when someone with bigger tits comes along!"

"Humph. You know I ain't tryin' to hear all of that," Zoe snapped.

"Yeah, well you better. You know as well as I do that Chris has always had a mind of his own. He's got to be the oldest young man I've ever met. Yeah, he listens to you, but then he just keeps on doin' what he wants to do."

"You've got a point there," Zoe sighed, reluctantly agreeing with her friend. It didn't matter how much she put her foot up Chris' behind, he took it like a man with hardly a whimper and then went and did what he wanted anyway.

"So how are your sisters doing since the funeral last month?" Tamika asked, abruptly changing the subject.

"Sara's hanging in there, but I can tell it's hard for her. Gina too, I guess. As for Steph, I have no idea."

"Oh? Why? What's going on?"

"Well, you know I told you that Sara and Theo were talking about going up to Dad's to start cleaning out some of Mom's things."

"Yeah? What's the problem?"

"The problem is Stephanie. She's acting like a total bitch about the whole thing."

"Why? That doesn't make any sense," Tamika commented, confused.

"It does if you let your big-ass funeral check bounce."

"What?! No she didn't!"

"Yes she did. After all that talk about 'I got this,' she didn't have shit! Now Dad has been embarrassed beyond belief and Sara and I are stuck with helping him pay off the bill. Sara volunteered to pay the whole damn thing but I wouldn't hear of it. He's my father too and I feel I should help. So we've worked out a monthly payment schedule with the funeral home."

"Umph, umph, umph! Gurl, wonders never cease! I would never have thought that she would do something like that. I'm really surprised at her," Tamika told Zoe.

Tamika and Zoe had been friends for years. And while Tamika knew that Stephanie could be a little rambunctious at times, she would never have believed that she would do something like this. Other than when she would get pissy-assed drunk at Zoe and Vaughn's parties, she was pretty cool. For the most part, Tamika wished she had an older sister as cool as Stephanie.

"Yeah, well, no more than we were. But you know the worst part about it?"

"No, what?"

"When Gina confronted Steph about it, at first she denied it. Then she promised to fix it."

"Well at least she's going to help."

"No, she's not."

"Wait, I'm missing something."

"Well if you would stop interrupting me, I could tell you," Zoe said, exasperated with the interruptions.

"Sorry! Go 'head," Tamika mumbled.

"Somehow, during her conversation with Gina, I guess she got pissed and then the *real* Steph showed up. She finally told Gina, 'I never liked his ass any damn way, so fuck him!' Well, you could have knocked me over with a feather when I heard that."

"Get the hell out of here! She really *said* that? Damn. That's some cold shit."

"Tell me about it. So I called her and got on her about the whole mess. She said she was going to send Dad a check. I asked him if he ever received anything and he didn't know what the hell I was talking about. When I spoke to her again, she got all nasty and shit with me. To say we had words is an understatement. And I haven't heard from her since."

"Damn! That's some deep shit, Gurl. Look, now I *know* you need to come out tonight. Come on, Girl. We could hit the clubs in Old City or Germantown."

"Naw, Girl. I think I'll stay right here. I can't leave Jonathan alone and I have to wait until Christopher gets home. You know I don't like going anywhere without knowing where my children are. Besides, Antonio should be home soon."

"Why can't he watch the kids?"

"Cause they are not his kids. I can't ask him to watch my boys so I can go party. That wouldn't be right."

"Alright, Girlfriend, but if you change your mind . . ."

"Yeah, I know. I'll give you a call," Zoe promised. But in her heart, she knew she probably wouldn't. Partying just didn't hold any appeal for her right now.

So much had shifted and changed for her since the funeral. She and Steph had drifted apart, yet she was closer to Sara than she'd ever been. As for her relationship with Gina, well, that was up in the air too. It was like family battle lines had been drawn: Zoe and Sara on one side and Gina and Steph on the other. Just because she and Steph stopped speaking didn't mean that she and Gina had to.

Sighing, Zoe glanced up at the clock on the kitchen wall. Muttering a curse, she was in the process of snatching the phone up to call Christopher's cell phone when he came sauntering into the kitchen.

"Where have you been, Boy? I was just getting ready to call you," Zoe fumed.

"I was over Tribby's house. I told you I was going over there," Chris answered in his smooth, deep voice.

"No, you told me you were going over to the mall. You didn't say *jack* about going over to *that* girl's house!"

"Chill, Mom. Dag. Why she gotta be *that* girl? Her name is Tribby."

"Whatever the hell her name is, you should have called me if you planned on changing your mind."

"I did try to call, but nobody was home," Chris told his mother defensively, avoiding her eyes as he spoke. Instead, he pretended to busy himself around the kitchen, as he pulled out a plate to re-heat the now cold food.

"Ah, hello! I *do* have a cell phone, you know. So don't even try it. If you wanted to reach me badly enough, you could have reached me by cell."

"Dag, Mom. I'm sorry. What's the big deal?"

"The big deal, Chris, is that I like to know where my children are."

Before Zoe could say anything else, the phone interrupted their conversation.

"Hello," Zoe snapped, after snatching the phone from Chris' eager grasp, giving her son the evil eye.

"Hi, Mrs. Knight. Is Chris there?" a female voice simpered over the telephone line.

"Who is this?" Zoe asked evilly, knowing good and well who it was.

"Tribby, Ma'am. Can I speak to Chris?"

"Damn! Didn't he just leave your house? What, you can't give him time to get in the door and get a bite to eat?"

"Moo-oom! Dag, you don't have to embarrass me like that!"

"Don't embarrass you? Boy, if you don't get out of my face," Zoe told her son, staring him down until he moved his hand away from the cordless he was trying to take away from her as Zoe walked further into the kitchen.

"Look, Tibby," Zoe started.

"Tribby," the girl corrected in her soft voice. Christopher looked exasperated at his mother's slip of the tongue.

"Whatever," Zoe went on. "Look, Christopher *just* walked in the house and we are getting ready to sit down to dinner. He'll call you later," she said before slamming down the phone, not bothering to say goodbye.

"Did you have to be so rude, Mom?"

"Honey, you haven't seen rude. That little hoochie acts like you're married or some damn thing. I mean, *damn*! You just walked in the freakin' door and she's on the phone already. Give me a break! Now fix your plate, sit down and eat, and don't aggravate me anymore tonight. And *don't* tie up the damn phone talking to that silly child!" Zoe commanded before marching out of the kitchen.

"What bug got up her ass?" Chris muttered as he punched out the warming time on the microwave.

Zoe sprinted up the stairs to the sanctuary of her bedroom, just barely restraining herself from taking out her frustrations by loudly closing the door.

Glancing at the pendulum clock on the wall near her side of the bed, she worriedly chewed her bottom lip. *Where was Antonio and why hadn't he called?* She had tried his cell phone, his mother, his grandmother, and his boy Kwame, and no one had seen him. She hadn't bothered calling either of his sisters. It was bad enough that she got a chilly reception from his mother. She wasn't up to his sisters' crap today. He should have been home at least two hours ago. It wasn't like him not to call her and let her know he was going to be late. She just hoped he was okay and that nothing bad had happened. But now that she thought about it, Kwame had sounded rather evasive, like he was hiding something.

Zoe was suspicious by nature. Especially after all the drama she had gone through with Vaughn and his cheating ass. Snatching up the phone, she was in the process of dialing Antonio's cell, *again*, when she heard the front door close. Terminating the call, she rushed downstairs to see who had come in or gone out.

"Chris better *not* have snuck back out to that little bitch again!" Zoe muttered to herself as she flew down the stairs.

As Zoe came around the curve in the stairs, she stopped a few steps from the bottom, surprised to see Antonio hanging up his leather *FUBU* bomber jacket.

Unconsciously, she repeated the question she recently asked her son.

"Where have you been, Boy?"

"Excuse me? I know I didn't hear you just call me a boy?" Antonio asked as he turned around to face her, one eyebrow up. "The last time I checked, I was neither a boy nor one of your children."

"I didn't mean it that way. But now that you mention it, you damn sure can act like one sometimes. I just had this conversation with Chris. You couldn't call and tell me you were going to be late? And just where in the hell were you, anyway?"

"Yeah, I should have called, but I didn't. So just drop it, okay?"

"Where were you, Antonio?"

"I went over my grandmother's house. Damn! I didn't know I was required to check in with you concerning my every move," he muttered.

Zoe could feel her temper building to the boiling point. She even recognized that she was fighting a losing battle with herself to keep it in.

"You went over your grandmother's house? Funny, when I called there, she said she hadn't seen you in a couple of weeks. Want to try that again? And don't tell me you were over your mother's house or with Kwame. None of them saw your ass either. So I'm going to ask you one more time. Just where the fuck were you?" Zoe practically screamed.

She moved off the steps and was all up in Antonio's face, her balled up fists on her slim hips. She was so busy getting into Antonio's world that she barely noticed Christopher slinking up the stairs to get out of the line of fire. As usual, Antonio refused to fight. He tightened his lips, walked into the kitchen, and began rummaging around in the refrigerator, looking for a Corona.

"Oh no you don't! Don't you walk away from me without answering my damn question!" Zoe told him as she followed him into the kitchen.

"Answer me, damnit!" Zoe hollered, pulling on Antonio's arm to make him turn around from the refrigerator and look at her.

Pulling his arm out of her grasp, Antonio looked down at Zoe's flushed, angry face. Moving away, he leaned up against the counter, and with one eye on the furious woman standing in front of him, he took a long swig from the beer, practically draining it in one swallow as he debated whether to answer her question truthfully. Deciding that the truth would only enrage her more, he evaded her question by saying, "I was out, aiight? Damn! Can't I have any time to myself? I don't grill you about where you go."

"You don't have to because I, unlike you, am courteous enough to let you know where I'm going or where I am. All I'm asking for is the same courtesy."

Zoe didn't know why she was so angry. Maybe because this felt just a little too much like one of the many conversations she used to have with Vaughn when he was cattin' around on her. The thought of Antonio sleeping with someone else made the hair on the back of her neck stand up. Not only that, she wasn't going through it again. She would rather be by herself than put up with another man's stupid shit.

For too many years she had watched her mother's heart break into tiny pieces over Phillip and his escapades. She swore back then that she would never go through that. She had her share of heartache and was tired of it. She almost killed her sons' father over it. She had put up with it from Vaughn because she had gotten too comfortable. And now? Well, she loved Antonio, and she certainly lusted for him. But she would be damned if she would put up with him cheating on her. She would buy something battery operated first.

"Look, Baby," Antonio said as he tried to pull her rigid body between his spread legs. "I'm sorry I didn't call. I just needed to clear my head a little, you know? My moms is getting on my case and you know all the stuff I'm going through on my job. I just turned off the phone and took a drive, okay?" he told her as he put his beer bottle down and started nibbling on her neck.

"Your mother is getting on your case? About what?" Zoe asked, pulling her neck away from his warm lips. In spite of herself, her body, the traitor that it was, was reacting in ways she didn't want it to.

"What else? About us. About our age difference," he explained with a sigh.

"Why don't you just tell your mother to mind her own business?"

"Come on, Zoe. You know I can't do that. She's my moms," he said, as if that explained it all.

Zoe sighed resignedly. They had *that* particular argument more times than she cared to admit and she didn't feel like getting into it again. Before she could say anything else, Antonio softly kissed her lips, saying, "I'm sorry, Babe. I didn't mean to make you worry and I didn't mean to snap at you. Forgive me?" he asked, looking into her eyes with such sincerity that Zoe felt her anger dissipating.

"Come on, now, stop," Zoe told him as he once again resumed nibbling on her neck, her protests not even sounding convincing to her own ears.

"You sure you want me to stop?" he whispered as he burned a slow trail from her neck to her lips before capturing them in a slow, sensual kiss.

Despite her feeble protest, Zoe felt her nipples harden and her panties moisten as she moved in closer to him. Reluctantly, her arms wrapped around the back of his head and she opened her mouth to deepen their kiss. As their tongues played with one another, she felt the evidence of his desire pressing against her stomach through the fabric of both of their jeans, causing her to grind sensuously against him.

When they finally came up for air, Zoe stepped away from him, mad at herself for letting him make her forget her anger. But she was even madder at herself because she wanted to believe him.

Trying to pull a cloak of dignity and nonchalance around her, she asked, "Do you want something to eat?" as she turned around to get a plate out of the cabinet next to the stove.

"Yeah, I'd like to eat you," was his low reply.

Zoe almost dropped the plate as a blush, quickly chased by desire, swept over her. She whirled around, peeking out of the kitchen door to make sure neither one of her sons had overheard that comment.

"Is that a fact?" She smiled.

"It's a fact," he concurred, as he removed the plate dangling precariously from her fingers, placing it on the counter next to her and pulling Zoe close to him.

Zoe looked into Antonio's eyes, searching them to reassure herself that what she was doing was right. Her vision blurred, then disappeared, as he leaned in to once again claim her lips. Before she knew it, they were ascending the stairs to her room. Just before going into their bedroom, however, she looked in on Jonathan and Christopher, where she found them engrossed in a Playstation2 game. She wished them goodnight before crossing the hall to her own room.

Upon entering her room she heard the shower running. After quickly disrobing she slipped in behind Antonio. Taking the already soapy washcloth from him, she proceeded to wash his back, stopping from time to time to sensuously rub her hardened nipples against him. Zoe heard the change in his breathing above the noise of the shower as she continued to rub the backside of his body, first with the washcloth and then with her bare hands. Gently pushing him to make him turn around, she was pleased to see the evidence of his desire bobbing in the air between their bodies. No doubt, she had his full attention now. Reaching around him, she poured more soap into her hands, and with her eyes locked on his, she slowly rubbed her hands over his smooth chest, down his hard stomach and further down to the object of her desire.

Zoe smiled slightly when she heard his indrawn breath as she softly but firmly stroked his hardness in her dainty hands. She employed a hand-over-hand technique, stroking him from his body to the tip of his penis, increasing the tempo of her strokes as she continued to look into his eyes. Finally breaking eye contact, she turned him around so the soap could rinse off his body, then turned him back to face her. Dropping to her knees in front of him, she teased the head of his penis with her tongue, swirling around and around, making him swell even more. Unable to resist further, she took as much of him into her mouth as she could accommodate and proceeded to bring him almost to the brink of climaxing. Antonio stopped her before she caused him to climax by pulling her up, pushing her back against the cold shower wall and making her gasp.

Leaning in, he kissed her deeply, letting his tongue play freely with hers while he pulled her legs up and around his waist. In one smooth thrust, he entered her hot, ready wetness. Moving his lips to her earlobe, he softly sucked it in and out of his mouth as his hips imitated his movements going in and out of her grasping body.

Zoe wrapped her arms around Antonio's neck, running her hands over his smooth, bald head as she held on for dear life while he proceeded to stroke her into mindless bliss. Like a piston moving inside a cylinder, Zoe could feel her heat building as he moved in and out of her body until she suddenly went rigid, her legs tightening around his waist as her climax hit her, causing her to contract against his iron hard penis and bathe it in her wetness. Soon after, Antonio shouted his own release before he collapsed against Zoe, who slowly lowered her legs, causing his now semi-soft penis to slip from her body. It was fast, hard, and furious, but to Zoe, it felt wonderful.

They silently bathed each other again before getting out of the shower, only to start all over once they fell into the bed, leaving their damp imprints on the sheets.

Antonio was like a man possessed as he made love to Zoe over and over that night. When they finally settled down to sleep, Zoe, while physically satisfied, could not seem to quiet the voice deep within her that was still shouting questions to her heart.

CHAPTER SEVEN
Say What?

"**O**kay, Granny. Thanks for the great meal. We really enjoyed ourselves," Antonio said, smiling into his grandmother's warm brown face before bending down to place a light kiss on her smooth, soft cheek. He gently caressed her other cheek. He always loved touching his grandmother's face. He found it fascinating that a woman of her seventy-six years could still have a face so smooth and line-free. But it was the texture of her skin that always drew his hand. It was as smooth and soft as the finest velvet. She was always slapping his hands away from her face, fussing at him to stop it, but they both knew she loved his displays of affection.

Zoe and Antonio had just finished spending an enjoyable afternoon keeping, as Zoe suspected, a lonely older lady company. Zoe didn't mind at all. Out of all of Antonio's relatives, his grandmother seemed to be the only one who accepted her and Antonio's relationship. His mother made no secret about her utter displeasure with Zoe. His sisters, Jayna, younger by two years, and Estelle, older by two years, weren't much better. They acted like their brother was the second coming and no woman, forget an older one, would ever be good enough for him. And then there was their attitudes, like they knew something that Zoe didn't. She figured they were trying to get a rise out of her, so she ignored their ignorant asses.

And Zoe couldn't *stand* how his mother always seemed to fawn all over Antonio. She thought his mother's public displays of affection were just a little too touchy-feely. Zoe had children of her own and never found it necessary to practically *pet* them whenever they were within reach. It was almost like she was trying to make Zoe *jealous*! Antonio, of course, just ate up all the attention his mother and sisters lavished on him and could never understand why it pissed Zoe off so much.

This was why Zoe found the time she spent with Antonio's grandmother such a refreshing change. She never looked down her nose at their relationship.

"Gotta take love where you can find it, Honey," she was fond of saying. "And you make my grandson happy and that makes me happy. Don't pay Pet no mind. She'll come around."

Pet was the name everyone called Antonio's mother. Zoe was almost sure she had never actually heard her real name. At first, Zoe thought they were saying *"Pit,"* until she finally realized what everyone was really saying. Zoe privately thought that *Pit* fit her personality better than *Pet* ever would. Even Antonio and his sisters called their mother Pet. After the first time she joked about it with Antonio she realized she was pissing him off and she never brought it up again. Such was not the case when she talked to her sisters, however. They would jokingly call each other Pet—when Antonio was not around, of course.

Zoe and Antonio spent the afternoon in his grandmother's tiny living room with the obligatory plastic covered olive green sofa and chairs, frozen in place on the much too old gold looped carpet, in a tiny house, on a tiny street in Old Germantown. The walls were a used-to-be eggshell that was now a nondescript yellowish white, along with the water-stained ceiling. The dining room was painted a faded yellow with heavy, dark furniture that was old, but still in excellent condition. The house might have needed an update, but it exuded a warmth Zoe found comforting and homey.

"Gon' wit'cha now. Just tryin' to sweeten up an old lady. I know your tricks, Boy! Shoot, I used to change your little stinky butt, so I know you better 'n you know yourself!" Vivian Wright play-scolded her grandson.

"You wound me to the quick, Granny," Antonio groaned, dropping his head, placing his hand over his heart, and staggering back, as if mortally wounded.

"How you put up with this silly boy, Zoe? Poor thing. He must wear you out with his foolishness," Vivian laughed.

"That he does, Mrs. Wright." Zoe laughed, smiling at Antonio's grandmother.

"I do declare! I don't even know why I let him come over here to bother me today. If I didn't like you so much, Zoe, I swear I would tell him never to darken my doorstep again."

"Yeah right! Until you needed something fixed!"

"That too!" his grandmother cackled, smiling up at her handsome grandson, as they all shared a laugh. After saying their goodbyes, Zoe and Antonio finally pulled away from his grandmother's small row house where she had lived for forty years.

"Lord, I'm tired. Too tired to cook. Let's get something to eat before we go back to the house," Zoe suggested.

"Sounds good. I'm still full from Granny's food, but I know that Chris, Jon, and Shanice will be looking for something when they get home."

"Tell me about it. Chris and Shanice are easy. They don't eat much, but Jonathan is a bottomless pit. I guess we could stop at a hoagie place and get something. If I don't get oil on the hoagies they should stay pretty good in the fridge until everyone is ready to eat."

"Or you could just wait until everyone is home and then order and have it delivered," Antonio suggested.

"Let me just call and see who's home," Zoe said as she pulled out her cell phone.

"Hey, Honey. I didn't think you would be back so soon. Your father just dropped you off? Okay. Are your brothers home? They are? Ask them what they want to eat," Antonio heard Zoe saying. After taking her children's dinner orders, she flipped her cell phone closed.

"Okay, Jonathan wants a cheese steak, Chris wants a hoagie, and Shanice wants hot wings and fries."

"Alright. And I think I'll pick up a hoagie." At

Zoe's incredulous look he explained, "For later. You know in about an hour or so I'm going to be hungry again."

"After all that food your grandmother fed you? I don't know where you put it." She laughed.

"Gotta keep my strength up. I happen to have a very demanding woman who just drains me," he said in mock seriousness.

"Is that a fact? Poor baby. Maybe I should call her for you and tell her to give you a break."

"Would you do that for little ole me?"

"And you know this, Baby!"

"See, that's why I love you."

"Gee, and here I thought it was because I gave such good head." Zoe laughed.

"Especially that!" Antonio quipped.

After directing Antonio to a steak and hoagie shop that Zoe favored on Stenton Avenue, they placed their orders. Then Zoe and Antonio started home with the mouth-watering fragrances of beef, fried chicken, onions, peppers, oregano, and fries teasing their noses. They were laughing and joking, their heads bobbing to the newest O'Jay's CD, when Antonio pulled up to a stop light on Stenton Avenue. Zoe was digging around in the bag of food, trying to steal a french-fry when she looked up and noticed a woman glaring at them and a little girl beaming. Without thought, she waved to the little girl who was enthusiastically waving back at them. Later, Zoe would remember that the more the little girl waved and jumped up and down, the more the woman beside her frowned.

Zoe mildly studied the child, who looked to be about six years old, with wild, unkempt hair and chocolate brown skin. She had on a coat that looked much too thin for the bone chilling temperatures outside. Her outfit was finished off by a thin pair of worn jeans. Without warning, the girl broke free from her mother's iron grasp and came sprinting toward the Cherokee. Zoe rolled down the window, thinking she wanted to ask directions, but she was floored when the girl finally reached the vehicle, grasped the window and chirped, "Hi, Daddy!"

Zoe could only gape at the child in stunned silence. Feeling like she was moving in suspended animation, Zoe slowly turned her head to see Antonio's dropped jaw as he mumbled "Shit, shit, *SHIT!*" under his breath.

"Did she just say 'Hi, *DADDY*'?"

CHAPTER EIGHT
Ain't This A Blip!

at Antonio's silent nod, Zoe felt the blood drain from her face. She could only stare at him, bug-eyed and rendered completely speechless. Suddenly hearing the irate sound of beeping horns, Zoe snapped back to reality and said through stiff lips that hurt to move, "I think you better pull over." She said it with hardly any mouth movement at all. Questions zigzagged and tumbled through Zoe's head, but she clamped her lips tight to keep them from spilling out of her furious lips. What she had to say could not be said in front of an innocent child. But oh, she had a lot to say, the minute the time was right.

"Ebony, Baby, move away from the car. Daddy's going to pull over," Antonio gently said with a small smile to the little girl, making Zoe's heart constrict.

After Antonio pulled over, the woman, whom Zoe had previously paid little attention to, huffed over to the vehicle, the little girl firmly in tow. Zoe briefly noted that while she had a very pretty face, she was a rather large woman. Not the kind of woman she would have pictured Antonio ever being involved with. She was light brown-skinned, with a ghetto-fabulous elaborate hairdo. She managed to squeeze her considerable hips into a pair of Guess jeans. A snug fitting First Down jacket, a turtleneck sweater that peeked out above the collar of her coat, and some slammin' boots completed her outfit. Zoe was immediately pissed to see that while this woman was obviously warmly decked out, the little girl was wearing what was almost nothing more than a spring coat.

In a flash, Zoe remembered how it had been when it was just her and her boys. She had gone without to make sure that they had what they needed. She even shopped at the Salvation Army a time or two to get herself a warm coat while she bought brand new coats, hats, scarves, and gloves for her boys to wear. And she had seen Sara and Gina do the same thing. No one ever talked about it. It was just something they instinctively did to make sure their children had whatever was needed. Maybe it was because they each saw Amanda do the same thing for them. She had worn white folks second hand clothes to ensure that her girls had whatever was needed to be warm *and* look good. Zoe could never understand a woman who put herself and her needs before the basic, fundamental needs of her children. Looking at this woman as she pranced toward the truck with the little girl shivering in the cold, Zoe felt an instant, deep dislike for her.

Before anyone could say anything, the woman

snatched open the back door and instructed the little girl to get in before hauling her own considerable weight into the back of the Jeep, causing it to lean noticeably to one side.

"Damn! It's cold as shit out there. Thanks for the ride, Baby. For a minute, the way you kept looking away, I thought you were going to act like you didn't know me. Who is this, your aunt? Naw, she can't be. Too high yalla. Ain't nobody in your family that damn light."

"No, this isn't my *aunt*," Antonio snapped. *What the hell is* she *doing in this part of town? And how am I going to get out of this one?*

"Hi, I'm Niambi. I'm his babies' mama," the obnoxious woman said, cracking her gum at the end of her sentence, extending a hand over the seat toward Zoe. Zoe looked at the outstretched hand with the obviously recently done talons, then up to the face of the woman leaning over the back seat. Zoe could have sworn this woman was smirking at her.

Ignoring her hand, Zoe snapped, "His *what*? Did you say *babies,* as in plural?"

Unfazed, the woman withdrew her hand, smacked her lips and said, "Oh yeah, Guuurl. I gots fo' kids by him. This one here, Ebony, she be five. And then there's Walter, who's seven and Akbar, who just turned eight and Antonio, Jr., who we just calls Tony, he be ten!" she finished proudly. "And just who are *you*?"

"Good question," Zoe mumbled.

"Where are you going, Niambi? We were on our way somewhere and we have to go."

"Yeah? What ever sistah-gurl got in them bags

sure smells good. We ain't had a steak sandwich in ages. 'Specially since I can't never seem to get no money from *you!* Shit, Niggah, you be ackin' like you ain't never got no damn money, but you ridin' 'round in this bad-azz ride and sportin' dat damn designer shit."

"Not now, Niambi. Where do you want me to drop you off?" Antonio asked through clenched teeth. He refused to turn his head and look at Zoe. Without even looking her way, he knew she was beyond pissed.

"Daddy, I'm hungry," Ebony's small voice said from the back seat. Zoe might have been mad as all hell at Antonio, but she could never stand to see a child go hungry. Reaching into the bag that had slipped from her numb fingers to rest haphazardly between her feet, she pulled out the chicken wings. Ignoring the woman, she turned around and smiled, "Do you like chicken wings?" At the child's eager nod and smile she passed them back to her. But before the little girl could take the proffered wings, Niambi snatched them from Zoe's hand and proceeded to stuff her own face with a wing.

Zoe, who didn't want to feel anything for the child, felt an uncontrollable rage flush through her body as she watched the woman unconcernedly eat without first making sure the little girl was fed. Turning toward Antonio she gave him a '*you better say something before I do*' look.

"Damn, Niambi! How fuckin' selfish can you be? That was for Ebony. Now give her the fuckin' chicken before I snatch your ass out the fuckin' car and whip the shit out of you like you stole something from me!" Antonio snarled, reaching to snatch the chicken from Niambi before gently giving it to Ebony.

"Here, Babygirl, go ahead and eat." He smiled at the child before shooting a deadly look at the mother.

Zoe was taken aback. She had never heard Antonio speak to anyone in that tone of voice or with those types of words. More shocking was how ugly he sounded with Niambi one minute, and then a split second later, how totally different he sounded with the little girl.

"That's okay. Momma can have it. I'm not that hungry," the child said, but you could see she was hungry by the way she longingly looked at the food.

"I said eat, Ebony. Your mother will get something later," Antonio said a little more forcefully than he meant to.

"Thank you, Daddy," she whispered, looking at her mother to make sure it was okay for her to eat before she daintily picked up a chicken wing, her hands shaking slightly.

"Gon' and eat girl. Damn! I gotta tell you everything?" she huffed, sucking her teeth. Turning her attention to Antonio she said, "I was gonna give her some. Damn! I told your ass I was hungry. Shit, we been standing out here for like, forever, waiting on the goddamn bus. I ain't got no money and she be whining about gittin' somethin' to eat. Shit, all she think about is her ass. I'm hungry too."

"I just gave you money last week, Ni, so why you tryin' to play me? You know goddamn well I give you money every week for those kids. So why is she," he thumbed his finger toward the child quietly devouring the chicken wings, "out here in that thin-ass coat and eating that food like she hasn't had a decent meal in days?"

"Shit, Niggah, what you give me ain't shit! You know how much it take to raise them damn kids? Oh, but you wasn't talking that shit when you was trying to get all up in my draws! Hell no, you was 'Baby this and Baby that.' Niggah *please!* And Ima ask one mo' time. Who is this bitch and what is she to you?"

"Excuse me? I know you didn't just call me a *bitch!* You don't know me, so I suggest you choose your words more carefully or your mouth might be trying to write a check your ass can't cash!" Zoe said, swinging around to stare the uncouth woman down.

"Like you could kick *my* ass!" Niambi scoffed.

"Don't let my size fool you," Zoe said with a deadly calm voice.

"Oh it's like that, huh?"

"Yeah, it's like *that.*"

"Humph. No wonder you don't have time no more for a plump sistah. You picking them slim now, huh? A little old too, I see," Niambi sneered but decided to leave Zoe alone.

"Just shut up, Niambi. Now either tell me where you are going or get the hell out of my truck."

"Take me to my Aunt Bessie's. You remember how to get to Aunt Bessie's don' cha? You should, as much as we used to sneak over there to get busy!" She was obviously trying to get in a dig at Zoe.

"Want me to drop you off before I take her where she's going?"

"You're kidding, right?" Zoe asked, ignoring the derisive, knowing snort she heard coming from the back seat. There was no way she was letting him drop her off. First, because she didn't want this woman knowing where she lived, and second because she had questions that she wanted answers to *now.* Or at least as soon as they were alone.

Without another word, Antonio checked his mirrors, pulled out onto Stenton Avenue and drove Niambi and his daughter to their destination. Niambi even had enough sense to finally shut up and leave them alone. The tension in the truck was as thick as a wet woolen blanket. The only person who seemed oblivious was Ebony, as she gave a contented sigh when she finally finished her chicken wings.

After they dropped them off, Zoe still refused to say anything. From the corner of her eye, Zoe could see Antonio continuing to throw glances her way. She knew the longer she said nothing, the more nervous he would become. *Good.* She wanted him to stew in his own juices. Antonio did not see the full force of Zoe's temper often, but based on the times he had, he knew that she was a force to be reckoned with.

Finally, unable to take the silence anymore, Antonio began his plea: "Zoe. Baby, I can explain . . ."

Then Zoe turned the full blast of her blazing eyes on him, causing him to sputter into silence. When they got to Zoe's house, she jumped out of the truck almost before it rolled to a complete stop in the driveway. Marching over to the trash can, she threw the food away, muttering, "Well, this is useless now."

After letting herself into the house through the

basement, she left the door open, leaving Antonio to decide for himself whether to come in or leave. He hesitated for a moment, turning to look at his truck longingly, tempted to bolt for safety. Shaking his head slightly, he quietly closed the basement door behind him, deciding the time for some truth was now, whether he was ready for it or not. When he got upstairs to the kitchen, he found Zoe on the phone. From the conversation, he deduced she was speaking to either Vaughn or her sister Sara.

"I'll be expecting you in a few minutes," Zoe said before slamming the phone down.

"Chris, Jon, Shanice!" she yelled up the stairs.

"Yeah Mom. I hope you brought something home. I'm starved!" Jonathan declared, bounding down the stairs, followed closely by Chris and Shanice.

"Where's the food, Mom?"

"I threw it away. I got . . . delayed . . . bringing it home and figured it was ruined. You can eat over your father's house. Get your coats. He's on his way over to pick y'all up."

"Dad's? I don't want to go over Dad's. My friend was going to come over to play my new PS2 game," Jonathan protested.

"Yeah, and I was going over Tribby's house tonight for a while."

"Dammit, don't argue with me! Just go get some overnight clothes and something for tomorrow. Let's get a move on. *Now!*"

"What's up, Mom? Why we gotta go over Daddy's? What's wrong?" Shanice asked. Sensing her mother's distress, she looked back and forth between her mother and Antonio, who was unusually quiet.

"Nothing, Shanice. Antonio and I got invited out tonight and I'm not sure how long we'll be and I don't want to leave you guys home by yourselves, that's all," Zoe said with a false brightness that none of her children were buying.

Something was up. They could almost smell it. For whatever reason, their mother wanted them out of the house. Christopher knew from before, back when things had gone bad with his mother and Vaughn, that there was about to be a showdown.

"Yo, Mom. I can stay here. Send Jonathan and Shanice. You know, in case you need anything," he said, flexing his biceps. He sensed that something was wrong as he leveled a menacing look at Antonio, trying to silently lend his mother support. He was ready to defend his mother against anything or anybody.

"That's not necessary, Chris. Come on, y'all. Get your stuff and your coats," Zoe repeated, checking out the window for Vaughn's car. As soon as she saw his headlights swinging into the driveway, she was shouting for her children to get a move on, hustling them out of the house. Before leaving, Chris once again asked his mother if she wanted him to stay.

"That's okay, Chris. Really."

"What's going on, Mom? He do somethin'?" he asked, jerking his head toward Antonio.

"Don't be silly, sweetie. I told you we're going out, and you are just going to make me late if you don't get out of here."

"Uh-huh. Call me if you need me, Mom," Chris said before kissing his mother's cheek and sprinting down the steps toward Vaughn's car. When he turned around to look at the door where his mother had been, he found the door had already closed.

For a moment, Zoe leaned against the front door, trying to gather her thoughts and control the temper that was raging through her. She managed to hide her anger in front of her children, but now that it was just Antonio and her, she was ready to explode. Pushing away from the door, she went in search of Antonio, who had managed to slink out of the kitchen without her seeing where he had gone.

Finding him laying across the bed calmly rolling a joint, Zoe exploded.

"You son of a bitch! How the hell can you have *four* damn kids and not tell me? We have been together for almost *four FUCKING years*, and somehow in all that time, you neglected to tell me you had kids? No wonder your mother and sisters were always so damn shitty. I thought it was the age thing, but now that I think about it, your sister was always hinting that I didn't know you as well as I thought I did. I guess not, since you couldn't tell me about Miami, Bambi . . ."

"Niambi . . ."

"Whatever! About whats-her-face and all those damn kids. Four! Four fucking kids and you never said a mumbling word!" Zoe was practically screaming at the top of her lungs. She paced around her bedroom like a lioness in a cage. Antonio knew that he had to choose his words carefully.

"Baby . . ."

"*DON'T* call me that! Baby my ass! Fool is more like it! I can't believe I trusted your ass!"

Starting again, Antonio tried to keep his voice even and well modulated. He had read somewhere that it helped to calm people down when they were upset. Although, even he had to admit, Zoe was way beyond being just "upset." She was full-blown livid, but he had to try anyway.

"Zoe, when we first met, I had no idea things would get so serious so fast. And then Niambi moved to South Carolina about a year after Ebony was born. I didn't even know where she was. So I thought, what was the point in telling you? I mean, as far as I knew, she wasn't coming back. It wasn't until she called my sister Jayna that I learned she was back in town. And then, I just didn't know how to tell you," he trailed off, hoping she would understand.

There was no sense in telling her that he had been to Niambi's house a few times recently. He only went to see his children and try to reconnect with them as their father. He wondered himself what he had ever seen in Niambi. She was foul, ghetto, and he was beginning to suspect that she was using drugs. He wanted to get his children away from her, but he didn't know how. Surprisingly, it had been his mother who told him the week before that he was wrong for not telling Zoe about his children. Pet urged him to tell Zoe before she found out on her own. For once, he wished he had listened to his mother.

He could have died when he saw Niambi and Ebony standing on that corner. But now that it was out in the open, he hoped that Zoe and he could work their way through it. However, that hope was dashed with Zoe's next words. Something in the way she said them sent a feeling of icy dread through his body.

"That is such a crock of shit! In almost four damn years, not once, did you find it necessary to tell me you had FOUR FUCKIN' KIDS? Not *once*? If you had just told me, I could have dealt with it, but you didn't. In essence, you lied. You've been lying to me since the beginning. And you know how I feel about liars," Zoe said with finality.

As far as she was concerned, it was over. She threw her head back and looked down her thin, keen nose at Antonio with icy disdain. Her heart was breaking inside, but she refused to let him see one tear.

"What are you saying?" he asked, unable to hide the panic in his voice.

"I think you had better go."

"Just like that? I don't get a chance to defend myself?"

"Defend what, Antonio? How you lied and deceived me all this time?"

"No," he sputtered, floundering for the words that would make her see his side and stop her from putting him out. "Look, just listen to me! It's not how you think!" He was damn near crying, begging her to listen to *him* and not her heart.

"Oh? So how is it Antonio? You have not one, two or three, but four, *four* children who I knew absolutely nothing about. Worse, their mother is the spawn of Satan. How you ever slept with that ghettofied hoochie mama is beyond me! But if you think that now that I know what you've been with that you could ever get with me again, you've got another think coming! Damn!"

"That was a long time ago, Zoe, and she didn't always look like that or act like that."

"Apparently not long enough. Isn't your *daughter* five? So up until at least a year before we hooked up, she was rockin' your boat. And here I thought you had some taste!"

"The only reason she got pregnant with Ebony is because she got me drunk and practically raped me!"

"Oh, please! Who do you think you're talking to? Do I look that stupid? Have you *not* been paying attention all these years? You can't shine shit, and this shit stinks to high heaven."

"Goddamnit! Why won't you fuckin' listen to me?" Antonio shouted, startling Zoe for a moment; but only for a moment. He could see the storm change in her eyes to a full blown hurricane. Her fair skin turned ruddy and he could almost feel the heat of her anger radiate across the bed.

"Who the hell do you think you're talking to? I know you don't have the nerve to be getting an attitude with me!" she railed, outraged by his display of temper.

"Because you won't listen! I keep trying to tell you. I *was* going to tell you, Baby! I just never found the right time. You were going through so much with Vaughn, and then it seemed like you were finally happy and I didn't . . . couldn't . . . wasn't going to be responsible for taking that away from you. I didn't want *this* to happen."

"You telling me would have been much better

than me finding out the way I did. And you can't tell me that bitch didn't know—couldn't *sense* that I didn't know what the hell was up! The fact of the matter is, you had plenty of time to tell me about her and those kids, and you didn't," Zoe said with finality and sadness.

Antonio was panicking. He knew she was pissed, but he didn't want to believe it was as bad as she was making it sound. His throat dry, his heart tripping like a jack hammer, he forced the words that were causing his stomach to churn and gurgle, almost rendering him sick, past his dry, heat parched lips.

"So what are you saying, Zoe? Are you trying to say it's over?"

Zoe stared at Antonio, letting her eyes roam over the planes and angles of his handsome face. She skimmed over his smooth bald head that she loved licking like a chocolate lollipop, and down his tight, muscular body, making herself skip over the physical part of him that had brought her so much pleasure. Slowly her eyes traveled back up his body until they locked with his.

She was oh so tempted to let it go. To tell him it was okay. But if she did that, then he had her. He would own her. She would never belong to herself again. No man could ever have that kind of power over her. At least no one so undeserving. He knew how she felt about liars. She had told him over and over again. If she gave in now, she would be no better than he was, because then she would be lying to herself. Against her will, she felt a solitary tear slide down her cheek that she quickly dashed away. The sight of that tear almost brought Antonio to his knees. He knew what it cost her to let him see even that one. He started to reach for her, but her next words brought him up short.

"That's exactly what I'm saying, Antonio. I think you better leave," Zoe told him quietly, all the anger spent, leaving nothing but tattered sadness.

"Baby, I. . ." Antonio tried to say, but was stopped by Zoe throwing her hand up, halting his flow of words.

"I don't want to hear it. I'm leaving. When I get back, don't be here. And don't let me find any of your shit here either." With that, Zoe whirled and quickly exited the room, flying down the steps on feet that barely touched the stair treads. Before she knew it, she was out the door and on her way up Route 309.

When Sara opened the front door, Zoe barged in saying, "You are not going to believe this shit!"

"Hi, Zoe! Glad you could stop by. I'm fine. Thanks for asking." Sara sarcastically joked, making her sister stop short.

"Sorry. Were you busy?"

"Not really. Theo and I were just watching a video in the family room and I was getting ready to fix us a snack."

"Where are the kids?"

"T.J. is over Carol's house, as usual, and Bethany's spending the night over a friend's house."

"Good. I'd hate to have to censor my language," Zoe muttered.

"Come on back," Sara said as she hung her sister's jacket up in the hall closet.

"Hey, Theo. Um, do you mind? I need to talk to my sister. Alone."

"Yeah, all right," Theo said, throwing a questioning look to Sara, who shrugged her shoulders and did her hands in an 'I haven't a clue,' gesture. After Theo went downstairs to the game room and home theater in the lavishly finished basement, Sara asked her sister, "What's wrong?"

"You are just not going to believe this shit!"

"Ah, you said that. What is it I'm not going to believe?"

"That bastard has *four fuckin' kids!*"

"What bastard?"

"Antonio, that's who!"

"What?! Get the hell out!! For real? Damn! That's some deep shit. How many did you say?"

"Four! Pay attention, Sara! Damn!"

"How did you find out?"

After Zoe related what happened, it was Sara who sank to the sofa, flabbergasted by what Zoe just told her.

"I swear to God, Sara, I started to jump out of that truck, open the back door, and give that woman a beatdown like she stole something from me. And in a way, she did. She stole my happiness and my peace of mind. If that little girl hadn't been there, it would have been on!"

"Holy shit! What are you going to do?" Sara asked, concerned for her sister, who was pacing around her family room.

"I told him to get out. What other choice did I have?"

"You could work it out, Zoe," Sara said gently.

"Oh come on, Sara! You would have done the same thing. Matter of fact, you probably would have opened a window and thrown all of his shit out on the lawn!"

Sara had to laugh because Zoe was right. She wasn't known to have the most patience in the world.

"You know the worst thing about all of this?" At Sara's negative shake, Zoe blew out a breath and said quietly, "Before I even thought about it, on the way up here, I started to call Mom and then I remembered I couldn't." Zoe sounded sad and tired, all at the same time.

The sisters looked at each other. A silent sadness settled between them, as they each once again mourned their mother's passing.

Laughing softly, Zoe said, "Mom had the best damn way of *not* giving advice to anyone I've ever known."

"Yeah, I know what you mean. She would let you talk and figure it out for yourself, but when you got done talking to her, it felt as if she had told you what to do, when in fact, you answered yourself."

"Yup. But she always used to say, 'you've got to do what's best for you! You have to do what feels right in your heart. But think long and hard before you make a decision.'"

Again, the sisters settled into reflective memories of the woman who had influenced them in ways they were only just now discovering.

"So, are you happy with your decision, Zoe, or do you think you should have thought about it some more?"

"I don't know, Sara. I'm just so angry and disappointed in Antonio. You know how I hate liars, especially after Vaughn. I don't have time or room in my life for that kind of bullshit!"

"I understand, but have you looked at it from his side?"

"What's to look at? He lied. He *hid* four kids from me. Worse, he hid that hoochie he had them with. I just can't believe that he could have kicked it with such a lowlife! Damn, what does that say about how he sees me?"

"As a lady and probably more than he could ever hope for?"

"Maybe. But the fact of the matter is, I can't deal with him or this shit right now."

"You can't or you won't?" Sara asked gently.

Zoe looked at her sister sharply, snapping, "Why are you taking his side? You don't even like him that much!"

"That's not true. I've gotten used to him, and yes, while I wasn't thrilled with him in the beginning, I see how happy he has made you."

"Yeah, well, all good things must come to an end, right?" Zoe asked sadly.

"Yo, Sara! Is that pizza ready yet?" Theo asked over the house intercom system.

"Oops! Sorry, Sweetie. I forgot to put it in. I warmed up the oven, though. I'll pop it in now," Sara answered back, speaking into the box on the kitchen wall that also tied into the stereo system in the house.

"Okay. Call me when it's done. I'm starved!" Theo laughed.

"Will do, Sweetie," Sara told him, a smile playing about her mouth.

"I always forget you have that damn thing. I almost jumped out of my skin when I heard him. Do you think he was listening to our conversation?"

"No, he wouldn't do that."

"I guess not. You'll probably tell him anyway!"

"Not if you don't want me to," Sara told Zoe, feeling a little insulted.

"Don't get all insulted. I know how couples share things. I really don't care one way or the other. He's going to find out soon enough when he notices that Antonio is no longer around."

Changing the subject, Sara asked, "Are you hungry? This is one of those big pizzas from Sam's Club. There is more than enough for all of us."

"Actually, don't mind if I do. I haven't eaten since we left Antonio's grandmother's house and I am a little hungry."

"Cool. This won't take long," Sara told her as she slid the pizza into the oven.

"Okay. Let me call Vaughn for a minute and check on the kids."

"Sure, the phone's over there," Sara said, indicating with her head the cordless phone on the wall between the kitchen cabinet and french doors leading to the patio.

Grabbing the phone, Zoe strode into Sara's seldom used living room.

"Hey, it's me. I was just checking to make sure the kids are okay."

"They're fine, Zoe."

"Did they get something to eat?"

"Of course. What? Did you think I wasn't going to feed them like you didn't?"

"Look, Vaughn, I'm not in the mood, alright?

I've had a shitty night and I don't feel like dealing with your bullshit too, okay?"

"Well excuse the hell out of me. Must be like Chris said. Did your boy-toy misbehave?"

"Fuck you, Vaughn," Zoe said, hanging up the phone.

"Goddamn it! I'm surrounded by freakin' morons! I fuckin' hate men! That's it, I'm going gay!"

"Yeah, right," Sara said dryly, taking a final peek at the pizza.

While they waited for the pizza to cook, they settled back down in Sara's comfortable family room.

"Speaking of gay, have you talked to Stephanie or Gina lately?" Sara suddenly asked, then laughed.

"See, you know you wrong! Steph would kill you if she heard you say that," Zoe scolded, but laughed despite herself. "Seriously, though," she said when she was able to stop chuckling, "Not since Stephanie and I had that blow up about her calling you to go up to Dad's house to help with clearing out some of Mom's stuff."

"I can't believe she acted like that. It is not our fault that her check bounced. All she had to do was tell some-damn-body she didn't have enough to contribute. Hell, Theo offered to pay for the whole funeral."

"Yeah, I know. But she refused to call Dad and apologize, and now she acts like we're trying to take all of Mom's stuff and leave her with nothing, when that couldn't be further from the truth," Zoe sighed.

"We could have used their help up there. I mean damn, we've been back a couple of times and we *still* have more stuff to go through. Shit, they act like it's been a picnic getting all dusty and dirty going through closets and drawers that haven't been touched in years."

"Tell me about it. I guess we're supposed to do all the grunt work and then bring them back all the good stuff and just hand it to them. Fuck that! If they want something, they can help with the cleanup!" Zoe snapped.

"Hey, don't take it out on me," Sara said, then laughed. "I've been helping the whole time, remember?"

"I know, Sis. It just bugs the hell out of me that Stephanie is acting like this. And I'm more than a little pissed that Gina seems to be taking her side."

"We don't know that Gina is taking her side," Sara said, feeling uncomfortable accusing Gina of something she wasn't sure about.

"Oh yeah? Well, has she called you lately? Cause she damn sure hasn't been ringing my phone off the hook!"

"Well, no, I haven't really talked to her. I left a couple of messages on her answering machine, though."

"And did she call you back?"

"No."

"Point made!"

"Point taken," Sara sighed, getting up when she heard the oven buzzer.

"Do me a favor and buzz down to Theo to tell him that the pizza's ready while I cut it up?"

"Girl, you know I don't know how that damn thing works. I'll just run down and get him," Zoe answered. When she got downstairs, she finally found Theo playing a solitary game of pool in the billiards room, after having looked in the theater room, the mini kitchen, the spare bedroom, and the bar area. Sometimes she forgot how large her sister's basement was. Picking up a cue stick, she told him, "Pizza's ready. Mind if I shoot a couple of balls? I would prefer if they were Antonio's, but these will have to do!" she quipped, setting up her shot.

"The way you hit that ball, I'm glad you're not mad at me," Theo grunted, wincing at Zoe's technique.

"Oooh, he's got jokes!"

"Want to talk about it?"

"Naw. I'll let your wife fill you in. Let's just say the honeymoon is over."

"Sorry to hear that."

"Yeah, me too."

"Well y'all were taking so long, I figured I'd bring the pizza to you," Sara said as she carefully came down the stairs with the sliced pizza. Placing it on the bar, she asked, "Anybody want something to drink?"

"I'll take a Corona, if you've got one," Zoe said, taking a healthy bite out of her slice.

"A soda for me, Babe."

"Oh snap! I forgot. A soda is okay for me too," Zoe said, trying to sound offhand.

"You can have a beer if you want, Zoe. It's not going to make me want a drink just cause you drink. You too, Theo. You know you love beer with your pizza," Sara said impatiently, frowning. It got on her nerves sometimes that everybody thought that the sight or smell of alcohol was going to send her off on a drinking binge.

"Soda is fine, Sweetheart."

"Just drink the damn beer and shut up, Theo," Sara snapped.

"Poor Theo. I don't know how you put up with my sister," Zoe laughed.

"Me neither." Theo grinned.

"Forget both of y'all!" Sara grumbled.

CHAPTER NINE

Finding A Way

*W*hen Zoe pulled into the driveway, she was both relieved and strangely disappointed to find Antonio's red Cherokee gone. For a moment, she sat in her car, unwilling to enter the empty house. It was late, cold, and she was glad she'd beaten the freezing rain home. According to the deep-voiced deejay on the radio, the rain would soon give way to snow. She supposed she should have felt more guilty than she did that the kids were stuck over at Vaughn's in his tiny apartment, but she didn't. She needed the time alone to think and get herself together. At least for a little while. Peering out the windshield, she noted how hard the rain was coming down.

"Great!" Zoe mumbled, finally rousing herself to get out of the car, she dashed to the basement door and entered the house before ruining her hair too badly. After she hung up her coat in the laundry room to dry, she trudged up the stairs to the kitchen where she put a pot of water on the stove to make herself a cup of herbal tea. The silence of the house settled around her and seemed to press down on her, interrupted only by the shrill whistle of the tea kettle.

She fixed her tea, went into the living room, and decided to start a fire. Turning on the stereo, she was surprised to hear her Blu Cantrell CD play. She was feelin' the songs "Waste My Time" and "Hit 'Em Up Style," thinking of ways that she could make Antonio pay for what he had done to her. However, when the track "I'll Find A Way" started, Zoe was brought up short. And before she knew it, all the hurt and pain she was trying to ignore came crashing down on her.

Staring into the dancing flames, Zoe thought about all the joy and good times she had shared with Antonio. She could feel all the hurt, betrayal, and lies welling up inside her. She fought with everything in her not to give in to it, but the more the song went on, the more she could feel herself giving in to the pathos of the words. And then the dam finally broke and she cried like she hadn't cried over any man since she had left Chris and Jon's father. Somewhere in her mind she recognized that these were no delicate, feminine, dab at your eyes type of tears like she shed at her mother's funeral. No, this was one of those ugly, makeup-running, snot-slinging, mouth-wide-open, gut-wrenching, gasping-for-air, falling-down-on-the-floor types of crying fits.

When she was finally spent and her head was pounding from having cried so hard, Zoe pulled herself up against the sofa, blindly staring into the flames of the fireplace. More than anything, she was grateful to be in the house alone, with no one to witness her moment of weakness.

"Wednesday's child is full of woe," suddenly zipped through her mind. "Thanks, God, for letting me be born on a Wednesday!" she railed, turning an evil eye upward. "Thanks for nothing," she mumbled. She remembered how Sara used to curse that poem. Zoe always thought it was kind of silly. But now, she was thinking maybe her sister knew something she didn't. The good Lord knew she had more than her share of woes. Jonathan and Chris' almost forgotten father and his cheatin' ass. Vaughn and his cheatin' ass. Her back injury. Her fight to get the money she had worked for. Vaughn. That little hoochie her son was so stuck on. Or maybe she should say *in*. Her mother's death. Steph and her bullshit. Vaughn. Why couldn't Gina have shaken her crystals or read some damn tea leaves and given her a heads up? Oh yeah, she wasn't speaking to her either. Vaughn. That's right, she said that already, hadn't she? And now Antonio. Damn him.

How had she allowed him to become so important in her life? After Vaughn, she had sworn to herself that she would guard her heart a lot better. Maybe she just wasn't meant to find love. She thought she had accepted that. But here she was again, heartbroken over some man whom she never should have allowed to get so close.

Sighing, she pushed herself up from the floor and went into the powder room to blow her nose and throw some water on her face. When she turned the light on, she almost scared herself looking at the mess she had made of herself.

"This is why I hate to cry!" Zoe muttered, shocked by her appearance. Her eyes were swollen, her skin blotchy, and her makeup had become a runny disaster. Quickly splashing water on her face, she blotted it dry, switched off the light without looking at herself, and walked back into her living room to retrieve her mug of now cold, barely touched tea. After washing, drying, and putting away her mug— because she always dried and put her dishes away immediately—she slowly trudged up the stairs to her empty bedroom. Looking around, she noted that Antonio had removed all traces of his ever being there. Gone were his many bottles of cologne. Gone were his clothes from the closet. Gone were his slippers by his side of the bed. He had even thrown his towel and washcloth in the dirty clothes hamper.

She didn't know what she had expected, but his thorough removal of himself from her life had not been it. She knew what she would find in the closet, but she made herself look anyway. As she suspected, there was a gaping hole where his clothes had once been.

Now she was pissed. "He could have at least tried a *little* harder to stay!" She knew it was irrational. After all, he had done exactly what she told him to do, but still, for some unfathomable reason, it just pissed the hell out of her.

Forcing herself to do something to make herself feel useful, she reached into the closet and rearranged and spread her clothes out so the empty space wouldn't be so glaringly obvious.

"That's better. Maybe my clothes will be less wrinkled for a change," Zoe muttered out loud without convincing herself. She thought about re-arranging the drawers, but decided that it could probably wait until another day.

Instead, Zoe decided to take a long, hot shower, hoping it would make her sleepy. All she wanted to do was fall into her bed and sleep. But when she finished toweling off, she felt more awake than tired. Turning on the television in the corner of her bedroom, she flipped through the channels and tried hard not to miss Antonio's weight on the other side of the bed. Before she allowed herself to get into the bed, however, she felt compelled to completely strip it, including moving the mattress so she could change the dust ruffle. The last thing she wanted was to smell Antonio's presence in her all too empty bed. However, she hadn't counted on his lingering scent seeping through his pillows. In frustration, she tossed them onto the floor on the opposite side of the room, as far away from her as possible.

By five o'clock the next morning, she'd bought an AB-Doer, an AB-Roller, a Showtime Rotisserie, two outfits, along with a pair of shoes from HSN, and a Diamonique ring from QVC that she figured was the closest she was ever going to get to a diamond in this lifetime. She bought some new pillows that happened to be the Today's Special Value and some crafty thing she couldn't remember, much less figure out what she was going to do with it. Maybe save it as a present for Sara. She was the Martha Stewart of the family. Well, the before-jail Martha anyway. Zoe wondered if she thought prison had been "a good thing." In between, she started and tossed aside three books and her ashtray was overflowing.

Sighing, she decided to give it up and just get up. After throwing on her most comfortable jeans and a sweater, she went downstairs to make a pot of strong coffee. While she waited for it to brew, she ran back upstairs, got the kids' dirty clothes, along with hers, stuffed them in the hamper, and dragged it down the curved stairway to the first floor and then down to the laundry room in the basement. She threw in the first load of white clothes. As she was separating the rest of the clothes, she checked pockets out of habit. She pulled something out of one of Jonathan's pocket and she was just getting ready to throw it into the trash can when something prompted her to look down at what was in her hand, just in case it was money. She gasped when she realized that she was looking at the packaging for a condom.

"What the hell?" A part of her mind knew what it was and the other part didn't want to accept it. Accept that her youngest son was having sex. But with who? As far as Zoe knew, Jonathan didn't even like anybody. She continued to stare at the empty package like it could give her the answers to her muddled questions. Finally, she decided that she would have to investigate further, and shoved the condom wrapper into her pocket.

After straightening up the basement, including cleaning the powder room, she went back upstairs and was grateful to see that the coffee was finally done. Sinking into the nearest kitchen chair, she blew on the scalding liquid, trying to ignore the pounding in her head from lack of sleep and tension. Then the phone rang, startling her. She cursed when some of the hot liquid splashed over her hand.

"Shit! Who the hell is calling me this time of the damn morning?" she snapped, flinging the offensive droplets of coffee off her hand as she jumped up to answer the phone and grab the damp dishcloth to dab at her burnt hand.

"Hello?" she almost growled into the phone.

"Well, damn! Is that any way to answer the phone? Maybe I should hang up and try again," Tamika said, laughing.

"Why are you calling me so early? Damn, it's not even eight o'clock in the morning!"

"I see we're in a good mood this morning," Tamika chided.

"What we? Maybe you are. I sure as hell am not!"

"Why? What's up? Antonio fall short last night?"

Zoe was quiet, not sure how to tell her best friend that it was over between her and Antonio. She didn't want to think about it, much less talk about it.

"Hello? You still there, Zoe?"

"Yeah, I'm here."

"What's wrong with you, Gurl? Damn! You sound like somebody died," Tamika said, concerned by Zoe's unusual behavior.

Sighing, Zoe told her friend, "I guess I might as well let you know that Antonio and I are over."

"What!?! Over? Aw, shit! What happened?"

"Four damn kids is what happened!" Zoe snapped.

"What the hell are you talking about?" Tamika practically screamed into the receiver.

"I found out yesterday that he has four kids. Three boys, one girl. And with a woman I wouldn't wish on my worst enemy," Zoe said bitterly through clenched teeth.

"Day-um! That is some fucked up shit, Girl. No wonder you sound like death warmed over this morning. So what are you going to do?"

"Do? Shit, I put his ass in the street where it belongs!" Zoe snorted.

"You did? Did he leave yet?"

"Yeah, he was gone when I got back last night from Sara and Theo's house."

"Where did he go?"

"Chile, I don't know! Nor do I care, just as long as his sorry ass ain't here!"

"Yeah, right. Come on, Zoe. This is me. I know you can't turn your heart off just like that"

"Well I did," Zoe said in a tone of voice that told Tamika to leave it alone. For now, anyway.

"Okay, girl, but you know I'm here if you need me, right?"

"I know, girl. Thanks."

After getting off the phone with Tamika, Zoe called Vaughn and explained that she had a lot of running around to do and asked if he would mind keeping the kids a little longer. The dire forecast had turned out to be a bust and the freezing rain had changed to regular rain overnight instead of the predicted snow, helping to alleviate her guilt at not bringing the kids home. He told her they had decided to go to the movies and then he was taking them to the mall. He generously told her to take her time. Zoe refrained from saying something smart. However, she made it a point *not* to tell him about the breakup with Antonio. She didn't feel like dealing with his "I-told-you-so" bullshit. Instead, she acted like she was too busy to stay on the line and quickly clicked off.

"None of his damn business any damn way," she mumbled to herself when she slapped the cordless telephone down on the kitchen table, causing her coffee cup to rattle a little.

Deciding it was time to get busy, she made herself go downstairs and finish her laundry. The next time she looked up, it was a few hours later. Her house was straightened from top to bottom, vacuumed, dusted, polished and wiped down. In between, there had been a couple of phone calls from Antonio, but every time Zoe heard his voice, she hung up on him. She finally left the phone off the hook, and made sure her cell phone was also turned off. Earlier in the day when she checked her messages, Antonio had filled up her voice mail with his pleas for her to just talk to him. Rather than listen to them all, Zoe opted to turn the phone off. She decided not to delete the messages because then he would just fill up her voice mail again.

Looking around her house for something else to do and finding nothing, Zoe turned her attention to her kitchen and food. Vaughn had told her he would be dropping off the kids sometime in the evening after he took them to TGIFriday's and she was startled when she realized that it would probably be sooner rather than later, given the time of day.

After baking a few batches of chocolate chip cookies and a peach cobbler, Zoe finally allowed herself to sit down and relax. She had been avoiding rest all day, afraid that inactivity would allow her to think and thinking was the last thing she wanted to do. Thinking led to feeling and she felt that right about then, she just couldn't stand the pain.

CHAPTER TEN

Jungle Boogie

Zoe, relaxing in a corner chair in her gleaming living room, had a small fire burning in the fireplace. The smooth jazz flowing from the speakers around the perimeter of the room was helping to fill the empty space. Before she realized it, she had drifted off into a fitful sleep. She wasn't sure how long she had been asleep before the chime from the doorbell startled her awake.

"Damn! Who could that be? I finally get to sleep and here comes some damn body," she fussed as she made her way to the front door.

"Hey, Girl! Well I'm glad to see that you're alright! Shit, I've been trying to call you for hours!" Tamika fussed, holding up a couple of bags before crossing the threshold and brushing past Zoe.

"Hey, Tamika. I was just starting to doze off. What's in the bags?" Zoe asked, yawning and stretching, trying to wake back up.

"Well what's wrong with your phones? I tried the

house and the cell, which is turned off, by the way," Tamika said, as if Zoe didn't know that.

"Obviously I have it turned off for a reason. Antonio is blowing up my mailbox and keeps calling the house. I got tired of hanging up on him, so I took the phone off the hook and turned off my celly."

"Hmm. Not talking to him is not going to solve anything, Zoe."

Zoe looked at her friend sharply, but said nothing.

"You can look at me like that all you want. You know it's the truth. And if your best friend, me, can't tell you that, who can?"

"What's in the bags?" Zoe asked again, ignoring what Tamika said. Before Tamika could answer, the doorbell rang again. This time it was Sara and her friend Danita.

"What are y'all doing here?" Zoe asked, bewildered.

"You know, you are starting to develop a problem with saying hello first," Sara said.

"Sorry. Hey, y'all!" Zoe said, smiling.

"Hey yourself. Somebody would think Mom didn't give you any home training!"

"Whatever. Hey Danita, wassup, Gurl?"

"Not a thang. I'm just hangin' with Sara. We wanted to make sure you were cool and all."

"Why is everybody all up in my business?" Zoe asked, looking at Sara.

"No, it ain't even like that. 'Mika called and said she couldn't get through. After a couple of hours we got worried. Dag!"

"Oh."

"Yeah, oh," Sara snapped.

"Break it up you two. We gonna eat or what?" Tamika said, stepping between the sisters, smiling.

"What's in the bags? I've only asked you that three damn times," Zoe reminded her friend.

"Well if folks stop interrupting me, I could get the food out. I've got corned beef specials and turkey specials. A side of cole slaw, some chips and, of course, a big ole juicy kosher pickle," Tamika said as she pulled the food out of the bags. "I once had a guy that looked like this pickle." She laughed, holding a big, fat pickle up as she turned it this way and that.

"He was green?" Danita asked, laughing, making everyone else burst out laughing.

"No, Gurl!" Tamika said, exasperated, rolling her eyes at Danita. "He was this thick! Thought he was gonna split me wide open. And let me tell you, it ain't easy tryin' to wrap your lips around a sucker like this!"

"Eewww. You are *soooo* nasty." Sara laughed. "I don't think I want any pickle now, thank you very much."

"Suit yourself." Tamika shrugged, completely unfazed, delicately cutting the pickle into lengthwise quarters.

After everyone fixed themselves a plate and settled around Zoe's kitchen table, Zoe asked between bites, "So, what's up for the night? Why don't we go to a club or something?"

"You can't be serious, Zoe," Sara said, looking at her sister like she had lost her mind.

"Who can't? And why not?"

"Well, I mean, damn! You just kicked the brother to the curb yesterday, and *tonight* you want to go to a club?" Sara couldn't believe her sister was serious.

"Damn, Girl! You startin' to sound as bad as me!" Tamika hooted.

"That is some cold shit," Danita said, chuckling.

"What, I'm supposed to sit around here mourning his lying ass? Please! Men are just like buses. If you miss one, another will be along soon enough," Zoe quipped. "And I feel like going out and catchin' me another bus!"

"Guuurl, you need to stop!" Tamika exclaimed, leaning up in her chair, staring Zoe down.

"You know your ass ain't hardly ready to jump back into the dating craziness. In case you haven't heard, it's a fuckin' jungle out there! And no offense, Gurl, but you ain't a spring chicken no more. Don't look at me like you're ready to kick my ass. I'm telling you the truth. Yeah, we all look good. Matter of fact, I think we look better than some of those young hoochies out there. But shit, brothers be looking for that new, fresh stuff. Bottom line. Forget that half of them don't know their ass from a hole in the ground, that's what these men want. And that's all you'll find at the clubs. Now if you're just looking for a piece of meat, then by all means, go 'head. Yeah, you might find another young stud, but he ain't gon' be about shit. He'll just want to run back to his dawgs and tell them how he turned this old-ass sistah out.

"See, you ain't like me, Zoe. I don't give a fuck. 'Cause most of the time, that's all I'm looking for, a good fuck. I know what I am. Ms. Party Girl. Ms. Good Time Thang. And I'm fine with that. I do what I want, 'cause I want to. You? Naw, Gurl, you can't go out like that. You a homebody. A mom and, as quiet as it's kept, a wife. Oh, you might not have been married to that young buck, but you might as well have been. Right now, you're mad as shit and you want revenge. Prowling the club for a fast fuck ain't the way to do it. Chile, this ain't like that *Sex and the City* shit."

Tamika sat back in her chair, her eyes never leaving Zoe's face. Sara and Danita nodded solemnly in response to Tamika's words. Sara was surprised. It was the first serious thing she had ever heard Tamika say. She was also impressed. Her respect for Tamika went up a notch.

"Damn, Tamika! I only wanted to go hang for a while. Shit! You make it sound like I'm looking for Mr. Goodbar or some shit!" Zoe told her friend.

While Zoe was feeling her friends words, she wasn't in the mood to *hear* them, let alone *listen* to them. She just wanted to go somewhere where the driving beat of a good song would replace the throbbing ache in her heart. She wanted to see and be seen. She wanted to surround herself with people who had nothing to do with Antonio and her memories. But she couldn't say those things to Tamika, Danita, or even her sister Sara. Those feelings and thoughts were much too private for Zoe to share. At least for right now. So instead, she said, "Look, y'all want to go or not? Cause you know I have no problem going out by myself."

"I could never do that. No matter how hard I tried, I've never been able to walk into a bar, club or even a house party by myself," Sara said, shaking her head at her sister's chutzpah.

"Humph. That has never been a problem for me. Sometimes I prefer it that way. I can stay as long as I like and I can leave when I feel like it.

Then again, sometimes it's fun to have someone to hang with." Zoe shrugged nonchalantly.

"Yeah, well, I've never been that adventurous," Sara commented, getting up to throw her plate and plastic fork in the trash.

"Well, I've gotten used to going to clubs by myself," Danita inserted, "since usually I'm singing in them. It was easier when I was with the band. When I first went solo, I used to be nervous, but it doesn't bother me anymore."

"How's it going by the way? When is your CD coming out?" Zoe asked.

"It's been going great! I almost have more bookings than I can handle. As for my CD, hopefully something will be out by the end of this year or early next year. I haven't even gotten in the studio to record yet. Contract problems. But Ben says that he's pretty much gotten all the concessions he wanted worked out on the contract. He's always negotiated excellent deals for my club dates so I'm pretty confident he'll get me an excellent recording contract. I'm glad my father assigned him to handle everything for me. He's very good at what he does," Danita said, looking dreamy. She didn't notice the looks that were passed around the table, she was so lost in her thoughts.

"Wow! That's great, Gurl! You know I'll be in line to buy a CD when they come out. Your voice blows me away," Zoe told Danita, smiling as Danita blushed her thanks.

"So, are we on for tonight?" Zoe asked, bringing the discussion back around to the original question.

"Naw, Girl. I'm going home. I got a date tonight with my hubby," Sara told them.

"Damn! All this time and y'all still got it like that?" Tamika asked, genuinely surprised.

"Oh yeah! Chile, please!" Sara laughed.

"Damn. I'd be sick of the same ole dick by now."

"Not if it was the right one," quiet Danita quipped, causing everyone to look at her in surprise.

"What do you know about good, bad or indifferent dick? I thought maybe your ass was still a virgin!" Tamika mocked.

"Just 'cause I don't talk about my shit like y'all do, doesn't mean I don't have it going on!"

"With who, that white attorney you got following you around like a whipped puppy dog? We saw that look you got on your face when you were talking about him. And if you ever did break down and give his ass some, he would probably have a dick like a skinny little hot dog!" Tamika cracked.

"He does *not* have a dick like a hot dog!" Danita exclaimed, then clapped her hand over her mouth, having inadvertently confirmed what they all suspected.

"I *knew* it! I knew y'all had something going on!" Tamika hooted.

"Come on, Danita. Give it up! You know we want to know if he's got it going on or not."

"I'm not telling y'all shit! I'm not like *some* folks I know!"

"I know you not tryin' to hold out on us, Girl!" Zoe exclaimed.

"I guess you mean me when you say some folks, huh? Shit, I've told you before, ain't no shame in my game! Sheeeet!" Tamika scoffed.

"Shut up, Tamika! Come on Danita, tell us. All

we want to know is does the man have skills or not?"

"Well . . ."

"Girl, stop acting like you shy and shit. Give it up! Does he have a little dick or not?"

Danita hesitated before answering their questions. Looking around the table she took a deep breath, causing the other ladies to hold their breath and to lean in toward her as they awaited her answer. Their expectant looks were almost comical, and Danita had to fight the urge to laugh at their wide-eyed looks of anticipation.

"Well," she repeated again, prompting Tamika to impatiently whirl the air with her hand in a hurry-up motion.

"Let me put it this way," she said slowly, only to be greeted with a chorus of "Yes?"

"My father has no idea what a gift he gave me by assigning Ben to handle my contract!"

"Oh yeah, like that tells us a whole lot," Tamika said disgustedly. "That ain't telling us shit!"

"Well what do you want me to say? That he's hung like a horse and has a tongue that can make you see stars?" Danita asked, exasperated enough to say more than she had intended.

"Now that's what I'm talking 'bout!" Tamika cackled.

"Is he hung like a horse?" Zoe wanted to know.

"Not exactly, but he could put some brothers I've known to shame!"

"Get out! For real?" Sara asked, amazed.

"Chile, please! Let me school y'all. Just like every black man doesn't have a big dick, every white man doesn't have a small one. Y'all feedin' into that stereotypical bullshit. Shame on you! Tamika, how many times have you complained about brothers who didn't know how to do shit in the bedroom? Or they got it goin' on in the boardroom, but are duds between the sheets? And Sara, how many times have you talked about some of the losers you've met over the years?" At their nods of agreement, Danita just said, "That's what I'm talking about!"

"Okay, girl, you've got a point. But do you really want to get it on with a white guy? Even if he is a hotty!" Tamika asked, referring to Benjamin Stockton's raven curls, rugged build, and piercing blue eyes. Handsome or not, the thought of tipping outside of her race caused Tamika to shudder slightly. She might have been a wild child, but there were just some things, or more specifically some guys, Tamika just wouldn't do.

"Why, Tamika? What difference does it make?" Danita asked, indignant, knowing before the words were spoken what was coming.

"You know why, Danita. Why you want to make me say it?"

"Because I do. Why?" Danita asked again, her eyes flashing in anger. This was why she had kept her relationship with Ben a secret. She didn't want to hear the shit she knew people would say. She knew they had no idea how deep she was into her relationship. So many times she wanted to say something, especially to Sara, since they were the closest, but something always made her hold back. As long as the outside world thought it was just a client-attorney relationship, things were fine. But the minute they thought it might be something else, she instinctively knew all hell would break loose. She thought—hoped—her friends would

understand. Out of them all, she thought Tamika
would be the least upset. She could give Samantha
from *Sex and the City* a run for her money. She assumed that Tamika must have had at least *one* interracial encounter. She realized now that she had
assumed wrong.

"Say it, damnit. Get if off your chest because
after you do, I don't ever want to hear it again!"
Danita huffed, her breath coming in short puffs of
anger.

"Chill you two, okay?" Zoe pleaded, holding her
hands up to both of them, trying to get them to
calm down. "Dag! What is wrong with the two of
you? Come on now. Leave her alone, Tamika.
What she does and who she does it with is nobody's business but her own."

"Come on, Zoe. You know as well as I do that
this just smacks of that ole Massa-slave thing. And
we all know that he's just in it for the thrill, that
jungle fever thing!" Tamika scoffed in disgust.

"You know, you don't know everything, Tamika,
and you *damn* sure don't know jack about me or
Ben!"

"You might be right; I don't know everything.
But tell me this, has Mr. Wonderful taken you
home to meet the folks? Or are you just his dirty,
but sexy, little secret? His piece on the side while
he escorts Buffy, Muffy, or Bitsy to the Devon
Horse Show?"

"Not that I owe you any explanations, especially
since you don't know me like that, but since you
asked, as a matter of fact, it's been *me* who has insisted on keeping our relationship a secret. Ben
wanted to tell his parents as well as my father for a
long time, but I asked him to keep it private.

Mainly because I didn't feel like having to deal with shit like this!"

"So tell me, what do y'all have in common? And if you tell me that 'love' shit, I swear to God I'm gonna have to reach across this table and smack the shit out of you!"

"We have a lot of things in common," Danita informed her indignantly.

"Yeah? Like what?"

"Art. Music. Books. Ambition. Especially ambition. We both strive to be the best at what we do and don't mind making sacrifices to get where we want to go," Danita proudly answered.

"And you really believe that when Mr. Bigshot Attorney gets to where he wants to be, you're going to be at his side? Yeah, right!" Tamika snorted.

"All right, that is *enough,* Tamika!" Sara shouted. When Tamika started to hotly protest, Sara said through clenched teeth, "I *said* enough! Damn! You act like it's the fifties or sixties, Tamika. Like the poor girl is going to get lynched if she's seen with a white man! Dag. Hello! There are plenty of interracial couples, and a lot of them are *black* women with *white* men. Get a clue for chrissake!" Sara snapped, as she put her arm around her friend's rigid shoulders.

"Okay, okay! I'll leave it alone. Except to say," Tamika stated, prompting everyone else to groan in exasperation, "just be careful, Gurl. Don't let it get too serious. Might as well enjoy it for as long as it lasts. 'Cause you know he's never going to actually marry you!"

"As a matter of fact, he did Miss Smartass!" Danita blurted out, throwing caution to the wind.

"WHAAAT?" they all screamed at the same time.

"That's right. He *married* me, Tamika. So much for your theory, huh? What do you have to say to *that*?" Danita asked in defiance, hand on her hip and her face so close to Tamika's that their noses were almost touching.

"Holy shit!" Sara mumbled.

"Well damn!" Tamika sputtered, uncharacteristically at a loss for words.

Zoe, recovering first, laughed and gave Danita a hug, while gently placing distance between the two combatants.

"Congratulations, Danita! That's wonderful," Zoe gushed.

Sara, finally snapping out of her shock, also hugged and congratulated her friend. Everyone looked at Tamika. Long moments passed as the silence and tension in the kitchen deepened. Finally Tamika said gruffly, "Oh, what the hell! You go, Girl! I just hope you know what you're doing," before quickly hugging Danita.

"You know I'm only trippin' cause I care," Tamika said.

"Yeah, I know. I just thought out of everyone, that you would be the one to understand the most."

"Oh really? Well, what about me? I *was* married to a white man before, remember?" Sara asked, indignant that her friend hadn't shared her news with her first.

"Chile, please!" Tamika said dismissively. "That marriage was over before it even started! So," she continued, trying to make peace, "where's the ring?"

Sighing, but smiling slightly, Danita looked around at the shocked faces intently staring at her.

Reaching behind her to retrieve her shoulder bag hanging on the back of the chair, she dug into her bag and slipped her rings on her finger before pulling her hand out to flash the set. Nestled in an obviously platinum setting was a round solitaire that had to be at least two carats surrounded by a baguette encrusted wedding band that swirled around the diamond, giving the set the appearance of being one ring.

"Well, damn! That's what I'm talkin' about!" Tamika exclaimed, impressed in spite of herself. Zoe and Sara also told Danita how pretty her rings were.

"So when are you going to tell your parents and when is he going to tell his?" Sara wanted to know.

"I don't know. We've been trying to think of the best way to do it."

"When did you get married?" Zoe asked, curious.

"Ah, about six months ago," Danita said quietly, almost whispering.

"Six months! Good Lord!" exclaimed Sara. "How on earth have you managed to keep it a secret for so long?"

"It really hasn't been that hard. His parents live way out in Ridley Park, mine in Cherry Hill, and we live in Blue Bell. Both of our parents usually call us on our cell phones and neither set of parents are the drop in kind. Well, Zenobia is, but I've finally gotten her to respect my space."

"Who is Zenobia?" Tamika asked.

"My mother. She can be a bit overbearing at times, but we've finally come to an understanding," Danita said, a ghost of a smile lingering around her mouth.

"Still, Danita, the longer you two wait, the harder it's going to be to tell them. I mean, six months!" Sara said again.

"I know. I just didn't want to have a scene like the one today," Danita stated, glancing at Tamika, who had the grace to look away.

"Yeah, but it's not like your father doesn't know Ben. He's been an associate at your father's firm for a few years now, right?"

"Yes. But that doesn't mean that my father will be any happier about it. He's just gotten used to the idea of me being a singer instead of going to law school like he wanted."

"What about his parents? How do you think they'll react?" Zoe asked.

"I have no idea. They seem nice enough, but you just never know. I'm not looking forward to a *'Guess Who's Coming to Dinner'* thing," Danita sighed, clearly upset and worried.

"Well, whatever you do, you know we're behind you, Girl," Sara said, giving her friend a reassuring smile.

"Thanks, y'all. It helps knowing I've got somebody in my corner. Even your evil ass, Tamika!" Danita laughed.

"Whatever!" Tamika quipped.

CHAPTER ELEVEN

Let The Games Begin!

Zoe stepped from the shower, a cloud of Beautiful scented steam swirling around her before dissipating into the warm, perfumed air. After quickly drying off, Zoe smoothed some Beautiful scented lotion over her body, followed with a quick spritz of the same scented perfume. Donning her black lace bra and matching panties, she then slipped into the sheer black pantyhose laid out across her bed.

Stepping back into the still damp bathroom, Zoe expertly applied her makeup, applying a hot, glossy red lipstick as her finishing touch. Checking that the light had gone out on her curlers, she quickly bumped her chin length bob before smoothing it with a comb.

Crossing her bedroom to one side of her bed, she picked up her short black leather skirt where she laid it out earlier with the matching jacket. After slipping into her red lace body suit, and donning both leather pieces, she stepped into her

black leather ankle boots with the three-inch
stiletto heels before going to her dresser to decide
what jewelry she wanted to wear. She finally settled
on her ever present tank watch, a pair of cubic zirconia studs, and a delicate silver choker with a
round cubic zirconia stone that nestled into the
hollow of her slim neck. Picking up her cordless
phone, she quickly dialed Tamika's number.

"Are you ready?"

"Yup, on my way out the door."

"Good. Me too. I'll meet you at the club."

"Want me to wait outside for you?" Tamika inquired.

"Naw, girl. It's too damn cold. If you get there
first, go 'head on in. I'll find you. Just make sure
you leave my name at the door," Zoe reminded
her, since it was a private club and she was going as
Tamika's guest.

When Tamika had initially suggested *Chez Nubian*, Zoe had wrinkled up her nose.

"Why you want to go to that bourgie place? The
men act like they are all that and the women look
at you like you just crawled out from under the
nearest rock."

"Girl, forget them hoes! They don't have
nothin' on us!"

"I'll never understand how you even got in!"
Zoe laughed.

"Because I came in the door with the power suit,
the correct briefcase and the corporate attitude, with
the corporate voice and corporate lingo, that's how.
How I speak and act around my peeps and how I
speak and act downtown are two different things."

"That just seems phony to me. Why can't you
just be yourself?"

"Because corporate America ain't ready for the 'real' me, girl. It's not being phony. Just think of it as being bilingual!"

"I don't know, Tamika. I want to go someplace fun, not somewhere with a bunch of uptight, I'm-better-than-you-cause-I-just-closed-the-deal-of-the-century-Negroes! Please! Their asses must hurt, being so anal retentive."

"Girl, get a grip. They can't get to you if you don't let them." Somehow Tamika had convinced Zoe to see things her way. As usual.

This was why Tamika was gaily saying, "Cool, later, chick."

"Yup," Zoe answered before clicking off the phone.

After Sara and Danita left, Zoe finally managed to talk Tamika into going out. Vaughn dropped the kids off and Zoe got into Chris' world about staying home and watching his brother and sister. She was grateful that none of the kids seemed to notice that Antonio was not around. If they had noticed, none of them had the courage to ask her about it. She knew that she would have to explain it to them, but for tonight, she didn't want to think about it. She also didn't like feeling like she had to explain herself to her children.

"It won't kill you to watch your sister and brother for a change. I'm only going to be a couple of hours. Hell, that's a short telephone conversation for you and Tibby," Zoe snapped.

"Tribby, Mom," Chris reminded his mother. He knew she did it on purpose, but felt compelled to correct her anyway.

"Whatever!" Zoe snapped. "In any event, I won't be long. And don't let me come back here and find out that you had that girl over here while I was gone. And I better not hear that you terrorized your brother and sister either!"

"Why not just take all the fun out of my life!" Chris answered sarcastically.

"Excuse you? I know you're not talking to me in that tone of voice. What did you say?"

"Nothin', Mom," he mumbled.

"That's what I thought you said. Nothing." Zoe gave him one of her looks that said he better not push her any more. Huffing, he had stomped off to his room, but just stopped himself from slamming the door. Almost immediately Zoe heard some stupid rap music blaring through the door.

Now, as she prepared to leave, she noted that the volume was turned down to a reasonable level. Knocking on his door, she opened it to find him on the phone (of course), smiling, as he bobbed his head to the beat of the music.

"I'm leaving Chris. Make sure Shanice and Jonathan don't kill each other or themselves. I think they're downstairs playing a video game."

"Okay, Mom. Whoa! Hold on," Chris said into the receiver, covering it with his hand.

"You're not going out like that are you?" he asked, frowning slightly.

"Ah, yeah. Why? What's wrong with this outfit?"

"You don't look like a mom, that's what's wrong with it! You look like a babe, Mom!"

Zoe had to fight to keep from laughing at the indignant look on her son's face. She would have if she didn't know he was serious. Still, she was touched.

"That's the nicest thing you could have told me," Zoe said with a smile.

"Mom! I'm serious. You can't go out like that!"

"So am I, honey, and yes I can. Bye!" Zoe said, leaving her son sputtering in his room. Now she was grinning as she went down the stairs.

"See you guys!" she hollered down the steps as she slipped into her faux black gama fur. She wished she thought to ask Sara if she could borrow her real mink.

"Okay, Mom. Have fun," Jonathan told her.

"Oh, I intend to!" Zoe muttered to herself, before closing the front door behind her.

Cruising up Germantown Avenue, Zoe blasted the music, singing at the top of her lungs while trying to drown out all thoughts of Antonio. Soon, however, she slowed her car as she looked for a place to park near the club. *Chez Nubian* was on a side street off Germantown Avenue, just before entering the Chestnut Hill section of Philadelphia. The owners bought three rundown rowhomes, gutted them out, combined them and now had one of the hottest private clubs in the city.

As luck would have it, someone was pulling out a few doors down from the club just as Zoe was pulling up. She slipped into the spot, just beating a brother in a Ford Explorer who tried to bogart the spot from her.

"Ha! Thought you had it, didn't you? But this kid was too fast for your ass!" Zoe whooped in the car, feeling cocky and arrogant. However, she still graced the brother with a dazzling smile and a shrug of her shoulders to take the sting out of her victory. Once she turned the wattage on, he could only helplessly smile back. After arming her car, Zoe quickly made her way to the club, gave the person at the door her name, and was quickly ushered inside.

After checking her coat, Zoe stepped into a large reception area warmed by the low light of the overhead crystal chandelier that reflected down onto the gleaming cream-colored marble floor.

As Zoe looked around, she noted the packed dance floors to the left and right of the reception area. Each had small tables and chairs hugging their perimeters. From what she could see, it appeared that every table was occupied. Directly in front of her was a large bar nestled between two sweeping, curved staircases that were littered with people laughing and chatting, but always conscious of being seen, as they slowly walked up or down the stairs.

The women sparkled like beautiful birds of paradise with their hot reds, bright pinks, funky oranges, and molten gold outfits. The men in their dark—but always designer named—suits, were handsome accessories to the women they had either come with or were discreetly trying to mack. The mahogany bar with the huge, gilt-framed mirror behind it made it easy for those who needed to constantly reassure themselves that they looked as fine as they thought they did. It was three deep with folks waiting to get their drink on.

Zoe just stood for a moment, a small smile on her face as she tried to make up her mind where she wanted to go first. The music was thumping and she was torn between moving toward one of the dance floors or ascending the stairs to the quieter live jazz room she knew she would find on the second floor.

The second floor, like the first, was divided into two rooms with live jazz on one side and piped in jazz music on the other. It was on this floor that patrons could get a bite to eat from the clubs limited, but excellent, menu while being soothed by mellow jazz sounds.

On the third floor, there were gaming rooms. These rooms included a billiards room, a video game room, and a room for those who enjoyed board games such as chess and backgammon. Similar to the first floor, the bar area, as well as the staircases, divided the areas on the second and third floor.

Instinct told her that she would probably find Tamika on the dance floor, but which one? Just as Zoe decided to check out the dance floor to the right, Tamika came dancing out of the room to the left.

"Hey, Girl! I was beginning to think you were going to change your mind," Tamika laughed, still dancing.

"Naw, Girl, I said I was coming. I've just been standing here checking out these bourgie folks and trying to decide which way I wanted to go. By the way, could that dress get any tighter? Damn, Tamika! I don't even know how you squeezed your butt into that dress. What did you do, grease up with some Crisco first?"

Zoe checked her friend out from head to toe. The short, burnt orange dress hugged her friend's curvaceous body with no mercy. The color of the dress complemented her copper skin beautifully. Its low, scooped neckline provided more than a modest peek at Tamika's very round, very full breasts.

The four-inch, jewel-colored stripped heels only highlighted Tamika's shapely legs. Tamika, who would add hair at will, had bronze, copper and gold curls cascading over her head and back from a jeweled headband *a la* Beyonce. She was causing a mild sensation in the reception area as men who should have known better were caught gawking by pissed off dates. Those who were single were starting to circle Zoe and Tamika like vultures moving in for the kill. The combination of Zoe and Tamika together was almost more than the men could stand.

"Don't start, Zoe. Just relax and have some fun! Come on, I managed to snag us a table," Tamika said over her shoulder before grabbing Zoe's wrist, as she turned around and began threading her way through the crush of people standing around the dance floor watching the ones shaking their booties.

Zoe ignored the "Day-um! Hey, Sweetness!" "Umph, umph, umph! You sure lookin' good Baby!" "Am I dying cause I know I'm lookin' at an angel! Aw man! TWO angels! Help me, Lawd!" and every other sorry line as she and Tamika moved deeper into the room. Personally, she would have preferred to go upstairs and chill in the live jazz room. She tried yelling that to Tamika over the blaring music, but either she didn't hear her or pretended not to.

When they reached the table Tamika had commandeered, she sweetly thanked the two guys who were holding the table for her, then shooed them away with a promise that they could come back later for a dance. Zoe could tell that they didn't really want to go back to holding up the wall, but after

Tamika whispered something to one of the men, he jerked his head for his protesting friend to get up.

After Tamika and Zoe settled themselves at the table and placed their drink orders, Zoe leaned toward Tamika and almost screamed in her ear about going upstairs instead.

"Later, girl," Tamika answered, popping her fingers to the music and looking around for a prospective partner. Whether it was for a dance or something else, Zoe wasn't quite sure. "And unball your face! Damn! How are you going to have a good time with your face all screwed up like that? Just get your drink on for a minute and your dance on and then we can go upstairs and chill with the rhythmically challenged brothers!" Tamika laughed, amused at her own joke. Even Zoe had to laugh at that one.

Before long, they were both asked time after time to dance. No sooner would they return to their table, than they would find themselves back out on the dance floor. In between dances, Zoe met an investment banker, a web site designer, a stockbroker, three CPA's, a questionable entrepreneur, two lawyers, and a doctor. As Zoe dropped yet another business card into her purse she had to laugh. Her purse looked like one of those jars found on takeout counters where business people dropped their cards in for a free lunch. The cards of the ones she thought might be interesting to check out if she really got bored, she moved into the zippered compartment of her purse. The others she decided she would toss out when she got home.

As for her friend, all night, whenever they were

at their table, men stopped by to greet Tamika. While she was nice enough to them, one by one, she blew them off. Almost every one of them left while begging her to call soon. Zoe's sides were sore from laughing so hard at Tamika's running commentary on them. "Little dick." "Can't fuck his way out of a paper bag." "Ugh! A kitty-licker!" "Two minute brother." "This one is worse. He's a minute and a half!" "He's really gay but won't admit it yet." "Needle-nose dick." "Spotted dick, and not the dish, either! Totally grossed me out. Ever seen a spotted dick? No? Trust me, you don't want to! The damn thing was pink and black and leaned to one side." "Good fuck, but married. Thinks I don't know. Found out after. Dammit. He had promise." "Bogus brother, pretends to have money, but he's a security guard at Rite Aid. Can't afford my monthly pantyhose bill."

Zoe chuckled to herself again as she remembered some of Tamika's biting, analytical comments.

"Whew! I'm beat! These shoes were not made for all this dancing! My feet are killing me! But the music is pumpin' tonight!" Tamika complained as she plopped in the chair opposite Zoe, sweating and out of breath.

"Tell me about it. I could feel my dogs starting to whine. That's why I sat out the last couple of requests. But I don't know what's worse: dancing on sore feet or trying to get the men to leave me alone!"

"Girl, you know how many women would like to have that problem?"

"Yeah, well, I forgot what it could be like out here."

"I tried to tell you. Some serious flakes. Makes you wonder how they are even allowed to go out alone." Tamika sighed, rolling her eyes and waving her hand dismissively.

"Tell me about it."

"Other than that, are you having a good time?" Tamika pressed.

"I guess. But I think I'm getting ready to call it a night."

"I thought you wanted to go upstairs for a minute."

"Maybe next time. I don't want to leave the kids too long at home by themselves."

"Didn't you call them on your cell?"

"Yeah, I did."

"And? What did Chris say?"

"He said that Shanice was in bed, asleep, and that he and Jonathan were watching some horror movie."

"Well, there you go. There is no need for you to rush out yet. Come on. Let's move this party upstairs. I think I'm ready for a little jazz so we can chill and hear ourselves think."

Sighing, Zoe picked up her drink and proceeded to go through the "'scuse me, pardon me, 'scuse me, oh I'm sorry! 'scuse me's" as she fought her way out of the dance room. Standing at the bottom of the stairs, she wondered how Tamika was going to navigate them without showing all her business to whoever might be coming up the stairs behind them. Zoe would bet her last dollar that her friend didn't have any underwear on under that tight-ass dress.

"Girl, walk behind me. I'm not puttin' on no

show for every-damn-body!" Tamika said, confirming her suspicions.

"Oh, like I want to watch your ass all the way up the steps. Gee thanks, Friend!" Zoe said in mock protest.

"You're welcome, Friend!" Tamika quipped. "For real though, girl, thanks."

"Uh-huh. Just get up the damn steps already. Jeez!" Zoe told her as Tamika laughed all the way up the stairs. However, when Tamika dropped her purse and stopped to pick it up, Zoe, who dodged out of the way to avoid Tamika's ample behind, was sure the guy behind her got a good look when he exclaimed, "Gotdamn! Holy shit!" When Zoe glanced over her shoulder, he was standing on the step, transfixed, as he watched Tamika's ass undulating up the stairs. Shaking her head, Zoe hurried the rest of the way up the stairs to join her friend, who was totally unaware of the damage she had caused.

"Live or recorded?" Tamika asked.

"Recorded. I think it might be a little quieter than the live band."

"Chile, please! If you wanted quiet, you should have kept your ass home!" Tamika said dismissively as she grabbed Zoe's wrist and pulled her toward the live jazz room.

"Then why did you bother asking?"

"Cause I wanted to see if I was right. And I was. I knew your tired ass was going to go for the soft and mellow!" her friend teased before pulling open the door to the darkened room. The bobbing heads gathered around small, intimate tables briefly turned their way before turning their attention back to the diva belting out an Etta James classic on the small, dimly lit stage.

Zoe and Tamika both gave the room a sweeping glance in search of an available table. Since all of the tables were full, they were getting ready to turn around and leave when the two guys who previously held a table for them downstairs gestured Zoe and Tamika over to their table.

Tamika and Zoe gave each other questioning looks. Zoe didn't really want to join them. One of the men, whom Zoe had dubbed Cheesey Chester, was sweating her all night. She found him to be a little too full of himself for her taste. He told her earlier that he was a sports agent and then regaled her with story after story about who he knew and where he'd been. His continued name-dropping got on her last nerve. Not to mention, he was just too goofy-looking for words. He looked like that guy, Bowfinger, Eddie Murphy portrayed in the forgettable movie by the same name. He had coke bottle glasses, really bad teeth, and a plaid jacket that was so loud, it practically screamed at you. His card was the first that she let slip through her fingers to rest on the floor under the table. His friend, Boring Bob, claimed he was a stock broker, but Zoe privately thought a stocking clerk was probably closer to the truth. However, Tamika was already threading her way through the tables before Zoe could stop her. Groaning, Zoe reluctantly followed her.

"Hey, foxy ladies! We were hoping to run into you again tonight!" Cheesey Chester exclaimed. He was grinning so hard, Zoe wondered why his face didn't split open. Boring Bob just nodded in mutual agreement, smiling a broad, gap-toothed grin. Zoe couldn't understand why Tamika would even deign to sit at the same table as these men. When she whispered that question to her friend, all Tamika said was, "Watch."

Forty-five minutes later, Zoe was laughing to herself. Somehow, Tamika got rid of the two bumbling idiots and Tamika and Zoe now found themselves surrounded by some of the finest men in the club. Actually, Tamika was holding court and Zoe was watching in amusement. Glancing at her watch again, Zoe signaled to Tamika that she was leaving.

"I'll call you tomorrow," Zoe motioned with her hand. Gathering her purse, she waved good night and almost sprinted for the door before Tamika could stop her.

As Zoe sped home, she laughed to herself when she thought about her conversation with Tamika in the ladies' room at the club.

"Why did you tell me to watch when we sat down with those guys?"

"If you want to attract the fine honeys in a club, make nice with the not so handsome ones."

"Why? That doesn't make any sense!"

"Girl, you have been away from the dating scene for a while, haven't you?" Tamika asked with exasperation. Glancing around for silent confirmation from some of the other ladies in the bathroom who were nodding in agreement, Tamika continued with, "Because, silly, it makes them wonder what the geeks have got goin' on that they don't. Then, it becomes a mission for them to move the geeks out of the picture."

"You got that right, Girlfriend!"

"Amen to that!"

"Ain't that the truth!"

Zoe laughed at the chorus of agreements Tamika's statement elicited from the small group. At the time, Zoe was amused. Now, however, she was less amused and a lot more tired. As much as she hated to admit it, Tamika was right. Clubbing was no longer her scene. All she had to show for it were tired feet and a purse full of business cards that would probably go out with the trash. Humming softly to herself as she neared home, she realized with a jolt that she hadn't thought of Antonio once. She wasn't quite sure how she felt about that.

CHAPTER TWELVE
Tell It To Somebody Who Cares

*D*ear Zoe:

I hope you will take the time to read this letter instead of going with your gut instinct and ripping it to shreds. See, I do know you better than you think I do. Anyway, I am writing this letter because you have consistently refused to speak to me when I've tried calling you. I'm begging you to please at least read this letter.

First of all, Baby, you have got to understand how sorry I am. I never meant for you to find out like this. I know I should have been more of a man and told you right from the giddy-up. I don't know why I didn't. I think because at first, it just didn't come up. You never asked me if I had kids. I guess because of my age. And I'm not saying that this is in any way your fault. I'm just saying, you not asking made it easier for me not to tell you. After a while I realized that I had waited too long. And then I didn't know how to tell you. But you must know that I never meant to hurt you like this. Baby, please! You have got to believe me when I tell you that I love you more than life itself. If I could change things, I *would. You know I would. What makes this situation even worse is that I was getting ready to tell you. I know you don't believe that, but it's true. Remember a couple of weeks ago when I came in late and you wanted to know where I had been? I went to see my kids. My sister called me on my cell and told me they were over my mother's house. I was all set to tell you when I got home, but then we got into an argument and again, like a coward, I decided that I couldn't tell you. Then we made love and that made it impossible to say anything. How could I ruin that moment with news like this? I know. I'm rationalizing my behavior when there is no rational reason for it.*

Anyway, as I said, when Niambi moved away, it made it easier for me to pretend that I wouldn't have to tell you. And even though she wasn't here, and things have long been over between us, I want you to know that I always did whatever I could to take care of my kids. Even when I didn't know where she was, I sent the money to her mother and assumed she was sending it to Niambi. At least I thought I was taking care of my children. I have been busting my ass for years sending her money, which I always assumed she was using to help with the kids. You saw how my daughter was dressed. Well, the boys aren't much better. I have come to the realization that I can no longer, in good conscience, leave my children with their mother. I don't know how I'm going to do it, but I have to get them away from her. I only wish that I had you beside me to help me figure out what to do. I know I have no right to ask for your help, and I'm not. It's just that I wish things could have turned out differently.

No matter what, please know that I will always love you, Zoe. I have never met any woman like you and doubt that I ever will again. (Smile). Please don't judge

*me too harshly. I know I was wrong for keeping my kids a
secret. I guess I should have listened to my grandmother.
She tried to tell me this would all blow up in my face.
Anyway, I'm sorry for any pain I have caused you.*

Loving you ALWAYS,
Antonio

"What a crock of shit!" Zoe spat, flinging the letter away from her like it was something too foul to
have near her. "How dare he! Oh, so I'm supposed
to get all weepy and call him and tell him that all is
forgiven? Like hell I will!"

"So who are you trying to convince, Sis? Yourself
or me?" Sara asked. She sat silently as Zoe sneer-
ingly read the letter. For all Zoe's disdain and
mockery as she read the letter, Sara felt Antonio's
sincere regret. Her sister, however, wanted no part
of it. Once Zoe made up her mind you were
wrong, you were tried, convicted and found guilty,
regardless of what you had to say. Forgiveness was
not in Zoe's vocabulary.

"Yeah, well, fuck him! He can tell that shit to
somebody who cares. I ain't the one! I'm done. As
Mom used to say, 'I don't chew my cabbage twice,'
and I know that's right!"

"Well, I think you need to give brotherman another chance," Tamika drawled.

"Funny, I don't remember asking you what you
thought!"

"Don't be getting all testy with me, Zoe. You
know I'm right and you just don't want to admit
it!" Tamika said, with hands on her hips as she
glared at Zoe.

Just because she had given her opinion was no

reason for Zoe to come off all snotty with her! *She* was only trying to help. She hadn't asked for them to come over here. She had been on her computer busy talking shit with this brother she had been chatting with for a couple of weeks and the conversation was just starting to get good and nasty when she was rudely interrupted by the insistent buzzing of her doorbell. Like a whirlwind, Zoe blew into her townhouse, dragging Sara and Danita along in her agitated wake.

"Okay, chill you two," Sara interjected, stepping between the two friends.

Deciding to give Zoe a minute, Tamika asked the room in general, "Anyone want a snack?"

"In here? You mean we would be allowed to eat in *here*?" Danita teased, looking around Tamika's seemingly all white living room.

In reality, it really wasn't all pure white, just many shades, tones and variations of the color. Tamika chose to do the living room and adjoining dining room of her smart Chestnut Hill townhouse in shades of white, cream, and taupe. Her floors were washed white oak. Tamika's walls were a rich shade of antique gold with a hand-rubbed, cream colored overlay, making them look like aged Tuscan plaster. The effect helped to warm up what would have been an otherwise cold room. Her sofa and loveseat were ultra-soft, ultra-plush, ultrasuede done in striped cream and taupe. Two velvet butter yellow club chairs, together with the other pieces in the room were placed around a tan and cream swirled abstract rug, which completed her seating arrangement.

A huge chenille textured ottoman in shades of tan, brown, green and blue presided in the center of the conversation area and helped to anchor the space. Since she lacked a fireplace, Tamika grouped her furniture around a large Italian handpainted pine armoire that housed her television, stereo and entertainment equipment. Wrought iron and sandstone topped tables dotted various corners around the room, with lamps of various faux stone finishes and softly translucent silk shades, gracing their tops. A hand crafted hanging glass and copper floor fountain was tucked in one corner, its softly soothing song barely discernable above the rocking reggae Tamika was playing on her stereo at the moment. Zoe used to tease her and say her townhouse was Spiegel's meets Crate & Barrel.

"I know you have lost your mind now, Girl. No, not in here. Come on back to the kitchen," Tamika told them, leading the way to her bright and airy kitchen.

It was immediately obvious that this was where Tamika really lived. When Tamika purchased the townhouse one of the first things she did was add a small den off the kitchen/dining room area by building onto the already existing patio space. The washed oak floors from the living room and dining area gave way to glazed sand-colored tiled floors in the kitchen and den that complimented the French vanilla walls and butterscotch colored stained wooden kitchen cabinets. A small open-shelved cabinet with a cream marble top served as her island and appliance center. Tamika may not have been very domestic, but her close friends and family knew that she loved to bake. She said it was how she worked off stress. That is, when sex wasn't available, of course.

Tamika's den consisted of a paprika colored

chenille sofa, a chocolate club chair, and a brass accented worn leather steamer trunk that served as her coffee table. At the moment, it was overflowing with papers, books and one of those oversized coffee mugs still half full with a tepid raspberry flavored coffee. Wedged into a corner near the French doors of the patio was a metal baker's rack with wooden shelves that Tamika painted a butterscotch color to match her kitchen cabinets. Tamika had since commandeered the rack to serve as her computer station. Again, the shelves not occupied with computer equipment overflowed with papers, books, and CDs. Metal baskets of varying sizes hung on either side of the rack to catch whatever overflow Tamika couldn't get on the already stuffed shelves. The room, while slightly messy, was very warm and comfortable. Unlike her living room, the den had a 'lived-in' feel to it instead of an 'on display' air about it.

Once Tamika added the den, the remainder of her fenced- in yard was converted into a stone covered patio space, with a pergola that extended from one side to the other. During the summer months, Tamika created a serene outdoor room with numerous pots overflowing with bright flowers and a sisal rug under her glass table and resin-coated, wicker looking club chairs. Above the set, hanging from the teak-stained pergola, was a tea-light candelabra. Tiny white lights ran up the posts and around the perimeter of the pergola. The effect, when lit at night with the citronella candles, was nothing short of stunning.

Looking out to the patio, Zoe asked, "Don't you miss having grass?"

"What do I care about having grass? It's not like

I'm planning on having kids anytime soon, if at all," she scoffed. "Chile, please! Look around this house. Does it look kid friendly? I just don't think I'm the nurturing, motherly type. I'm too selfish!" She laughed. "When I get a 'mommy' urge, I go visit one of my triflin' sisters houses. If that doesn't work, I take one of their bad ass kids for the weekend. That usually cures me for about a year. They have got some of the worst kids you ever want to meet. Please! But that's not what we are here to discuss. When did you say you got this letter?"

"It was waiting for me when I got home from work yesterday. I should have gone with my first instinct and thrown it in the damn trash!"

"Work? I didn't know you went back to work," Danita said, surprised.

"I had to go back. They cut my benefits off on some bullshit, so I had no choice. Actually, it hasn't been that bad. They have me training new phlebotomists and helping in the mobile unit with assignments," Zoe said with a shrug.

"Yeah, yeah, yeah. Y'all can play catch up later," Tamika said.

"Damn, Tamika! Don't be so cold," Danita said, rolling her eyes.

"As I was saying," Zoe interrupted, cutting her eyes at Tamika and Danita, "I should have thrown that damn letter down the disposal and shredded it. Or at least flushed it, cause it sounds like shit to me," Zoe said with disdain.

"Girl, you know you are too damn nosy for that!" Sara said, laughing at her sister's indignant expression.

"Um, I think you have me mixed up with Stephanie, Ms. Thing," Zoe shot back.

"Oh yeah. She is nosy as all hell, ain't she?"

"Will y'all stop?" Tamika interrupted. "What are you going to do, Zoe?"

"Do? Do about what?"

"Why, Antonio, of course," Tamika said.

"I'm not going to '*do*' a damn thing about Antonio. I meant it when I said it was over. My name is Bennett, 'cause I ain't in it!"

Tamika refrained from saying anything. Zoe made it absolutely clear that she no longer wanted anything to do with Antonio. She loved Zoe to death, but sometimes her stubbornness could be a bit trying. Still, she felt that Zoe and Antonio really had something, and despite their age difference, Antonio was the best thing for her. Not to mention, she had other reasons for wanting Zoe and Antonio to get back together.

CHAPTER THIRTEEN

We Are Family!

*T*he doorbell rang just as Danita nervously looked around her spotless living room one last time, satisfied that even Zenobia couldn't find fault with her home.

From the gleaming golden hardwood floors, soft lavender-blue walls, and muted cotton floral upholstered pieces in washed shades of light sage green, lavender, and ivory to the creamy pale blue vases overflowing with lavender hydrangeas, the room exuded quiet taste and homey comfort. Pale sage green sheers filtered the bright sunlight streaming through the oversized Palladian window in the living room, casting a soft glow about the room.

Columns, faux painted to look like marble, separated the living room from the dining room. Glancing into the dining room, Danita was satisfied with the table laid out with her best china for the brunch she prepared, though she doubted any eating would actually get done. What a shame, especially since Tamika had even baked one of her outstanding cakes. Danita looked at the cake again. At first glance, it looked like she had a large woven basket overflowing with colorful roses, gardenias, mums, and calla lilies as her centerpiece. In actuality, the centerpiece was the breathtaking cake Tamika prepared for the occasion. Danita's pearl white china trimmed in gold gleamed softly from the muted light coming through the bay window in the dining room. The plush cream Aubusson area rug muted Danita's final walk around the table as she straightened settings that were already perfect and swept away nonexistent pieces of lint from the snowy white table cloth.

Glancing in the mirror above the receiving table in her small entry, Danita inspected herself one final time before walking to her front door on legs that threatened to send her toppling over at any moment. The thought actually brought a brief smile to Danita's face. Zenobia would be horrified to think a child of hers could be that graceless.

After taking a deep breath, pulling her shoulders back, and stretching a smile across her lips, Danita threw open the door.

"Danita, Darling!" Zenobia exclaimed, lightly hugging her daughter as they exchanged air kisses before she swept off her ranch mink and handed it to her daughter. Smudging Zenobia's perfect lipstick would never do.

"Mother. Hi, Daddy!" Danita greeted as she stepped from her mother's perfumed cloud into her father's warm and *real* embrace. Danita lingered for a moment, almost hiding herself in her father's massive chest and arms, not wanting to deal with the very petite woman standing at his side. Her mother, however, had other ideas.

Looking around, Zenobia's eyes swept the living room, searching for any flaws. Seeming almost disappointed she said, "The place looks lovely, dear. Let me get a look at you, Danita. It has been *months* since we've seen you! Why, I don't know. I mean, it's not like we live on the other side of the country. I can see you maybe not visiting more, although it would be nice, but you could at least pick up the phone and *call* once in a while!"

Silently groaning, Danita pulled away from her father's embrace, turned around, and headed for the sofa and coffee service already set up on the coffee table.

"Coffee anyone? And Mother, you really have to try one of these pastries. They are absolutely divine!" Danita chattered nervously. She just knew this visit was going to be a disaster. She could feel it in her bones.

"Obviously, you must really like them. Picking up some weight, Danita?" Zenobia asked, her critical eyes passing over Danita's figure. Danita fidgeted under her mother's scrutiny as she unconsciously tugged at her loosely cut coral colored jersey knit top and smoothed the wrinkles in the matching linen pants with slightly damp hands. Glancing at her mother, Danita noted her mother's classic Chanel winter white suit that accented her trim figure to perfection. Zenobia's matched pearls and her discreet pearl stud earrings were understated and elegant. Zenobia's short, soft halo of curls even seemed to lie perfectly. Now that Danita knew all about the finer points of passion, she wondered if her mother ever looked mussed, even after sex. Somehow, she doubted it.

While she was what they called "stacked," Danita knew that anyone who wasn't a size four like her mother was considered fat. Danita's size twelve wasn't fat by any stretch of the imagination. However, she had always battled with her weight. Stress and her crazy hours as a singer sometimes caused her to eat things that she shouldn't and then the battle would be to get those unwanted pounds off. However, if she was looking a little "full" at the moment, she didn't care. She actually welcomed the added weight. It was worth it just to see the look on her mother's face. Before she could address that little snipe, Zenobia was on to her next favorite subject.

"And when are you going to give up this foolishness and go back to school so you can get a real job? I still can't believe you waited until your *fourth* year of college to drop out. You asked us to give you three years and if you didn't have a recording contract in that time, you would go back to school. And you can't tell me that you meet any decent men at those seedy places you sing in. But your father is a soft man when it comes to you girls and it's only because of him that I let you have your way. Well, your time is up. It's time to move on, Danita," Zenobia said firmly before raising the cup of coffee to delicately sip the steaming brew.

Before Danita could answer her, however, the sound of a key being inserted into the front door lock caused all of them to look in that direction, Danita with expectation and her parents in surprise.

As Benjamin Stockton entered the Laura Ashley

meets Martha Stewart inspired condo, Danita could hear her father saying, "Well I'll be damned!"

"What are you doing here and why do you have a key?" Zenobia rudely asked.

"Isn't it obvious, Zee?" Steven said, chuckling in spite of his own consternation. It wasn't every day that someone got the best of his wife, but he had to hand it to his daughter, it looked like today might be the day.

"Excuse me? Could someone tell me why this man has a key to my daughter's apartment?"

"It's a condo, Mother, as you very well know," Danita said with a sigh. However, she chose not to answer the real question at hand.

"Apartment, condo, whatever! Just tell me why in hell this white man is walking into this place like he owns it?"

"Because he does, Mother. We both do." There. She'd said it. And yes, the look on her mother's face was worth it. If she had the nerve, she'd take a picture and have copies made to give to her sisters to prove that yes, Zenobia Wingate could be rendered speechless.

Ben looked at his wife and was blessed with one of her beautiful smiles. Danita's father, Steven, noted that the moment his young associate stepped into the room, both he and Zenobia ceased to exist. As much as Steven didn't want to see it, the love his daughter felt for this man was almost a palpable thing in the room.

"Ben! You're finally here!" Danita said in a rush as she flew into his arms. After a brief kiss, Ben led his reluctant wife back over to the sofa and Zenobia's direct line of fire.

"Sir, Mrs. Wingate," he said, nodding to each in turn.

"I think you have some explaining to do, Benjamin, and I want to hear it now!" Steven demanded in his gravelly voice. He rarely spoke loudly, yet he had a voice that commanded respect, always got the attention of whomever it was directed at, and had caused many a juror to sit up and take notice. Ben knew he was getting ready to get grilled like he was a criminal on trial, but he felt pretty confident he could handle himself. After all, it was this man who had been his mentor. However, before he had the chance to say all the things he wanted to say for months, he was interrupted by the buzzing of the doorbell. With a quick glance at Danita, and a slight nod from her head, he crossed the living room in a few quick strides and pulled open the front door.

"Benjamin! What a surprise to get a call from you. Give Mother a kiss!" Emily Stockton demanded of her only son. After bending down to kiss his mother's smooth, plump cheek, Benjamin then greeted his father. The only difference between Adam Stockton and his son were Adam's shock of white hair and a weathered, just beginning to line, face. It was obvious that he was a man who took care of himself and enjoyed outdoor sports.

As the group moved into the living room, Adam stopped briefly, surprised to see his partner, together with his wife and daughter, in his son's condo.

"What a lovely surprise! Good to see you, Zenobia. Steve, what are you two doing here?" Adam inquired, feeling a vibe in the room he couldn't quite place. It was like walking into a conference room when the other counsel was getting ready to throw him a nasty surprise. Adam hated surprises; in his cases and in his life.

"Wait. Let me guess. Danita has finally gotten a studio contract and this is a celebration. Am I right?" Adam asked, smiling warmly at Danita.

"Ah, not exactly, Dad," Ben hedged.

"You got that right. Your son here was getting ready to tell me why he has keys to, and is part owner of, my daughter's condo. I want an explanation and I want it now!"

"What? Steven what the hell are you talking about? This is Ben's condo. I call here all the time. I've never once talked to Danita. If she lived here, wouldn't I have spoken to her at least once?"

"Not really, Dad. We've only given you all our cell phone numbers. That is why you were guaranteed not to get the other on the phone."

"What? Ben, you are not making any sense! Is this your place or Danita's?"

"It is both of ours."

"Oh dear!" Emily exclaimed, fanning herself with her hands.

"What exactly are you trying to tell us?" Zenobia snapped, not wanting to believe the obvious.

"I'd like to know that also. I think you need to explain yourself, Benjamin!" Steven growled.

"Yes, Sir, I agree. I do owe you an explanation. I guess the easiest and most straightforward thing to say is that I love your daughter. Pure and simple."

"Is that a fact?

"It is an absolute fact," Ben said quietly, pulling Danita closer.

"Okay, so what has that got to do with you having keys to this place?"

"We live together, and have for quite some time."

To say all hell broke loose would be an understatement of gigantic proportions. First, there was absolute silence and then the room erupted into a cacophony of very unhappy sounds. However, in the middle of it all, Danita maintained the most serene look. One that finally caught her mother's attention.

"Damnit, Danita. You are looking entirely too calm. There's more, isn't there?" Zenobia asked with dread.

"As a matter of fact, Mother, there is." Standing up, she reached into her back pocket and quickly slipped her ring on her finger before flashing it before the stunned parents' eyes.

"Oh my God," Zenobia and Emily moaned in unison.

"Have you lost your damn mind?" Steven and Adam asked in unison.

"Not at all," Ben answered, starting to get a little pissed with the other two men's attitudes.

"Can I speak to you in the other room?" both sets of parents asked their respective offspring.

"I see you all must have read the same Parents-in-Crisis handbook. You guys need to take this show on the road. Did you practice long, or do the responses in stereo just naturally happen?" Danita asked sarcastically.

"Now is not the time to be a smart ass, Danita!" Zenobia snapped, itching to slap the taste out of her silly daughter's mouth.

"Seems to be as good a time as any, Mother." Danita almost burst out laughing at the affronted look on her mother's face.

However, after giving each other an imperceptible nod, Danita silently led her parents into the master bedroom while Ben and his parents stayed in the living room. The bedroom door had barely closed before Danita's father tore into her.

"Danita, what is the matter with you? Are you trying to deliberately ruin your life? Is this the thanks your mother and I get for letting you have some independence?"

"Nothing is the matter with me. The fact of the matter is that I love Ben, Daddy. Can't you understand that?"

"Please," Steven scoffed. "You're just getting lust confused with love."

"Trust me, Daddy, I know the difference between the two!" Danita snapped, surprising her father. His daughter had *never* used that tone with him before.

"Is that a fact? I most certainly doubt it," Zenobia said. "Girl, I thought I taught you better than this! Well, there is no question. This will just have to be annulled."

"Too late, Mother. We've been married for almost a year."

"Good Lord! How the hell have you been married for almost a freakin' year and didn't tell us?"

"Because I was trying to avoid a scene exactly like this. Now you both need to get over it and accept it. Especially since you are soon going to be grandparents!"

"Oh my God!" Zenobia said again as she dropped down on the chair in the bedroom.

"Well that can be easily fixed. All you have to do is get an abortion and have this farce of a marriage annulled," Steven said coldly.

"How could you even say something like that, Daddy? Especially after what *you* did? How dare you!" Danita cried, making her father remember his own indiscretion. Steven had the grace to flush.

"That was between your father and me, and I'll thank you to stay out of it, Miss." Zenobia said, springing to her husband's defense.

"How can you say that, Mother? It affected all of us. Need I remind you how badly it affected Lilly? Sasha? Not to mention the rest of the family? So don't come up in here trying to get all high and mighty with me! Benjamin Stockton is my husband and the soon-to-be father of my child. Either you learn to accept it, or we no longer have anything else to discuss!"

"You watch how you speak to your mother!"

"Give it a rest, Daddy. You two act like I'm some pregnant teenager without a clue. I'm a grown woman. A grown, *married* woman. This afternoon wasn't about what we are going to do about my pregnancy. It was about finally letting you know that I was married *and* pregnant. I was hoping, foolishly I see, that my parents could share in my joy."

Danita glared at her parents, furious with them and undeniably hurt. Her sister Simone tried to tell her that it would be like this. But Danita was convinced that once they knew about the baby, all would be well. She couldn't have been more wrong.

As Danita tried to deal with her parents in the bedroom, Ben wasn't faring much better in the living room.

"Son, you know that Steven and I have been

partners for years. He's been like a brother to me. He's my best friend, for God's sake."

"So then I fail to see what the problem is, Dad."

"Under normal circumstances, I would be ecstatic. But Ben, have you thought about the problems you and Danita are bringing on yourselves?" Adam asked, hedging.

"Yes, we've talked about it. Come on, Dad. This isn't the 1950s. People are more tolerant of mixed couples now."

"Be that as it may, why put yourselves through that?"

"Because, in case you haven't been listening, I love her, Dad. Plain and simple. End of discussion."

Glancing at his wife, who appeared to be on the verge of having a case of the vapors, Adam pulled his son into the dining room, near the bay window, leaving Emily to weep into her already shredded tissue.

"Look, son, I'm going to tell you something your mother knows nothing about." At Ben's raised eyebrow, Adam cleared his throat and continued, "Son, I understand the attraction. The mystic of, you know, being with a, um, woman from another race." As his son continued to stare at him, Adam rushed on.

"Son, we all wonder about those who are different from us. I mean, I'm sure you've heard the stories, just like I did when I was a young man. Why, I remember this fine, dark-skinned girl who helped me get through many a lonely night in college. But as much as I liked her, I knew that nothing could ever come of it. So did she. We both understood the rules. It's only natural to want to take that walk on the wild side. But son, you don't marry your curiosity. You fuck it, date it maybe, but you don't marry it."

"You hypocritical son of a bitch! How can you say something like that when you just told me that the man in the other room is your best friend? Oh, he's your best friend as long as I'm not in love with his daughter? He's your best friend as long as he's helping you to get city contracts when you want to prove how progressive you are. He's your best friend as long as it helps your political career to say 'some of my best friends are black.' But his daughter is just another piece of ass when it comes to me deciding who I want to spend the rest of my life with? I never thought I'd see the day when I would realize what an utter asshole my own father is!"

"Just you wait one moment, young man! Who do you think you are talking to?"

"At this moment, I haven't a clue," Ben said sadly, seeing his father through different eyes.

"Well at least come to your senses. Have this farce of a marriage annulled."

"I don't think I can do that, Dad. Especially since I will soon be a father myself," Ben all but shouted.

"Are you telling me that she's pregnant?"

"Give the man a cigar! Yes, Dad. We are having a baby!"

"Baby? Did I hear you say baby?" Emily asked from the living room.

"Yes, Emily, a baby," Adam told his wife in disgust.

"A baby! That's wonderful! When is it due? Have you picked out names yet? A baby!"

"For God's sake, Emily! Get a hold of yourself.

You act like this is the second coming. Don't you realize what a disaster this is? My God. I just want to go on record saying that I believe you are making a huge mistake."

"The record has been duly noted. That is your opinion, and as such, you are entitled to it. I just hope you get over this feeling before the baby gets here. I really do want you and Mom to be part of his or her life."

Before Adam could answer his son, his partner and "friend" was standing before him.

"I can see from that look on your face, you've heard the happy news," Steven said grimly.

"Yes. I have. I guess that makes us in-laws and future grandparents."

"So it would seem."

Emily, who had miraculously recovered from her shock, now looked around the room at the gloomy faces of her husband, Steven, and Zenobia. She also noted the stony expressions of both her son and Danita. *His wife.* Wordlessly, Emily walked over to Danita and enfolded her in a soft embrace.

"Welcome to the family, Danita. I don't know why you want to subject yourself to us, especially after the way my husband has acted today."

"Thank you Mrs. Stockton." Danita said quietly before moving back to the circle of her husband's arms.

"Please, call me Emily."

"Glad to see you are so happy about this, Emily! Like everything is so hunky-dory! Please!"

"Oh get over yourself, Adam! I don't want to hear another word. Danita may not have been the woman we would have chosen for Adam. But let's face it. It was never our choice. We all know the problems of an interracial couple. But those are problems they have to face *out there*. It shouldn't be a problem they have to deal with within their own families. All of you should be ashamed of yourselves! It is not just about us, or even them, anymore. It is about a baby that didn't ask to come here, and most assuredly didn't ask to be scorned by its own family! Now, we all need to come to grips with this and stop fighting about it. It's a done deal. Whether we like it or not, we are about to be grandparents."

"That was beautiful, Emily. Thank you," Danita said, tears of gratitude springing to her eyes.

"Oh for God's sake, Emily! Will you get your head out of your Pollyanna cloud?! Don't you ever get tired of thinking everything and everybody is sweetness and light? Like I'm supposed to believe that you will be parading your nappy-headed grandchild up in that fancy-smancy country club of yours. Yeah, right!" Zenobia disdainfully snorted at Emily.

"Don't you ever get tired of being a bitch, Zenobia?" Emily snapped.

"Oh no she didn't go there!" Zenobia shouted, jumping up from the chair where she was sitting. Zenobia was about two seconds from forgetting all of her so-called "breeding."

"Okay, that's it! I'm asking everybody to leave now. You've upset my wife enough for one day. Mother, thank you for your support. I—we appreciate it more than you know. It's funny. You think you know your family and then you find out that you don't have a clue. All my life I thought my father was an equal rights, progressive, fair-minded man who believed that all people should be judged by who they are, not the color of their skin. Today I learned that to him those principles only apply when it's not in his own backyard and that he is the worst kind of racist there is: the kind that doesn't even know it, or at least, won't admit it to himself. I'm not even sure I want my child around a person like that. You all can fight and bicker amongst yourselves. Steven, I have come to you for advice before my own father at times and this is how you feel about me loving your daughter? To say I'm shocked is an understatement. I thought out of everyone, you would be the most understanding. Who would have thought that it would be my whiter-than-white-bread mother? And you wonder why we didn't want to tell you."

Ben looked at the faces before him, saddened by what he saw. Looks of embarrassment and almost shame passed between Steven and Adam.

"Well, I most certainly don't have to stay here and listen to this crap. Let's go, Steven," Zenobia fired over her shoulder as she marched to the door and snatched it open.

"I'll talk to you later, Miss!" she told her daughter before regally sweeping out of the apartment, Steven trailing behind her. He turned briefly to look into his daughter's hurt eyes, wanting to say something, but not finding the words. When Danita turned away and buried her face in Ben's chest, his shoulders slumped as he reluctantly followed his wife out the door. In his heart, he felt he had failed his daughter and wasn't sure if he could ever make it right.

"Son, you know I only want what's best for you. Surely you can understand that."

"Danita *is* what's best for me, Dad. Can't *you* understand *that?*"

"Adam, do something! I will not lose my son over your foolishness. As the kids say, get a grip and act like you know!"

Danita burst out laughing, at both the look on her father-in-law's face and Emily's unexpected street slang.

"Let's go, Emily," Adam said, steering his wife toward the front door. Pausing before opening it, he added, "Son, we'll talk. Danita," he nodded in her direction before almost pushing Emily out the now open door.

"Danita, I'll be calling you soon, Dear!" Emily sang as her husband hustled her out the door.

After a moment of silence in the now still apartment, Danita drawled, "Well, that went really well."

CHAPTER FOURTEEN

What's New, Pussycat?

I can't believe I'm doing it again! I swore to myself that this would never happen again. Yet here I am, succumbing to his kisses, his touch. I must be insane! Oh, but damn, the way he makes me feel. I can't stand it. I've never had a man touch me like this. And his shit must be dipped in gold cause what it's doing to me should be against the law!

"Yeah, that's it, Baby. Aaahhh shit! Stroke it! Stroke it. Fuck the shit out of me!"

The man continued to move against the woman's fevered skin, enjoying her moans and cries of ecstasy as she writhed beneath him. Feeling her stroking him like a soft, moist hand as she expertly worked her muscles around his hardness was driving him to distraction. It took all of his concentration not to explode into her more than willing body. Finally, with relief, he felt her most powerful convulsion and he succumbed, climaxing with a strangled shout that almost drowned out her high-pitched moan of pleasure.

After a moment, she pushed against his chest. He wordlessly pushed off her body, rolled over, and threw his arm over his eyes. She looked at him and allowed her hungry eyes to travel down his body.

What was wrong with her? It was like he was her new drug, and she couldn't get enough. If she had any pride at all, she'd get up, get dressed, and leave. Yeah, that's what she would do. She'd get up and . . . oooh, damn! Now he was running his fingers over her already hyper-sensitive nipples, causing a shudder to ripple through her. And he was leaning over, his tongue teasing her neck and the outer shell of her ear. And he was turning her over and running a trail of hot, moist kisses down her back, and why didn't he stop teasing her cheeks like that? Why did he have to reach around to her front and tease her bud like that? Now he was making her get up on her knees and she could hear the foil packet being ripped open and she pictured it as the condom was rolled down over that big, beautiful, engorged dick that she couldn't seem to get enough of. And she almost cried out in joy when she felt him slip into her, still wet, hot, and ready from their last bout. She loved it doggy style. But she knew what was coming. He wouldn't be there long. He had something else in mind and she was almost breathless with anticipation. She loved it and hated it all at the same time. She loved it because it was so forbidden. She hated it because it seemed to certify that she was the freak everyone thought she was.

Don't tense up. It only makes it hurt worse. Breathe deeply. That's it. Relax. Just relax. Oh my God! It wasn't supposed to feel this good and she knew that she was not supposed to enjoy it that much. As he inserted himself inch by slow inch, she could feel herself slipping away on a sexual haze. It was times like these that she didn't even know who she was. Time ceased to exist as it seemed he stayed in that hot, tight space to the point of almost making her sore. Feeling him grow even bigger and harder, she gasped as he suddenly pulled himself out, fought to get the condom off and then rammed himself inside of her vagina. She wanted to tell him to stop, to put another condom on, but they were both too far gone. Neither had the will or the power to stop. A few short moments later, she moaned deep and low as wave after beautiful wave broke over her, almost making her pass out from the intensity. He quickly followed with his own howl of release.

Later, after waking up from her short nap and untangling herself from their jumble of legs and arms, she winced when she got out of bed and padded into the bathroom. After quickly taking her shower and getting dressed, she briefly stood over him, watching him sleep. He was undeniably one of the finest men she'd ever seen, but it wasn't just his looks that attracted her to him. She reached out a hand to shake him awake, but slowly let her hand drop. She knew she had to tell him, but she couldn't. Not yet. What could he do? Nothing really. No one could get her out of this madness but her.

CHAPTER FIFTEEN

My old new friend

Zoe pulled into her driveway, put the car in park, and just sat there, slumped over the steering wheel. After almost a whole week of doing doubles at the hospital, she was tired to the bone. Even her good news couldn't seem to give her more energy. She just hoped the kids would be as happy about the news as she was. It was time for a change.

Looking to the left, she eyed the door to her basement entrance. Looking straight ahead, she thought about the stairs, one step landing, a turn, and then five more steps to her kitchen door. If she went in through the basement, she still had stairs to navigate. Groaning, she opted for the door closest to her. After passing through her small laundry room on legs that felt like she had weights tied to them, she made it through her finished basement and had one foot on the stairs when she detected the most delicious aroma coming from upstairs. With more pep than she thought possible, she almost ran up the stairs, only to stop short at the sight that met her eyes when she skidded to a halt in the doorway to her kitchen.

"Hey, Babe. Took you long enough to get in the house. I was just getting ready to send Jonathan down to make sure you were all right," Vaughn said, smiling, waving a tomato sauce stained wooden spoon around.

"Vaughn, what are you doing here?" Zoe asked, surprise evident on her face. In fact, she was so surprised that she forgot to put on the sour expression she usually wore whenever she looked at her ex-husband. Vaughn immediately noticed that her face hadn't balled up into that look he hated and dreaded, and he was encouraged.

"Well, you know I've been picking the kids up almost every night and we were all sick of cheese steaks, hoagies, and Mickey D's, so I thought I'd come over and cook while they did their homework. You used to like my spaghetti so I thought I'd whip some up. This way, you won't have to cook for a coupla days, you know?"

He looked so anxious to please, even Zoe couldn't find it in her heart to fuss or say something smart. The food *did* smell good, and she realized that she was starved. So instead, all she said was, "Thanks, Vaughn. I appreciate the help."

"You do? Wow. Cool!" He was grinning so hard, and in spite of herself, Zoe found herself smiling back.

The dinner that followed was one of the most relaxing Zoe remembered having in long time. Shanice and Jonathan were pleased as punch to have both of their parents sitting at the same table having an actual conversation and not screaming at each other. And as much as he tried to play it off that he could care less one way or the other, Chris was also secretly happy. He was glad to see his mother looking happy and relaxed. Since her break up with Antonio, he noticed how sad she seemed to be all the time; when she wasn't working, of course. Zoe was always the first to volunteer for overtime.

Everyone was surprised when she suddenly went back to work. Things fell into place for her when Elkins Park Hospital found a position for her to train the new phlebotomist and to work in the Mobile Unit department. She was actually making more money than before, and she didn't have to lean over beds drawing blood, which would have been too big of a strain on her injured back. Worker's Compensation was happy and she was happy to find a way to fill up her days again. She would do anything, it seemed, so she wouldn't have to be home too long. Usually by the time she got in, she would be so tired she barely had the energy to eat and briefly check on the kids before falling into bed, exhausted. She knew she couldn't keep this pace up. She just needed some help getting over the hump. Maybe with the coming spring, her mood would lighten with the lighter days.

At the moment, however, she was extremely surprised she was actually enjoying Vaughn's company. But Zoe began to think she was living in the twilight zone when the kids, including Chris, volunteered to clean up the kitchen. Zoe felt so good she even asked Vaughn if he cared to share a glass of wine before he left.

"I'm sorry, but do I know you? I could have sworn this was my ex-wife's house," Vaughn joked, laughing.

Looking at him, Zoe was a bit startled. Sometimes she forgot how good looking Vaughn was. And the divorce seemed to have helped. He went back to working out and it looked like he was back to the size he had been when they first met. Discreetly looking him up and down, she noted that brotherman was looking *tight*. Damn. Either he was looking really good, or it had been too long since she had some. Pushing those thoughts aside, she led him into the living room.

"Hey, don't look a gift horse in the mouth. Tomorrow the war may be back on. Think of this as a temporary cease fire," Zoe drawled, settling herself in her favorite chair in the living room. "On the serious tip, Vaughn, I do appreciate what you did tonight. It helped more than you know."

"Glad I could help. At least I finally did something right."

"Don't spoil it, okay?"

"Yeah, aiight. Old habits die hard."

"Ah, there's something I wanted to talk to you about. Your being here tonight actually saves me the trouble of having to ask you to come over."

"Yeah? What's up?"

"I've been thinking, and ah, I think I'm going to put the house up for sale and move."

"Move? Move where? Why would you want to do that? The kids love this house and all of their friends are from the neighborhood."

"I put in for a job at Doylestown Hospital and I got it," Zoe said quietly, carefully watching Vaughn's reaction.

"Doylestown Hospital? As in Doylestown, Bucks County?" Vaughn asked, stunned.

"Yes."

"But why? You've been at Elkins Park for years. You have seniority!" Vaughn knew he was grasping at straws, but at the moment his brain couldn't seem to come up with a better argument for her not to take the job.

"Be that as it may, I feel the need for a change," Zoe hedged.

"It's that asshole, isn't it? You are doing this to get away from memories of him, aren't you?" The hurt in Vaughn's voice was almost more than Zoe could bear. "I don't believe this shit! Oh, you had no problems staying here after we broke up, but now, now that you've seen what a gigolo he is, just what I've always known him to be, *now* you can't stand to be here? Ain't this some shit?!"

"Vaughn, keep your voice down!" Zoe hissed, glancing into the kitchen that was suspiciously quiet. "Look, if we can't discuss this like civilized adults, then maybe you'd better leave."

"I ain't goin' no-damn-where! How you gon' take my kids all the way up there, Zoe? You know half the damn time that piece of shit I call a car doesn't work. And why doesn't it work Zoe? I'll tell you why. Because almost all of my damn check finds it way over here before I even get the summa'bitch, that's why! And now you want to make it even harder because that bastard broke your heart? I'll be damned!"

"Damn it Vaughn, lower your voice! Just bring your ignorant ass upstairs so we can discuss this in private," Zoe demanded, marching over to the foot of the stairs.

Whirling around, she told the three surprised onlookers standing in the doorway, "And would you three busybodies in the kitchen go downstairs and watch television, or play Nintendo, or something?!" Zoe said in exasperation.

"Are we moving, Mom? I don't wanna move," Shanice cried, tears welling up in her eyes.

"Yeah, Mom, me neither. My team is here. All of our friends, everything," Jonathan protested.

"And what about me and Tribby? How am I supposed to see her if we move all the way out to Doylestown? It's not fair. You didn't even ask us!" Chris announced.

"I was going to talk to you all about it, I just haven't had a chance," Zoe defended herself, feeling uncomfortable under all the hostility that her kids were directing toward her.

"See what you're doing, Zoe? None of the kids want to go. Why can't you just forget this foolishness? I don't want my kids that far away."

"You, upstairs," Zoe snapped at Vaughn. "You three," Zoe stabbed a finger in their direction, "Go on downstairs like I said."

Zoe's expression and tone brooked no arguments from the children. She figured with them in the basement and Vaughn in her bedroom, she would have the first floor as a buffer for the screaming match she felt was coming. Chris opened his mouth like he wanted to say something else but one step toward him by Zoe made him change his mind and he herded his brother and sister down the stairs instead.

After leading Vaughn upstairs and firmly shutting her door, Zoe turned on him, her small face tight and her gray eyes almost black with pent-up anger. Whether it was all directed at Vaughn, Antonio, the world, or whoever, it didn't matter. She just felt the need to lash out at *somebody*.

"Goddamnit, Vaughn, why did you have to get so loud that the kids overheard? I wasn't ready to tell them yet. I shouldn't have said anything to your ignorant ass either, but I was trying to be nice. But *nooooo*! You just had to spoil it when we were finally having a civil-fuckin'-conversation! Jesus H. Christ! You would think I would have learned my lesson by now!"

"Bullshit, Zoe! As usual, you want everything your way and fuck anybody else's feelings! I don't want my kids that far away!" Vaughn thundered, the veins in his thick neck bulging out.

Zoe, her voice dripping with sarcasm replied, "Technically, Vaughn, only one of these kids is yours anyway, so I fail to see why you are getting your draws in a bunch! This is really about Shanice. You could care less about my boys and you damn well know it!" Zoe knew she'd crossed the line when she saw the devastated look on Vaughn's face.

"I don't believe you said some shit like that. I have cared for, and loved, Jon and Chris like they were my own flesh and blood. Yeah, I know Chris and I have had problems sometimes, but I don't think it's any different than it would be with any father and son. Maybe one of the reasons we haven't been as close as we could be is because of *you*!"

"Me? What the hell did I do? Don't put that shit on me, Vaughn. You did fine by yourself proving to them what an asshole you can be!"

"Bullshit, Zoe. If you hadn't been so busy over the years telling them, especially Chris, that the only person they had to listen to was you because I wasn't their father, maybe he and I could have been closer. Yeah, you thought I didn't know about that, didn't you? You know goddamn well that I'm right!

Jonathan, however, has always thought of me as his Dad. I've known the boy since he was in diapers. I never understood that, Zoe. Why were you so adamant about Chris not thinking of me as his dad, but you didn't have a problem with Jon?"

"You're talking stupid, Vaughn! This has nothing to do with me wanting to move. And just for the record, Antonio has nothing to do with it either. I got a great job as head of the mobile services department at a suburban hospital, where I'll be making a lot more money. Not only that, the schools are better, the sports are better, and I think it is an all around good decision for me and the kids," Zoe explained, feeling like she had to defend her position.

"Yeah? Then why didn't you make this move when we split up?" Vaughn challenged.

"I don't know! Look, I didn't go looking for this job. It was more or less handed to me. I didn't really think they would seriously consider me, but they did. I thought it was an excellent opportunity, so I took it."

Zoe started to sit on the side of the bed, thought better of it, and bounced back up. Maybe bringing Vaughn upstairs hadn't been such a great idea. Being in the room she shared first with Vaughn, and then with Antonio, was just too strange for words. Vaughn, however, in his agitated state, didn't seem to notice Zoe's sudden discomfort.

"How long have you known about this?"

"I just got word a couple of days ago that I got the job."

"Come on, Zoe. Isn't there some way we can work this out? Look, I understand you're hurting, but don't do this to the kids. They need some stability in their lives, and for what it's worth, that stability has always been this house."

"Then why don't *you* buy me out?" Zoe suggested with sudden inspiration.

"Me? With what? *You* take almost all of my money, remember?"

"Give it a rest, will you? Damn. There must be some way you can get the money."

"This wouldn't even be an issue if you would just drop this foolishness, Zoe. Why can't we just leave things like they are?"

"'Cause it is time for a change, Vaughn. You may not like it and the kids, well, the kids will get over it. But I gotta do this for me. Can't you understand that?" Zoe pleaded, trying to make him understand.

She wasn't angry anymore, just tired; tired of always having to explain herself and her motives to everyone. When did she get to do what she wanted, when she wanted to do it? Before she knew it, she was crying. Vaughn looked at his ex-wife helplessly, not sure if it was in violation of some code he was unaware of to comfort one's ex-wife. After a moment's hesitation, he pulled her down next to him on the bed and into his arms to let her cry. After a while, her cries quieted down to low snuffles and then just a ragged sigh.

"Feel better?" Vaughn asked, a smile in his voice.

"Yeah, I do," Zoe answered, looking up at him. For a moment Vaughn was transfixed as he stared into Zoe's now clear, sparkling gray eyes. Wordlessly he leaned down and lightly brushed his full, soft lips over Zoe's. The spark of electricity they each felt surprised them both. Vaughn hesitated, then proceeded to kiss Zoe liked he used to do back when they first met and he was trying so hard to win her over.

Zoe couldn't believe the feelings that swept through her. Unconsciously, she raised her hand and placed it on the back of Vaughn's head, inviting him to deepen their kiss. Soon that kiss led to another and another and yet another. She was barely aware when they fell back on the bed. Or of how her uniform top ended up on the floor, with her bra quickly following. Clothes, shoes, stockings, and under-things were flying all over the place.

Vaughn was paying tribute to Zoe's engorged nipples and his hand had found its way between her legs. Listening to her moans and watching her body writhe with need beneath his hands again almost brought him to tears. He was just about ready to move between her legs to take them to the next level when an insistent knock at the bedroom door served to act like a very large bucket of cold water. The shock brought them both back to their senses.

"Who is it?" Zoe asked weakly as she scrambled to put her uniform back on. She had to keep from laughing as she watched Vaughn struggling to get his Timberlands back on without stamping his feet, a sure sign to anyone listening that the shoes had been off in the first place.

"Ah, it's me, Mom. Ms. Linda from up the street wants to know if she can borrow your punch bowl." Jonathan answered from the other side of the door.

Chris, who followed Jon upstairs to make sure Zoe and Vaughn hadn't killed each other, smacked Jonathan on the back of the head. He had a pretty good idea of what was going on before they got there, and if he had gotten there before Jon, there would have been no way in hell he would have interrupted for a stupid punch bowl.

"What?" Jonathan whispered, rubbing the back of his head. "What did I do?"

"Didn't you notice there was no arguing going on, you moron?"

"Yeah, so what?"

"Come on, Jonathan. You may be young, but you are not *that* young! Think about it," Chris told his brother, trying to get him to think without coming out and saying it.

"Huh? I don't get it," Jonathan answered. Suddenly, comprehension dawned and he could have kicked himself.

"Damn! I mean, darn!" he whispered.

"Tell her I said she can use it, Jon. Oh, and give her the ladle and the cups as well. Everything should be in the buffet. Tell her to call me if she needs anything else," Zoe called through the door.

"Okay, Mom! Will do," Jonathan told his mother. Zoe listened as she heard not only Jonathan's footsteps, but a second pair as well, retreat back down the steps. Mortified, she realized that Christopher must have come upstairs trying to check on her on the sneak-tip.

"Damn, that was close!" Zoe sighed.

"Tell me about it. So, what are we going to do? Are you still determined to do this?"

"Yes, Vaughn. I have to," Zoe said quietly, hoping another argument wasn't about to start. "But I'll tell you what I'll do. I'll try to find some place between here and Doylestown, so you won't have to travel so far to see or pick up the kids. Deal?"

"Deal," Vaughn agreed, resigned. Once Zoe

made up her mind about something, it would be a miracle if Jesus Christ Himself could change it.

"And if we put our heads together, maybe we can figure out a way for you to buy me out of this house. At least that way, when the kids do come to visit, they could see their old friends," Zoe suggested.

Nodding his head thoughtfully, Vaughn was surprised at Zoe's willingness to work with him instead of fighting with him like usual.

"Cool. That will work. Okay, I think I can deal with that."

"Good. And, Vaughn, um, one more thing. Would you mind looking over the house when I find it? Just to, you know, make sure everything is in good working order?" Zoe didn't know what possessed her to just ask that. She had originally planned on having Sara and Theo help her, but here she was extending another olive branch to her ex-husband.

"No problem, babe," Vaughn assured her as he followed her out the door and down the steps. Vaughn ran downstairs to the basement and spent a few moments with the kids before saying his goodbyes. After coming back upstairs he joined Zoe near the front door.

"Feel better?" he asked with a smile.

"Yeah, thanks," Zoe answered, a blush spreading on her pale cheeks at the memory of what they had almost done.

Bending down to give her another kiss, Zoe stopped him with, "Oh no! That's what almost got us into trouble earlier!"

"Hey, a man can try, can't he?"

"Goodnight, Vaughn!"

Vaughn just laughed as he left, glad to have survived the storm called Hurricane Zoe. After closing the front door, Zoe leaned her back against it and smiled, feeling better than she had in a long time.

CHAPTER SIXTEEN
Oh Drama!

"So that's about how it went," Danita said, having recounted the fiasco at her house a few weeks earlier.

"Damn, girlfriend. I really feel bad about coming down so hard on you now. I hope you know you can count on me. On all of us. You know we got your back," Tamika said, as Zoe and Sara nodded their agreement.

"Thanks, y'all. You know I appreciate it and all, but . . ."

"Ain't nothing like family, right?" Sara said.

"Yeah," Danita sadly agreed.

"Has your mother come around yet?"

"Mother is going through one of her diva moments. Half the time she's not speaking to me and the other half I wish she wasn't!"

"Do all of y'all call her 'Mother,' or is that just you?" Tamika wanted to know.

"I guess we all call her that. Or Mom. But never, ever, Ma, Mama or Mommy. She doesn't like it and refuses to answer if you do call her one of those variations."

"Damn! She sounds like a character."

"That she is. A real diva! And you better not forget it, either. She would be mortified if she knew we called her 'the Mean Queen' behind her back," Danita said, smiling sadly.

Once again, she'd gone and disappointed Zenobia. No matter what she did, it never seemed to be good enough or quite right, at least not in her mother's eyes. She had an awful feeling that as far as her mother was concerned, she was an abysmal failure and disappointment. Danita was tired of beating her head against the wall trying to make her mother love her for who she was, not for who Zenobia thought she should be.

"Well, at least your mother-in-law has been supportive," Zoe said.

"Please. Almost *too* supportive. She's getting on my damn nerves. Every time I turn around, there she is. I swear to God, if I have to go to one more of those tired, boring luncheons or dinners with another one of her clubs, I'm going to kill somebody. Three luncheons and two dinners in the last three weeks is more than enough for me, thank you very much!"

"Has it been that bad?"

"You don't know the half. Do you know I actually heard one of those stuck up bitches say, 'at least she's not one of those *dark-skinned* Blacks!' Like that makes it more acceptable, less of a threat, or easier on the eyes or something. She tried to act like she was whispering, but that bitch said that mess loud enough for me and everyone else in the room to hear it. I was insulted and mortified."

"I know you told her off, didn't you?" Sara wanted to know, feeling her own temper kicking up a notch.

"No."

"No? What do you mean *no*? Girl have you lost your mind? I would have been all over that snotty bitch like white on rice!" Tamika said, indignant.

"I can just imagine," Danita laughed, picturing Tamika snatching off her earrings, ready to do battle. Continuing, she explained, "I didn't have to say anything. Emily did."

"*Emily*? What did she say?" they all asked.

"She said, 'Why thank you, Babs. The ignorance I was always sure you possessed has finally been confirmed. By the way, I understand that you'll have to sell that custom house you recently built since Bill didn't get that appointment he was sure he was going to get in the Governor's office, huh?' And that woman lost all of her color and said that the decision hadn't been made yet. Then Emily kind of gave her this cold smile and responded, 'Oh, but it has.'"

"Chile, I thought I was going to pee myself. The other women kind of gasped, and then suddenly, we were surrounded by all these fawning women who couldn't say enough nice things to me or Emily. And of course, once they heard that I sing, well, you would have thought I was Whitney or some damn body."

"Damn, so that's how they do that shit, huh?"

"I guess. Most people think it's the *men* who run this country. Ha!" Danita laughed.

"Emily got juice like that?" Tamika wanted to know, a calculating look in her eye. Here was a possible unexpected business connection that she might be able to use. One never knew from where the next 'in' could come.

Not noticing, Danita laughingly replied, "Yeah, at the moment at least. Adam is so busy trying to make up with her, she could ask for a piece of the moon and he'd find a way to get it for her. And to look at her, she seems kind of quiet and mousy. Who knew?"

"So have father and son made up?"

"I guess. But Ben seems to be handling his father with a long-handled spoon."

"A what?" Tamika asked.

"My mother used to say that!" Sara and Zoe said at the same time, and then laughed.

"Nice. That's still not telling me what it means."

"Think about it, Girl. It means keeping someone at a distance. DUH!" Zoe teased her friend."

"Remind me why we're supposed to be friends?"

"I don't know. Why are we?"

"Whatevah!" Tamika answered.

"Well, Zoe hasn't been handling Vaughn with a long-handled spoon," Sara interjected, a mischievous twinkle in her eyes.

"Thanks, Big mouth!"

"Hey, I can't help it if you had a close encounter of the weird kind!" Sara said before bursting out laughing.

At the confused looks from Danita and Tamika, Zoe rolled her eyes at her sister and then explained what happened with her ex-husband, her new job, and her moving.

"You, in suburbia? Oh, Lawd! I'm sure when

Vaughn heard about that, it went over like a fart in church!" Tamika said, cackling.

"Very funny. *Anyway*," Zoe went on after silently giving Tamika the hand, "I told Vaughn about this special mortgage program, so he's checking it out. And my sister," waving a hand in Sara's direction, "has agreed to help me find a new home. A friend of Theo's is a real estate agent. He's going to work with me and he thinks he may have already found something. He said it was a hell of a deal. The kids weren't too happy to hear about it, but I think they're starting to come around. Shanice is hoping for a bigger room. Jonathan can't wait to finally have his own room and Chris is just pissed. But he'll just have to get over it. Anyway, I'm getting really excited about it. It's time to make a change."

"That is so nice, Zoe! You go, gurl! I'm really happy for you," Danita told her, nibbling on a baby carrot.

Danita was always nibbling these days. But she was trying really hard not to go overboard with the sweets and salty stuff. She had seen too many women blow up while pregnant and then have to fight like hell to get it off. Some never did. She couldn't take that chance, mainly because of her career. Already, her manager was fretting about her video image. And God help her if she was less than perfect. Zenobia would have a field day! At the moment, while her sisters were sorry to see their mother coming down so hard on Danita, they were grateful it was keeping Zenobia's attention away from them.

"Yeah, well, what about lover boy? Have you talked to him?" Tamika asked, watching Zoe intently.

"No. Enough said," Zoe replied shortly, looking away.

Zoe knew, sooner or later, that she was going to have to talk to Antonio. But the longer she waited, the easier it became *not* to talk to him. Yet still, in the darkest part of the night, she knew, without a doubt, she missed him. She wasn't sure, though, if she would ever be able to forgive him. Her mother would tell her that she was letting her pride stand in the way. Thinking about Amanda just made her sadder, so she tried hard not to let her mind wander there. She never realized how much of a comfort it was to have Amanda as a sounding board and as a constant source of wisdom and good common sense. That is, not until she was gone. Sighing again, she returned her attention to the present.

"Hey, I'm hungry. Anybody want to order Chinese?" Danita wanted to know.

"That sounds good. I could go for some cashew shrimp with snow peas," Sara added, rifling through her 'menu' drawer.

"Mmm, some shrimp with lobster sauce might taste good," Zoe added.

"Ewww," Sara said, wrinkling her nose in disgust. "Isn't that the dish where it looks like the shrimp is floating around in snot sauce?"

"Snot sauce? That's disgusting, Sara!" Danita laughed.

"Well that's what it looks like. I ordered that once at a luncheon. Girl, I was sick for the rest of the afternoon, every time I thought about what that shrimp looked like in that mess! Yuck!" Sara told them, shuddering at the memory.

"Well, I like it," Zoe mumbled.

"Fine, but if you plan on eating at *my* house

tonight, you won't be ordering it! I'll be damned if I'm going to get sick looking at that snotty looking stuff."

Before Sara could fuss anymore, Tamika jumped up and ran for the bathroom.

"What the hell is wrong with her?" Sara wanted to know.

"Beats me," Zoe answered, unconcerned as she looked over the menu trying to find something else. "Does Happy Family meet with your approval, Ms. Thang?"

"That'll work. And you're getting your usual sesame chicken, Danita?"

"And you know this," Danita laughingly agreed.

"Are you all right?" Zoe asked Tamika when she returned to the billiard's room in Sara's finished basement. They were half-heartedly shooting pool as they caught up with the events of the last few weeks.

"I guess. I don't know what's wrong with me lately. I think I must be getting a stomach virus or something. I can't keep a damn thing down, and when y'all started talking about that, you know, sauce," Tamika said gesturing with her hand, unwilling to say the word "snot" for fear that she'd get sick again, "I don't know, something happened with my stomach and I just barely made it to the bathroom!"

"Sounds like you're knocked up to me," Danita joked, rubbing her own tiny protrusion.

"Who? I *know* you are not talking about *me!* Chile, please! That's absurd. There is no way . . ." Tamika started to protest and then her voice drifted into horrified silence, before she whispered hoarsely, "Oh my God! *Oh my God!*"

"I was just kidding. Are you serious?" Danita asked, concerned by the look in Tamika's eyes.

"Well you knew it had to happen sooner or later, girlfriend," Zoe told her.

"Bullshit. I've always been so careful."

"First of all, you need to be sure," Sara told her.

"Right. Right. I need to be sure," Tamika agreed, her eyes wild.

"You need to call your doctor and get a test done," Danita gently suggested.

"Right. Right. A test."

"Forget all that. Just go to the drugstore and pick up a home pregnancy test," Zoe told her.

"Right. Right. A home pregnancy test."

"*Tamika!* Girl, will you snap out of it? You sound like a freakin' zombie!" Zoe told her, snapping her fingers in front of Tamika's frozen face.

Tamika zoned everyone out. All she could think about was what she had done and who she'd done it with. It was bad enough that it even happened. Now, if what her friends were saying was true, she was carrying around a little reminder of her bad judgment. Her friends. She couldn't even look them in their faces. Especially not the one she had betrayed. She couldn't be pregnant. She just *couldn't* be!

CHAPTER SEVENTEEN
Something Old, Something New

Zoe hurried from the hospital, eager to meet Sara for a look at the house Theo's realtor friend wanted Zoe to see. She was hoping it would be all that Sara said it was. It sounded like a dream come true, and right about now she needed some good news. Hopefully, it would be enough to make the kids stop being so mad about moving, period.

Just that morning she was forced to get into Christopher's world. She was getting just a little sick of his snarky, sullen attitude. She'd told herself that he was acting that way because it was spring and maybe he was feeling a little rammy. That, she could understand. She always felt that way herself at the beginning of spring. She loved spring and after being confined to the house during most of the winter, as soon as the temperature started its upward climb, it was all she could do to make herself go to work. She would usually try to sneak and take a day off from work, rent a convertible for the day, put the top down, and go for a ride from Philly to Wildwood just for the joy of being alone and free. Of course, since she recently went back to work, she sadly realized she probably would not get to do that this year. That was how she exorcized her rammy feelings, but Chris' sullen mood was really starting to get to her. She made a mental note to talk it over with Vaughn. She had an idea that just might make everyone happy, but she wanted to see what Vaughn thought first.

As she was digging around in her purse looking for her car keys, she came to an abrupt halt when she walked into a solid chest. She mumbled an apology as she stepped around the person. But when she looked up she saw that the person was Antonio.

Frowning, she asked, "What are you doing here?" She glanced around and noted that the area was flooded with other employees hurrying to their own cars.

"I didn't know what else to do. I had to see you, baby, I mean, Zoe," he hurriedly said when he saw her frown increase.

"Look, Antonio, there's nothing to talk about. It's over, done, finished. See? End of discussion."

"Aw, come on, Zoe! I did like you asked, I left you alone. I thought by now you would have calmed down."

"Guess it didn't pay for you to think!" Zoe snapped, attempting to step around him. When he grabbed her arm, Zoe stopped and looked from his hand to his face with an expression that should have slain him on the spot.

"Let go of me," Zoe hissed through clenched teeth.

"Damn it, Zoe! Will you stop fighting me and just listen?!" Antonio asked, frustrated, his voice booming out across the hospital parking lot. Everyone still in the area stopped and looked in their direction. Zoe cursed under her breath when she saw her supervisor, Jill Stevens, hurrying toward her.

"Is everything all right?" Jill asked in her clipped English accent.

"It's fine, Jill," Zoe assured her, smiling. Jill always reminded Zoe of Julie Andrews. She looked amazingly similar to the star and sounded just like her. Zoe was going to miss Jill when she left. They had become very good friends over the years.

"Are you sure?" Jill eyed Antonio up and down, a small frown marring her features, before looking at Zoe with concern again.

"Oh, hey, Jill. Nice to see you again," Antonio said.

"Antonio."

"Really, Jill, everything's cool. Really," Zoe tried to reassure her supervisor.

"Well, if you say so. I'll see you tomorrow, Zoe." After giving Antonio another once over, she turned and walked away, but kept looking back as if to make sure no harm came to Zoe.

"Well, I hope you're satisfied! Thanks a hell of a lot for coming to my job and acting like an ass!"

"You made me act like an ass! Wait, that didn't come out right."

Even though she tried not to, Zoe burst out laughing.

"What? Oh, just kick a brother when he's down and tryin' to come correct. Yeah, aiight," Antonio said, trying to sound hurt, but smiling anyway.

After a moment, the laughter faded away and they were left just staring at one another. But the air between them felt less electric. Calmer, a little clearer.

"Want to go across the street for a drink?" Antonio gently suggested.

"Actually, I can't. I'm already late as it is. I'm supposed to be meeting Sara in Ambler and I should have been there fifteen minutes ago."

"Oh." Zoe noticed how his shoulders slumped in disappointment. She started to invite him to come along until she remembered that she already asked Vaughn to meet her there.

"Look, I'll call you later. Where are you?"

"At my grandmother's. Call me there."

"Will do. Please tell her I said hello."

"I would if I could, but Ms. Lady is on a two week cruise."

"Get out! Go 'head, Mrs. Wright! Did she go by herself or with her senior group?"

"Naw, she went with Pet."

"Nice. Anyway, I really do have to run, but I'll call you later, okay?"

"Cool. I'd like that," he told her, grinning. His good mood was infectious, and Zoe found herself smiling back as she slipped into her car.

Zoe's mood was lighter than it had been in a long time. She found herself turning the radio up to a level she usually fussed about, and sang with almost every song at the top of her lungs. She didn't bother to stop and think about why she was so happy, she just knew that she was.

When she pulled into the driveway alongside the house, she hopped out of the car, her step lighter and quicker than it had been recently. Looking around, she noted that Sara and Vaughn's cars were already there. As she stepped lightly toward the front door, Zoe noted the trim front yard with the modest landscaping on either side of the cemented front steps. She liked that there was a peaked roof held up by two ionic columns that covered the front door. At least her guests wouldn't get drenched in the rain waiting for her to answer the door, should she choose to buy.

Upon entering the house, Zoe stopped in the entryway, already liking what she saw. To her left was the stairway leading to the floor above. Directly in front of her was an open hallway with gleaming hardwood floors. To her right were the living room and dining room, which were separated by square pillars. Afternoon sunlight from bay windows flooded both rooms from the front, making the rooms appear bright, warm, and inviting. A green marble fireplace graced one wall in the living room. You could access the kitchen from the hallway or through the dining room. Zoe nodded her head in approval as she walked toward the rear of the house to the kitchen, where she found the agent, Sara, and Vaughn waiting.

"There you are! I've been trying to reach you on your cell phone," Sara told her.

"Oops. I forgot to turn it on when I came out of the hospital. I was, ah, distracted."

"Oh? How so?"

"I'll tell you later. I don't want to hold this gentleman up any longer than I already have," Zoe said while putting her hand out to shake the stranger's hand and flashing him one of her smiles.

"Not a problem at all. We've only been here a short time ourselves. I'm David Culvert, and I am very pleased to meet you. Very pleased," the tall, blonde giant said, still holding Zoe's hand, as his deep blue eyes smiled into her startled gray ones.

"Yes, well, Zoe, let's look at the house," Vaughn broke in, stepping between them to break the contact.

Zoe shrugged in helpless apology as Vaughn dragged her down to the basement to start the tour. By the time they looked the house over from top to bottom, inside and out, Zoe was sold. Zoe felt that the gods were finally smiling her way. And when David told her the price, she almost fainted. Not from it being too high, but because she would actually be able to afford it, even with the obvious upgrades that she could see were already included with the house—upgrades such as the granite countertops in the kitchen, the hardwood floors, and the crown moldings throughout the first floor. She was glad that the house was all white. At least she wouldn't have to worry about primer. She was already picturing what color each room would be.

"How can it be that price? What's wrong with it? There's a creek running under it, isn't there?" Zoe asked as she looked out the sliding glass doors in the family room to the deck, craning her neck back and forth, searching for one of those tension wire frames. "Or we're near all the electrical thingies and everybody's going to get cancer, right?"

Laughing, David rushed to assure her, "No, there is no creek, no high tension wires. This is a bank repo. The people who originally bought it were dot-commers. When the company the husband worked for went belly up, things just unraveled. I don't know all the particulars, just that the bank is selling the house for what is still owed. The house is only about eight years old. As you can see, they upgraded it pretty well. Judging from the price, I can only guess they must have either paid a substantial down payment or they were trying to cut the mortgage time down by paying extra."

"I wonder how they came to lose it? That is such a shame!" Zoe commented. But as she looked around the kitchen, breakfast room, and family room again, Zoe continued with, "Well, I'm sorry for them, but I'm damned happy for me!"

"I told you David would hook you up. I also told you that you would love this house!" Sara said, then laughed while hugging Zoe.

"Yes, you did," Zoe said, hugging her sister back.

"And it's great that it has a family room and a finished basement," Vaughn commented.

"It is great," Sara continued, "because then the kids can have another place to go when the grown folks are up here. Or when you just want them out of your hair, and want the family room to yourself. Let me tell you, when Bethany and T.J. are home, Theo and I are glad they have the lower level, instead of them being all up on us when we're trying to watch a movie in the family room. And you know how it is when we all get together. All the women are upstairs in the kitchen and family room, and all the men are down there screaming at whatever sports thingy is on."

"And a laundry room, right off the kitchen, so I don't have to constantly run up and down the steps."

"This is nice, Zoe. Not too far from where the old house is and not too far from your new job. Lots more room, too," Vaughn said, sounding a little disappointed things were turning out so well.

Zoe chose not to let Vaughn's tone get her down. She was flying high and wanted to enjoy it. Instead of getting pissed, she said, "Yup, it sure is, Vaughn. Especially since you got the loan and can buy me out. Everything has worked out perfectly!"

"Yeah, perfectly," Vaughn said dryly.

Handing Zoe a business card, David said, "Call me tomorrow so we can set up a time to get everything signed. Make sure you tell your loan officer that it will be a thirty day closing so they can get the inspector out here as soon as possible and do the title search. I hate to rush you folks, but I have another appointment. Sara, give Theo my best," he said before lightly kissing her on the cheek. After shaking Vaughn's hand, he turned to Zoe again, a smile playing around his mouth and eyes.

"I look forward to seeing you soon," David said, his tone sounding almost flirtatious.

Zoe felt herself blush, before saying, "Thank you so much for everything, David. I'll call you in the morning."

After he left, Zoe, Vaughn, and Sara lingered outside of the now locked house. Zoe looked up and down the street at the beautifully manicured front lawns and drew in a deep breath that smelled of newness and renewal. As hard as Zoe tried, she just couldn't get the stupid grin off her face as she gazed at the house. It was more than she ever thought she would have.

"Well, Zoe, you can't stand out here all night

gazing at this house," Sara teased. "You guys want to come by the house and have dinner with us?"

"I guess you're right. I can't stand out here all night. Thanks for the invite, but I have to get home and feed my own crew. Vaughn, do you want to come for dinner? I need to talk to you about something."

"Ah, yeah. Sure. I'll follow you to the house."

The sisters kissed and hugged again before everyone got into their vehicles.

After Zoe and Vaughn got to the house, Zoe quickly threw dinner together for her kids, who tried to act like they were dying of starvation.

"Well, if you were that damn hungry, why didn't you just eat a bowl of cereal until I got home?" she grumbled as she opened two cans of Manwich sloppy joe mix to pour into the ground beef simmering on the stove with onions and green peppers.

"We did. But we're still *famished* Mommycandescent!" Shanice said. Shanice recently discovered the word *incandescent*, and fell in love with it. Consequently, anything that was really cool, pleasing, or just struck her in a particular way, she tacked 'candescent' onto the end of it.

Zoe smiled, even though she tried hard not to. She was in too good of a mood. She couldn't wait to tell the kids about the house. She and Vaughn briefly discussed it when the kids hadn't been around, and even though she was bursting to tell them, he suggested waiting and showing them instead. It would probably help to win them over far easier than just telling them about it.

Zoe was impressed with his reasoning and readily agreed. She was suspicious, however, as to why he was being so helpful. Years of being adversaries made it awfully hard to be compatriots now. But as her mother would have told her, she had to stop looking a gift horse in the mouth. She needed to admit that it was nice not to expend so much energy fighting. She was tired of fighting. It was time to do some living.

After the kitchen was cleaned up and the kids scattered to different parts of the house, Zoe and Vaughn sat at the kitchen table, not really paying much attention to the soft droning of the television in the background as they idly chatted and shared a glass of wine.

"So, what did you want to talk to me about?"

"Oh, that. Nothing really. We can talk about it later."

"I see. Are you sure?"

"Yeah. Well, see, I had this thought . . . oh, never mind. It probably won't work, and well, never mind."

Before Vaughn could comment further, Chris briefly looked in and mumbled, "Later."

"Whoa! Get back here, Chris. Where are you going?" Zoe asked.

"Out, okay?"

"No, it's not okay. When I ask you where you're going, I expect a civil answer. Don't make me ask you again."

After a few seconds of stony silence, he mumbled, "Over Tribby's, okay? Dag!" As he turned away, he mumbled, "Does everything have to be a fuckin' inquisition?"

"Oh no his narrow behind didn't! What did you

just say?" Zoe demanded, jumping up and heading her son off at the front door.

"Nothin'."

"You know, I'm about sick of you and your smart-ass mouth, boy."

"Yeah, well, I'm sick of you always tellin' me what to do."

"What the hell?!" Vaughn said, before jumping up. "Boy, I know I didn't just hear you talk to your mother like that."

"You don't know how it is with her, man. All she do is fuss and complain about stupid stuff. I know what the real reason is for us moving. Because she can't stand my girl. That's the real deal."

"Oh, for God's sake! Will you get a grip, Chris? I could care less about that little chippy! News flash! The entire world does *not* revolve around you. If your lazy behind was less worried about gettin' some ass and more concerned about your school work, or an after school job, you would realize that."

"Can I go now?" he said, sounding disinterested, like he had heard it all before.

"I feel like telling you no, but I think you need to get out of my face before I slap the taste out of your mouth," Zoe threatened as she stood staring him down by the front door. She stepped aside and let him dash out of the house.

"That boy is going to be the death of me yet!" Zoe said in exasperation, returning to the kitchen. "That's what I was going to talk to you about earlier."

"I don't follow. You mean about Chris?"

"Yeah. I was thinking that maybe, if it was okay

with you, maybe I should let him stay here. He only has one more year of high school, and I know he really wants to graduate with his class. But I didn't want to impose . . ."

"Funny you should say that. I was going to suggest it, but I thought you would hand me my head." Vaughn laughed at the expressions that chased themselves across Zoe's face. He could tell that she didn't want to admit he was right, but at one time, she *would* have handed him his head. Zoe had some serious control issues.

"Really? You really wouldn't mind? I mean he can live with me during the summer, and of course I would want him to come up sometimes on the weekends. But I want him to get an after school job as a condition of him staying here. Is that a deal?"

"Again, we're on the same page. He should have to do something for, as you say, getting his own way."

"Not only that, next year is graduation, so that means prom, after-prom, school trip, and if he thinks I'm paying for all that, he's got another thing coming! I may be getting a bargain with that house, but it still costs more than living here."

"I understand, babe. Wow. We got through a whole discussion and you didn't cuss me out once. Where's the calendar? I want to mark this date down!"

"Ha-ha. He's got jokes."

"Seriously, you know Shanice and Jon are going to raise all holy hell."

"Yeah, but I can deal with that. Jon is starting high school next year anyway, and Horsham-Hatboro

High has a better athletics program. After the wrappers I've been finding in his jeans, I think it will be best to get him in a new environment anyway."

"Wrappers? What are you talking about?" Vaughn asked, confused.

"I found a couple of condom wrappers in Jon's jeans."

"What?? Jonathan? Our Jonathan? Jonathan who only thinks about sports and video games, Jonathan?" Vaughn asked, shocked.

"One and the same. I finally broke down and asked him about it. He was all embarrassed and said that he was only 'trying them on.' I told him to get real, that I wasn't stupid. He never would tell me with whom he'd been using them. I hope to God it was with a girl."

"Zoe! Why would you say something like that?"

"You know how some of those supposed jocks are. Closet jills. I just don't want anyone experimenting with my baby boy. And honestly, I've never seen Jon demonstrate the slightest interest in a girl."

"Damn. Why didn't you tell me about this before?"

"I don't know. I was trying to handle it myself."

"Would it matter if he's gay?"

"Honestly? I don't know. I would like to think it wouldn't, but I really don't know. He's a football player and he has real potential. He doesn't need the added stress of being a closet *gay* football player. It would ruin his chances for college scholarships and maybe one day the pros. I don't want to see him go through that. It would crush him."

"Hmmm, I see your point. Maybe it is just a phase. Boys go through it just like girls do."

"Maybe," Zoe said, not wanting to discuss it anymore. Instead she continued with, "And I think Shanice will do better in the middle school out there, especially since it has such small class sizes. She performs much better with one-on-one attention. Not only that, her new school has a gymnastics program, and I know she's been wanting to do that for a while. It's gonna be a lot easier winning Shanice and Jon over than Chris."

"I see your point," Vaughn said, letting the matter of Jonathan drop. He decided the next time he got to spend some time with Jon alone, they were going to have a man-to-man conversation that was long overdue.

"And I think they are really going to like the house and their new neighborhood."

"That Dave guy said it was a real family-oriented neighborhood with a lot of kids."

"Sara told me it was pretty racially diverse in that area too, and that's really important to me."

"That was one of the main reasons we bought the house here, remember?"

"Yeah, I do," she answered with a smile. They stayed silent for a few minutes, remembering back when it had been good between them. Zoe a little wistful and Vaughn regretful, for what he had and for what he now knew he had thrown away.

He was looking forward to moving back into the house, though. However, the first room he planned on redecorating was the master bedroom. He didn't need the ghost of Antonio driving him crazy at night with thoughts of what he and his ex-wife did in that room. He and Zoe discussed leaving the kids' furniture so the rooms would feel familiar when Shanice and Jon came to spend the night. Zoe fretted at first about the replacement cost until Sara asked if she could do the kids' rooms as a housewarming present. Pride almost made her turn Sara down until she heard Amanda's voice telling her to stop being silly and get over herself. After going back and forth with Sara on the phone, she called her sister and graciously accepted.

"What made you change your mind?" Sara asked, curious.

"Mom."

"Ah!" Sara said, not needing further explanation.

Vaughn was just relieved that he wouldn't have to come up with money he didn't have to buy furniture he couldn't afford.

"Well, let me get out of here. Thanks for the dinner, babe. I enjoyed it." Vaughn said, getting up and slowly walking toward the front door.

"It was the least I could do. Thanks for looking over the house today. I really appreciate it. You know I don't know a thing about plumbing and wiring and all that stuff."

"No problem, my pleasure." He stood awkwardly at the door.

"Well," he said.

"Well," she said, at the same time.

They laughed nervously. When Zoe leaned up to kiss Vaughn on his cheek, he turned his head at the last moment and her lips lightly brushed his.

Zoe stepped back quickly, momentarily startled. Then she playfully swatted at him and said, "Oh you! Tryin' to be Mr. Slick. Gon' witcha' now!"

"A little is better than none!" Vaughn teased as he stepped through the door.

"Night, Vaughn!" Zoe mock admonished as she firmly shut the door.

But the smile on her lips lingered long after she heard his car pull off.

CHAPTER EIGHTEEN
Friendly Strangers

Tamika impatiently paced back and forth in front of her living room window with the cordless phone pressed firmly against her ear.

"Come on, come on! Pick up the damn phone," she hissed.

"Hello?"

"Thank God! I was just about to hang up," Tamika said, relief evident in her voice.

"Oh, it's you. What do you want?"

"Yeah, it's *me*. Damn! Why you gotta say it like that?"

A lengthy silence on the line was followed by an even longer sigh.

"What do you want, Tamika?"

"I need to talk."

"About what?"

"Not over the phone. This is a conversation we should have in person."

"You know what happens every time you come over here."

"And that's my fault?"

"Isn't it?"

"Maybe the first time. But no one held a gun to your head. And, um, it wasn't me who started it the second, third or fourth time. So stop acting like a punk and admit you wanted it as much as I did. Damn! All this shit is not just my fault, so don't get it twisted!"

"Calm down, baby. It's just, well, you know, I feel so guilty. I know things are over between Zoe and me, but I still feel like it's not right. You know what I mean?"

Tamika was quiet, consumed with her own guilt. Never a religious person, she still found herself praying God would forgive her for what she had done to her sister-friend.

Shaking it off, she said, "Well, too late to cry over spilled milk now. Look, I'm on my way over."

Before he could say anything, Tamika hung up the phone. She wanted to get this particular scene over with. She knew that he would probably expect her to terminate the pregnancy. She could understand that, it was her first knee jerk reaction as well. But the more she thought about it, the more she was leaning toward keeping it. She didn't know who she surprised more when her doctor had confirmed her suspicions: herself or her doctor.

"I assume that you will want to terminate as quickly as possible? I can have my nurse schedule you as early as next week."

"Hold up there, Doc. I'm not so sure that I want to do that."

"What? Are you sure?" Dr. Elizabeth Connors asked, looking up quickly from the notes she was jotting down in Tamika's chart. Her expression was almost comical before she regained her professionalism and smoothed out the surprise from her eyes and mouth.

"I'm just as surprised as you, Dr. C." Tamika said ruefully, turning her head and looking out the window.

"Are you sure you want to do this, Tamika?"

"No, Dr. C, I'm not," Tamika answered with a deep sigh.

"If you don't mind me asking, what about the father? Do you think he will be pleased?"

"Probably not."

"Does he have other children?"

"Yes, he does. He doesn't live with them. He's not with his kids' mother anymore."

"I see."

"No, you don't, but that's okay," Tamika told her, looking away again. After a beat she swung back around and in a defensive tone said, "He's not a dead beat dad, okay? He takes care of his kids."

She surprised herself at her defense. She knew the doctor was probably thinking the father was another black man who made babies and then walked away from them. But one of the things she really liked about him was that he wasn't like that. No matter how hard it was, he still tried to do right by his children.

Thinking back on that as she drove to his house, Tamika was more than a little apprehensive about how he would receive the news that he was going to be a daddy again.

By the time she got to his spot, Tamika was a wreck. She had to sit in her car for a few minutes to gather herself. Finally, she took a deep breath, got out of the car and made her way to his door.

When the door opened, they eyed each other before Tamika, in her usual smart ass manner, asked, "Well, are you going to invite me in or just look at me all night?"

Laughing slightly, he stepped aside and swept his hand out in a gesture of welcome.

Tamika barely noticed her surroundings because she couldn't help but focus on the specimen in front of her. He only had on a pair of pajama bottoms, leaving his muscular chest and arms bare. No matter how hard Tamika tried to resist, she felt compelled to reach out and touch.

"Stop it, Tamika. Let's not start that shit again, okay?"

Instantly angered, Tamika felt her hand curve into a weapon and she almost succeeded in raking her talons down his chest, but he grabbed her wrist. She cried out when he applied pressure to it, before allowing her to snatch her hand out of his grasp.

"No marks, Tamika. I may be seeing . . . , well, never mind. I'm not in the mood to be pawed at and scratched up by you tonight."

"I'm sorry, baby. Look, I don't know what's wrong with me. Please, let me make it up to you," she pleaded.

Dropping to her knees, she quickly pulled his pants down and had him in her mouth before he could stop her. In a matter of minutes she wakened his sleeping giant and was struggling to keep from gagging on his length. But Tamika was an expert at this. She could deep throat better than any woman he had ever met. In no time, she had him moaning sweet and low. His hips started a dance of their own as he worked himself in and out of her hot and willing mouth.

Sensing he was about to explode in her mouth, Tamika suddenly stopped, turned around on her hands and knees, and flipped her short skirt up. Pulling her thong aside, she was an open invitation.

Hard and throbbing, and desperate for completion, he dropped down behind her and entered her wetness in one powerful thrust, almost bringing her up off her knees. Tamika nearly fainted from the intensity of having him fill her to capacity. Looking almost like two wrestlers rather than lovers, they fought their way to climax. He expressed his in a short shout; she, in a low moaning scream. Even after they came, he continued to pump and she continued to move against his still hardness, milking him for every drop of his essence, until he finally went limp and slipped from her body.

Tamika inched forward until she was prone on the floor, and he collapsed next to her. For a while the only sound in the room was the harsh rasp of their breathing.

Tamika closed her eyes and felt a tear slip down her cheek. This was not how she meant for this to go. She had to tell him. And she had to do it now, before she chickened out again. But at least she could wait until after she washed up a bit. She felt him stir beside her and keeping her eyes closed, she heard him stand and pull his pants on. Rolling over onto her back, she opened her eyes and looked at him standing over her. Silently he reached down to give her a hand up. Just as silently she went to the bathroom to fix herself and her clothes.

When she returned, he was sitting on the sofa, idly channel surfing. She stood quietly to the side until he finally deigned to look at her.

"You going to invite me to sit down?"

"Why I gotta 'invite' you? Damn, Mika. Didn't I just fuck the shit out of you? So why we gotta get all proper and shit now?"

"Whatever," she said, waving her hand in the air. "What did you want to talk to me about?"

"I'm pregnant." There. She'd said it. She hadn't meant to say it just like that, but hell, there really wasn't any other way to say it.

"Come again? You're pregnant? Oh, and just like that, I'm supposed to believe it's mine? Come on, Tamika! Bitch, I know you. Been knowing you for a while now. I know how you roll. You fuckin' niggahs left and right. So why you want to play me?"

"I don't believe you said some foul shit like that! So what are you trying to say? That I'm a whore?"

"Well, if the designer shoe fits, baby, then wear it!"

"So what does that make you?"

"I don't know, horny?" He laughed, but it wasn't a sound of amusement.

They glared at each other, both breathing hard for a different reason now.

"Look, I know that I've got some issues, okay? But ever since we started this . . . thing," Tamika said, flinging her hands in the air indicating her inability to define exactly what their relationship was, "I haven't been with anyone else. I make it *look* like I am, trying to protect your ass like you wanted. God forbid anyone should know that *we* have a thing goin' on! Oh no. Can't be seen with Tamika. People might talk. *Zoe* might get upset. Don't get me wrong. I love Zoe like a sister. But shit happens. We got involved. *So what!!* But I guess I should have known better. Stupid me thought maybe we could have something. Stupid me thought maybe I was *feeling* something. Stupid me was dumb enough to fuck around and fall in—well, never mind. Stupid me," she finished in a whisper, fighting hard not to let loose the tears that were burning her eyes. "Forget it. I'll deal with this myself," she said, jumping up and running for the front door.

"Tamika! Wait. Look, I'm sorry, okay? I shouldn't have . . . look; you didn't get into this mess by yourself."

Tamika stopped, but wouldn't turn around. She couldn't. She didn't want him to see the tears running unchecked down her face.

"What are you going to do?" he asked, his voice a lot quieter now.

At least he isn't screaming at me anymore, she thought to herself. But she was incapable of answering, so she just shrugged, struggling to get herself together. She felt him come up behind her.

"Hey, come sit back down," he said, his voice gentle. Still, she didn't move. And when he put his arms around her, she wanted to let herself melt against his chest, but instead she held herself rigid and stiff.

"Stop being such a bad-ass, Tamika. Why do you always have to be so tough?" he asked, his voice sounding teasing and seductive to her ears. But it made her give up a watery laugh and relax, at least a little.

Dashing her tears away, she allowed herself to be led back to the sofa.

"Okay, so you say this baby is mine. You're going to have an abortion, aren't you?"

"Why would you assume that?" Tamika snapped, getting pissed all over again.

"Well, come on, Tamika. You've never had the slightest inclination to be a mother. You're a workaholic and a party animal. How you manage to find a balance is beyond me. But you've said yourself that you hate kids."

"I don't hate kids! I never said that. Okay, well, maybe I did. But a woman can change her mind, you know," she said primly.

"Tamika, I mean no offense, but you are much too selfish to have a kid. And what about that monument to yourself that you call a townhouse? I've been there. It is not exactly kid friendly."

"I can move. I'll buy a house in the suburbs. Yeah, like Zoe. I certainly make enough money. I can more than afford it."

"Haven't you done enough like Zoe?" The minute he said it, he regretted it.

"Ouch. Did you have to go there? I was just trying to be a friend. That's all. To both of you. Who knew all of this would happen?" Sighing, she got up and walked around the room, idly picking up and putting down things. "Would it really be that bad for me to have this baby?"

Blowing out air hard through his mouth, he was silent for a moment before saying tiredly, "I don't know. I'm catching hell as it is now. But let me ask you something. What are you going to tell Zoe?"

"That's what you are really worried about, isn't it? What Zoe is going to do or say or feel."

"A little. You should be the one worried, though. You know how she feels about liars."

"Yeah, I know. But I can't worry about how pissed off Zoe is going to be. This is something I have to decide for myself. I want this baby. This may be my last chance to be a mother. And this baby isn't just some Joe Schmoe's baby. It is *your* baby. I think you are a hell of a father, and even though we may not end up together, I know, without a doubt, you would be there for this baby."

"I hear you, and I appreciate that you think that of me. But Tamika, lives are going to be affected by this. The shit is going to hit the fan. Are you prepared for that? Don't you even care?"

"I care. And I've done nothing but think about it. The only alternative I can see is for me to have an abortion. I'm not willing to do that. I could tell her that I don't know who the father is, but won't it be a little strange when she sees you with a baby that happens to be mine? So you can forget that noise. She's going to have to know. Don't you think I realize that this has cost me my friend?"

They were quiet for a moment, each of them thinking about the consequences of their actions.

The sudden blaring of the phone caused them both to jump. Then Tamika heard him say, "Zoe! You're on your way over? Now? You're where? A couple of blocks away? No, no problem. Okay. I'll see you in a few."

"Zoe's on her way over here?"

"Yeah, so you have to go."

"But why? We might as well tell her now and get it over with."

"Don't start, okay? We haven't even decided anything and you want to tell her? What if there is nothing to tell?"

"So if there's no baby, you still want to keep it on the down low? Is that what you're trying to say?"

"Well, yeah. Why do we have to say anything if we don't need to?"

"Because I'm sick of being in the damn closet, that's why!"

"I don't have time for this now, Tamika. I'll get at you later, okay? But you have got to get your ass out of here now."

Tamika could tell from his tone that he was not in the mood to hear any arguments. She could just wait outside and confront Zoe herself, but she didn't really want to do that. Besides, she reasoned, it wouldn't help her cause any. Resigned, she gathered up her purse and car keys to leave.

"We'll talk later? Can you come over?"

"It's already late," he hedged.

"Bring a change of clothes and stay at my place."

"I thought that was a no-no."

"I don't want to be alone tonight. Is that so hard to understand?"

Looking at her glistening eyes, he was a little surprised. Tamika all soft and vulnerable. Who would have thought it?

"Naw, Baby. It's not hard to understand," he said before kissing her soft lips. The passion that immediately flared between them still surprised him. Damn. What was it about her that made him as horny as a teenager? He could feel his sleeping four inches trying to stretch out to its raging ten.

Down boy, he silently willed himself. Wouldn't do for Zoe to walk in with him at attention. Stepping back from Tamika he said, "I'll call you when I'm on my way. I want to finish this discussion tonight."

"Okay, Sweetie. I'll see you then," Tamika said, smiling before hastily leaving.

CHAPTER NINETEEN

Twilight Zone

"Okay, Sis. I'll swing by in a few. No, I don't mind letting Bethany spend the night. It helps to keep Shanice out of my hair," Zoe said, talking with her sister on her hands-free headset for her cell phone as she swung in and out of traffic. "Let me drop Jonathan over Vaughn's house first. Then I have to make a stop for, oh, about half an hour, and then I'll come to your house. Is that okay?"

"Sounds like a plan," Sara said. Her curiosity got the best of her and she asked, "I know it's none of my business, but where do you have to go before you come here?"

"I'll tell you later," Zoe whispered, as much as she could with a hands-free device.

"What?" Sara shouted into the phone, unable to hear as the phone faded in and out.

"Never mind. Later!" Zoe shouted back, and then disconnected the call.

She clicked the on button again and said "Vaughn!" then waited to be connected.

"Hey! In your rush to leave, you forgot to take Jon with you," Zoe told him, laughing.

"Oh, hey, Zoe! You're on your way over?"

"Yup!"

"Now?"

"Yes, now. Is there a problem? I'm only a couple of blocks away."

"You're where? A couple of blocks away? No, no problem."

"Why are you repeating everything I say? Do you have company or something?"

"No, no. Not at all. Umm, okay. I'll see you in a few."

"Yup!" Zoe said, ending the call. A few minutes later she ushered Jonathan into Vaughn's apartment.

"What was the matter with you? Why were you acting all weirded out on me?" Zoe asked, trying not to notice Vaughn in only his pajama bottoms and a sleeveless tee shirt that he had hastily put on before opening the door.

"I just woke up. Sorry. I came home and sat down and was out like a light. Every time the president puts the country on High Alert, we end up pulling double, sometimes triple time. I'm just wiped out. Hey, Jonathan. How's it going, Buddy?" Vaughn asked his son, giving him a playful one-two punch lightly to his stomach.

"Okay I guess," Jon told him, grinning. He dropped his bag near the front door, walked over to the sofa, turned on the television and started playing a video game.

"Umm, excuse me. Does this bag belong here?" Zoe asked, tapping her foot.

"Ah, Ma! I'll get it in a minute," he answered, never taking his eyes from the mesmerizing action on the screen.

Zoe walked over and blocked his view. "Move the bag, Jon. Now! You don't do that at home and you will not do it here. Now!"

"Dag, Ma!"

"And stop calling me 'Ma.' What's up with that?"

"Okay, *Mom*," Jonathan said. Getting up, he snatched the bag, took it to the spare bedroom, and threw it on the bed. Coming back he said as he passed his mother, "Satisfied? Dag!"

"Boy, I know you are not sassing me."

At his sullen silence, Zoe started across the room to pop him upside his head. Vaughn stopped her and shook his head. Tilting his head toward the kitchen, he pulled her into the small space.

"Leave him alone. I'll deal with him later."

"Yeah, whatever. Between him and his brother, I'm about ready to put my foot up some ass."

"They're boys, Zoe. They're just feeling their oats."

"Yeah, well, if they keep this shit up, they will be feeling my foot!"

Vaughn laughed, causing Zoe to smile in spite of herself.

"Always so feisty! See, you got too much energy pent up. Want me to help you work some of that off?" Vaughn offered, leering at his ex-wife, as his eyes swept her slim form from head to toe.

"Okay! Time for me to go!" Zoe declared, pushing Vaughn out of the way. Walking back to the living room, she went over to Jon and kissed the top of his head.

"Hey! What was that for?"

"Cause no matter how much you piss me off, you are still my baby boy and I love you," Zoe told him, laughing at the confused look on his face.

"Aw, Ma, I mean, Mom," Jon said, blushing. "Love you too," he mumbled, dropping his head.

"What? What was that? I thought I heard you say the "L" word! Naw! Couldn't have been. Not my big ole macho son!" Zoe teased him.

"You are so silly, Mom!"

"Gotta be, with y'all running me crazy," Zoe said as she waved goodbye. Turning around, she saw that Vaughn was still standing in the doorway watching her as she walked down the hall to the rickety elevator in his building. Waving, she turned back around and added just a little more dip in her hips as she switched away. She heard him laugh before he closed the door.

When she was almost to Antonio's grandmother's house, she thought maybe she should call rather than just drop in.

"Hi! It's me. Are you busy?"

"Zoe!"

"What's up?"

"I thought I'd stop by for a minute."

"You're on your way over? Now?"

"Yeah. I'm not far. Maybe two, three blocks away. Is it okay to stop by?"

"You're where? A couple of blocks away? No, no problem."

"Cool. See you in a bit."

"Okay. I'll see you in a few."

After Zoe hung up the phone, she had a feeling of deja vu.

Didn't I just have that same conversation with Vaughn? That was just too strange. My life is starting to feel like I'm in the Twilight Zone! Zoe thought to herself. However, as she navigated her way down the narrow street where Antonio's grandmother lived, she forgot about the parallel conversations. But the minute Antonio opened the door, she began to feel like her name was Alice and someone had dropped her down the rabbit hole.

"What is up with everyone in their pajama bottoms today?"

"Excuse me?" Antonio asked.

"I just left Vaughn's house, where I dropped off Jonathan, and he was in pajama bottoms and a muscle tee shirt and here you are in the same thing."

"Actually, these are sweat pants."

"Sweats, pajamas, same difference."

"I was working out in the basement," Antonio explained.

"Oh. Well, never mind. It was just weird."

"So, what made you come by?"

"Well, I did say earlier that I would call you. I was out this way, soooo . . ."

"Out this way for what, Zoe?"

"Does it matter?"

"No, I suppose it doesn't."

They stood around awkwardly for a moment before Antonio remembered his manners.

"Uh, sit down. Do you want something to drink? I made some lemonade earlier."

"Thanks. Yes, I'd like something to drink. Lemonade sounds fine."

While Antonio was in the kitchen Zoe tried to

gather herself. She was thinking maybe coming to see Antonio wasn't such a good idea.

If he wasn't parading around here looking like a big ole chocolate bar, maybe this would be easier. Damn, I sure would like to lick . . .

"Here you go," Antonio said, thrusting the glass of lemonade under Zoe's nose, causing her to jump. Her hand instinctively came up and she knocked the glass of cold, sticky liquid all over herself and him.

"Oh shit! Oh shit!" Zoe screamed, jumping up and leaning forward to get her now cold, wet shirt away from her.

Antonio was caught between embarrassment and wanting to laugh. Finally the urge to laugh won out over the embarrassment and he laughed so hard he had to wipe the moisture from his eyes.

Zoe was less than amused. She stood in front of Antonio holding her top out from her, tapping her foot and waiting for Antonio to bring himself back under control.

When he finally settled down, she asked sarcastically, "Are you through?" At his silent nod of affirmation, she demanded, "Give me a tee shirt or something so I can get out of this soggy mess, please!"

"Yeah, aiight. Come on upstairs so you can wash off," he told her as he removed his own shirt.

Trying to bring her temper under control, Zoe closed the bathroom door behind her. This was *not* what she came all the way out to Germantown for. Looking down, she tried to assess the damage. Her top was soaked, but her pants weren't too bad. If she hadn't jumped up so fast, they would have been just as soaked.

"I knew I should have taken my black ass home," she mumbled to herself, even though the color of her derriere was closer to the other end of the spectrum. Zoe was grateful that her shirt was a button up instead of a pullover. She was glad she didn't have to worry about ruining her hair.

She found a washcloth in the small linen closet and some of Antonio's grandmother's fragrant gel soap. Quickly divesting herself of the offending top and wet bra, she made short work of lathering up and lightly bathing her upper torso. She had just finished rinsing off and was reaching for the towel to dry herself when Antonio barged into the bathroom, causing Zoe to jump and drop the towel.

"Here, I hope this will work. I know it'll be . . . oh, shit! Damn, I'm sorry!" Antonio said as he stood in the doorway, staring at Zoe's exposed breasts.

Antonio always loved Zoe's breasts, and was endlessly fascinated with how pale they were and how her nipples looked like they had been dipped in dark chocolate. The contrast drove him nuts and he felt an instinctive tightening in his loins. He was unaware of the way he repeatedly ran his tongue over his lips, as if he could almost taste them.

"Uh, uh, here," he said.

Zoe bent over to get the towel and heard his sharply indrawn breath. In spite of herself, she smiled. However, all traces of her smile were gone from her face when she straightened back up. Tucking the towel around her, she took the shirt, noticing it was his favorite Sixers jersey.

"I can't take this. It's your favorite. Don't you have anything else?"

"Nothing that's clean. I haven't done laundry in a while," he admitted.

"I see. Are you sure?"

"Yeah. Hey, I'm just lending it to you. I want it back!" he said, laughing.

Smiling, Zoe said, "Yeah, alright. Ummm, are you going to close the door so I can put it on?"

"Right. Yeah . . . ah, okay." Still he stood there staring at her. Before he lost his nerve, he took the two steps into the small bathroom, swept her against his hard frame and kissed her.

Zoe, taken completely off guard, opened her mouth to protest but suddenly found it full of Antonio's tongue. For a moment, she just stood there, letting him thoroughly kiss her, not knowing what to do, until her body started reacting to his kiss.

This is NOT what I came over here for! she thought to herself, as her one arm lifted and found a perch on his shoulder.

Isn't it? a little voice asked, as the other arm followed the first onto the other side of his neck while she pulled him closer into the kiss.

She barely noticed when the towel slipped from between them until she felt her nipples harden from the contact against his naked chest.

I have to stop this before it's too late! Zoe thought to herself, right before she realized it already was.

Antonio was the first to break the kiss, but only for a moment. Backing out of the bathroom, he led Zoe to his room. Before she could protest, he gently pushed her back on the bed and began to worship her breasts. He licked and sucked until her nipples became hard and sensitive to every stroke of his tongue against them. Gasping for breath, she didn't protest when she felt him unzip her pants and tug them away from her inflamed body.

Nor did she protest when he pulled her to the edge of the bed and positioned himself between her legs while he began a hot trail of kisses from her feet to her thighs. First he went up one side and then the other. He kissed, licked, and gently sucked on her thighs until she was shaking with anticipation. He kept getting closer and closer to the object of her moist desire, but he never actually let his lips part hers.

Zoe thought she was going to scream in frustration if he didn't bury his head where she wanted it soon. She could feel that she was already swollen and wet. She almost cried in relief when she felt him slowly pull her lips apart. Glancing down she saw that he was intently looking at her as if he was memorizing how she looked there. She began to feel slightly embarrassed, but it turned her on too.

Closing her eyes, she waited. She almost came off the bed when she felt his tongue make one long sweep between her parted lips. Over and over he did that, lightly at first and then applying more pressure each time.

Zoe moaned as she parted her legs more to allow him easier access. When he gently blew on her bud and sucked on it, she could feel herself losing all control. And when he slipped first one, and then two fingers into her, moving them in and out while flicking his tongue all around, it sent her over the edge. She clutched at the bed and felt her body buck with the force of her climax.

Before she realized it, Antonio stood up and replaced his fingers with himself. She gasped when he entered her in one powerful thrust. Zoe opened her eyes and saw him as he sucked her essence off his fingers. She widened her eyes in surprise. He just laughed and pulled her closer to the edge of the bed, placing her legs so that her feet were on his shoulders, allowing him to move deeper into her throbbing wetness.

Zoe gasped again when Antonio pulled out of her. Instead of entering her again, he teased her swollen bud with the tip of his hardness. Every time she thought he was going to enter her again, he would just barely dip into her wetness and then go back to teasing her. Over and over Antonio teased and tormented Zoe with his wicked dance, making her think he was going to give her what she wanted and then taking it away. When he felt she was on the brink of madness, he finally slipped slowly, but steadily, into her trembling body. Rewarding her with stroke after stroke, he alternated between moving fast and then excruciatingly slow, in and out of her body. Wound tighter than a drum, Zoe finally felt herself reaching climax after climax while her own wetness slid between her ass cheeks and soaked the bed linen beneath her. Just when she didn't think it could get any better, Antonio pushed her up on the bed, briefly laid on her and then rolled over until she was on top of him. Incredibly, Zoe felt him push even farther into her as she slid all the way down on his hardness.

"Oh, it's on now!" Zoe said as she proceeded to ride Antonio for all she was worth. Antonio lifted his legs, causing Zoe to lean forward. Grabbing the headboard for support, Zoe gave him some of his own medicine as she tortured and teased him the way he had her. But when he pulled her down so that he could let his tongue play with her sensitive nipples, she forgot about payback and concentrated on riding the waves. Her moans were soon drowned out by his when he finally gave in and had his own climax that seemed to go on forever.

Zoe lay spent but satisfied on Antonio's chest, feeling him soften in slow degrees inside of her. As she struggled to get her breathing back to normal, she wasn't sure if she was elated or appalled by what had just happened.

With as much dignity as she could muster, she climbed down from him and winced a little when he slipped from her body. She was surprised at how sore she was. The time that passed since the last time they made love was longer than she realized, and her body was no longer used to his girth.

She could feel his eyes on her as she walked out of the room and went to the bathroom to wash up. When she returned she wore his shirt that was left on the bathroom floor, forgotten in their love play.

As far as Antonio was concerned, she didn't need to put anything else on. He liked how his shirt looked on her. Zoe rooted around the room, retrieving her panties and pants. Slipping them on, she sat on the edge of the bed, not looking at Antonio. He said nothing, waiting. He knew she was trying to gather her thoughts.

"I didn't come here for this today, you know," she said finally, turning to look at him.

"I know. But I can't say that I'm not glad it happened, Babe."

"I'm sure you are!"

"I don't mean it like that, Zoe. I think this was

exactly what we needed, to remind us of how good we are together."

"This," she said waving her hands around, indicating the bed and what had just happened, "has never been a problem for us. Hell, we damn near scorched the paint off the walls!"

Antonio laughed, knowing she was being serious, but he had always loved her sense of humor.

"So what's the problem then, Zoe? I lied about my kids. I am sorry. I can't send them back. And whether you want to admit it or not, you still love me. And I have always loved you. So as the song says, where do we go from here?"

"I don't know, Antonio! I just don't know."

"What is the real problem, Zoe?"

"What do you mean?"

"I think you probably already forgave me or you wouldn't be here. What happened never would have happened if you hadn't forgiven me. So, what is the *real* problem?"

At her silence he leaned up and grabbed her by the back of her neck, giving her another one of his toe-curling kisses. When he let her go, she didn't have the strength at first to do more than just stare into his eyes. She could feel his breath on her cheek when he asked her again, "What is the real problem, Zoe?"

Sighing, she pushed herself up and resumed her position on the edge of the bed.

"What's going on with your kids, Antonio?" she asked him finally, looking him in the eyes.

"I . . . they . . . what do you mean?" he hedged.

"Just what I said. What's going on with your kids? More importantly, what's going on with you and Miami?"

"Niambi."

"Whatever. What's the deal?"

"I've given it a lot of thought, and I think I'm going to sue for custody."

"Sue for custody? Why?"

"You met her. You have to ask me why?"

"Good point. But being a ghetto bitch is not enough reason for a judge to just separate a woman from her kids."

"I know that!" Antonio snapped, sounding insulted. "But being mentally and physcially abusive is enough. Being a druggy is enough. Since visiting every one of their schools and making myself known to the teachers, which was another trip, I realized those kids are never going to make it if they stay with her."

"How so?"

"Wait, let me get up and we can go back downstairs," Antonio said. Zoe moved out of the way. After going to the bathroom to clean up, he came back into the room and slipped on a pair of sweat pants, not bothering with underwear or a tee shirt. After they got downstairs, Zoe joined him in the kitchen, where he got her another glass of lemonade. They settled themselves at the small wooden table and Zoe asked again, "So, what did you mean?"

"She doesn't feed them all the time, only when she feels like it or remembers. Every time I see them, they look dirty and unkempt. The teachers say that the other kids complain that they smell, which is no surprise since they are never made to take baths, let alone brush their teeth."

"Damn! Now that is a sorry-ass woman."

"She didn't used to be like that. I can only assume that it's the drugs that have made her indifferent."

"Hhmm," was all Zoe said. She had other thoughts, but opted to keep them to herself.

"How are you going to be able to deal with four kids by yourself, Antonio?"

"I don't know. I'll just have to figure that out as I go along. But I sure could use your help," he said hopefully.

"Raising my own kids wears me out, Antonio. I don't know if I have it in me to help you with yours."

"I'm not asking you to help me raise them, Zoe."

"Aren't you?"

"No, just help a brother out every now and then. Like with my daughter. What do I know about little girls?"

"I would say that you're getting ready to find out quick, fast and in a hurry. Are you sure there's no other option?"

"Zoe, you don't know how they beg me not to take them back every time I have them. Or how they beg me not to leave when I stop by to drop something off. When I take them food, I have to stay and fix it for them to make sure they even get to eat it. And every time I leave and see them standing in the doorway crying, it just tears me up inside. I have to take them. I don't have any other choice."

Zoe hated seeing him so torn up about his kids. It made her heart go out to him. But she knew she was going to regret her next words before they even left her lips.

"I'll help as much as I can, Antonio, but understand," she cautioned when she saw his eyes light up, "there will only be so much that I can do to help. My own kids come first."

"Hey, I'll take whatever I can get!" he said, elated.

I just know I'm going to regret this! Zoe thought to herself.

CHAPTER TWENTY
Movin' On Up!

"That's the last box!" Sara sighed.

"Thank goodness! Now I remember why I never wanted to move," Zoe said, collapsing on top of another huge box. She didn't know what she would have done without all the help. She was shocked speechless when she turned around that morning and ran almost head on into Antonio as he was coming into the door. She was struggling through the door with an unwieldy box of books. She hadn't bothered to ask him for help because she knew he was supposed to have his children that weekend.

In between handling her issues with buying a house alone and helping Vaughn get through buying her out, she also helped Antonio find and secure a three bedroom rowhouse in the lower Northeast section of Philadelphia. His attorney advised him that he needed to show both proof of steady employment and ownership of a house in order to prove that he was more than capable of providing for his children. Being employed as an ironworker who made almost two thousand dollars a week certainly helped Antonio's case. There were so many construction sites in and around the Philadelphia area that finding work was never a problem. Ever since he'd made it into the ironworker's union, he had almost more work than he could handle.

Antonio, with Zoe's help, was lucky enough to find a house within walking distance of a nearby elementary school for the younger children, and a one-bus ride to the middle school for the older ones. His mother, Pet, helped him purchase new and used furnishings to fill the house and make it look homey. Between Zoe and Sara, they provided and hung all the curtains in the house and Zoe filled his kitchen with all of her old pots, pans and dishes. She didn't mind giving these items away since Sara and Danita gifted her with all new items for her new kitchen.

Still, even with all Zoe did to help Antonio, she continued to avoid a sexual relationship with him. She was still sorting out how she felt about him. In her mind, helping him was one thing. She was doing that for the sake of his children. Sleeping with him was another thing entirely. Zoe realized, however, that if she was completely honest with herself, there was a part of her that craved nothing more than to fall back into bed with Antonio. The man had serious skills. Stereotypes were made of the stuff he was packing. Her thoughts of Antonio and his endowments was what almost made Zoe drop the box she was carrying when she ran into him.

"Whoa! Let me help you with that," he laughed, taking the box from her.

"Thanks. What are you doing here?"

"I came by to see if you needed any help."

"Where are the kids?"

"My mother has them right now. She wanted to spend some time with them, so her and my grandmother took them shopping for some badly needed underwear and clothes."

"Were they that bad?"

"Please. I have better looking rags for my truck."

"Damn. How did you know I was moving today?"

"I, ah, somebody told me. I don't remember who," he said with a slight smile.

"Uh-huh. I bet it was your grandmother. I talked to her earlier this week."

"I don't know. Maybe. Anyway, need some help?" he asked again.

"Hell yeah," Vaughn said as he and Ben came down the ramp leading into the moving truck.

Zoe shot Vaughn a look that clearly said she could have slapped him. He gave her an innocent "What?" look back. Zoe wasn't fooled. He'd done it on purpose. It made her wonder why Vaughn was being so nice to Antonio all of a sudden and why it seemed like he was almost trying to push them together. She finally decided she was probably overreacting.

Now, she had to admit, Antonio's help was probably a lot of the reason why everything was completed so quickly.

"Dinner's here," Theo boomed as he, Ben, Antonio, and Vaughn walked in the kitchen from the garage with two pizza boxes, a bucket of hot wings, and a big bag of sandwiches, chips, coleslaw, two-three liter bottles of soda and two-six packs of Corona.

"Dag, the kitchen looks good," Theo said glancing around. There wasn't one box to be seen and the canisters, toaster, and other kitchen stuff were already arranged around the gleaming countertops.

"Thanks to Tamika and Ms. Preggie in there, who we had to practically threaten with a beat down to keep from lifting stuff out of the truck," Sara informed her husband, laughing as she took the hefty sandwiches out of the bag.

Danita just smiled, glad to have been able to help. Tamika, however, winced at Sara's words, but said nothing. She started to beg off helping with the move by claiming that she had a project due. But she couldn't stay away. She had to see if Zoe was suspicious about anything. So far, it didn't seem she was. But Tamika did think she saw Zoe throwing curious glances her way. Up to this point Tamika had avoided discussing her pregnancy and decision to keep the baby with Zoe.

"You must have gone to the Pickle Barrel Deli. These sandwiches are huge! But why it took all four of you to go is beyond me," Sara teased.

"Well, you know. Male bonding and all that," Ben said, laughing. "And unlike you women, we had a plan. Theo got the sandwiches, Vaughn and I got the pizza and hot wings, and Antonio got the beer and sodas."

"Yeah, yeah. Whatever," Sara said, acting like she wasn't impressed. They all worked hard today. Trying to move Zoe into her new house, Vaughn out of his apartment and back into his and Zoe's old house, which was now *his* house, was a lot of work. Whew! Sara felt like she needed a score card to keep up. She was shocked, however, when she learned that Christopher was staying with Vaughn.

"I thought they didn't get along?"

"Sometimes, but Chris said he wanted to stay so he could graduate with his own class next year. He'll come to this house on the weekends. Well, most weekends. I'm sure he'll find reasons not to come here so he can be near that damn Tibby, Tabby, Truvy. You know, whatsherface."

"Tribby."

"Whatever."

Sara laughed. By now Zoe had to know her son's girlfriend's name. She felt that Zoe messed up the girl's name just to be smart. Sara remembered seeing Tribby a couple of times and she had to agree with Zoe. There was something about the girl that didn't sit right with her. She would be just as upset if T.J. brought home a girl like that. Although the ones T.J. was meeting weren't that big of a prize either. And if she had to walk in on the family room or basement in total darkness one more time, there was going to be hell to pay. She and Theo were already starting to bicker about it.

Sara wasn't stupid, and she knew very well the smell of sex. Standing at the top of the basement stairs and having that particular odor practically run up and smack her in the face was enough to make her almost lose it. She told Theo, in no uncertain terms, that if he didn't do something about it, *she* would. She also told Theo that she hoped he had the good sense to tell T.J. to wrap it up. She wasn't looking for him to be bringing any babies home.

Like Chris, T.J. was one year away from graduating high school. And he was already looking forward to going to college to become an architect. Sara made a mental note to pull him aside and talk with him herself.

But Sara pushed those thoughts away now as she strode over to the french doors to tell the boys to come eat. Jon, Chris, and T.J. were tossing around a football in Zoe's spacious back yard.

"Why are they out there playing instead of in here helping?" Vaughn wanted to know.

"They helped. All of the furniture is pretty much how and where I want it. All the boxes have been put in the correct rooms, so we told them to go outside. They were in the way."

"Is Jonathan's room all unpacked?"

"Pretty much. He can do the rest tomorrow," Zoe said, getting paper plates, napkins, and plastic utensils from the top of the refrigerator.

"I'll get Shanice and Bethany," Sara said, walking to the end of the stairs and calling for the girls.

Once everyone found a spot to settle themselves either around Zoe's new farmhouse table that sat eight, or her counter that sat five, there was very little conversation as everyone attacked their food with gusto. Zoe, however, was puzzled when it seemed that Tamika purposefully took a chair at the counter rather than one at the table with her. When she thought about it, it seemed that all day, Tamika had been avoiding her. Every time Zoe walked into a room Tamika was working on, Tamika would mumble that she forgot something, was looking for something, or whatever, and would rush out of the room. Zoe wondered about it, but was much too busy to really give it any thought. Even now as she ate and joined in the happy conversations, she once again pushed Tamika's behavior to the back of her mind.

When she finished eating, Zoe sat back with a happy sigh, not just because of the good food, but also because her friends and family surrounded her. She looked around her new kitchen, breakfast room, and beyond into her family room, and despite her best efforts not to, she grinned.

Sara quietly observed her sister and smiled to herself. She understood how Zoe felt. The difference, however, was that when Sara got her house, Theo bought the sample, brand spanking new. Zoe's new house was about eight years old. Still, Sara knew that her sister never thought she would have something as new as that. Sara was glad for her sister. The weeks leading up to Zoe moving were hectic, harrowing, and downright nerve-wracking. Zoe was on the phone constantly with Sara, obsessing about every little detail.

"I'm sorry I'm being such a pain in the ass, but I've never been through this before," she told her sister.

"What about when you bought the house you're in now?"

"Vaughn handled everything. He just told me where to sign and that was it."

"Yeah, I know what you mean. Theo did the same thing. Actually, he *bought* the damn house before I even knew about it."

"I still think that has got to be the most romantic thing I've ever heard."

"Yeah, me too." The sisters giggled, remembering when Theo presented Sara with the keys to the house they now lived in.

They shared a moment of sadness, though,

when Zoe said wistfully, "At least Mom got to see your house. She loved that house. She used to like my old one, so I know she would be thrilled to see this one."

"Yeah, I know," Sara said sadly. "But she knows. I'm sure of it. I talk to her every day, did you know that?"

"No, I didn't. I did when she first died, but I haven't lately."

"Every single day I look up and say, 'Hey Mom. How are you today, Ms. Lady? I sure do miss you.' And then I proceed to tell her what's going on in my life. It makes me feel like she's still close to me. I guess that sounds silly, huh?"

"Not at all. We all knew how close you and Mom were, Sara. You were the baby of the family and mostly had her all to yourself growing up. It's only natural that it would be hard for you."

Zoe was touched that Sara shared those feelings with her. They went on to discuss other things and eventually the conversation came back to the house.

"And I hate to keep asking Vaughn," Zoe said. "I mean, we're cool and all, at least, more than we used to be. I called Dad a couple of times, but for real, he hasn't been much help because Mom used to handle the housing. So I'm stuck with asking Vaughn. I'm not too keen about having him all up in my business, if you know what I mean."

"I can understand it, Sis. I'll try to help as much as I can," Sara promised.

"But, umm, from what I hear, Dave has gone above and beyond the scope of being helpful!" Sara said, teasing her sister.

"Dave? Oh, you mean *David*! Yeah, he's been just great. What a sweetheart!"

"Umm-hmm. He had to bring his car into Theo's shop last week. Theo said all he did was ask questions about you and talk about how nice and fine he thinks you are," Sara informed her sister, waiting for some juicy information.

"Really? Interesting."

"Interesting? That's it? That's all you have to say? You're kidding, right? You *are* going to tell me what's up, right?"

"There is nothing to tell. He's a nice guy. He's my real estate agent. End of story."

"Yeah, well, from what I hear, sounds like he wants to be more than just your realtor."

"Chile, please! What would a guy like David want with me? I'm divorced, the mother of three, and oh yeah, I'm Black."

"Apparently none of the above is bothering him, so why is it bothering you?"

"It's not!" When all Zoe heard was silence stretching across the phone line, she sighed. "Okay, maybe a little."

"What's bothering you? That you're Black or that he's White?"

"Well it's a little late for me to be bothered about being Black now, ain't it? It's not like I can *change* it! DUH, Sara!"

"I guess that did sound a little stupid," Sara admitted ruefully before laughing. "But you know what I meant, wench, so don't get it twisted. Does it bother you that he's White?" Sara continued, wanting to find out how her sister really felt.

"No, not really, I guess. I don't know. I don't

think him being White has anything to do with it. I'm just not ready to get involved with him or anybody else right now."

"I hear that. I don't blame you."

Sara understood perfectly. Before she met her husband, Theo, she had all but completely sworn off men. After what she went through with her loser first husband, she didn't want to be bothered with anybody else. She resigned herself to a life alone, save that of her daughter. But Fate planned otherwise. The 'otherwise' included her husband, Theo, their beautiful new home, and the peace of mind that Sara never believed she would know. She just hoped that fate would do the same for her sister.

Thinking back on the past few weeks, Zoe knew she had earned the right to smile. When it looked like Vaughn was going to have a problem getting approval for his loan, Zoe was convinced that the entire plan was unraveling. Thankfully everything worked out. Zoe was happy Vaughn was able to get out of that dumpy apartment and back into the house. At least the kids would still feel comfortable when they stayed with him. He was leaving their rooms just as they were.

After everyone finished eating, the ladies quickly shooed the men and children out of the way so they could clear all the debris of the meal and get back to work. At one point, Zoe looked around and realized that she was alone in the kitchen with Tamika. Tamika must have realized it also because she was in the process of trying to leave when Zoe stopped her.

"Tamika, wait."

Tamika reluctantly halted her escape and slowly came back into the kitchen.

"What's up Sistagurl? You've been avoiding me all day. Is there a problem?" Zoe asked.

"No I haven't. And no, there's not any problem."

"That's bullshit, 'Mika, and you know it. Didn't nobody twist your damn arm to help today. If you didn't want to do it, all you had to do was say so!"

"It ain't even like that, Zoe. You are seriously trippin'!"

"The hell I am. Don't insult my intelligence, okay? Now, if you have a problem with me, I want to know what it is."

"Nothing, Zoe. I just have a lot on my mind, okay? News flash! The whole damn world does not revolve around you, your drama, and your woes. Other people have problems too, you know!"

"Excuse me? I don't know what you're talking about, Tamika. I've been trying for *weeks* to talk to you about whatever is going on with you. Every time I call you're either not home, or you rush me off the phone. Why? You act like you are pissed with me about something. If you are, I just want to know what it is."

"Hey, Zoe, where do you want me to put . . . whoooops! Guess I better come back later," Sara said when she walked into the kitchen. Zoe was on one side of the island, Tamika on the other. Sara could almost smell the tension in the air.

"Is everything alright in here?" she asked before leaving.

"Yes, Sara. Everything is *fine*," Zoe said, never taking her eyes off Tamika.

Tamika looked away. She wanted to tell Zoe her secret so badly it was making her stomach churn. Sooner or later, she reasoned to herself, Zoe was going to have to know. And since all of the affected parties were there, now was as good a time as any to get it all out in the open.

"Are you sure?" Sara asked, not liking the vibe she was picking up.

"Excuse me, ladies, I hate to interrupt, but I think we're going to be leaving," Ben announced as he strode into the kitchen, Danita close on his heels.

"I hope you don't mind, Zoe. But I'm done!" Danita said, laughing.

"Can't have my wife falling out on me," Ben said, chuckling and pulling Danita back against him into the circle of his arms.

Zoe forced herself to relax and turned to Danita and Ben, saying, "Thanks, you guys. I really appreciate all the help today. This house practically looks like I've been living in it forever! I couldn't have gotten anywhere near this much done without your help."

"Our pleasure. You know we only wanted to hurry up and get it done for you so we could have a place to hang out," Danita teased.

"You are both always more than welcome."

"Nice neighborhood you've got here, Zoe. Danita and I want to drive around and check it out. We've been looking at houses close to where we live now, but I think I kind of like it out here. We already know there is no way we want to raise our baby in a condo. By next year this time, he or she should be walking and we want to have a yard."

"Here," Zoe said, pulling a business card out of

one of the kitchen drawers, "Call David. He's really good. He'll hook you up!"

"Cool! Thanks," Danita said before giving Zoe a kiss on the cheek. Ben bent down and did the same, yelling goodbye to everyone who hadn't migrated back into the kitchen as they slipped out the door.

Tamika decided she would tell Zoe later, when there was less confusion. Instead, she also pleaded tiredness and quickly left.

When everyone wandered back to whatever they were doing, Zoe found herself alone with her sister in the family room. Sara was helping her hang curtains.

"What was that all about?" Sara asked, openly curious.

"I have no idea. I asked Tamika why she had a bug up her ass."

"What did she say?"

"Nothing really. I think she was getting ready to tell me something, but then we got interrupted," Zoe said, giving Sara a hard look.

"Whoops! Sorry. I didn't know y'all were in there getting into some deep shit."

"Yeah, I know you didn't. Ha! Neither did I. Maybe it was that whole pregnancy thing."

"Isn't she still pregnant?"

"I don't know. I assumed she had an abortion. You know Tamika and kids just don't mix."

"I don't think she did. Didn't you notice how tight those jeans were fitting? And she had her top on the *outside* of them." Sara noted.

"Well, Mika's jeans are *always* tight. Shit, that ain't nothing new. But now that you mention it, she was looking a little, I don't know, *something*.

And you are right. I kept looking at her today trying to figure out what was different. Her face did look a little fuller. But I still can't believe she would carry a baby to term. Tamika?"

"I don't know, Zoe. Maybe her biological clock is screaming at her."

"Yeah, right! If it was, my girl would throw that sucker right out the window," Zoe said, laughing. "And why would she have a baby when she doesn't even know who the father is? Hand me that panel over there, please?" Zoe asked, pointing to a sheer butter yellow curtain folded over the back of the sofa.

After handing her sister the curtain, Sara said, "How do you know she doesn't know whose baby it is? Maybe she does and that's why she decided to keep it."

"I don't know. Could be. I just assumed she wouldn't know. You know how Tamika rolls. Shoot, I've seen her do two, three guys in the same *day*. And that was only a couple of years ago! I don't think she's slowed her roll that much."

"You never know," Sara said, shaking her head.

"As you like to say, true dat!"

CHAPTER TWENTY-ONE

Mr. Telephone Man

Sipping on a cup of bland, tepid tea, Tamika sighed, glad that it was Sunday and she didn't have to go to work. But she was especially grateful she had finally stopped throwing up. For the umpteenth time, she questioned her decision to have her baby.

"I wish you were here, Big Mommie, to tell me what to do," Tamika whispered, talking softly to her deceased grandmother.

After years of listening to her parents scream and fight with each other, Tamika never forgot how devastated she was when her mother suddenly up and left the family. Then when her father was beaten to death for cheating a man using his "special" dice, Tamika's care, as well as that of her sisters, fell to their grandmother. Big Mommie, as everyone called Bertha Washington, was a maid during the week, head of bible study on Wednesdays, host of the weekly bake sale at the community center on Saturdays, and a deaconess in her church on Sundays. While poor, she gave her granddaughters all the love she could. Tamika was grateful, but those hard times convinced her that she never wanted to have children. Recognizing her intrinsic selfishness, Tamika decided that motherhood was not for her. Also, the fear of finding out that being a bad mother might be hereditary kept Tamika from wanting to have children.

Tamika always scoffed at the notion of a biological clock. Since she never entertained the thought of having a child, it made no sense to her. She flushed more babies down the toilet than the law should allow. That whole biological clock shit was a bunch of mumbo-jumbo that white men talked about to make white women feel guilty for wanting to be as successful as the men were, as far as Tamika was concerned. Black women didn't buy into that. They had their babies whenever they damn well pleased; from fifteen to fifty. And quite a few of them hadn't let having babies stop them from reaching the top. How their children felt was an entirely different subject.

But for Tamika, all she ever wanted to do was reach the top, unencumbered by a baby at her teat. Until now. Over and over again she asked herself why she decided to let this one live. Was it the timing or was it the man?

Sighing, Tamika got up and threw the rest of her bland tea down the drain and sat the cup in the sink to wash later. Idly wandering from her kitchen, she passed through her small den into her dining area and eventually sat in her rarely-used, pristine living room. Looking around, she decided that her home was far from kid-friendly. She was going to have to make some changes, and soon. She could just see a toddler, on short, fat legs running from her into her all white living room with a cup of juice, which would naturally be red, then falling and spilling said red juice all over her snow white carpet. Rather than worrying about that happening, she decided to have the carpets changed to something like Berber carpeting, so that the baby could still have something soft underfoot, but the carpet would be a lot more durable.

Who would have thought that she would even consider doing something that would accommodate someone else? Certainly not her. To her surprise, she was looking forward to the baby's birth. She couldn't wait to see what she had created. Reluctantly she admitted that she had not done it all by herself. But she knew she had to be prepared to handle this all by herself. While she hoped, wished, and prayed that she would not be alone, there was that possibility. She wondered who the baby would look like. If it looked like her, she could keep her secrets. If it looked like *him*, well, she couldn't do anything about that. It would be out there for everyone to know.

She decided that she had to tell Zoe who her baby's father was. Tamika was still hoping that there would be a way for them to salvage their friendship. She loved Zoe. She was the sister Tamika wished she had. Hers were a bunch of flakes who didn't know their asses from holes in the ground. Tamika had little time or patience for their foolishness. They accused her of thinking she was better than them because she lived in a townhouse in Chestnut Hill while they all lived in public housing in North Philly. She did think she was better, but only because she had worked like a new slave to put herself through school at Temple for her business degree. Now she was a junior vice president at one of the local insurance companies that was a global name, and she was proud to have brought herself this far.

She had no idea what she was going to tell her boss. On Monday she needed to find out about the company's maternity leave policy and what she would have to do to add her child onto her health insurance. On second thought, maybe she should wait on that. Rumors ran around her company faster than news of imminent layoffs. The last thing she needed was to have some nosey-ass people all up in her business.

Glancing down at her once flat stomach, she supposed it really was a moot point because sooner, rather than later, people were going to notice. Normally Tamika couldn't give a rat's ass what people said about her. As long as it didn't affect her upward mobility, they could talk until their tongues fell out. This time, however, it wasn't just about her.

"Wow. I guess I'm turning into a mother after all," she said out loud. Tenderly she rubbed her stomach as the realization slammed into her that a life dwelled within her.

"I'll *never* leave you, my sweet baby. I promise you on my life. No matter how bad it may get, it is you and me, all the way!"

Having come to terms with her pregnancy, Tamika decided it was time. She had to tell her girl, her friend, her *sistah*, before Zoe found out on her own. Maybe since the father was no longer in Zoe's life, she wouldn't care. Tamika prayed that would be the case.

Walking over to the cordless phone she had

thrown down on the sofa, she bent over to pick it up. Dialing the digits she knew as well as her own, she paced as she waited for Zoe to pick up.

"Hey, Gurl," she said when Zoe answered.

"Hey, Tamika. What's up?"

"Not much. I was just calling to see what you were up to."

"I was getting ready to go over Vaughn's and then I might stop by Antonio's. Why?"

"Vaughn and Antonio? Wow. What's up with that?

"Gurl, it is stranger than shit. I've been getting along with both of them and they have both been trying to get with me. What's really strange is I like it," Zoe said, laughing.

"Really? But I thought things with you and Vaughn were deader than dead. Same with you and Antonio. I know brotherman has been trying big time to get back with you," Tamika said casually, trying not to let her prying sound obvious.

"Yeah, I know. I thought I would go to my grave hating Vaughn. As for Antonio, I just don't know. He's a great guy and all, but I'm afraid to trust him again."

"It's not like he was cheating on you, Zoe. Not like what you went through with Vaughn."

"I know. But enough about them. I want to talk about you," Zoe said, changing the subject.

"Me? What about me?" Tamika asked, unable to keep the attitude out of her voice as her guard immediately went up.

"Yo, chill, Girlfriend," Zoe said, picking up on something in Tamika's voice. "I just wanted to know what was the matter with you the other day and why you've been avoiding my calls."

"Nothing was the matter with me. I was just stressed and very tired. I probably should have just stayed home."

"Hhhmmm. I just wondered. Look, there isn't any way to ask this but straight out."

"Ask what?"

"Are you still pregnant, Mika?"

For a long moment, Tamika said nothing. Finally, she answered with a sigh, "Yes, I am."

"Wow. I'm shocked. I thought you didn't want kids. Why did you change your mind?"

"I don't know. I didn't want kids, but, well, let's just say shit changes."

"I see. And you didn't feel like sharing this with me?"

"Is there some rule that says I have to get permission from you, Zoe?"

"Damn, why do you have to be all like that? I just asked. I *thought* we were best friends!"

"I . . . look, you're right. I'm sorry. I guess it's the raging hormones or something."

"Don't think just because you're pregnant that I won't slap the shit out of you, Mika!" Zoe said in a joking tone.

When Tamika didn't come back with a smart answer, Zoe knew something was wrong.

"What is it? What's the matter?"

"Nothing. I'm just trying to adjust to all of this, I guess."

"Mika, who is the father?"

"I'd rather not say."

"What the hell does that mean?"

"This is not a conversation I wanted to have on the phone, Zoe," Tamika hedged, afraid now to tell Zoe. It was the reason she had called, and now she couldn't do it.

"What the fuck? You're scaring me, Tamika. Who is the father of your baby?"

"I'd rather not say," she repeated.

"Fine, don't tell me then. I just thought we were cooler than that."

"Look, Zoe. Don't start, okay? I'm tired, I'm grumpy and I don't feel like fighting with you."

"Well, excuse me, Miss Thing, but *I* didn't call you. *You* called me!"

"So what does that mean? That I'm supposed to tell you everything? Since when?"

"I don't need all this damn drama, Tamika. Shit."

"Fine!"

"Fine!"

"Goodbye!"

"Whatevah!"

Zoe slammed the phone down, totally exasperated with her friend.

"What in the name of Hell was that all about?" she wondered aloud.

On her end, Tamika slowly hung the phone up as a tear slipped down her smooth cocoa cheek.

"I wish you were here, Big Mommie, to tell me what to do," Tamika repeated again.

Tamika was startled by the sudden ringing of her doorbell. Hurrying through her house to the front door, she peeked out to see who it was. Smiling in recognition, she opened the door and flung her arms around her unexpected, but very welcomed, guest.

"I'm so glad you came by. I was just getting ready to call you to see if you could stop over."

"I'm always happy to make a lady smile," her guest answered, as he dropped his keys and cap on her sofa table near the front door. His deep voice soothed Tamika's distraught spirit.

Smiling even wider she led him upstairs to her bedroom that he knew as well as his own. Tamika felt some tender lovin' care was exactly what she needed at that moment. Everything, she reasoned to herself, would work out, one way or another.

CHAPTER TWENTY-TWO
Me And My Girlfriend

"*O*h no she didn't! I can't believe that wench! If she wasn't pregnant, I swear I'd go over there and kick her natural black ass!" Zoe fumed out loud, her tires spinning and screeching as she rapidly backed out of her driveway.

As soon as she ended her conversation with Tamika, Zoe raced out of her house. Neighborhood kids, alerted by the car's sound, quickly jumped out of the way as she wildly backed into the street, fishtailed for a moment, righted her car, and zoomed up the street.

"I swear to God, I don't know why I'm even friends with her triflin' behind," Zoe mumbled as she whipped out of her development and swung her car onto Cowpath Road.

I might as well stop by Vaughn's house before going over to Antonio's grandmother's house to help him decide on a color to paint her living room, Zoe thought to herself, as she zoomed down Route 309.

As mad as she was at the moment, she regretted agreeing to help Antonio in the first place. As for her ex-husband, he was increasingly insinuating himself back into her life. The change in their relationship was subtle, but steady. Vaughn fixing her car. Vaughn picking up the kids when she had to work overtime. Vaughn inviting her to stay for dinner when she had to get Shanice and Jon after a weekend at his house. Vaughn surprising her with a new microwave after Jonathan put a carton of left over shrimp fried rice in her old one, forgetting about the metal handle. Vaughn cutting her grass when Antonio didn't beat him to it.

And thinking about Antonio, she realized that she was now looking forward to his evening phone calls. Things had gone from hate to like and maybe more. She was amazed the two men she thought she was completely finished with were now vying for her attention. It was like they were having a pissing contest. She laughed out loud as she remembered the waiting contest they engaged in the weekend before.

Vaughn brought the kids home as usual on Sunday evening. As had become habit, instead of scowling him out the door, she offered him dinner with a smile, actually glad to have his company. As everyone was enjoying the sundaes they concocted after dinner, Antonio's unexpected appearance interrupted the cozy, almost forgotten family atmosphere.

Shanice was especially displeased with Antonio's appearance. Things were going so well with her parents she started to think they might get back together. That night, Shanice was extremely rude and bratty, causing Zoe to level a threatening gaze on her youngest child. With a toss of her head, Shanice ignored her mother, declared her sundae gross, dumped it in the sink, and stomped upstairs. Jonathan was dismayed with his sister's wasteful ways, hoping to finish her sundae himself. After finishing his, he loaded the dishwasher then dashed upstairs to his room and his Game Boy II, leaving the adults to fend for themselves in the family room.

Zoe watched in amusement as Vaughn and Antonio tried to engage in idle chit-chat, watch a movie, and then play cards. Zoe finally threw them both out when she declared she was tired and had to get to bed because the next day was a work day. It was all she could do to keep from laughing when she almost heard the wheels turning in both their minds as they tried to think of a reason to stay. They both finally left together.

It was during the chit-chat part of that visit that she somehow agreed to help Antonio with the paint color selection. Honestly, she thought maybe she did it more to annoy Vaughn than anything else. She hadn't thought Antonio would actually hold her to her word until he called earlier in the week and reminded her of her offer to help.

Maybe it was just what she needed to get her mind off her fight with Tamika, she decided. Thinking about that fight only served to piss her off all over again. Suddenly deciding to get off at the Mount Airy exit, she barely missed a Ford Expedition as she screeched across the highway in order to get to the exit she almost passed. Unconcerned with the finger the driver threw up, she turned onto

Cheltenham Avenue North, traveled down Ivy Hill Road and then made a right onto Stenton Avenue, riding toward Chestnut Hill and Tamika's townhouse.

Pulling into the parking lot near Tamika's townhouse, Zoe was oblivious to any of the other cars in the lot. She only had one thing on her mind and that was to have it out with Tamika. Not only was she pissed, if she really wanted to admit it to herself, she was hurt by her friend's cavalier attitude.

Zoe laid on Tamika's doorbell, becoming increasingly angry when Tamika didn't immediately answer. She retraced her steps to the parking lot, and after scanning the cars, saw that Tamika's car was parked in the area where she generally parked. In her anger, she missed what should have been a warning.

Thoroughly pissed off, Zoe stomped back to the door and proceeded to bang on Tamika's door. Finally, Tamika slowly opened the door, one hand clutching the short satin robe covering her lush, bronze body.

"Zoe. What are you doing here?" she asked nervously, glancing around her to see if any of her neighbors were summoned by Zoe's rude knocking.

"Isn't it obvious why I'm here, 'Mika? After that conversation, I wanted to talk to you and find out what in the name of hell is your problem. I *know* you are not in here gettin' busy, are you?" Zoe asked, shocked.

Continuing without waiting for an answer, she said, "I mean, damn! We just got off the phone, what, fifteen, twenty minutes ago and you're knocking boots already? Damn!"

"What I'm doing in my own damn house is really none of your business, Zoe. Ummm, I don't recall you paying the note on this spot, so I suggest you don't get it twisted, okay?"

"See, this is just what I'm talkin' about. What is your damn problem? When did you start gettin' all secretive and shit on me? And are you going to let me in, or are we going to have this conversation out here so all your neighbors can get a taste?"

"Okay, but you can't stay long. I do have company," Tamika told Zoe, looking up the stairs and willing her company to stay put.

"Gee thanks. I was beginning to think you didn't want me in your house," Zoe snapped.

"Zoe, look, I'm really not up for this right now," Tamika said, uneasy, knowing something was getting ready to jump off.

"Tamika, I just want to find out why you've been so distant lately. That's all. Was it something I did? Are you mad at me about something? What's the deal?"

"No! You didn't do anything," Tamika said, wanting to reassure Zoe. She really felt like shit now. How could she tell her best friend what she'd done? She couldn't even bear to look Zoe in the eye. She looked everywhere else but directly into Zoe's eyes, no matter how hard Zoe tried to catch her eyes and hold them.

"Then what is it? Is it because of your pregnancy? Girl, you know I'll be here for you. You are my best friend. I can't believe you decided to go full term, but hey, I'm down for you. Just tell me what you need and I'm there. I know things have been crazy lately for me, but now that the kids and

I are settled into the house, things are calming down. So, what's the deal? Are you freakin' out 'cause you're pregnant? And how come you can't tell me *who* got you pregant?"

"Zoe, I . . . I just can't tell you! I promised . . . I want to, but . . . no, I can't. You must understand, I didn't want this . . . see what happened . . ." Tamika stammered, ready to cry.

"*Why* can't you tell me? Is it somebody I know?" Zoe asked, consternation twisting her face.

"Oh yeah, you know me very well," a deep voice said from the stairwell.

Turning her head in slow motion toward the too familiar voice, Zoe gasped and fell back against the front door where her and Tamika had remained after Tamika finally let Zoe in. Zoe gaped, unable to process what she was seeing. Not wanting to believe *who* she was seeing and *what* she was hearing. Here was the father of Tamika's baby. He was the last person she expected to see strolling down her supposedly *best friend's* stairs, resplendent in his paisley green boxers, his chest hairs slick and matted down like they were recently licked or he was sweating profusely. His face, she noted, looked glazed, like it was still coated with Tamika's juices.

"He hadn't even bothered to wash his face before coming downstairs!" Zoe wildly thought.

Zoe shook her head, not wanting to believe her eyes as they literally bugged out of her head. Looking from Tamika's ashamed face to his resigned one, Zoe felt her mouth go dry and her tongue stick to the insides of her mouth as she fought to articulate her surprise and outrage. Her rage, betrayal, hurt, and shock all fought for dominance, effectively shutting down her vocal chords. Finally, after a supreme effort, she managed to get one word to pass through her stiff lips.

"Vaughn?"

CHAPTER TWENTY-THREE

And In This Corner . . .

"Zoe!" Vaughn and Tamika cried out when Zoe's knees buckled and she hit the floor. Hard. Violently shaking off their efforts to assist her back to her feet, Zoe sprang back up, and as she did, her temper washed through her, forcing her back ramrod straight.

"Aw *hell naw!!* You son of a bitch!" Zoe hissed, right before she drew her hand back and knocked the shit out of Vaughn. Somehow, between the drawback and the actual hit, she managed to knot her hand into a solid fist, catching Vaughn under the eye and stunning him with the force of her blow. Zoe groaned inwardly when she felt a pain in her back that she knew she was going to pay for later.

Vaughn, taken by surprise, rocked back on his feet for a moment and knew her blow was going to leave a mark when he felt his cheek almost immediately swell. When she went to hit him a second time, he caught her by the wrist and held it, forcing Zoe to twist her wrist out of his vice grip.

Pleading, he tried to make her understand.

"Baby, it ain't like you think. Seriously. You have to calm down and listen to me."

"I don't have to listen to shit, you sorry ass motherfucker! How dare you try getting in my pants when you've not only been fucking this bitch, but you *got her pregnant!* Fuck you and that sorry ass, broke down, two bit fuckin' horse you rode in on!"

Turning her attention to Tamika, she wanted to give her what she had just given Vaughn. About to forget all the home training Amanda tried to instill in her, Zoe was ready to pounce, not caring about Tamika's pregnancy. A red haze settled over her and she was ready to draw blood.

"You fuckin' skank-ass bitch! My friend, huh? What utter bullshit! How could you do this to me, Tamika?

"Zoe, I swear to God, I never meant for this to happen! You have to listen to me. I didn't mean to fall in love . . ."

"Fall in love? Are you serious? You must be out of your fuckin' mind! Fall in love? With Vaughn? Vaughn is my *husband,* you bitch!"

"Your *ex*-husband, Zoe! Come on! You think he wasn't supposed to have a life after you?"

"Of course I know he is entitled to a life after me. Just not with the likes of *you!*" Zoe spat.

The two women raged at each other, forgetting that Vaughn was even in the room. This was a territorial fight. A female pissing contest. They squared off like two tigers, sizing each other up, waiting for the perfect time to spring. And like two tigers, the battle was over meat with Vaughn as the meat in question. Zoe wasn't sure whether she wanted Vaughn or not. But she knew, without a doubt, she did not want Tamika to have him.

"What? Have you already fucked every man in Philly and the surrounding counties so that now you had to resort to boffin' my rejects?"

"Hey, I'm hardly anybody's reject!" Vaughn protested.

Ignoring him, Zoe continued to taunt her opponent.

"Are you that hard up, that desperate to be me that you had to fuck my ex-husband, Tamika? Are you that vindictive, that jealous, that *sad* that you had to fuck *Vaughn?*"

"Damn, Zoe. Why you gotta say it like I'm third prize at the fair? Shit, I remember I used to make you holler!"

"That's called *acting*, Vaughn!" Zoe snapped, not caring whether she hurt his feelings or not.

"Yeah well, maybe something was wrong with you, because I ain't never had to *act*. Ain't that right, baby?" Tamika said spitefully, having grown weary of Zoe's venom, moving into what she hoped was the safety of Vaughn's arms, who was now standing at the bottom of the stairs.

It was all Zoe could do not to rush over and tear Vaughn's arms from around Tamika and swipe the smug look off her so-called fickle friend's face.

"So it's like that, huh? Then what was that all about when you were trying to get in my pants, Vaughn?"

"Zoe, I . . ." Vaughn said, trying to find the words to explain himself.

"Save it, Vaughn. I don't want to hear shit you have to say! As for you, my *friend*, I can't believe you would do this to me. That you would actually violate The Code. I loved you like a sister. And this is how you thank me? Well fuck you!"

With that, Zoe spun around, snatched open the door, and sped down the steps to the parking lot, hoping she could remember where she had parked her car. Tears of anger, remorse, and betrayal stung her eyes.

Before she knew it, she was banging on Antonio's grandmother's door. When Antonio finally answered, she fell into his startled arms. He was shocked at Zoe's mascara streaked appearance and her heart-wrenching tears.

"Zoe! What in Heaven's name is the matter? Talk to me, woman!" Antonio said, trying to calm her down.

"I can't believe this shit! I just can't believe it!"

"Believe what? Baby, please. You're scaring me!"

"Vaughn. Tamika. Her baby."

"What? You are not making sense. What about Vaughn and Tamika? What baby? Baby, you are not making sense."

Sighing a mighty, shaking sigh and taking the balled up toilet paper Antonio pressed into her hand, Zoe blew her nose long and loud, trying to gather her dignity. After a moment, she took a deep breath, blew it out, and cleared her throat. Speaking slowly, she wanted to make sure he understood so that she would never have to repeat the foul words about to exit her mouth.

"Listen to me, and don't ask me to repeat what I am about to say. If I have to repeat it, I just might be sick all over your grandmother's rug."

"Okay, give it to me."

"Vaughn, my ex-husband, the father of my daughter, and stepfather to my sons, the two-timing, cheating, son of a bitching, no taste having, motherfucking bastard who was acting like he changed, fuck-face son of a bitching, lying, cock sucking, dick head is the father of Tamika's baby!"

"Get out! Oh shit! No wonder you're so upset. Damn, Baby. That's rough. Tamika and Vaughn, huh? Damn!"

"Yeah, *damn!*"

They sat in silence, Zoe's head on Antonio's strong chest. Gradually, listening to his steady heartbeat calmed her down at least enough to make her not have thoughts of committing murder.

"They ain't worth it any damn way," she muttered, not realizing she said it out loud until Antonio said, "What? Who's not worth what?"

"You don't want to know. I might have to kill you if I tell you," she halfheartedly joked.

"Oooookay. Feeling better now?"

"Not really. Some. No. Yes. I don't know," she said, her answers and feelings scattered like pieces of mercury.

Sitting up with her forearms resting on her thighs, her hands dangled between her open knees and her head was so low that her chin almost touched her chest.

"My best friend. I can't believe my best friend did this to me," she whispered hoarsely, as unchecked tears rolled down Zoe's soft cheeks and splattered on the floor between her feet. Even Antonio rubbing her back in an attempt to comfort her did nothing to relieve the pain she felt. Still, he kept rubbing as she kept crying, only stopping occasionally to shove more toilet paper into her hand so she could blow her nose. She was so upset she never saw his slight grimace as she kept handing him the balled up pieces of used tissue. Silently he accepted them and gingerly placed them on an unused piece of tissue to dispose of them later.

After a while, she calmed down again and asked for a glass of ice water. When he came back from the kitchen and saw the empty living room he thought she had left. Looking out the window, he saw that her car was still a few doors up the street. Just as he was putting a foot on the bottom step to look upstairs for her, she came back down.

"Looking for me?" she asked, slightly amused by his worried look.

"I thought you left until I saw your car was still outside."

"I went to the bathroom to repair my makeup. I was looking a hot mess!"

"Feel better?"

"No, but I'll live. I don't want to talk about it."

"Where are the kids?"

"Jonathan and Shanice are over Sara's and Chris is at work."

"Work? Since when did Chris start working?" Antonio asked, surprised.

"Since he decided he wanted to go to three proms this year and I told him it wasn't up to me to foot his bill for his decision to be mister man about town. His prom, I could see, but for the other two, uh-uh."

"I can understand that," Antonio laughed.

"I hope I'm not keeping you from anything. I know we were supposed to meet today, but I can't remember for what," Zoe told him, her voice trailing off as a pained expression marred her features.

"You were going to help me decide on a color to paint in here. We can do that another time. I thought you weren't coming and I was getting ready to go pick up . . . ah, never mind."

"A date?" Zoe asked, curious and disappointed at the same time.

"Ah, no. Not exactly," Antonio hedged. He didn't want to tell her, seeing how well they had been getting along.

"Oh. Well, let me get out of your way then," Zoe said, bristling. Snatching up her purse, she attempted to open the door when Antonio held it closed.

"It's not what you think, Zoe."

"Hey, what you do is no longer my concern, right?"

"It can be. You decided that you wanted it this way, not me," he said quietly. Zoe thought she heard hurt in his voice. Before she could comment he informed her, "I'm getting ready to go pick up my kids. But I didn't want to tell you because I know you don't want anything to do with them." Now Zoe thought she detected a note of bitterness in his voice.

"I never said that! How dare you accuse me of that!"

"Maybe not those exact words, but throwing me out of *your* house, as you reminded me, was the same thing as saying you didn't want to be bothered with them or me!" Zoe drew back, surprised that he had hollered at her.

"No, I threw you out because, *just like Vaughn*, you lied to me! It didn't have anything to do with those kids!"

"No? Then how come you never ask me about them? How come whenever I mention them, you change the subject? How come when I call and you hear them in the background, you rush me off the damn phone? Huh? How come, Zoe?"

"I . . . I . . . I don't do that. Do I?" she asked, frowning, thinking back over the last few weeks. Slowly walking back into the living room, Antonio following behind her, she sat down, suddenly realizing that she had been avoiding any discussion with Antonio about his children.

"I didn't mean . . . I didn't know I was . . . I'm sorry, Antonio. I guess I just couldn't deal," she told him.

They sat in silence for a while before Antonio finally asked, "Do you really hate my kids that much, Zoe?"

"I don't even know your kids, so how could I hate them? And they're kids, Antonio. Give me a break. I may be a bitch, but I'm not *that* damn bad!" Zoe told him, affronted by his remark.

Chuckling at her returning attitude, Antonio reached over and squeezed her hand.

"Can I come with you?"

"To meet my kids? You'd really do that?" he asked, surprised.

"No, to meet the man on the moon. Yes, to meet your kids. I wouldn't have asked if I didn't want to do it. It is past time that I met them and I may have some selfish reasons as well." At his puzzled look, she told him, "I need something to keep me from thinking about Vaughn and my bitch-in-heat, supposedly best friend." Zoe's face flushed in renewed anger.

"Okay, let's go," Antonio said, pulling her up from the sofa and toward the door, determined to keep her mind off all that.

As Zoe walked toward the front door, she suddenly stopped.

"Oh my God!"

"What? What's the matter," Antonio asked, wondering why she seemed to be rooted to the floor.

"I just realized that Tamika's baby will be Shanice's half sister! Aww hell naw!"

"Later, Zoe. Think about it later. There's nothing that can be done about it right now."

"You think so, huh? Well we'll just see about that!" Zoe said, sounding ominous.

"Come on, Zoe. You can't let this eat you up. You know how your stomach and your back get when you get upset."

"You remember that?" Zoe asked, surprised.

"I remember everything about you," Antonio said, pulling Zoe into his arms and surprising her with a passionate kiss. He kissed her past her protest. He kissed her past her tension and anger and he kissed her until he felt her body grow limp with desire.

Finally, he lifted his mouth from hers. Seeing her eyes half closed, he smiled.

"Ready?" he asked, grinning at her slightly dazed look.

"Huh? Oh, yeah. Sure," Zoe answered, sounding flustered. Antonio could turn her on faster than any man she'd ever met.

Antonio just continued to smile as he grabbed Zoe's hand, happy to have her finally willing to meet his children.

CHAPTER TWENTY-FOUR
The High-Priestess of Hoochies

*J*he ride to pick up Antonio's children passed mostly in silence. Zoe was beginning to second guess her decision to take this plunge. She was also trying to fight the image of seeing her ex-husband with her ex-friend. As far as she was concerned, she and Tamika were through. Zoe didn't think there was any way she could ever get over what was the ultimate betrayal. Every time that situation tried to take dominance in her mind, she pushed it back, choosing not to deal with it at the moment.

Before she knew it, they were parking before a house that was in sad disrepair. The front steps were leaning to one side and didn't look safe enough for anyone to navigate. The porch had cracked and peeling black paint, missing floor boards, and looked plain tired, sagging, and well past its former glory.

Zoe reluctantly got out of Antonio's jeep and followed him up the mishapen steps. She waited as he banged on the dirty, scarred, windowless front door.

Zoe damn near gagged when the door was thrown open and Niambi stood before them in all her ragged splendor. Zoe gaped as she took in the torn men's tee shirt that barely concealed Niambi's massive, pendulous breasts. Below the dirty, stained, and ripped tee shirt, Niambi had on a pair of sweat pants that probably fit two sizes ago. In the space between where the shirt ended and the pants began, hung a large, saggy, and very unattractive stomach that looked like a road map of harsh, ugly stretch marks leading to nowhere.

Licking the fingers of one hand and running her other fingers through a badly done maroon weave in desperate need of a redo, Niambi stood in the doorway, a belligerent look resting on her bloated, unmade up face.

"Humph. About damn time you got here. These mu'fuckin' kids 'bout ready to work a sistah's last fuckin' nerve. To hear them tell it, you would think yo' azz was the second-fuckin' comin'! Oh, I see you brought Ms. Priss with you. Humph. Thought your azz had run for the hills when you found out 'bout dem kids. What up, gurlfriend?"

"Ain't nuthin' but a thang," Zoe answered her dismissively and stood with her legs apart on the pitiful porch in an obvious challenge. She had the satisfaction of seeing the surprise on Niambi's face by her use of slang. Zoe was in no mood for more bullshit and was actually spoiling for a fight. She *wished* Niambi would come out her mouth the wrong way. She needed to get some shit out of her system, and kicking Niambi's ass would be a wonderful start.

Instead, Niambi must have seen something in

her eyes as she replied, "Yeah, heard that." Turning around, she screamed, "Yo! Hurry up, you little bastards! Your daddy's here. Don't make me have to call your sorry asses again!"

Zoe cringed as she watched the cowed children scurry to snatch up their meager belongings that were in grocery store bags. They gazed at Zoe, awestruck by the sight of her. She looked like a slim, golden goddess who had suddenly glided into their dark, dank, messy living space.

The children glanced at their mother in all her unkempt glory as she picked her bottom teeth using her pinkie finger's two inch blue and silver nail, and then proceeded to suck up whatever it was that was now under that nail. Then the children looked at Zoe, who stood by the front door in hospital scrubs that were neatly pressed, her blinding white sneakers and her simple, but elegantly, bobbed hair. They didn't know what to think. One, because they had never seen Zoe before. And two, because other than their sister, none of them had ever seen their father with a woman other than their mother. Instinctively, they were drawn to Zoe's warmth.

The children were lined up like stair steps, waiting. The boys gawked and Antonio's daughter, smiling shyly, stepped forward and said, "I remember you. You were in the car with my daddy the night he gave us a ride home."

"Yes, that's right. How are you? Ebony, right?"

Pleased that the nice lady remembered her name, Ebony's face broke into a wide grin. Getting ready to speak, she was rudely interrupted by her mother's harsh tones.

"You got money for me?"

"When I bring the kids back, Ni. I told you that earlier."

"Why can't you give it to me now? I thought you was gonna give me something now, so I can go grocery shopping while the kids ain't here," she wheedled. She had plans for that money, and she needed it now, not later.

"Y'all go on out to the truck," Antonio instructed, walking to the door and hitting the key fob to unlock his vehicle.

Whooping, the kids pushed and stumbled to get out of the house and down the rickety steps to their father's truck. As Zoe turned to follow them, she heard Antonio use that voice he seemed to reserve only for his children's mother.

"I ain't giving you shit! Do I look fuckin' stupid? Naw, bitch, you ain't gon' take my hard-ass earned money and go get high. Fuck that!" Antonio yelled.

"See, it ain't even like that, baby. Look, okay, see, I need to get right. Come on, Antonio. Help a sistah out. I won't spend it all. I swear to God. I'll really go grocery shopping. I promise."

Zoe stopped in mid stride and turned around, unable to believe her ears. She turned around just in time to see Niambi step up to Antonio as she tried to clamp her hands on his pants over his privates.

"Bitch, please. Get the fuck away from me!" Antonio bellowed when she grabbed for him, totally ignoring Zoe's shocked face.

"I'll suck your dick for you, Baby. You know you used to love how I sucked. Come on, Antonio. Your old ass bitch can watch. Yeah, I bet she's a freak like that. Shit, she might learn a thing or two 'bout how a dick should be sucked proper."

"Oh no she didn't!" Zoe said, advancing on Niambi. "Bitch, don't make me kick your ass in your own fuckin' house!"

"Don't even go there with her, Zoe. I got this," Antonio said, shoving Niambi so hard she landed on her ample ass.

"Niambi, don't you *ever* come out your mouth like that to this woman. This, you stupid, ignorant, low class bitch, is a *lady*. Look at her long and hard. It's the closest you will ever get to one. Let's go," Antonio said, grabbing Zoe by the elbow and quickly escorting her out of the house.

"This is why I have to get my kids away from her triflin' ass," Antonio said tightly as he tried to relax his face for the four anxious faces inside his truck that watched his every move. He smiled, acting like everything was fine. Under his breath he said, "They have seen and heard too much, too soon. It's gotta stop."

Silently, Zoe nodded her head, feeling sorry for the thin, pitiful faces staring back at her.

When they got in Antonio's truck, Zoe's breath was snatched away from her. Confused for a moment, she quickly realized that the stench of unwashed bodies and pissy drawers was coming from the back seat. Looking at Antonio, he just gazed back at her for a moment before dropping his head so she couldn't see the tears that quickly sprang to his eyes. Without a word, they held a whole conversation. However, in desperation Zoe eased down the window, gulping in fresh air.

Antonio got back to his house as quickly as the evening traffic would allow. As diplomatically as he could, he told the children that they had to take their baths first.

"But we ain't got nuttin' else to wear," Akbar said, looking from Antonio to Zoe.

"None of y'all got any clean clothes?" Antonio asked, stunned.

"Nope," they all answered.

"What's in your bags?"

He was answered with shrugs and feet dragging back and forth.

"Let me see your bag, Ebony," Antonio gently asked his daughter.

Handing it over to him, she watched as he opened the bag. Reaching inside, he pulled out two mismatched, dirty socks and a torn pajama top. Quickly looking through all their bags, he was dismayed to find the boys belongings weren't in much better condition.

"Where are the clothes your grandmother bought you last month?"

"Gone," Tony, the oldest at 10, answered, sounding bitter.

"Gone? What do you mean gone?" Antonio snapped, his voice rising with his panic. Zoe placed a hand on his tense shoulder, trying to silently get him to calm down when she saw he was frightening the children.

"She, I mean Ma, sold most of it. Right after we got home. Said she needed the money to keep the water on. Only the water got turned off anyway," Tony said, looking down.

Leaving the children and a bewildered Zoe in the upstairs hallway, Antonio strode into his bedroom, returning in a few moments with white tee shirts in his hands.

"Okay, start taking your baths. Put these on

while I wash your clothes." Antonio announced, frustration evident on his face.

"While you oversee that, give me their sizes and I'll run over to Wal-Mart or Target on the Boulevard," Zoe volunteered.

"I can't ask you to do that, Zoe," Antonio protested.

"You didn't ask," Zoe said firmly. Looking the children over, she pulled out a pad and pen and asked those who knew, what their sizes were and guessed on the little ones.

In a softer tone, after the older kids went to help the younger ones get undressed, Zoe told Antonio, "Look, I can see you are overwhelmed. And you know I can't stand to see kids without. So stop looking at me with those puppy dog eyes, and give me your charge card!"

"Always keeping it real, aren't you?" Antonio said, handing over the gold.

"No doubt," Zoe quipped, laughing as she ran down the stairs.

"Oh, what's your limit?" Zoe asked, looking up the stairs.

Seeing her animated face, softly illuminated by the lamp on a table by the stairs, momentarily took Antonio's breath away. Sometimes he forgot just how beautiful Zoe was. He'd missed her, even her snapping at him about silly, small things. That was just Zoe's way. And whether he liked it or not, he still loved her.

"Hello? Yo! Did I lose you, Hon?"

Snapping out of it, he mock-grimaced and said, "I was trying to calculate what I might have left on that card. Don't hurt me too badly, Zoe. I think I may have seven or eight hundred dollars on that card."

"That'll work." Turning away, she abruptly turned back around. Motioning for him to come down, he glanced toward the bathroom and then hurried down the steps.

"What is it? I don't want to leave them unsupervised too long."

"I know. They're not going back, are they?"

Surprised, Antonio could only stare at Zoe for a moment. "No," he answered quietly.

"Good. Something will work out. But at least I know what to get."

"Just get enough to get them dressed. I'll worry about the rest later."

"How about pajamas and stuff for tonight and something for tomorrow? That way, they will at least look decent when you take them shopping."

"Cool. Thanks, Zoe. I really appreciate this. I owe you one."

"No problem. It's keeping my mind off other things," she said with a sad smile.

"Ouch. Didn't mean to make you think about that."

"You can't stop me from thinking about it, Antonio. It is what it is. Look, I'll see you in a few. You'd better get back upstairs," she told him, listening to the squawks of protest from Walter on the way Tony was giving him a bath. Kissing his lips quickly, and almost laughing at his look of surprise, she left him momentarily stunned.

Two hours later, Zoe struggled through the door, laden with bags that were bursting with clothes. She sniffed the air appreciatively, heavy with the aroma of spaghetti sauce bubbling on the stove. She was tired after fighting the crowd in the closest Wal-Mart, and her feet and back hurt.

"Hey, Babe! I thought I was going to have to send out a search party for you," Antonio said as he stole a kiss and took the heavy bags from her hands, this time startling her.

"I'm exhausted!" Zoe said, falling into the nearest chair.

"What did you get?" Antonio asked, upending the bags and dumping the contents all over the sofa and floor.

"I know you were supposed to be taking them shopping tomorrow, but they were having a sale and once I started, I couldn't stop," she said ruefully, laughing at herself. "You still have to take them shopping for school uniforms, though. Each child got a pair of pajamas, a three pack of underwear, undershirts and socks, two pairs of jeans, a pair of chinos, three tops, a sweatsuit, and a pair of sneakers. Oh, and a bathrobe, slippers, and a toothbrush," Zoe proudly told him.

"Damn, Babe," Antonio said, awed. "I could never have done all of that in just a couple of hours. I don't know how to thank you," he said, his voice sounding suspiciously shaky.

Brushing off the awkward moment, Zoe said, "A plate of that scrumptious smelling spaghetti would be a nice start."

Before they could move toward the kitchen, however, Antonio's children came into the living room and went crazy when they saw all of their new clothes. After giving each child his haul, they bounded up the stairs, eager to put their new pajamas, robes, and slippers on. Moments later they reappeared, grinning and running their hands over the softness of their robes, looking proud and grateful for their unexpected windfall.

Shyly, each child gave Zoe a hug and thanked her for getting them their new clothes.

"You are most welcome. But really, your father paid for it all."

"But *you* picked it out," Tony, the oldest, insisted.

"Miss Zoe, how did you know that purple is my favorite color?" an awed Ebony asked, looking down at her purple flowered pajamas, purple robe trimmed in white piping and her purple bunny slippers.

"I don't know Ebony. Just lucky I guess," Zoe said, fighting the tears that suddenly sprang to her eyes when the child looked at her.

The look on the little girl's face was so full of awe and delighted surprise, it just pulled at Zoe's heartstrings. Zoe watched, bemused, as they struggled to eat the spaghetti and not get any on their new pajamas. She didn't think she had ever seen children eat that carefully. It was almost sad that they had so little in their lives that a pair of pajamas meant that much.

"Okay guys, go on up to my room and watch some television. I'll be up in a few to check on you. Let me get the kitchen cleaned up and Ms. Zoe a plate," Antonio instructed when the children finished eating.

Zoe silently watched him. This was a new and different Antonio that she would have to get used to. That thought startled her. It implied that they had, or would have, a relationship. But she wasn't sure if she was ready for that.

After eating her fill of his delicious dinner, she leaned back in her chair with a contented sigh. Her contentment, however, was quickly replaced with tension as she recalled the day's revelations. Her anger still simmered below the surface, but more than anger, she was deeply, profoundly hurt.

"I'm sure there's an explanation, Zoe," Antonio said quietly, after watching her for a few moments. He knew the exact moment she went from contented to vexed. He could see the lines of tension that held her body tight, whereas only a few moments before, she was loose and easy. Without her saying a word, he knew what caused the change in her. Sighing, he crossed the room and carefully sat down across the table from her.

"What is really the problem, Zoe? You and Vaughn have been divorced for a long time. Did you think you were the only one who could move on? Did you expect him to remain single and pine away waiting for you to come back to him indefinitely?"

"Of course not!" Zoe sputtered, stung. Or had she? Had she expected Vaughn to wait for her to come back to him? The thought stunned her, causing her to snap her head back and her eyes to widen. *Had she?*

"Look, I gotta roll. I've got my own kids to worry about," Zoe said abruptly, getting up and looking around for her purse.

"Don't go mad, Zoe. I'm just trying to help you put things into perspective. I saw when you moved that you and Vaughn didn't have the animosity there that was present for so long. That's why I stopped calling as much. I thought that maybe you two were working it out and might be getting back together. I didn't want to interfere with that, you know?" At Zoe's slow nod, he continued. "Obviously, the niggah was hedging his bets. He was playing you and Tamika. Damn, I can't believe he got with Tamika! I know that was your girl and all, but I wouldn't fuck her with somebody else's dick! Oh, she fine as hell, but knowing about Tamika like I do? Sheet, ain't no way in *hell* I would have gotten with her!"

Zoe started to open her mouth and defend her friend out of habit and then she remembered Tamika was her *used* to be friend. Try as she might, she couldn't stop the burning anger that swept over her like a hot flash, causing her to break out in a sweat. With great effort she pushed the anger down, realizing there really was nothing she could do about it. And she didn't want to go off again with Antonio's children in the house.

"Stop! My brain can't take anymore tonight," Zoe said tiredly. "I'll be lucky to make it home, I'm so tired."

"Maybe you should stay here," Antonio suggested. Zoe just raised her eyebrow and walked toward the front door saying, "Tell your children I said goodnight. I'm glad I finally got to meet them. But Antonio, I have to tell you, you've got your work cut out for you."

"Yeah, I know. But I knew what I was getting myself into when I bought this house. Again, thank you for helping me get it. Your realtor friend was great, calling his friend down here in the city to help me find this house. I wish I didn't need to have all the boys crowded up in one room, but in a few years I'll probably move the two oldest to the basement. I plan on expanding that half bath down there to a full bath, so that will help. And you know my mother works for the Department of Children Services, so she's been a big help in guiding me through the ins and outs of the court system."

"But if you don't take them back, won't you be endangering your case?"

"Maybe, but I don't have a choice anymore, Zoe. I can't take them back to that bitch! You saw how she was today. She's been getting worse and worse. I think she's on crack or something. All I know is, I can't, in all good conscience, take them back to that hovel she calls a home."

"I don't know much about the law, Antonio, but I would think you are taking one hell of a gamble."

"I doubt she'll even notice they're gone, until she needs more money. I'm glad I gave her checks instead of cash. At least I can prove I've been paying support."

"Thank goodness for that!"

"Yeah, hopefully by the time she notices, we will be in court. And listen, let me just say again, thanks for your help today. I really appreciate it," Antonio said, standing close enough for Zoe to feel his body heat.

"Ah . . . yeah. Sure . . . no problem," Zoe said before clearing her throat. "Umm, I really should be going," she said, not moving.

"Yeah, I don't want to keep you," Antonio said low, moving in closer and slowly lowering his head, his lips almost touching Zoe's. He was so close their breaths mingled as he hesitated for a long, emotionally charged moment.

"Daddeeeeeeeeeeee!!! Tell Akbar to stop teasing meeeeee!" screeched Ebony as she raced down the stairs with Akbar, devilment dancing on his face, chasing her as he jiggled a huge, black plastic spider.

Sighing, Antonio mumbled, "It never stops."

"Welcome to parenthood!" Zoe told him, laughing at his woebegone expression. "Look, you need to give them some attention and I need to get home. I'll talk to you later, okay?"

"Bet. I'll catch you later," Antonio told her, a small smile on his face as he watched her hurry down the steps.

Turning around, he stood still for a moment listening to the cacophony of sounds assaulting his ears. Ebony was still screeching and Akbar was still laughing. Upstairs, Tony and Walter were arguing and the television sounded like it couldn't go another decibel higher. It was utter chaos. And Antonio loved it.

CHAPTER TWENTY-FIVE

Uncomfortable Genes

"**I** tell you, Sara, if that woman wasn't my mother, I don't think I'd ever speak to her again!" Danita declared between sniffles.

"Oh, Danita! I'm so sorry to hear that. My mother and I were so close. I hate it when I hear about a mother and daughter at odds," Sara told her friend, holding the tissue box out for Danita to snatch another one.

Sitting in the breakfast room in Sara's kitchen, they barely paid T.J. and Bethany and their gang of friends any attention as they played a game of soccer in Sara's spacious back yard. The thick glass of the french doors muffled most of the squeals, grunts, and laughter as they raced all over the yard.

"Yeah, well, you had a mother who treated you like you had some sense. My mother doesn't have children. She has pawns on a chess board. And when we don't move the way she wants, she has a fit. I thought she had finally gotten used to the idea of Ben and I being together. *Not.* But this latest stunt is just too much!"

"Well, maybe she just wanted to give you your baby shower, Hon. I'm sure she didn't call the country club and cancel it out of spite," Sara told her friend, not believing her own words.

Zenobia didn't play. And when she was mad, she could be downright vicious. Sara could only imagine how pissed she must have been when she found out that Danita's mother-in-law was giving Danita her baby shower. Sara was going to throw it herself until she spoke with Emily Stockton, who begged Sara to let her do it.

"Well, didn't Emily call your mother to see about doing it together?" Sara asked now.

"I don't know. I assumed she did. Actually, I'm sure she did. If nothing else, I am sure Emily strictly adhered to protocol. And knowing my mother, she probably rudely hung up on her or blew Emily off."

"Well, why would the country club cancel the event without checking with Emily first? That doesn't make sense."

"It makes sense if you are on the board of directors, like my mother is."

"*Damn.* I can't even begin to understand how any of that shit works. It's out of my league," Sara joked.

"It's really no big deal, Sara. I told you I could get you and Theo in if you want. I think it would be good for Bethany and T.J. T.J. could meet some nice young ladies and Bethany is old enough to be part of the debutante ball next year."

"Girl, please. We are just plain folk. Not only that, it's bad enough T.J.'s looking at them white girls in his school. I don't need for him to be around a bunch of stuck up ones looking to satisfy their Mandingo curiosity."

"Our club is mixed, Sara." At Sara's raised eyebrow, she amended, "Okay, maybe there are only like, including us, three black families registered, but it is getting there. That is why you and Theo should join. Bring some new blood to the place."

"Yeah, right," Sara said, snorting. "And I bet every one of the men are either doctors or lawyers. Am I right?"

"Ah, let me think. Ummm, well, Daddy is a lawyer and Mr. Robinson is one and there are the Pettigrews, and yeah, he's a doctor."

"Umm-humm. That's what I'm talking about. What in hell are they going to think about Theo, who for all intents and purposes, is a mechanic? So what that he now owns like five shops and could be as big as Jiffy Lube? And so what if he's grossing some serious paper? To them, he's blue collar, and we don't belong in their white collar world. Period." Sara said, sounding a little bitter.

"But you have a flourishing interior design business, Sara. You deal with a lot of people, both black and white. And didn't you tell me you just got a deal with that guy who found Zoe's house to do his sample homes? He's getting to be a big name in real estate. Talk about impressive! That would definitely look good."

"I am *not* trying to impress any-damn-body, Danita. You know me. People can take me as I am. If they can't, then fuck 'em," Sara told her friend.

Danita looked at Sara, and then burst out laughing. "You may have a point, Sara. I don't think the club is anywhere near ready for *you!*"

After they shared a laugh, Sara got serious again.

"So, what are you going to do about your mother, Danita? Sooner or later, you have to have it out with her."

"I know. But it's hard, you know? She *is* my mother, and I try so hard to be what she wants, but sometimes I have to ask myself, when do I get to be what *I* want? It's not like I'm a bad daughter. Ben was telling me about his secretary, Lydia. You won't believe this. Lydia's daughter, Jasmine, stopped speaking to her, because Lydia's husband, while doing a favor for Jasmine, hurt himself in Jasmine's house. I think Ben said he broke his leg falling down some steps. Anyway, when Lydia asked her daughter for her insurance information, Jasmine jumped to the conclusion that her mother wanted to sue her!"

"What? Well, that's just plain stupid and ignorant!"

"That's what I said. But Ben said that Lydia has been just heartbroken because not only did her daughter stop speaking to them, she returned her key to their house, changed her phone number, and won't let Lydia or her husband, Jasmine's stepfather, anywhere near their grandchildren!"

"Oh that is just *awful!* I would *never* treat my mother like that. You only get one mother."

"I know. And Zenobia can drive me crazy, but I would never, *ever* treat her like that. Good, bad, or ugly, she's my mother and as such, deserves my loyalty and respect."

"That's so ugly. Damn. I would give everything I have to spend one more day, hour, hell, even a minute with my mother," Sara said, tears filling her eyes.

The past few months had been hell for Sara. She missed Amanda more than she could ever articulate. She couldn't understand how anyone could ever turn on their mother like that. It was beyond her comprehension. She was always so close to her mother; even when Amanda got on her nerves, she loved her mother with everything she had in her. And Bethany loved her grandmother so much, no way would Sara *ever* have kept them apart on purpose.

"Ben said that Lydia came into his office practically hysterical the day after her birthday."

"Why?" Sara asked, almost afraid to hear the answer.

"You are not going to believe this. Not only did Lydia's daughter *not* call her on her birthday, she didn't allow Lydia's grandchildren to call her either!"

"What?! No! You have got to be kidding. No one is *that* cruel."

"Well, apparently, that little bitch was."

"Damn. Are they speaking now?"

"I don't think so. Lydia's husband raised Jasmine from the time she was eight or nine. So basically, James was the only father she'd ever known. She never called and asked how he was doing. Never gave them the insurance information, and didn't let the grandchildren, who Lydia said adore him even more than her, call him for his birthday either."

"Dag, that is really nasty. I don't even know that lady and I feel like crying for her. Umph, umph, umph!"

"See, that's what I mean. At least I'm not a daughter like that. I respect my mother, and Lord knows, I do love her. I just don't always like her. But when I hear stories like that, I think that I should just try harder. Only problem is, sometimes I feel that no matter how hard I try, it's never going to be enough," Danita said, her voice dropping to a hoarse whisper, as a fat tear slid down her soft, pregnancy-plumped cheek.

Sara hugged her friend and let her cry on her shoulder.

"I have the solution. We'll have your shower here. No ifs, ands or buts about it. End of problem. This way, neither your mother nor Emily feel like the other one has more control. Your best friend is giving you a shower. End of discussion. And you know," Sara said, getting up and rushing to the desk drawer in her kitchen. Snatching it open, she let her sentence hang as she frantically swished papers and pens around the shallow drawer.

"Ah-ha!" she said triumphantly. "Two of my Valley Dolls have an invitation business. They do fabulous work. I'll call Shelly and see how fast she can whip up some invitations for me. When do you want to have it?" Sara asked a stunned Danita as she started dialing the phone number on the smart business card.

"Sara!"

"What?"

"You're moving too fast for me. Hold up a minute!"

Clicking the phone off, Sara watched as Danita paced back and forth across her kitchen.

"What's the matter, Baby Girl?"

"It can't be that easy, can it?"

"Yup. And I bet if I call my Dolls, they will have this thing organized and done in no time flat. You should see these ladies. They are amazing!" Sara said, laughing.

"Who are they?" Danita asked, curious.

"My Huntingdon Valley friends. I was introduced to them through my old boss, Sandy Brownstein's wife, Sheila. They are the nicest bunch of ladies. I really enjoy their friendship. Each has her own business or talent and they just blow me away. They remind me of us, except they happen to be Jewish. Each one has a rich husband who is either a doctor or a lawyer or some big time business mogul, and you would think they would be stuck up, but they aren't. They are so down to earth. Even with the big-ass rocks they have. How come you don't have a huge rock like that? I mean yours is nice, but girl, you should see the rings these chicks are rockin'! Whew! They must be five, six carats. I know, I'm hatin'. Now their country club, I would join. Well, maybe not. Just because they are nice doesn't mean the rest of their club would be. And I don't think Jewish clubs have blacks in them anyway. Well, unless maybe you're a judge or head of the United Way or something like that," Sara rambled as she paced, her mind racing, mentally making a list of things to be done.

"We have Jews in our club."

"Really? Well, that shoots that theory to hell. *Anyway*, getting back to you. When do you want to have this shower?"

"I don't care. At this point I just want it over!"

"I heard that," Sara said as she again dialed her friend's number. When the call was picked up, Danita heard, "Shelly? Hi, Sara Watkins. Listen, have I got a job for you . . ."

CHAPTER TWENTY-SIX

Everything Ain't Everything

Sara bustled around, greeting guests and checking with the caterer to make sure everything was on schedule. It was a beautifully balmy day and she wanted to make sure that Danita's shower was perfect. They ended up having the event at the Melrose Country Club instead of Sara's house. It turned out that Sara's friend, Shelly, who did the invitations, knew somebody who knew somebody who was letting them use the garden room at the club for next to nothing. Sara was sipping on a much-needed raspberry flavored iced water and idly chatting with some of the guests when she heard, "*What* is *she* doing here?"

Sara turned toward Zoe. Shocked, Zoe looked across the veranda and saw Tamika breezing through the door, sipping on a clear drink that Zoe assumed was soda or water with a bright slice of yellow lemon floating in it. Tamika looked around, and spotting the table already overflowing with presents, sailed toward it. A flushed-faced

young man tried to keep up with her as he struggled with a huge, oversized, gayly wrapped present. *Leave it to Tamika,* Zoe thought viciously, *to
buy the biggest, most expensive gift on Danita's list.*
What was worse, Tamika looked luminous. Zoe
cursed under her breath, pissed that Tamika had
the nerve to show up at Danita's baby shower, and
even more pissed at how she looked.

"How come every other pregnant woman looks
worn out and pale in her early months and this
bitch looks like she just got back from two weeks in
Negril?"

Sara politely excused herself from her guests
and turned to give her sister her undivided attention.

"She's here because her name was on the list
that Danita gave me." Sara answered Zoe's first
question and ignored her second.

"*Why?* Doesn't 'Nita know?"

"No, she doesn't. I never told her. I felt it wasn't
my tale to tell."

"That's a first. You tell every damn thing else!"

"Um, Zoe? Don't start with me today, okay?"
Sara said, wagging one finger in front of Zoe's
face, her other hand on her hip. She might have
taken that when they were kids, but now they were
older and, as Sara felt, equal, so she wasn't putting
up with Zoe's shit anymore.

"I've been working my ass to the ground trying
to pull this thing together. I understand and appreciate how you feel about Tamika right now.
But, like it or not, you are going to have to deal with
it. And, ummm, while you're at it, deal with this:
her and Vaughn's baby *will* be related to Shanice.
And I'm sure my niece is just tickled pink to find

out that she will no longer be the youngest sister. But for today, put it aside. This is for Danita and I'm not having it spoiled by you or Zenobia!"

"She doesn't know."

"Who doesn't know what?"

"Shanice. She doesn't know."

"*What? What do you mean she doesn't know?*"

"Just what the hell I said. She-doesn't-know," Zoe repeated, making like she was doing sign language in front of her sister's face.

Sara swatted her sister's hand away from her face, staring at her, waiting for Zoe to explain. As the silence between them ripened, Sara crossed her arms in front of her, rolled her neck, and began tapping her foot in an exaggerated manner, indicating that she was getting tired of waiting to hear what Zoe had to say.

"What?" Zoe asked in mock innocence.

"What, my ass. Why haven't you told her? She's going to find out sooner or later. Do you want her to find out by going over to her Dad's and finding Tamika there?"

"Why would that happen?"

"Why wouldn't it? I mean, since they have been outed, they no longer have to hide, right? So I'm assuming they will be more open about their relationship, right?"

"I have no idea. I haven't spoken to either of them since this happened."

"Well, hasn't Vaughn been over to pick up the kids? And isn't Chris still living with him?"

"No and yes."

"Huh?"

Zoe sighed as she watched Tamika direct the

young man to put the present down, making sure it was prominently displayed.

Dragging her eyes away, Zoe fought hard to turn her attention back to her sister. Making a slight sucking noise, she said, "No, he hasn't been over because I have forbidden him to see Shanice or Jonathan. I have also forbidden him to say one freakin' word about this mess to Chris. However, since school is now over, I have let Chris know in no uncertain terms that I want him to move into the house. Chris, of course, doesn't want to because then he'd be away from his precious Tibbles."

"Tribby," Sara automatically corrected.

"Whatever," Zoe automatically responded. "*Anyway*," she continued, "things have been . . . tense, to say the least."

"Doesn't he have a court order to see Shanice?"

"And?"

"And you don't want to mess with that, Zoe. You could really fuck yourself if you do."

"Whatever," Zoe replied airily, indicating to Sara that she wasn't the least bit worried.

"I'm serious about that, Zoe," Sara insisted to her sister, trying to make her see the gravity of the situation. Before she could say anything else, however, Danita's mother swooped down on her.

"Sara! Sweetie!!! This is *wonderful!* Almost as nice as if I'd done it myself," she simpered, acting like she'd given a compliment, her smile about as sincere as a Siamese cat playing with a hapless mouse.

"Thanks, Mrs. Wingate," Sara said dryly. "No way was I going to let my girl *not* have a baby shower. That would have been just *awful*, wouldn't it?" Sara said, slipping in her own dig.

She saw Zenobia open her mouth to retort, but before she could let her venom drip, she walked off, leaving Sara and Zoe to stare after her. Shrugging their shoulders, both women turned in opposite directions and went in search of new conversations.

Zoe, however, was careful never to be near Tamika. Try as she might, she just couldn't seem to trust herself to say a civil word to the person whom she'd thought was her best friend. This was Danita's day and she didn't want to do anything to ruin it. However, that didn't stop her from seething every time she glanced Tamika's way. What really pissed her off was how cool, calm, and collected Tamika seemed. To Zoe, it was almost as if she were flaunting her affair and subsequent pregnancy in Zoe's face. Not able to take much more without having her head explode, Zoe excused herself before the presents were opened.

Tamika, watching Zoe's ramrod-straight back as Zoe walked through the patio doors into the dim recesses of the country club, fought to keep the tears back that threatened to race down her overly warm cheeks. Tamika was dismayed at how quickly things had deteriorated with Zoe. She was calling, e-mailing, and damn near begging Zoe to talk to her. All to no avail. Zoe was avoiding her like the plague. Not that she could blame her. Turning away from the happy people milling about the sun-drenched terrace, Tamika stared over the greens of the golf course, seeing neither a player's triumphant hole-in-one, nor hearing his shouts of jubilation. She was barely conscious of the low hum of conversation around her. Instead, she was thinking back on her relationship with Vaughn, again questioning if it had all been worth it.

"*Yes!*" she hissed to herself. Never had she felt so much for someone other than herself. And she felt Vaughn had finally admitted to himself that he cared for her as well.

Tamika continued to blindly stare over the course replaying conversations in her head between her and Vaughn, particularly those concerning Vaughn, Zoe, and the kids.

Vaughn swore the only reason he tried to get back together with Zoe was because of Shanice and Jon's constant pestering. At least that was what Vaughn told her once right before plunging deeply and forcefully inside of her ready wetness. At the time, she hadn't cared about anything other than having him fill her to capacity. Over and over again. The odd thing about the entire situation was that up until the time she accidently bumped into him, she'd never had any interest in Vaughn whatsoever. He was her best friend's husband and then ex-husband. End of story.

Tamika probably wouldn't have given him another thought, except one day she ran into Vaughn at the grocery store. He looked so morose that she felt sorry for him. His car had died in the parking lot of the store and she gave him a ride home.

Tamika remembered it was early summer and Vaughn offered to cook for her. They were sitting out on his patio as steaks sizzled on his tiny hibachi balanced precariously on a rickety, rusted three-legged table, while they downed glass after glass of sweet, chilled wine Vaughn bought from somewhere in Bucks County. Some place Theo turned him onto. Tamika, who could drink with the best of them, was surprised by the punch the light, fruity wine delivered. She really felt it when she went to stand up and go into Vaughn's apartment to pee. Surprised, she had flopped back down into her chair, hoping Vaughn hadn't seen her faux pas. Unfortunately, he had. Laughing, he'd asked her, "what, can't handle your liquor?"

"Liquor, I can handle. Wine, I can't," she answered ruefully, laughing at herself. After helping her up, she lurched her way into Vaughn's bathroom. When she finished, all she wanted to do was have a moment to lie down. Stumbling into Vaughn's messy bedroom, she fell face first onto his bed. She didn't recall stripping off her suddenly constricting clothes, nor sighing in relief when she was free of them. Before she knew it, she was softly snoring into his sheets.

She awoke to the soft caress of Vaughn's hands across her aroused nipples. Startled, she looked down and discovered that not only was she on her back, spread eagled, but she was also naked. Scrambling, she pulled the sheet up over her nakedness and away from Vaughn's seeking hands.

"Vaughn! What are you doing?"

"What I thought you wanted. You're in my bed, naked, wet and ready. Don't front. You know you want this."

"No, I don't!" Tamika protested weakly. "I was drunk and wanted to sleep it off. You know Zoe is my best friend and, and, ooooh! Damn, stop that! Uummmm, ummmmmm, oh shit! Damn, that feels, mmmmm, so fuckin' goooooooooood!" Tamika moaned when Vaughn slipped a finger deep inside of her and began to stroke her G spot, forcing her, against her will to move against his insistent finger until she shouted her satisfaction when she climaxed so hard it made tears spring from her eyes. At that point, she was too far gone to care anymore and she only wanted as much satisfaction as she could get. Moving into Tamika mode, she proceeded to show Vaughn her bag of tricks. She showed him all the tricks that would make him moan, groan, and grunt her name over and over again. She was on a mission to prove to him her worth. And prove it, she did. But to her surprise, Vaughn showed his worth as well. After a while, she forgot he was Zoe's ex-husband and only dealt with this sensuous man who could match her position for position.

The dawn found them exhausted, satiated, and asleep, their limbs tangled and numb from their all-night workout.

After that, despite their best efforts, they met again and again, and each time, the sex just kept getting better and better until they were addicted to each other. Then, to their surprise, they discovered they actually *liked* each other and that they could converse and relate to each other outside the bedroom. But the best thing was that Vaughn could make her laugh. Gut-busting, tears-running-down-her-face laughter. No man had ever done that. He also taught her how to laugh at herself and not take herself so seriously. He made her want to learn who *Tamika* was, minus the sexy siren role she played so well for so long.

In return, she gave him the ear Zoe had not; she listened to him talk about his job, his dreams, his aspirations, and goals. She worried every time there was news that a police officer was down or shot. He was a straight up guy and she felt safe when she was with him. She tried to make their times together as stress free as possible, and she was careful never to demand more than she thought he was prepared to give, even when she worried that he and Zoe might actually get back together. It took all of her self-control not to tell Zoe what the real deal was when Zoe went on and on about Vaughn sweating her and trying to get her into bed. It ripped her heart to shreds to think Vaughn was only using her for sex. While her doubts and fears wreaked havoc with her mind, her body betrayed her over and over by always succumbing to his calls.

She remembered when she mentioned the possibility of Vaughn's being with another woman to Zoe and asked her how she would feel about it.

"Gurl, any woman stupid enough to get with Vaughn deserves whatever the hell she gets. Humph! He can't be faithful. And he's a lousy fuck on top of it. Yeah, he looks good, but he just didn't do it for me in the bedroom," Zoe confided.

Tamika thought she was crazy. Shit, Vaughn had shown *her* a few new tricks, and that was saying something. She wondered what the problem was with Zoe.

"Really? I thought things in that department were cool with you and him," Tamika replied, digging softly.

"It was alright, but he was into too much freaky shit for me. I'm not into all that weird stuff. I don't like the back door stuff, and there are just some positions that are too demeaning for me."

"Hhhmmm, I hear you, Gurl. But my policy is, if it feels good, then go for it. Sexual pleasure can come in many forms, and plain old sex is boring to me."

"You always were a freak, Mika. That ain't me. I like plain old ordinary sex. If you know what you're doing, it can be quite stimulating."

"Uh-huh," Tamika answered, glad they were on the phone and Zoe couldn't see her face. Just thinking about her and Vaughn's last time together was enough to make her moist and her cheeks warm. In any event, she'd let the matter drop and never brought it up again.

But now Zoe knew and Tamika was frantic to find a way for them to salvage *their* relationship. She was so confused and conflicted. She wondered how things had gotten so out of control. Her curiosity had bitten her in the ass and she had become entangled in more than she bargained for. But she didn't want her friendship with Zoe to be one of the casualties. It would sadden her greatly if they could no longer be friends. On the other hand she recognized that maybe, just maybe, she had a chance to have something she never thought she could. What was she to do?

Thinking about that, Tamika wrinkled her brow in anger. Hell no, it wasn't fair. How dare Zoe even put her in that position? *But you put yourself in this position,* a small voice in her subconscious whispered. Waving the voice away, Tamika refused to believe she'd done anything wrong.

Tamika decided she'd had enough of the baby shower. After saying her goodbyes to Danita and Sara, and promising to give Shelly a call the following week to talk about her own shower, she left the country club. She was eager to get home and get out of her three inch heels, constricting panties, and bra that was driving her pregnancy-sensitive nipples crazy, and slip into something loose and flowing, or maybe nothing at all. That sounded good, but then she decided against it.

Might as well start getting used to acting like a mom. And moms can't walk around their houses naked with a small child in the house. No sense in scarring the child if I don't have to! Tamika thought to herself. *I'm sure he or she will have enough to tell a therapist without that. I must be out of my mind to think I can be somebody's mother!* Tamika fretted again.

She was so busy thinking about her impending motherhood, Vaughn, and Zoe, that she didn't notice when she zoomed right through a stop sign. That is, until the sudden blaring of a horn to her right and a Ford Expedition bearing down on her snapped her back to the present. Mashing her foot on the gas, she shot forward, the Ford just missing her by inches. However, she over-wheeled her car, hit a soft patch of dirt, and before she knew it she felt her car go into a spin. Fighting for control, she turned her wheel into the spin, righted her car, and then brought it to an abrupt stop, causing her to hit her head on the steering wheel. For a few minutes she rested her head on the top of the wheel, trying to calm her nerves and gather herself. The guy in the Ford blared his horn again as he shot by her, cursing and flipping her the bird.

Tamika ignored him, drawing in a shaky breath. She couldn't believe how close she'd just come to losing her life and that of her unborn child. If she had any lingering doubts about keeping the baby, that near miss made up her mind for her. Pulling herself together, she eased back onto the road and drove cautiously home.

Tamika let out a small sigh of relief when she shut the door to her townhouse behind her. She almost poured herself a glass of white wine to calm her frazzled nerves when she remembered she couldn't drink. She had her cordless in her hand and almost completely dialed Zoe's number when she remembered she couldn't do that either.

Tamika thought about calling Vaughn, but he was supposed to have Shanice and Jonathan this weekend. He promised to break the news to them since it was obvious Zoe had not been so inclined. Chris was still in California visiting his father, and Vaughn planned to tell him when he came home the following week.

Still, Tamika's curiosity was threatening to get the best of her and she had to force herself not to pick up the phone. If he was telling them, she didn't want to be the one to stop his flow. Instead, she took a long hot shower. Feeling refreshed, albeit a little sore, she then made her way back downstairs and fixed herself a light dinner of grilled chicken and a salad. She was finding that eating healthy was a lot easier than she thought it would be, now that she was eating for her and the baby, and not just for herself. She was appalled at her past eating habits. It was a wonder that all the fried and high carb foods she used to eat with abandon hadn't caused her to have a heart attack. But she was pleasantly surprised at how many things she was changing about herself now that she was pregnant.

After she finished her meal and cleaned up her kitchen, she wandered aimlessly around the first floor of her townhouse. She really was going to have to get serious about finding another house. She loved the neighborhood Zoe lived in and even liked where Vaughn lived. She wondered if she and Vaughn would ever live together. That would never happen, she reasoned to herself. Vaughn only recently got that house back. And she would be *damned* if she was going to live in Zoe's old house! Maybe they could both sell their homes and find something really nice outside of Philly. But she was getting ahead of herself. She and Vaughn really needed to have a serious conversation about their relationship and where it was going. It was time for her to stop being afraid of rocking the boat and to start acting like she knew. She needed to know what his intentions were. She knew he was prepared to do for their child, but what about *her*?

CHAPTER TWENTY-SEVEN
You Are My Friend

"Zoe, you can't keep avoiding my phone calls. Come on now, pick up the freakin' phone!" Vaughn said through teeth clenched so tightly his temples were throbbing.

"Fine, be like that. I'll just come to your job . . ."

"Hello? Vaughn, don't you dare!" Zoe hollered, just catching him before he hung up. Or so she thought.

"I thought that might make you pick up," he stated dryly.

"I'm not in the mood for your shit today, Vaughn," Zoe snapped.

"Oh, but I'm supposed to take all of your shit?"

"Just go to hell, Vaughn, you hear?"

"Only if you lead the way, Zoe."

"Fuck you, Vaughn."

"You wouldn't. That was part of the problem, remember?"

"How dare you!"

"I dare. Now are we going to talk about Tamika and me or what?"

"I've got nothing to say. Except if you want to lay down with a common bitch in heat, don't come running to me when you get up full of fleas. Or God knows what else she might have."

"Damn, Zoe. That's cold. I thought she was your best friend."

"So did I, until I found out she was fucking my husband."

"In case you've forgotten, we've been divorced for years, as you constantly reminded me when Antonio was in the picture. How come you suddenly want to think of me as your husband when you find out Tamika wants me, but when your boy-toy was in the picture, you could barely give me the time of day?"

"Don't do that. Don't try to turn this shit on me. I *never* slept with any of *your* friends. Maybe I could have dealt with it better if either of you respected me or my feelings by coming to me and telling me. But you didn't. You, I could see being a sneaky bastard. But Tamika? Uh-uh. She should have said something. She was like another sister. What she did is unforgivable. She violated the Rules."

"The Rules? What rules?"

"Oh don't be such an ass, Vaughn. You know damn well what I mean. The girlfriend rules! They are the same as y'all's: thou shalt not sleep with somebody your friend was involved with. *You know!*"

"Jesus, Zoe. Do you know how stupid that sounds? That's so *high school*. You are always so busy telling everyone else to grow up, why not try it yourself?"

he asked, his voice low and angry. "You are so good at finding fault with everybody and their mama, but you've always refused to look in the mirror and admit you're not the perfect person you think you are!"

"Oh, and this is coming from Mr.-I-Always-Think-With-My-Dick! Negro, please!"

"I'm not doing this anymore, Zoe," Vaughn said, his voice sounding weary and strained. "The fact of the matter is, Tamika is pregnant with my child and you're pissed. I can accept that and I can even understand it. But Shanice is my daughter and she has the right to interact with this baby. Now we can do this the easy way or the hard way. I really don't feel like going back to court, but I will. It's your choice."

"Fuck you, Vaughn," Zoe said, her own voice sounding resigned and tired. She had already come to the same conclusion, but it didn't stop her from being angry.

"Ahhh! She thaws!" Vaughn chortled, realizing that even though she hadn't said it, Zoe had finally given in.

"Now what?" he asked.

"Don't push it, Vaughn. I don't know what. I need time. Be happy that I have accepted your little bastard and that I won't stomp Tamika's bitch ass the next time I see her!"

"Wait. Hold up! First of all, get that phrase 'little bastard' out of your vocabulary. Second, neither of the mothers of my children are bitches. Do we understand each other?"

"Whatever."

"I'm serious, Zoe. I have never let anyone call

you a bitch, even when you may have deserved that title, and I will not let you call Tamika that either. Are we clear?"

"Now wait just one damn minute . . . !" Zoe sputtered.

"*Are we clear?*" Vaughn thundered, taking Zoe aback.

"Yeah, we're clear," Zoe answered. *Damn. When did Vaughn get all those big-ass balls? Shit. Maybe if he'd been more decisive while we were married, we would still BE married,* Zoe thought to herself, seething. *Great. Tamika gets the new and improved Vaughn. Wonderful.*

"Are we done? 'Cause I got shit to do," Zoe snapped, wanting to bring their conversation to an end.

"Yeah, we're done. Just to clarify, I can tell the kids about the baby and Tamika and I don't have to sneak around anymore, right?"

"Whatever," Zoe answered, slamming down the phone before he could say anything further.

Striding over to her mini bar with the wine refrigerator under it, she pulled out a bottle of Niagra that Sara bought her from the Buckingham Winery. If she knew that winery was a favorite of Tamika's and Vaughn's, she probably would have dramatically poured the wine down the drain, no matter how badly she wanted a drink. Instead, she rummaged around her kitchen drawers until she found the fancy-smancy wine opener that Sara insisted she needed, and after a few minutes of trying to figure out how it worked, she gave a small sigh of relief when the soft white grape flavor finally slipped down her throat.

Now what? Zoe asked herself. How was she supposed to resign herself to Vaughn's new bundle of joy? Maybe it would have been an easier pill to swallow if it had been anybody but Tamika. Tamika and Zoe had been friends for so long, Zoe no longer remembered how they met. What she did remember was that after awhile, Tamika was more like a sister than just a friend. They had trashed Vaughn together, Zoe remembered as she drained her wineglass. So knowing as much about Vaughn as she did, how had Tamika allowed herself to become involved with him? It just didn't make any sense.

Filling her glass back up, Zoe sat at her table in front of the patio door gazing unseeing at the deck and yard beyond. How had her life gone so wrong? With all of her heart and soul, Zoe longed to talk to Amanda, the only woman she had ever known as her mother. Once again, she bitterly regretted the petty differences she let fester between them. She wished she had the chance to say she was sorry. But more than anything, she wished she could feel one of Amanda's hugs, just one more time. Comfort and peace could always be found in Amanda's arms.

Maybe it was the wine, but Zoe found tears spilling down her cheeks. She was so tired of the losses, the battles not won, the being alone, and mostly, being lonely. *Wednesday's child is full of woe,* at least in Zoe's case.

Although she knew she was being melodramatic, she felt like her life was destroyed. But hadn't she felt like that when her marriage with Vaughn had disintegrated? She would have gone mad if it hadn't been for . . . damn! She didn't want to let herself admit it, but if it hadn't been for Tamika, she was not sure what she would have done.

When Vaughn first found out about Antonio, it got downright ugly. There was a lot of cussing, a lot of threats, and a lot of court dates. Through it all, Tamika was right there with Zoe, even taking days off from work to be by her side in court for moral support. That was why Tamika's betrayal cut her to the quick.

Zoe drained her glass and poured another. *Damn! This shit's got a kick to it,* she thought when she stood up and swayed a little. "I need a joint to smooth this wine out," she said to herself.

She thought about that for a minute and decided she was too toasted to climb the stairs to her room to retrieve her stash. She decided maybe she needed some food first. Weaving to the refrigerator, she rummaged around inside until she found some sharp cheese, some grapes, and some cold roasted chicken. Next to the refrigerator was her pantry from which she pulled out a box of cheddar cheese crackers. Pulling down one of her new Italian hand-painted plates that was a housewarming gift from Sara, she arranged some grapes and crackers on the plate. Sara was always drumming in her head, "It's the presentation that matters!" She had to admit, sometimes making things look a little fancier did seem to make them taste better.

She was in the process of slicing the extra sharp Vermont cheddar cheese when the knife slipped and she nicked her index finger.

"Ouch! Damnit!" she cried, sticking the injured digit into her mouth and sucking on it. Working in a hospital, she knew better, but it started bleeding so fast, it was her first impulse. She was on the way to the powder room to retrieve her first aid kit when her doorbell rang. Muttering and wincing she snatched open the door and was shocked to find Tamika standing on the other side. So shocked in fact, that she just stood there, until Tamika cried, "Zoe, you're bleeding all over yourself!"

"What? Damn!" Zoe exclaimed when she looked down and saw the blood dripping onto her golden bamboo wood floor. Leaving Tamika at the door, she rushed back to her powder room and turned on the faucet to rinse her injured finger. Once the blood was washed away, she saw that the injury looked worse than it was, and the bleeding had already started to slow. Reaching under her sink, she pulled out her well stocked first aid kit and a bottle of hydrogen peroxide. Working in a hospital did have its benefits. She was struggling to get the bottle open with her uninjured hand when Tamika pushed her hand aside and said, "Here, let me do it." They were silent as Tamika popped open the kit and gestured for Zoe to hold her hand over the sink so she could pour some of the peroxide over the open wound. She ignored Zoe's sharply indrawn breath, let the peroxide bubble and foam, and then poured some more to make sure the wound was properly cleaned.

"It doesn't look too bad. I don't think you need stitches, but I would watch it for a couple of days," Tamika said as she put a bandage on Zoe's finger.

"Yeah. Thanks," Zoe mumbled. Wordlessly, Zoe turned and walked back into her kitchen. Picking up her glass of wine, she drained it in one gulp.

"Want some? Oh wait. You can't drink, can you?" she asked snidely.

Tamika just looked at her and shook her head slightly.

"How could I have forgotten you got a bun in that tired ass oven? It's a wonder it still works. You've sucked almost as many babies out of it as all those dicks you enjoyed sucking off."

Tamika took a step back, Zoe's words stinging like a slap to her face.

"That's enough, Zoe! Look, I didn't come here to be insulted like this," Tamika said while fighting hard not to let Zoe hear the hurt in her voice. She had told Zoe personal, intimate details about herself because she trusted her. She never expected her so called best friend to throw those details back in her face.

"Why did you come, Tamika? Huh? What is the point? It's over. Finished. Done. I have nothing to say to you. Okay? *Nothing!*"

"But I have something to say to you, Zoe. Please hear me out. You at least owe me that much."

"I don't owe your sorry ass a fucking thing, so let's not get it twisted," Zoe spat.

"Yes, you do. You owe me because you were, *are*, no matter what you say, my friend. Yeah, I know you are pissed with me, but deep down, you still love me as much as I still love you. Come on, Zoe. We been through too much shit together to let this come between us."

"But you weren't thinking that when you were boning my husband, were you?" Zoe snarled, not wanting to hear anything Tamika said.

"He's your *ex*-husband, Zoe. Your *ex*. Why do you keep referring to Vaughn as your husband when you couldn't wait to get rid of him? Why do you only want him when you think somebody else does?"

"That's not true! It was a slip of the tongue, pure and simple."

"Yeah right. You have done nothing but revile and ridicule Vaughn ever since your divorce. I did too, 'cause you were my girl. But then I got to know him for myself. The first time we slept together, I was drunk, I'll admit it. And then, me being me, it was about the sex."

"I don't want to hear this," Zoe said, putting her hands over her ears.

"No, you need to hear this," Tamika said, prying Zoe's hands from her ears.

"You better be glad your ass is pregnant. 'Cause if you weren't, you'd be getting a serious beat down right about now."

"While I have no doubt your threat is real, whether you would be able to beat me down is debatable," Tamika told her dryly, causing Zoe to pause. Despite herself, she laughed, until she remembered she was supposed to be mad at Tamika.

"Whatever. I just want you to leave my house."

"And I will. But I want you to be perfectly clear on how I feel about Vaughn. I think I love him, Zoe. I never meant to fall in love with Vaughn, but I do believe that what I'm feeling is for real. The one thing I am absolutely sure about is that whether Vaughn and I stay together, I have fallen madly and completely in love with this baby. I don't know jack shit about having a baby. I was hoping my best friend would be there for me like I was once there for her."

Silence reigned supreme in Zoe's kitchen as the

two women stared at each other. Tamika felt she had said all she could say. Zoe, however, was a mixed cauldron of emotions. The flavor of forgiveness kept fighting to take over while she kept pushing it to the bottom of the pot by heaping more doses of anger and betrayal on top. But instead of the pot boiling over, it seemed to be fizzing out to something that was leaving a stale and flat taste in Zoe's mouth that had nothing to do with the wine she was drinking. The bitter taste of salt from the unshed tears she was trying so hard to swallow were choking the back of her throat. Turning, she waved Tamika away, hoping that she understood it was time for her to go.

Tamika hesitated for a moment then turned to walk away, before turning back around. Rushing back toward Zoe she threw her arms around her. Zoe stiffened for a moment and then the dam broke. Turning around, she and Tamika hugged and swayed together, crying in the middle of Zoe's kitchen.

When the storm finally subsided, they broke awkwardly apart. Tamika noticed that Zoe was swaying slightly and when she looked at her, she saw how exhausted Zoe was.

"You need to sit down. When is the last time you ate?"

"I'm fine. I don't remember. Yesterday, I think."

"Yesterday? Where are the kids?"

"They went to the shore with Sara and Theo. Well, Shanice and Jonathan did. Chris went out to California to visit his father."

"And how much of that wine have you had?"

"Dunno. Maybe a bottle or two or three . . ."

"You need some coffee. And something to eat."

"I'm fine, Tamika. Look, just 'cause I didn't throw you out on your ass and just 'cause we had a little cry-fest doesn't mean it's all happiness and sunshine, you know," Zoe told her, her words sounding slightly slurred.

"I know," Tamika said, fighting the urge to laugh, as she pulled out a half loaf of wheat bread and sliced the cold roasted chicken and cheese Zoe had taken out earlier with some tomatoes and lettuce. Pushing some jars around, she pulled out some Hellman's. Filling the coffee pot with water, she poured it into the Brewmaster and carefully measured out the aromatic coffee. She then proceeded to make the sandwiches after the bread popped up from the toaster.

Zoe watched Tamika move around her kitchen as she pulled out plates and mugs and silverware and she said nothing. She was too emotionally drained and just plain tired.

When Tamika placed the thick sandwich in front of Zoe, with the bunches of grapes around the plate for garnish, along with the steaming mug of coffee, she was surprised when her mouth watered and her stomach growled.

"How's your finger?"

"It hurts. But it's okay. Thanks."

"You're welcome."

They ate in silence for a few minutes, not sure what to say. Zoe hated to admit it, but it was just what the doctor ordered. Even her hand felt like it had stopped throbbing as much.

"Do you remember that time I was having my twenty-fifth birthday?" Tamika asked suddenly.

"Oh, Lawd! Do I! Everything that could go wrong did!"

"You were supposed to bring the food and the DJ and you went to the wrong place."

"And idiots that they were, they let me in and I set up everything. And then all these people came and started getting their grub on and their drink on and proceeded to party like nobody's business. And I'm wondering who all these people are and where the hell were you," Zoe said, chuckling.

"Yeah, this was before everybody and their mama had a cell phone. And I'm at the right place with no food, no DJ and no liquor. There were some hot niggahs up in that piece that night!"

"Thank goodness I went home to check my answering machine. But damn, did you curse me out when I finally got there!"

"You had it coming, too! Thank God for that guy I was dealing with back then. He must have spent a fortune buying all that KFC and running over to Jersey to get the liquor."

After that, they went from one "hey, do you remember" story to another until the early hours of the next day. Some time during the night Sara called with the news that Danita had given birth to a healthy baby girl. When Zoe told her sheepishly that Tamika was there, Sara was surprised for a moment and then she just said, "Good!" Tamika and Zoe celebrated the arrival of Danita's baby with a click of their coffee mugs.

The early morning sun was just breaking over the horizon when Zoe let Tamika out. Zoe leaned back against the door, a look of contemplation on her face. She wasn't sure if she would ever be able to completely forgive Tamika, but there was hope.

CHAPTER TWENTY-EIGHT
New Beginnings

"*I* want to thank you for coming to court with me today, Zoe. I couldn't have done it without you," Antonio said, beaming as they walked down the steps of the family court building at 1801 Vine Street, the building known to Philadelphians as just 1801. Everybody knew that was where you went for domestic disputes.

"I didn't do anything, Antonio. I was just here for moral support."

"Yeah, well, you helped me get a decent lawyer."

"Actually, that was Sara's old boss. He knows everybody."

"I don't think I would have stood a chance if it hadn't been for Jerry. Thank goodness I had somebody like him in my corner."

"Now what?

"What do you mean?"

"Are you sure this is what you want to do? I mean, it's a lot of responsibility. You've only had them for sporadic weekends. Dealing with kids on a daily basis is no one's picnic. How are you going to deal with four?"

"Well now that I've finally won custody, I was hoping maybe you would be there to help me."

Zoe didn't answer him. Instead, she watched as his kids ran around people who were exiting the large, impressive building. Antonio seemed oblivious to the children running around like wild Indians, whooping and screaming and prompting people to shake their heads and step lightly to the side in order to avoid being trampled. He didn't even turn around to tell them to come with him as they walked toward the parking lot. It took all of her self control to keep her lips pressed together as she watched them. She would never have allowed her children to behave like that in public. Like she and her sisters were taught by Amanda, she had taught her children public decorum. They were nice enough kids, but they were in serious need of a firm hand to teach them and control them.

As she kept glancing at them, it was like they were totally unaware that their lives had completely changed a few minutes earlier. Maybe they didn't understand that they would no longer live with their mother. Or maybe they did. Maybe that was why they were running and playing with such unbridled glee. Zoe didn't know how Antonio was going to deal with it all.

They were undisciplined, underdeveloped, and educationally challenged. And they had almost no home training. She had seen that enough for herself. Antonio was constantly telling them to flush the toilet and wash their hands when they got done going to the bathroom. They had to be shown over and over again how to make a bed and Antonio couldn't just tell them to take a bath or shower. He learned the hard way that they would just run the water and pretend to wash. He had taken to washing each of them, even the oldest, until they finally got the picture that he meant business about them being clean.

Finally, Zoe couldn't take it anymore, and said to Antonio, "Aren't you going to call them? Look at them. They're running all over the place, not caring who they bump into or almost knock down. Oh my God! Did you see that? They almost pushed that lady down!" Zoe exclaimed, watching horrified as an elderly lady tottered precariously on a step before regaining her balance.

"Yo! Y'all get over here before I tear your little behinds up!"

"Are those little heathens yours?" the lady called to Antonio.

"Yes, Ma'am. I apologize for their behavior."

"Apologize my ass. You need to teach the little bastards some manners!" With that she turned and stomped the rest of the way up the steps, grumbling about ignorant-ass people and their ignorant-ass kids.

After Antonio rounded up his children, they all proceeded to the parking lot at 18th and Market Streets. They walked in silence for a few moments, watching the children running and laughing in front of them.

"So, you never answered my question. Can I count on you?"

"I don't know, Antonio. We'll have to see. I hope you didn't do all of this just to get me back. If so, you are doing it for all the wrong reasons."

"No, I'm not just doing it for that. I'm doing it because I could no longer stand by and watch what that woman was doing to my children. I couldn't look myself in the mirror if I continued to let them live in those squalid conditions. You saw her house. Hell, you saw her. You know she's just a triflin'-ass junkie who cares more about herself, gettin' high, and the next party than she does about whether those kids are clothed, fed, and educated."

"Ssshhh! Whatever you do, don't ever let your children hear you talk about their mother like that. Right or wrong, that is still their mother, and kids, especially boys, are mighty funny about their mothers."

"But I don't believe in hiding the truth from them."

"Maybe. But let them draw their own conclusions. They will learn as they grow up. Better they figure it out for themselves. It will hurt, true, but at least they won't be able to say that you turned them against their mother."

"And does that advice apply to you as well, Zoe?" he asked her quietly.

"I don't know what you mean," Zoe said, looking away.

"What will you tell Shanice about her father and his new baby? More importantly, how will you tell her? As you say, it is in the telling."

"Touche´," was all she said quietly, but she refused to answer his question.

Realizing that it was futile to push her any further, Antonio sighed.

"Hey, how is Ms. Vivian doing?" Zoe suddenly asked.

"She's hanging in there. She finished her

chemotherapy, and it wore her out. She's moving in with my mother because she can no longer care for herself," he told her sadly, remembering the robust, smiling woman his grandmother used to be.

"I can't believe Ms. Vivian has cancer. I am so sorry to hear that."

"She told me to tell you to visit her sometime. You know how much she likes you."

"Yes, she does. And I like her. Your mother, however, is another story altogether. And you know I'm not too keen on her, or your sisters, for that matter. They knew about those kids and thought it was funny as hell that they knew and I didn't."

"That's not true. They felt it was up to me to tell you about them. But I don't want to get into that particular argument again. Please?"

"Whatever. You know you were wrong for that, though," Zoe said, needing to have the last word.

Antonio looked away. He learned a long time ago that it was useless to argue with Zoe. She wasn't one to let things go. She *said* she did, but she didn't really.

They reached the parking lot and found they were on opposite sides of the lot.

"Sooo," Zoe said.

"Sooo," Antonio said. They both laughed a little nervous laugh.

"Can you come over for a while?" Antonio asked deep and low, his bass voice plucking that chord within Zoe.

"I can't, Antonio. I, ah, I have things to do."

"Please? Once I get the kids settled, I think we have some things to talk about."

"I can't, Antonio. I'm not ready for this. I didn't

mind helping you get custody of your kids, but us? Naw. I'm just not ready to deal with it."

"Why, Zoe? What can I do to get you back? Don't you still love me?"

"Whether I do or not is not the issue, Antonio. I can't trust you. You lied to me. You know how I feel about liars."

"I thought we were past all that."

"So did I, but I guess I'm not," Zoe told him sadly. She missed Antonio. She really did. But at this point she was sick of men using and abusing her love and trust.

"Look, I don't think this is the time, nor the place, for this discussion," Zoe continued, nodding her head toward his jeep where his children were becoming increasingly impatient and rowdy.

"I know. That's why I'm begging you to please come by my house. We really need to talk, baby."

Looking at his expectant face, she noted he was giving her the dreaded puppy dog eyes. Zoe heaved a huge sigh and reluctantly agreed to meet him later.

She had the day off and wasn't sure what to do with herself. When she reached her car, instead of turning it toward home, she went farther into the downtown area. After finding a parking garage on Locust Street, she walked up to the Barnes and Noble on Walnut Street across from Rittenhouse Square.

Picking up about ten new books by some African American writers, she stopped at Bleu, a restaurant overlooking Rittenhouse Park, and enjoyed a leisurely lunch by the window while she perused her new books. They all sounded so good, she didn't know which one to start first.

She was enjoying a delicious creme brulee and still checking out her books when she felt a soft touch on her shoulder.

Jumping slightly, she looked up into the startlingly blue eyes of David Culvert, the agent who found her house for her.

"David! What a pleasant surprise. What are you doing here?"

"I had a meeting with an insufferable client. Thank goodness she's leaving," he said nodding toward where a very statuesque brunette was sweeping out the door looking like a Jackie O. wannabe. Whipping out a pair of black framed sunglasses, and slapping them on her face, she stepped to the curb to hail a cab. As she stepped into the cab, Zoe noted that she looked vaguely familiar.

"She's very beautiful from what I could see. Is she a model?"

"Yes. And if I ever take on another one as a client, may lightening strike me where I stand!" he said dramatically, one hand over his heart and the other raised toward Heaven.

Laughing, Zoe said, "Is it that bad?"

"Worse! But enough about the ice princess. What brings you all the way downtown?"

"I was helping a friend out earlier and decided to treat myself to a leisurely lunch. And some books."

"I see," David responded, picking up various titles and actually seeming to read the back synopses.

"Wow, some of these sound really good. Maybe you'll let me borrow them when you're finished?"

"How about you support the authors and buy the books for yourself?" Zoe countered.

"Touche´. Maybe I will. Will you help me pick them out? I've been hearing a lot about this Zane person," he said, skimming the back of *Nervous*. "I hear her stuff is really hot. And this book, *Ride or Die*, by Solomon Jones. He's from Philly, right?"

"Oh yeah. He's awesome. And if you like something different, you have to get *The Minion*, *The Awakening*, and this one, *The Hunted* by L.A. Banks, who is really Leslie Esdaile, and she's from Philly too. Now Zane is not somebody you want to read alone. You might want to make sure you have your little black book handy when you read her!"

"I'll keep that in mind," David said before directing his megawatt smile at Zoe.

Damn! Zoe thought to herself. Talk about one fine-ass white man. Zoe had never been into white men, even though quite a few made passes at her. She always figured it was her very light skin and gray eyes. But she noticed that David had a very self assured air that she liked. Not to mention his height, his build, and his almost too beautiful blue eyes and blond hair, which complimented his slightly tanned skin. *Brad Pitt doesn't have a thing on this man*, Zoe thought to herself, and Brad was one of her all time favorites.

"Mind if I join you for a cup of coffee?" he asked, waiting for Zoe's response.

"Not at all," Zoe responded enthusiastically, thoughts of Antonio slipping from her mind.

Soon coffee was replaced with glasses of wine and then appetizers appeared, followed by dinner. After scrumptious desserts, David insisted on picking up the bill. Since it was a beautiful, balmy spring evening, they decided to stroll around Rittenhouse Park. Neither thought much about it as David grabbed her hand and they proceeded to walk everywhere holding hands. Other mixed couples looked at them and smiled. Those who weren't, smiled anyway at how animated Zoe and David appeared to be. To the outside eye, they made a striking couple.

David offered to see her home, but Zoe insisted she was fine. She hadn't had *that* many glasses of wine that she couldn't drive. She couldn't wait to get home to have a couple of hits on a "tree" as she and Antonio used to call them.

"Shit! Antonio!" she muttered under her breath as she turned the key in the ignition. She completely forgot that she was supposed to meet Antonio at his house. Turning her cell phone back on, she noted that he had called her five times.

"Damn!" Zoe cursed out loud. She debated for a moment as to whether she should call him back or not. If she was honest with herself, she really didn't feel like being bothered. She just had fun with David. David was also single, never married, no kids, no baggage. He was looking better by the minute. He was established, had his own house, his own business, and was damned successful at it. Hell, he probably even had good credit!

Damn, Zoe, why'd you have to go there? Zoe thought to herself. The one thing Antonio didn't have to worry about was credit. Not with the kind of money he made as an ironworker. Still, Antonio did have his issues, and that's why Zoe went there—issues she didn't necessarily feel like dealing with. Issues like four damn kids. Issues like baby mama drama. Issues like not having enough private time for her now because he had all those kids. And Zoe didn't even want to think about the problems associated with those kids. They had no home training to speak of. Antonio felt so guilty about how they had been living that he just let them run all over him. Zoe could already see they were developing bad habits which would take years to break.

With all these thoughts swirling through her head Zoe dialed Antonio's number. When he finally answered, she listened to him rant and rave and after he finally started to wind down she asked, "Are you finished? You sure? Good. We need to talk."

CHAPTER TWENTY-NINE

Exhaling

       Jamika hummed a little song to herself as she moved around her home, watering her plants. She smiled a soft smile as she looked down at her round stomach and rubbed her protrusion as she had done so many times over the last few months. Things had finally settled down, and while Zoe hadn't completely forgiven her, at least they were speaking. All in all, things had worked out even better than Tamika could have hoped. This seemed to be the time for new beginnings. A new baby, a new home, a whole new life. She had done it. She'd actually pulled it off.

    She strolled upstairs to retrieve some papers she was working on the night before for a video conference the next day. It was a quiet, soft June evening and she had just finished another day of work. Her commute was about as short as it could get since she had stepped out on faith and started her own insurance brokerage firm from her new home office. Her clients came mainly from the Internet, and she would place them with insurance companies that matched their particular needs. She was in the process of training an assistant to take over for her when she first came home with the baby. If the trainee, Aslynn, worked out, maybe Tamika would make her a permanent assistant. She really liked Aslynn, who was Danita's youngest sister. Seeing Danita's happiness over her new baby was making Tamika eager for her own. It seemed that babies had the effect of smoothing relationships over. It looked like it was working for Danita and her mother. Tamika hoped it would do the same for her.

Her doctor's appointment was in the early afternoon and Tamika was relieved when the doctor assured her that all was well with her health and that of the baby's. Before she went into her sumptuous lavender and green plaid bathroom, she couldn't resist taking another look at her baby's nursery.

She had to admit, Sara had done her thing. She wasn't sure at first whether she should even ask for Sara's help considering she was Zoe's sister. And there was the fact that Sara lost her own baby several years ago. She could tell that Sara hadn't really wanted to take the decorating job, but Tamika offered her so much money, it made it damn near impossible for Sara to turn her down.

Looking around, Tamika felt herself becoming more relaxed in the room's atmosphere. All of the furnishings were done in antique white. The walls were done with murals painted all around the room, showing woodland themes with Disney-type animals that seemed to gambol and play from scene to scene. The window valance, crib skirt, and glider material were all pale yellow and white stripes with white baby rabbits on them. The crib sheets and comforter were pale blue like the ceiling above. Sara cleverly painted the ceiling so that it looked like lazy clouds were drifting across its surface. The floor was a gleaming yellow pine covered with a large, sumptuous area rug with soft green, blue, yellow, and cream blocks. Two bookshelves, filled with every child's and baby's book imaginable, flanked the large window.

Sara had taken a page from her own book, and like she had done with her own baby's nursery, she filled this room with lots of stuffed animals, many from the pages of the books placed in the bookshelves. Velvet rabbits, woolly sheep, and soft, squeezable spotted cows resided right along with friendly lions, fat, cuddly bears, and inquisitive cats. It was a room any child would love to live in. This room would definitely inspire countless hours of imagination.

Tamika gave the mobile over the crib a few turns and let the melody of "Twinkle, Twinkle, Little Star" fill the quiet room. She was just settling into the gliding rocker when the ringing of her cell phone interrupted her quiet musings.

"Hey, baby," a deep voice purred on the other end of the line.

"Hey yourself," Tamika answered, all her nerve endings suddenly becoming aware.

"How's it going?"

"Okay, I guess. I was just admiring the baby's room again."

"Sara did a nice job. She's got mad skills."

"Yeah, she does. I'd been hearing how good she was, but I didn't know she was *that* good. The finished job certainly exceeded all my expectations."

"And how is my baby today?"

"Which one?" Tamika asked.

Laughing he said, "Both. But I was really asking about the bambino."

"Oh, she's fine."

"You mean *he* don't you?"

"I guess we'll just have to wait and see, won't we?"

"I guess," he answered. There were a few minutes of silence on the phone before he asked, "You home by yourself?"

"Yes. Why?" Imagining that she could almost see him shrug before he said, "I thought I'd swing by for a few."

"I hope longer than a few."

"If you want."

"I do. Come on. Only you have to promise not to tease me for being so fat."

"You're not fat. You're carrying my baby. I think you are voluptuously beautiful and I can't wait to be in you."

Tamika's breath caught in her throat. His words made her instantly moist and throbbing. She found her libido had elevated significantly since she became pregnant. Any little thing set her off. Maybe it was the luxury of not having a period. Maybe it was her elevated hormone levels. She didn't know. All she knew was that whatever it was, she was far worse now than she had ever been before. But she was in a committed relationship with Vaughn. Only problem was, with his hours, when she was home at night, he was at work.

Tonight, however, it seemed things were most definitely looking up.

"Really, Baby? How far away are you?"

"Not far, almost around the corner. Meet me at the door. Naked."

"Naked? Are you crazy? I look too fat to come to the door like that!" Tamika told him before dissolving into laughter.

"Ah come on, baby. For me," he coaxed in the low deep voice he knew got to her.

"I'll see what I can do," Tamika told him, breathless. He wasn't even there yet and she could already feel his lips on her body.

"How far away are you?"

"Three minutes tops."

"See you in a few," she told him before hanging up.

She crossed the hall and walked as fast as her added girth would allow back into her bedroom. Standing in front of her spacious walk-in closet, she lightly ran her hands over her many negligees. For some odd reason she remembered that Blanche from *Golden Girls* used to have an impressive amount of negligees. Looking at her collection, she thought Blanche would have been green with envy.

She finally chose a sheer black robe shot with copper threads that complimented her skin. She decided not to put on the gown with the plunging neckline and split up the right thigh. Slipping out of her clothes, she pulled on the gossamer robe, sprayed her favorite perfume, Jean Paul Gautlier, in front of her and then quickly walked through the perfumed cloud. Going back downstairs she turned the lights down low and loaded up the CD player with her favorite mix of slow jams that played over the whole-house system. Perfect.

Tamika was trying hard to tamp down her excitement. It had been a while since she saw her baby's father. Things were hectic lately, with his schedule and her job. She was beside herself. She couldn't wait to have him in her arms, in her bed, inside of *her*, again.

Instead of using the key she gave him, he rang the doorbell. Killing the lights in the living room, she slowly opened the door and surreptitiously looked around, noting that the street appeared empty and all of her neighbors were safely tucked in the backs of their houses, kitchens, or family rooms.

Throwing her head back, she let her long, enhanced tresses softly caress the gossamer material covering her still thin, curvaceous back, while allowing the edges of the robe she was loosely holding to slip out of her fingers. It didn't take much to make the edges part. Her belly certainly took care of that. Like Demi Moore, Tamika was actually proud of her obvious badge of impending motherhood. She had come to terms with her pregnancy, and for someone who had long claimed she never wanted a child, she was eagerly anticipating its arrival. She even opted to go the old fashioned route and wait until her baby's birth to be surprised as to whether it was a boy or girl. But she was secretly hoping for a girl.

All thoughts of the baby, however, were quickly swept out of her mind when she was pulled into a strong, but careful, embrace and then engulfed by a soul-stirring, heart-racing kiss that damn near made her toes curl. They didn't have time for words as he walked her back into the house, their lips still locked while he impatiently pushed her robe off her now heated flesh.

"Wait!" Tamika said, trying to slow it down. "Don't you want a drink or something to eat?"

"Later. Right now, all I want is you. Come here, woman!"

Tamika giggled at his attempt to be macho, but it did turn her on a little more.

Before she could suggest they go to the family room because she felt that there was no way in hell she could navigate the stairs and look sexy, he swept her up in his strong arms and carried her up the steps. Tamika was mortified. She felt like she must have weighed a ton, when in actuality she was only about twenty-five pounds heavier than before her pregnancy. She was, as the old ladies say, "all baby."

In the blink of an eye, she felt the warmth of his skin next to her as he pressed the front of his body along the back of hers. Gently turning her over onto her back, he turned her head toward him and once again drugged her with kisses as his soft lips caressed her own. Soon Tamika was drawing his tongue deeply into her mouth, suddenly famished for the taste and texture of him. She cried out when he pulled his lips from her and began kissing her all over her face, neck, and shoulders before dipping down to draw one of her swollen, distended, ultra sensitive nipples into his warm, moist mouth. Tamika almost strangled on her in-drawn breath and then found all she could do was pant as wave after delicious wave of pleasure spread from her nipples throughout her now gyrating body. Tamika was loving how he paid such wonderful homage to her twins until she found herself becoming impatient and pushed his head lower. Laughing soft and low, he obliged her, but proceeded to torture her with his slow and leisurely path to where she really wanted him to be.

Finally, after teasing her to the point of distraction, he slipped between her trembling thighs, the insides of which were already slick from what his fingers forced from her body. Tamika was almost embarrassed by how wet she, and the sheet below her rounded bottom, were. The man had barely started and she had already cum an ocean! She nearly caused him physical harm when his mouth finally made contact with her swollen bud. Holding her as still as he could, he proceeded to bring her to climax after climax as he adored her with his lips, his tongue, and his mouth.

And just when Tamika thought she could stand it no more, he stopped and gently motioned for her to turn over and get up on her hands and knees, taking her doggie style. When he slid into her she shoved the pillow into her mouth to muffle the scream of pleasure that ripped through her. Tamika could tell that he was holding back, afraid that he would hurt her or the baby. Still, that didn't stop her from pushing back on his hardness or twisting her hips to make him lose his hard-won control.

Soon, however, neither thought about anything as pure physical need took over. They moaned and groaned and stroked each other until Tamika felt that something bigger than herself was slowly infusing her body. A pleasure so intense, slowly, and then with increasing speed, swept over her body. And at the moment she felt herself sliding into the most incredible climax she had ever experienced, she felt him stiffen even more inside of her as he cried out her name. She felt a love so intense, so overwhelming, all she could do was cry out as the tears streamed down her flushed cheeks, "Oh God! Oh, God! I love you so much, Vaughn!"

CHAPTER THIRTY

A Brighter Day

"*H*ey, Sis, what's up?" Sara asked, surprised to hear from Zoe.

"Girl, I finally did it. I didn't think I could, well I did, but I knew it was going to be kind of hard, even though I couldn't help but realize it was the only logical thing to do. And it was hard, but I finally did it," Zoe said dramatically, sounding all mysterious.

"If you don't stop playing with me and just tell me what you did, I swear I'm going to come over there and slap the mess out of you," Sara mocked-threatened.

"Well if you would wait a minute, I'd tell you. Dag, so impatient!" Zoe said, laughing because she knew she was further infuriating her sister.

"What the fuck are you talking about, Zoe? This guessing shit is getting on my damn nerves. If you don't tell me, I'm hanging up," Sara told Zoe, starting to get more than a little pissed off. After all, Zoe had called her, not the other way around.

"Okay, okay. Remember I told you that I was helping Antonio get custody of his kids?"

"Yeah, there was a court hearing or something the other day, wasn't there?"

"Yes, and he won. Which is nice for him, but puts a different spin on him and me."

"Why is that?"

"Don't get me wrong. They are nice kids, when they aren't acting like wild animals. But that's just it, they are *kids.*"

"I don't get it. You have kids, he has kids. What's the big deal?"

"Most of his kids are younger than Shanice and therein lies the problem."

"Still no comprende, Sis."

"Okay, let me break it down to you. Chris is getting ready for his last year in high school, Jonathan is almost in high school and Shanice is in middle school. I'm on countdown. My kids are big enough to be damn near self sufficient if they have to be. Oh, they still need discipline and guidance, but it's not like I have to bathe them. And when they're hungry, they can just pop something in the microwave. Not so with Antonio's kids. And I am not kidding when I say these kids have no home training at all, Sara. I mean, I know it's not their fault, having a mother like Miami."

"You mean Niambi," Sara interjected.

"Whatever," Zoe said, dismissing the correction before continuing, "He's got his hands full and I just don't think I'm the one to help him take up the slack."

"Soooo, what did you tell him?"

"I told him I couldn't do it," Zoe said quietly, sighing deeply.

"Whaaaaat? For real?" Sara exclaimed, practically squeaking, her voice rose so many octaves. Clearing her throat, she continued, "So what does this mean? Is this it?"

Zoe sighed deeply again, a catch in her own throat. She hadn't stopped to think about it. She hadn't really stopped long enough to allow herself to think about anything since her conversation with Antonio.

After she left from downtown she started to go to Antonio's house when she realized that she had drank too many glasses of wine. She called Antonio back and promised to meet with him the next day instead. She wasn't sure what she wanted to say to him, but she knew she wanted a clear head when she said it.

Thinking back, Zoe winced when she remembered the scene at Antonio's house. If things were different, she was sure she would have joyfully taken Antonio back. But she just could not deal with his children. She hoped they could at least remain friends.

All of these thoughts skipped around Zoe's mind as she reluctantly mounted the steps to Antonio's house. What used to be a welcoming facade suddenly turned cold and foreboding in her mind as she made her way to the front door.

Zoe shivered slightly in the heat as she waited for Antonio to answer the staccato ring of the doorbell. Her stomach was twisted in knots and she felt positively ill. Zoe was digging around the bottom of her handbag as she waited on the stoop for Antonio to come to the door, frantically looking for the roll of antacids she was sure was in there somewhere.

"Digging for gold?" Antonio asked, amusement dancing behind his words.

"Damnit to hell, Antonio, you scared the mess out of me!" Zoe snapped. Seeing the look on his face, she tried to soften her tone. "I'm sorry. I was looking for some antacids because my stomach seems to be acting up again."

"That's not good. What's the matter, Zoe? If memory serves me, your stomach usually only bothers you when you are worked up about something or worried about something. Which is it?"

"Nothing," Zoe mumbled, avoiding his eyes as she eased past him into his house. Still, she couldn't stop the errant thought, *Damn he looks good*, as she walked by him. Just looking at Antonio was enough to make a sensible woman want to do wrong. It, *he*, was oh so tempting. Maybe she needed to rethink her position.

When she came in, the first thing that struck her was how quiet it was.

"Where are the kids?" she asked, curious.

"My mom and my sisters came and got them to take them shopping."

"Oh. I noticed how quiet it was in here."

"Yeah. That's one of things it's been hard for me to get used to. The noise. I never had to deal with that before."

"Mmmm," was all Zoe said.

She was thinking that she never dealt with it either. Maybe because she only had three children as opposed to four, but it seemed to make a hell of a difference. Or maybe it was because all she had to do was give her children a look and the decibel level would drop considerably. Her children knew better. Antonio's, on the other hand, didn't have a clue. They freely "expressed" themselves. Quite vocally. Much more than Zoe could deal with. More than she *wanted* to deal with. Talk about BeBe's kids. Antonio's kids would give BeBe a run for her money. Zoe felt bad, but on a few occasions she felt like she was looking at criminals in the making. She just knew that if Antonio didn't start to get a grip on them, some of them could possibly end up in juvenile court or worse. And she just could not invest that kind of time or emotion into a losing battle.

Of course, thinking all of those things was a lot easier than actually saying them. Who wants to tell someone that she can't deal with your children?

"Come on in the kitchen. I thought you might want something to eat, so I was making some of my famous beef stew."

"I thought I smelled something good. But I don't know if my stomach can take that right now. I will come in and keep you company, though," Zoe told him as she cleared her throat.

"What's going on with Ms. Viv's house? I know it must be hard to go in there. It's like when I go to visit my dad. I hate walking into that house. It just doesn't feel right, knowing Mom won't be sitting in her favorite chair in the kitchen. Or that there won't be something delicious smelling cooking on the stove or in the oven, you know?"

"Yeah, I do know. My mother and I are slowly cleaning the house out so it can be sold. Gran signed it over to my mom so she could handle everything unencumbered. She's hanging in there, but her treatments are hard on her. They just drain her, but she's trying to stay upbeat. You know what she always says," and they said it in unison, "If God brings you to it, He'll bring you through it!"

Both chuckled and let thoughts of his grandmother drift through their minds. Zoe didn't want to, but suddenly she was flooded with thoughts of Amanda. She felt a physical ache from missing her so much. She felt bad because she hadn't spoken to her father in a while, whereas right after Amanda's death she spoke to him no less than twice a week. Now she let inconsequential things get in the way of that. Her children and sisters were here in the Philly area, whereas her father was in, as Sara would say, small-ass Athens, Pennsylvania, all by himself. All he had were a few friends. Loyal friends were great, but still, they weren't family.

"Zoe, are you okay? Why are you crying?" Antonio asked, alarmed at the tears he saw running unchecked down Zoe's cheeks.

"Crying?" Zoe asked, touching her cheek and looking with surprise at the moisture on her fingers.

"I didn't realize that I was. I was thinking about my mother and how much I miss her. And my dad. I haven't talked to him in a while. I've let other things get in the way. We were starting to build something, finally. Sara too. I haven't been close with my little sister in a long time. And neither one of us were close with our dad, but for a while we were getting pretty close. I don't want to lose that. Which brings me to us," she told him, holding his hesitant brown eyes with her suddenly clear gray ones.

"I've thought long and hard about us, Antonio. While I will always have a place for you in my heart, I can't go back, even if your ass is fine as hell."

"It's because of my kids, isn't it?" he asked, ignoring her compliment.

"Partly," she said succinctly.

"What's the rest? I think I have a right to know."

"Do you, now? I guess that's a matter of opinion. But you know why, Antonio. You lied to me. How do I know that you're not hiding something else from me? I don't think my heart could take being ripped out like that again. No, this is just a matter of self preservation. As for your kids, while they are nice enough, they need a lot of work. And I am sure your mother and I would be clashing all the way. It's an aggravation I don't need in my life right now. I've got enough going on with my own kids. I can't deal with anyone else's."

"You are using my kids as a shield, a weapon to keep us apart, Zoe, and I think that you're full of shit!"

Zoe blinked at his vehemence. This was an Antonio she didn't know.

"Excuse me?"

"You heard me. I thought I was dealing with a real woman, a woman who would make a hellified mother. But instead, I see you are the shallow, selfish bitch my mother always said you were."

"Ah hell naw!" Zoe shouted, jumping up from the table. "You and your ignorant-ass mother can just kiss my natural black ass, Antonio! How dare you come at my neck like that? I was hoping we could remain friends, but I see that we can forget that noise. Oh yeah, fuck you!" Zoe shouted as she snatched up her purse and made her way to the front door.

But Antonio was faster than she anticipated. Before she could snatch open the front door, he reached over her and held it closed.

"What are you going to do, Antonio? Huh? So you're bigger and stronger than me, now what?" Zoe asked derisively, looking up at him mockingly. She expected to see him puffed up with rage. Instead what she saw was a look of sorrow and regret.

"I'm not going to stop you from leaving, Zoe. I . . . I'm . . . I just wanted to say I was sorry for saying those things. I don't know what came over me. I didn't mean it. Please forgive me, baby. You know how much I love you, right?"

"I don't know shit. All I do know is that I think I made the right decision and that I want to go. Good luck, Antonio. With those kids, believe me, you're going to need it. Oh, and I meant it when I said to tell your mother to kiss my ass!" Zoe's gray eyes were icy shards as she waited for him to drop his arm and get out of her way.

Antonio looked down into Zoe's tight, closed-off face. He'd blown it. He finally got it. It was over for him and Zoe. Zoe used to tell him that she was not a very forgiving person. He wondered how he forgot that. Even with everything he had done, he thought Zoe would always be there for him. And she probably would have been had he not acted like a complete idiot. His mother always told him his temper would get the best of him. How was he supposed to deal with his kids without Zoe? *Stupid, stupid, STUPID*, he thought now.

Dropping his arm, he allowed Zoe to leave. He watched her stiff back as she marched to her car. She looked back once, and for a moment he thought her face softened. He started to run out to her car, but then he saw her flip him the bird. *Wow, she really was pissed with me,* he thought. No matter. He had a few other things up his sleeve. All was not lost. He would find a way to win her back. He just *had* to!

Zoe knew none of the thoughts that were going through Antonio's mind as he watched her leave. She expected to feel remorse, sadness, grief, *something*. She was astounded to realize she felt nothing. Maybe a slight regret, but she understood that whatever it was she felt for Antonio, it was gone.

She was free. It was over with Vaughn and it was over with Antonio. As far as Vaughn was concerned, they would forever be tied because of Shanice. More importantly, she had finally made peace with the fact that he was the father of her best friend's baby. It still stuck in her craw, but overall she was making herself accept it. Until all of this, she had loved Tamika like a sister. Zoe didn't know if they would ever have the same type of relationship, but she hoped they could at least be civil. It wasn't likely, but she could hope.

So, this is it. Wow. The two men who have influenced my life the most are gone. Now what? Zoe asked herself. Where was she supposed to go from here? Maybe she needed to finally live her life without a man. What a novel idea.

Zoe thought one last time about Ms. Vivian and said a silent prayer for her. Ms. Viv reminded her of Amanda. Finally, fully, Zoe knew, appreciated and understood that Amanda always was her mother. Zoe never knew her own mother. She had died when Zoe was only three. Amanda was the one who was always there. Good, bad, right, or wrong, Amanda was her mother. Zoe loved and missed her with all her heart. But Amanda had raised strong, independent women, so very different from what Amanda herself had been. Their independence was Amanda's legacy. Zoe felt a tear slip down her cheek.

"Thanks, Ma," she said out loud.

Before she could pull off her cell phone rang. She almost ignored it, thinking it might be Antonio calling to beg her to come back in the house. Squinting at the tiny screen, Zoe was surprised at the number displayed.

"David! What a nice surprise. I was just thinking about you. . ."

Zoe started her car, looked up through the windshield, winked, and drove into her future, confident that yes, there was a brighter day ahead.

About the Author

Gayle Jackson Sloan is a native of Philadelphia, but has lived in Akron, Ohio, Pittsburgh, and Washington, DC. Gayle has loved to read and write since she was four years old. Growing up, she used to write volumes and volumes of poetry that was inspired by the syncopated rhythms of Maya Angelo and the freestyle of Nikki Giovanni. Life, however, has a way of sometimes getting in the way and she put aside her poetry to raise her daughter. When she picked up *Disappearing Acts* by Terry McMillan, she said to herself, "I can do this!" Encouraged by her mother and husband, she started two books that were still languishing in the bottom of a drawer. However, it wasn't until the passing of her beloved mother that she finally finished her first novel, *Saturday's Child*, which she first self-published. Amid personal tragedies, upheavals, and general chaos, she struggled tenaciously to finish her second novel, *Wednesday's Woes*, which is a follow up—not a sequel—to her first novel. She attended Philadelphia University where she studied interior design. She is currently a legal assistant at a prestigious law firm. When she is not writing, reading or gardening, she is teaching her grandchildren to say "Nana is a Diva!"

You can read excerpts of her upcoming works at: www.gaylejacksonsloan.com.

She is currently working on her third and fourth novels, *Dancin' In My Shoes* and *Let the Necessary Occur.*

Attention Writers:

Writers looking to get their books published can view our submission guidelines by visiting our website at:
www.QBOROBOOKS.com

What we're looking for: Contemporary fiction in the tradition of Darrien Lee, Carl Weber, Anna J., Zane, Mary B. Morrison, Noire, Lolita Files, etc; groundbreaking mainstream contemporary fiction.

We prefer email submissions to: candace@qboro books.com in MS Word, PDF, or rtf format only. However, if you wish to send the submission via snail mail, you can send it to:

Q-BORO BOOKS Acquisitions Department
165-41A Baisley Blvd., Suite 4. Mall #1
Jamaica, New York 11434

*** By submitting your work to Q-Boro Books, you agree to hold Q-Boro books harmless and not liable for publishing similar works as yours that we may already be considering or may consider in the future. ***

1. Submissions will not be returned.
2. Do not contact us for status updates. If we are interested in receiving your full manuscript, we will contact you via email or telephone.
3. Do not submit if the entire manuscript is not complete.

Due to the heavy volume of submissions, if these requirements are not followed, we will not be able to process your submission.